INVASION

INVASION

LUKE RHINEHART

TITAN BOOKS

Invasion
Print edition ISBN: 9781785651755
E-book edition ISBN: 9781785651762

Published by Titan Books
A division of Titan Publishing Group Ltd
144 Southwark Street, London SE1 0UP

First edition: September 2016
1 3 5 7 9 10 8 6 4 2

A CIP catalogue record for this title is available from the British Library.

Printed and bound in the United States.

To my wife Ann, who despite my continual complaints that I was dead, kept insisting that I was still breathing.

"IF GOD CREATED MAN IN HIS OWN IMAGE,
THEN WHO THE HELL CREATED THE FFS?"

Anonymous Human

"HUMAN BEINGS ARE THE PLANET'S
WAY OF COMMITTING SUICIDE."

Anonymous FF

CHAPTER OUTLINE

66. BILLY. Can Billy and the FFs save the Central Park Nation from massacre?

NOTE ON BOOK TWO

ONE

My name's Billy Morton. When I met Louie I was captain of my own small fishing boat that runs out of Greenport on the North Fork of Long Island. I'd take her out into the Long Island Sound or over east of Montauk, and me and my crew of two happy-go-lucky nobodies would run out our nets and see what we could pull in. Might be out there three days, but now that my health isn't all it should be, usually only two. I used to own two boats and actually make a bit of money, but a lot of the fish got tired of getting dragged up out of the water and chopped up into cat food, and they sort of began to go extinct. Had to sell half my fleet and settle for running just *Vagabond*, a thirty-five-footer whose diesel engine had been built during the Civil War, and the wood that went into her frame was so old the trees that provided it are extinct. But at least she was mine.

I run a tight ship but a relaxed ship. I'm the boss and the guys know it. But they also know they can hack around a bit or take a ten-minute break without getting shouted at. In fact if they didn't hack around a bit I'd never have hired them. Don't like fellows who are too serious. As long as the work gets done, how it gets done don't worry me much.

So when Marty Beck said to me that some swell-belly fish had "climbed up on the coach roof," I assumed Marty was having some fun and thought he was being clever. Marty's a good man but cleverness isn't one of his strengths. I knew, and he knew, that fish didn't get from the working deck to the coach roof unless they were thrown there.

But when I saw Sam Potter listening soberly as Marty reported the climbing fish, I thought either the whole crew was trying to pull my leg or that Marty was serious.

"Fish got onto the coach roof, huh?" I said.

"Yep," replied Marty, scratching the inside of his right thigh through his rubberized overalls. "Bounced there."

"Bounced onto the coach roof," says I.

"After rolling away from us when we tried to throw him overboard again," says Sam, nodding seriously, intent on getting the story straight.

"Again."

"I threw him overboard," Sam says. "Damnedest looking blowfish I ever seen. Big fella, like a basketball, but he looked useless. Tossed him off the stern and went back to work."

I was at the wheel at the time facing my two guys and waiting patiently for them to finish the story, still not sure if it was an elaborate joke or what.

"Fish came back," says Marty. "Popped up over the coaming and plopped right back onto the deck."

"Fish jumps up into the boat," says I, still waiting for the punch line.

"He did," says Sam.

"And then, when you tried to throw it overboard again, it hopped up onto the coach roof."

"Right. Bounced there with one bounce."

"Did it say anything?" I ask.

The two men looked at me. They knew I was a kidder but were sometimes a little slow to pick it up. Sometimes wish there were brighter guys who wanted to work sixteen hours a day for peanuts, but then of course they wouldn't be bright.

"Let's take a look," says I.

I turned the wheel over to Marty and went out of the cabin with Sam.

When I looked up to the coach roof what I saw was a hairy basketball. Larger than a basketball, more like a beach ball. Covered with short silver-gray hairs. No blowfish.

I reached up to take hold of the… thing, and it rolled away from me to the right. It had no mouth or fins or limbs or eyes, so how he saw me reach for him was a puzzle.

So I moved myself a couple of steps to my right and reached up again. The thing rolled back to where it had been before.

"Doesn't want to get thrown overboard again, I guess," says Sam.

"What the fuck is it?" asks Marty from the helm.

What the fuck indeed. I'd seen a lot of strange things dragged up from the deep but never a bouncing fish without fins, scales, eyes, or anything else that was fish-like. Just a stupid beach ball with a lot of smooth, fine hair.

After staring at it a long time and trying to come up with something brilliant to say, I sighed and moved away.

"It's probably just another creature from outer space," says I, and went back to the wheel.

My two guys looked at me, then up at the beach ball on the coach roof. Then they went back to work.

Dockside, Marty and Sam unloaded the crates of iced fish into Sam's big truck, cleaned the decks as well as it could be done, and then, it already getting dark, headed off to deliver the fish and then to their homes. Before they left, they each took a peek at the thing on the roof, and at me, and then went off trying to look cool and unconcerned.

Cool and unconcerned is always a good strategy for a man, especially when he hasn't the foggiest idea about what's going on. I stood on the deck and looked up at it.

"I'm heading home," says I aloud. "You gonna hang out here?"

The thing seemed to expand upwards a half foot, making itself look like a big hairy egg three-feet tall standing on end, then settled back down into a sphere.

"Well, suit yourself," says I.

I went and got my duffel bag, walked aft to the ladder that led up to the dock, and climbed ashore. It was late, and my boat was docked off in a corner of the marina where most of the other boats seldom saw any more action than an occasional marina drinking session. And in late September, most boats had retired for the year. So there wasn't anyone around when I got up on the pier and looked back.

The thing fell or leapt or slid off the roof, hit the deck, and bounced neatly up onto the dock six feet from my boots.

I nodded, as if it were a perfectly normal thing to have a fish bounce twelve feet off a boat as if it wanted to follow me home.

After looking around to see if anyone else had seen the fishy acrobatics, I began to move off. As I walked to my pickup truck, the thing rolled along behind me.

"Want to hang out a little longer, huh," says I.

At the truck I threw my duffel in the back, unlocked the passenger-side door, and then held it open. The thing, five feet behind me, stayed still a moment then rolled forward and bounced into the cab.

Off to my right I noticed another guy opening his car door staring over at what had happened, but when I casually closed the passenger-side door and gave him a little wave, he nodded and got into his car. Guess he figured that if a self-hopping beach ball didn't bother me, it wouldn't bother him.

I got into my pickup and started the engine, then I turned and stared at the furry fish sitting beside me.

"Yep," says I.

And drove home.

Our home is a mid-nineteenth-century farmhouse that has seen better days but is still breathing. When we bought it, it was one of the last surviving farmhouses on the North Road, most having long been torn down to make way for the wineries that for more than thirty years had spread across Eastern Long Island like the plague. Good plague, I guess, especially if you like wine, but it meant the death of the potato farms and the old farmhouses.

Except ours, which squatted determinedly on only half an acre. But on one side was a vast field of grape vines, so close I could lean out our living room window and pick grapes whenever I got the urge. On the other side of our farmhouse was a big spread of lawn owned by the rich guy who lived next door—next door being two hundred feet away. And his house was a hundred feet off the road where ours was so close we could eavesdrop on conversations in the cars whizzing past.

That early evening out on the back porch I wondered what I was doing. The beach ball was only five feet away sitting on the top step. Something that had come from the sea had followed me home. It wasn't close to anything I'd ever experienced or heard of—except in the *National Inquirer* or a sci-fi novel. But for some reason I wasn't scared.

So I clomped into the kitchen the way I usually do, letting the screen door bang behind me, and tossing my duffel into a corner. Carlita was at the stove stirring something in a frying pan, and I heard our two kids arguing happily in the living room.

Usually I march over to the fridge and pull out something cold and alcoholic, but this time I stopped in the middle of the kitchen and looked back at the screen door. The thing was sitting just outside it on the porch. I'm tempted to say "staring at me" but since the thing had no eyes, it made it tough for it to stare.

I turned to Carlita.

"We got a visitor," says I. Lita glanced over at me and waited for me to explain. She's almost twenty-five years younger than me, bright and a tough cookie who doesn't put up with much bullshit.

I looked at her and then marched back to the screen door and swung it open. The thing hesitated about a second and then rolled in and stopped ten feet from Carlita. Gotta hand it to her, Lita stood her ground, although I think she did raise her spatula into a defensive position. After giving the thing a long stare she turned to me.

"What's the joke?"

I moved past her to the fridge.

"No joke," says I. "The thing jumped into our boat off Fishers Island and then followed me home."

When the "thing" rolled four feet to stay closer to me, Lita took a step back away from it. She followed it with her eyes, still not decided whether to laugh or scream or start yelling at me to get the damn thing out of her kitchen. She was a lawyer once, so she's careful not to make quick decisions.

"What is it?" she finally asked.

I took a beer out of the fridge, popped it open, and looked down at the thing.

"Beats me."

She looked at me, then the thing, and then went back to her frying pan.

"Well, until you figure out what it is, keep it in the basement."

I nodded. Lita always has been the practical one.

Actually I'd converted a small part of the dark, damp basement into a sort of rec room for the kids, putting in a couple of windows, a plywood floor covered with wall-to-wall carpeting whose color had originally been an off-white but was now, after a decade of kid use, closer to an off-brown. When I got to the bottom of the steep stairs, the thing bouncing behind me, Lucas was at his computer and Jimmy was feeding his goldfish. Lucas is almost twelve and the serious sort, always reading books and wanting to chat about ecology and karma and things that I sometimes have to look up to find out what he's talking about. Jimmy's only eight and is all imagination and impulse. Thinks his brother is dull.

Lucas is built pretty much like me: wide shoulders, strong upper body, a mop of wild, dark hair. His skin is even darker than Lita's, having a lot of Hispanic genes from Lita's mom's Cuban side of the family. Except for coloring, Jimmy's more like his mom, small, lithe, and cute. Jimmy's a little darker than me, but not much. So Lucas is the only family member who occasionally gets called "nigger" or "wetback."

After they'd greeted me with "Hi, Dad" they noticed the hairy ball. At first they were both amazed, especially when it bounced up onto the back of the settee.

"What is it, Dad?" Lucas asks.

"It's some sort of newfangled pet I picked up today at a tag sale," says I. Since they were used to my saying things that had no particular relation to reality, neither of the boys believed this for a second. They just stared at it up there on the back of the settee.

"It looks yucky," says Lucas.

But then the thing rolled off the back of the couch onto the cushions and then to the floor and finally up close to Jimmy. The kid stood his ground. The thing stopped right up against his legs and, after only a brief pause, Jimmy reached down and petted it. Gotta hand it to the kid: he was a lot cooler about it than I'd been.

Well, in the next few minutes something happened that changed our lives forever. Damned if it didn't turn out both our kids liked the thing. Within minutes of my bringing it down to the rec room, they were acting as if it was a toy. They played with it like with a puppy, the thing rolling and bouncing as they chased it, the boys laughing away until, after ten minutes, they began to get frustrated. The next thing I knew—I'd been sitting at the foot of the basement stairs watching all this—the thing abruptly let itself be captured and rested without fuss in the arms of Jimmy, as Lucas patted and petted it. I think it was then that I realized that this thing might be pretty smart.

When the boys got tired of playing with the "Funny Fish" as they called it, Lucas went back to his computer and Jimmy turned on the TV to watch some documentary about seals in the Antarctic. For reasons I suppose I'll have to get into later, Carlita didn't let the kids watch much regular television, so for Jimmy and Lucas, documentaries were their sitcoms and thrillers. The Funny Fish sat on the sofa next to Jimmy and seemed to be "watching" too—although how a creature watched with no eyes, I hadn't figured out. But I felt the thing was no threat to the kids, so I clomped back up the stairs to have some supper.

In the den that first night after the boys had been sent to bed, I sat on the couch with the thing watching some boring TV program about the benefits of nuclear energy, when I decided it was time to try to find a few answers.

"Mind if I touch you?" says I, knowing that the thing had no ears that I could see but figuring he must be absorbing info from some source in his hairy body.

Naturally the thing didn't answer.

So I slowly reached out with my right hand and touched it with my four fingers. The hair was very soft and fine, and there seemed to be more hairs per square inch than on any animal I'd ever seen or felt. The hairs were only about a half-inch long.

I pressed my hand against the thing a little harder and damned if my hand didn't sink into its body as if it were made of tapioca pudding—hairy tapioca pudding—something soft that partially swallowed up my hand when I pressed it in.

I had thought the thing would be hard, so this softness

was a bit unnerving. Still, I didn't say anything but pressed my hand in further. The next thing I knew my whole right arm was buried right up to the armpit. Scared the bejesus out of me—thought I was going to be the first human eaten by a beach ball. I tried to pull my arm out, but the thing seemed to have me in an iron grip. I stood up and the thing lifted off the couch still wrapped around my arm. It had lost its beach-ball shape and was now a sort of oval, about three foot long, with more than half of its body wrapped around my arm. It felt like a furry, eyeless alligator was swallowing my limb—no pain but the whole arm felt squeezed.

I wanted to scream and shake my arm and run the hell out of there, but screaming and running is not cool, and running is something that at my age I try to avoid, so I just stood there and let my arm and the thing fall to my side.

Then this "Funny Fish" let go of my arm and, resuming a spherical shape, bounced twice away from me, then up against the brick façade above the fireplace, then back to the floor and then off the opposite wall and then, before I'd absorbed much of any of this, back to wrap itself again around my arm exactly as before.

I plopped back down on the couch and laughed. This thing was a real card. What it seemed to be telling me was "Hey, old man, don't worry about my grabbing your arm 'cause it doesn't mean any more than my bouncing off walls. It's just one of the fun things I can do."

Next, the thing let go of my arm and again became a beach ball sitting on the couch beside me watching television. After a few seconds I reached out and put my arm around it the way I'd seen the kids do once or twice. Damned if the thing didn't snuggle closer to me.

I just sat there for about half a minute and then gave it a little squeeze.

"Louie," says I, "I think this is the beginning of a beautiful friendship."

I hoped Louie would laugh, but I guess he'd never seen *Casablanca*, so my joke went right past him.

Which is where most of my jokes go.

The boys called the thing "FF" for "Funny Fish," and my wife called it, "that interesting something," and me, I didn't call it anything at first but began to think of it as "Louie." I knew it wasn't a fish and was a lot more than a beach ball, and a lot more than anything I'd ever known. I would have thought it was a creature from outer space, but they all had big ping-pong-ball eyes and big heads and skinny arms and legs, and didn't look at all like Louie.

It watched television most of the first day in the house—my wife even let him watch the junk TV on the networks—but late in the evening of the second day I caught it reading *Penthouse*. I was a bit surprised and disappointed and wondered how he planned to get his end into one of those sexy gals when he didn't have any end to get in with, but a couple of hours later I found him reading one of the volumes of an old encyclopedia set we had down there. And later I caught him leafing through an old *Progressive Magazine* Lita had left lying around.

I say "reading" but of course what I actually saw was the thing on the couch, the magazine or book lying in front of it, and every couple of seconds it somehow configured its belly into a limb which reached out to turn a page. Then another.

I wasn't scheduled to take the boat out again until the following week so had a lot of free time, but it wasn't until noon the next day that I figured maybe I ought to Google this strange creature.

You might wonder what an old geezer is doing knowing anything about Googling, but that's the advantage both of marrying a young wife who's brainy and educated, and having two kids in the house. Both my boys can Google circles around me, but still I think I'm pretty good for someone who wasn't brought up suckling on an iMac, didn't have a computer in my teens to watch porno, don't use one in my business to do spreadsheets, and don't have an iPhone or iPad attached permanently to my hand so I can communicate with anyone in the universe whenever I get an impulse.

So I went into my study (our bedroom) and Googled "hairy beach ball." Well, I'm proud to report that that request pretty much gagged Google. Top on its list was this:

"A larger woman's hair-covered pubic area bulges outwards creating a spherical shape. Add the vaginal slit and that area looks like hairy wedges tha…"

You gotta hand it to Google: they'll give you something even if it has nothing to do with what you said you wanted to look for. I browsed through a lot of irrelevant things like a "woman's hair-covered pubic area" but didn't get anything that had anything to do with FF. They came up with a lot of links that wanted to discuss "hairy balls" but that was a subject that didn't catch my fancy so I moved on.

I tried: "round hairy fish"—although I was pretty sure Louie was no fish.

Google struck out again. There was one link to a site that said "avoid hairy fish" that I thought I ought to check out, but it didn't really tell me why I should avoid hairy fish.

So I began to retreat and Googled "strange-shaped fish." No big hairy round fish. Got a nice picture of a big blowfish that looked exactly like FF except it had eyes, a mouth, a tail, fins and no hair. And I bet it didn't cuddle nice either.

So I figured that our creature was a one-off.

And I liked that.

I told Lita and the kids that I was pretty sure that our new friend wasn't a fish so we couldn't call him FF anymore. We agreed we couldn't call him "beach ball" because that really didn't capture what we knew about him or the way we were beginning to feel about him. My wife suggested we call him "the hairy computer," but the boys still wanted to call him FF 'cause they were used to it, so I surrendered and told them FF could stand for other things besides "Funny Fish." They asked for an example, and I says "Well, 'Fat Friend,'" and Lita says "How about 'Fun Friend,'" and Jimmy says "'Fantastic Friend!'" which we all liked, and then Lucas suggests "How about 'Fucking Funny Friend,'" but Jimmy pointed out that would mean FFF and be too big a mouthful.

We finally agreed that our new buddy was FF, which, depending on what mood we were in, could mean anything from "Fun Friend" to "Fucking Fascist," to "Fierce Foreigner," to "Furry Flip-flopper." We came up with more than fifty possible meanings of FF before we got bored and realized we weren't making much sense.

• • •

That night lying in bed with Carlita, I realized that both of us were wide awake, and sure enough, soon as I had that thought, Lita spoke up.

"I think FF is a lot smarter than he looks," she says.

I looked over at her in the dim light and, thinking of how FF looked, we both laughed.

"I think FF is a very special being," she says. "Really, it's something of a miracle creature."

"Yep," says I.

"But I think it might be dangerous," she says.

"Hasn't been so far," says I.

She was quiet for a bit and then says, "Not so far. But when I went down to pick up the kids' dirty clothes, he was working the computer, and unless he was just randomly hitting buttons he was surfing that computer faster than anyone I've ever seen."

"Yep."

"I think he understands us much better than we understand him."

"Yep."

For a while the two of us stared up at the ceiling.

"I think it means trouble, Billy," she finally says.

"Yep."

And we turned to each other and went into a big hug.

TWO

(From *THE OFFICIAL HISTORY OF THE ALIEN INVASION, Volume 1,* pp. 66–69)

(BEING AGENT MICHAEL JOHNSON'S INFORMAL NOTES ON THE FORMATION OF UNIT A.)

The National Security Agency didn't develop a special unit to investigate alien terrorists until 2015. Were they asleep at the switch? I don't think so. The idea that visitors from outer space might work secretly against the United States was not a common train of thought, so when the idea of a special unit to investigate such a possibility was first raised there was much healthy skepticism. But the desire to leave no stone unturned and no bureaucracy unexpanded in our War on Terror was too great. A unit was formed.

At first the primary task of the unit was to determine the right name for itself. This was three weeks before I was assigned to the unit, so I plead "not guilty" to all the wasted time. After two weeks they finally settled on a brilliant compromise: they named themselves Investigations Unit A.

Notice how much is achieved with this title: there is no mention of aliens. The "A" of the Investigations Unit would appear to be a simple letter to indicate primacy. Moreover, as the unit evolved, it became clear that their initial investigations were into anomalies: patterns, usually patterns involving violence that could not be explained by normal human activity and motivations. So the "A" could stand for anomalies and did so until the discovery of actual alien terrorists justified coming out of the closet.

Initially, Unit A combed the internet and worldwide media for stories that were so strange that the possibility of alien interference had to be considered. For a while they investigated all the reported abductions by aliens, interviewing many of the abductees to see if previous questioners had overlooked something.

In the first two years there were two "anomalies" that garnered our time and analysis. The first was the death of almost one hundred tribesmen in Bongulu, a remote village in the north-eastern Democratic Republic of Congo. Since only three of the villagers had survived whatever had killed their kinsmen, the United Nations Health Organization sent a small team of specialists to investigate. The specialists were unable to determine what had killed the tribesmen. "Unknown causes" concluded the report. Now this particular tribe was not involved on any side in any civil war. The people had lived in peace and poverty for almost two centuries—since the last slavers had retired. They were Muslims, and thus unlikely to be the victims of ISIS terrorists or their brethren.

So the question naturally arises: could this be aliens trying out lethal methods on some obscure tribe in some obscure location in order not to attract attention to their experiments? Unit A looked into it. But found nothing.

The second anomaly occurred in Siberia. In a remote village in the Sredinny Hrebet Peninsula, a strange creature suddenly appeared in the village that neither the villagers nor anyone else could make head nor tail of. This creature was brought to the attention of the more civilized world when a Russian health worker went to the village on his semi-annual visit to see if he could improve public health. The villagers claimed that the creature continually changed shape, could form a ball and roll at fifty miles per hour, could stretch up like a giraffe and pick fruit from the tops of trees and seemed even to be able to read, although the villagers disagreed on this point. The creature seemed to love to play hide-and-seek, although neither the villagers nor the creature had ever heard of the game. In any case, when the health inspector went to see this strange being, it couldn't be found. Or rather, it could be seen by a villager, but the moment he pointed it out to the health inspector, the being would disappear. He reported that once he saw a silver-gray beach ball roll very rapidly across the muddy street fifty feet away that the villagers claimed was the thing in question, but he believed they may have been trying to fool him by rolling a big muddy ball for him to see.

After three days of fruitless efforts to see the little bugger, a little bugger that the villagers, especially the children, seemed to see all the time, the health inspector had to leave. In his report on the village's health he said the most serious new development was a bad case of mass hysteria, with group hallucinations uncommonly common.

His report was picked up by an enterprising reporter for the *Ubiskitan Times and News Report Herald* with a medium-sized headline reading: "Alien Being Visits Odipac." The Investigations Unit A Google Sweep Team picked up this article and reported it to unit headquarters.

But nothing much came of our investigations until it was my good fortune to come upon a new development that was to make Investigations Unit A the biggest guy on the block in all of the NSA.

THREE

(From Billy Morton's *MY FRIEND LOUIE*, pp. 18–25)

Louie loved water. He hopped in a bathtub filled to the brim with cold water at least three times a day and just lay there underwater like a round gray rock. So Jimmy asked if he could take Louie for a walk through the woods to the sound. If there was no one on the lonely stretch of beach then Louie could go swimming to his heart's content.

So Jimmy set out walking in the woods behind our house with Louie rolling along beside him. The woods run along the winery property line almost to the Long Island Sound, which is only a half mile away. The rich guy owned the woods but didn't send in a SWAT team when me or the boys went hiking through it. Jimmy didn't normally go to the sound without either me or Lucas because twice over the last year he'd run into two or three slightly older kids who liked to tease him and threaten to rough him up. Once when he was walking his Aunt Juanita's dog, the bullies began to hit the dog with sticks, and when Jimmy tried to stop them, they began beating him up and sent him running full speed for home with their laughter trailing after him.

Jimmy traipsed happily along with Louie rolling beside him or bouncing a few feet ahead. Jimmy picked up a stick and flung it out in front of them and, sure enough, Louie rolled quickly to it, picked it up, and rolled back to hold it up for Jimmy in two little pincer-like things that he projected out of his top—if you can say that any part of a beach ball is the top.

Jimmy laughed and was about to fling the stick again when he saw three fifth-graders, two of 'em kids who'd bullied him before, coming his way through the woods on the trail from the sound. He knew I'd told him not to let other kids know about Louie and was frightened. But when he looked down he saw that the little bugger had sprouted four legs and a head, and had a tail whipping back and forth like an erect windshield wiper. It looked something like a weird dog, but without eyes or ears and with something that Jimmy thought must be intended as a tongue drooping six inches out of the front of the face—Louie the dog looked more like a creature from outer space.

The three ten-year-olds came to a halt and stared at the dog. Louie doubled the speed of his tail wagging.

"What the fuck is this?" asked the biggest kid, who was mostly the biggest because he was fat.

"It's my new dog," says Jimmy.

"Dog, my ass," says fat boy. "That's not a dog."

Another of the boys picks up a stick and pokes it at FF.

"Hey, doggie, what's your name?"

The three boys laugh, and fat boy picks up a thicker and longer stick and slaps it across FF's back. FF just sits there wagging its tail.

"Hey, speak, weirdo!" says the second boy.

Fat boy strikes again with his heavy stick. FF's tail stops wagging. Fat boy raises his stick again.

"AHHGGRRRHHRRGGRR!" comes from someplace out of FF, a roar that may have been heard in Lower Manhattan.

The three boys drop their jaws, drop their sticks, and begin backing away.

"He won't bite," says Jimmy.

"AHHGGRRRHHRRGGRR!" says FF.

The three boys turn and run.

At first Louie raised his eyeless head to look up at Jimmy and then he began tearing forward in an awkward run after the fleeing boys. He looked more like an epileptic centipede pared down to only four legs. When the kids looked back and saw this weird creature chasing them down, they turned up the afterburners and ran faster than any ten-year-olds in the recent history of mankind.

"FF!" shouts Jimmy.

And FF comes screeching to a halt. He turns around and trots back to Jimmy, again wagging his tail.

"Sit," says Jimmy. And FF squats a very unconvincing dog sit.

"Wow," says Jimmy.

Well, you might think no harm done, but that's because you haven't been paying attention to how life works. The next day five kids, most of them near Jimmy's age, one of them part of the gang that had seen FF as a dog in the woods, arrive at the back kitchen door and tell Jimmy they want to play with his new dog. Jimmy comes and asks me what he should do. I knew we couldn't keep FF hidden forever, and I'm a sucker for giving in to whatever Jimmy wants. And I knew he was probably hot to show off FF to his friends. So I march down into the basement den where Louie is working on the computer and tell him he's got visitors. Wanted to see what he'd do.

He hits a few keys on the computer, then bounces out of the chair and up the steps to the kitchen. And then bounces out of the house for recess.

FF and the kids began playing some game that was sort of "tag" I guess, but it soon became clear that all the fun was having all five of the boys be "it" and run after FF to try to tag him. And with five screaming and laughing kids chasing him, FF bounced and rolled and slithered and climbed trees and knocked boys' feet from under them and dodged so quickly it was like he was made of quicksilver. At one moment FF had bounced into one of our apple trees and was shaking a branch so some of the last apples fell on the kids' heads, and the next moment he'd wrapped himself around Jimmy so completely that the only parts of the kid that showed were his head and his feet, and somehow the combo of FF and Jimmy still managed to elude the taggers.

Finally, since when FF was "it" he could tag anyone he wanted within about a millisecond, the kids began to get tired and bored with the game.

The next thing I knew they had divided into two teams and were playing soccer with Louie as a rather oversized soccer ball. The kids loved kicking Louie and he seemed to love it too, but the game was sort of different, since a boy would kick the ball straight toward the goal but two-thirds of the way there the ball, FF, would swerve off in any direction it felt like, or might bounce over the goalie's head. Or some poor boy would take a vicious swing with his leg at FF who was lying there right in front of him, and the damn "ball" would duck—shrink down to a flat rectangle close to the ground and the kid would miss and fall flat on his ass.

The game ended when FF rolled into the legs of a kid named Donny, and the boy fell to the ground and began crying. Twisted a knee or something. Couldn't even walk. The other boys looked worried so I came down the porch steps, looked at Donny's knee—nothing to see—and then carried him to my pickup to take him home.

Louie came rolling along with me and, after I'd put Donny in the passenger seat of the pickup, and I'd gotten into the driver's seat, he hopped into the back of the pickup.

It was then I realized what trouble we were all in. Donny's parents were going to ask what happened and Donny was going to say "FF knocked me over." "Who's FF?" "FF is a beach ball that can climb trees and dodge and wrestle and run faster than a horse and bounce higher than a house and…"

And that would be the end of our new friend.

I got out of the truck and went back to the pickup bed and stared at Louie.

"Stay here at the house, Louie," says I.

For a moment or two he didn't move, but then he bounced out of the truck and began rolling slowly back toward the house.

He understood exactly what I'd said. I'd known he was smart, known he was learning a lot, but that he understood everything I said, I hadn't yet figured.

I drove Donny to his parents' house and carried him in and set him on the couch and apologized, but it was even worse than I expected. Mommy got hysterical and screamed "My son can't walk!" and Daddy glared at me as if I had personally shot his son in the leg and was claiming the gun went off by accident. When the dad began questioning Donny about what had happened and Donny began squawking about how FF had clipped him on purpose, I knew we were in trouble.

"Who's FF?" the dad naturally asked.

"He's a bully," said Donny. "A basketball bully."

The dad didn't absorb too much of that, so he turned to me. "Who's this FF?"

I looked back at him with my usual grumpy-old-man scowl, one that usually works to make people tread lightly around me, but I knew wasn't going to work here.

"Well?" says Dad.

"He's a pet Bulgy I bought in New London last week." I don't have the faintest idea where this lie came from, but out it came.

"What the hell is a pet Bulgy?" asks Dad.

"It's an Arctic dog that evolved over the years into having no legs and gets around by rolling and bouncing. It's shaped like a beach ball. It evolved into a beach-ball shape so it can move on snow, ice, and water. And floats good."

To come up with a lying piece of bullshit like this you have to have years of practice. And I had it.

"Well, that dog seems to be something of a menace, doesn't it?"

"Well, maybe, but he's so smart we call him Dr. Bulge." When I get into a good lie I just can't stop myself from rolling with it.

"I don't care if you call him Einstein, he's a menace."

"Yep, you're right. I'll keep him tied up and away from kids from now on," says I, almost smiling at the utter impossibility of anyone ever tying FF up.

"I think you'd better," says Dad and, having shown he was the man of the house, he turned to put a supportive hand on his wife's shoulder and the two of them comforted Donny.

I hurried away. Didn't want to hear how Donny explained to Pop about all the incredible things this Arctic dog could do. And the fact that the dog was most of the time missing legs, a tail, eyes, a nose, ears, and just about anything resembling a dog. And I also was worrying about my sudden memory that Donny's father worked for the Riverhead newspaper, an editor or manager or something.

Back at my house, I located Louie in the rec room perched on Jimmy's desk while Jimmy and Lucas were doing something on the computer. I pulled up a chair beside them. My youngest son turned to me, but all FF did was squiggle a bit—otherwise didn't change his position.

"We're in a bit of trouble, boys," says I. "Other humans will want to talk to FF and may cause us trouble, may want to take FF away from us."

"No!" says Jimmy.

"We've got to be sure that we can hide him on short notice whenever someone comes along we don't want to see him."

"We can do that," says Lucas.

"Won't be easy," I says. "Not many creatures like FF lying around in a house on the North Fork."

Next thing I knew, FF rolled toward the couch and, just as I thought he was going to get up in Lucas's lap, it was as if he suddenly melted: he disappeared under it.

"See, he can do it!" Jimmy said excitedly.

I walked over, bent down, and looked under the couch.

There was a hairy something, three-feet long but flat as a small boogie board.

Now hiding under a couch—if you can do it—isn't the most advanced form of hiding known to mankind, but it showed that FF knew what I was talking about.

"He's smart," Jimmy said proudly.

Oh yeah, I thought.

When FF slid out from under the couch and resumed his spherical shape, I turned to the boys.

"I told Donny's folks that FF is a rare breed of dog from the Arctic. Said it was a Bulgy. It won't take them long to realize that there's no dog ever been created anyplace that is a sphere and plays video games on a computer."

They were listening.

"We're going to tell anyone who asks… that our Bulgy ran away and that we don't know what happened to him," I says. "Think that'll work?"

"We could say he got hit by a car and we buried him," says Jimmy.

"They'll ask where we buried him," says Lucas.

"We buried him at sea!" says Jimmy.

I got two pretty sharp kids considering the genes they got from the male side.

FOUR

(From Billy Morton's *MY FRIEND LOUIE*, pp. 25–32)

Two days later things started to fall apart. 'Course things are always falling apart, so I just mean that the collapsing went into avalanche mode. Not only did the local dog catcher show up, but the sheriff and a local reporter from the *Riverhead Express and Tribune*. I guess Donny's father knew a potential hot news story when he heard one. I knew the sheriff pretty well, but the dog catcher and reporter I'd never met. The reporter was so young I wondered if he was writing for his high school paper.

"Hi, Billy," Sheriff Coombs greets me, putting out his big paw to shake hands. "Seems to be a bit of trouble about a dog that isn't a dog."

"I'm here to examine the mammal that hurt Donny Arkin," the dog catcher says, "and if so, to determine whether he's a threat to the community."

This DC was a small man whose chin looked as if it was permanently frozen in the belligerent position.

"Well, boys, I'm afraid you're out of luck," I says. "Damn dog got run over by a car yesterday. Buried him at sea this morning."

All three of them stared at me.

"Mind if we come in, Billy?" says the Sheriff. "Little chilly out here."

"Come on in," I says. "Beware of the dog."

After a brief start, Sheriff Coombs laughed, but the dog

catcher's chin expanded another centimeter. The kid reporter just looked blank. IQ puts him maybe reporting for a junior high paper.

They all troop into the house and, after a few awkward moments, I get them to take seats in our living room, the sheriff and the kid on the couch and the dog catcher in the one straight-backed chair in the whole house. The sheriff and me had known each other for almost forty years, even went hunting for deer together in Upstate New York for three or four years before I met Lita. She informed me that killing deer wasn't nice unless you ate their meat. Venison makes me fart for six weeks, so I gave up hunting.

"Get you fellas a drink?" I ask.

"Well," the sheriff says, "I got off duty ten minutes ago so I'll have a bourbon."

"We're here to search this house for a dog," says the DC. "Not to socialize."

"A dog that can bounce fifteen feet high," adds the kid, proving he could talk, "can change shapes, and likes to play on computers."

"Ah, *that* dog," says I.

"Unfortunately, Teddy," says the sheriff, "the dog got killed and has been deep-sixed." Apparently the kid's name is Teddy.

"This man lied in claiming that the creature was a dog," says the DC. "There is no such animal as a Bulgy."

"And Marty Beck says the dog is actually a fish your men caught on your last trip out," says the kid, making me wish he was as stupid as I'd first thought.

"How'd Marty get involved in this?" says I.

"Small town we got here, Billy," says the sheriff. "Kids talk.

Parents talk. Marty gave me a ring to give me his two cents' worth about the round blowfish that hurt Donny."

"I want to search this house, Sheriff," says the DC. "I thought you said you'd help me."

"Well, I think it would be nice if you could have a look around," says the sheriff, "but we don't have a warrant. Billy'll have to give you his permission."

So the DC glares at me.

I'd warned Louie that there might be visitors and I knew he'd hide. 'Course if he couldn't think of anything better than sliding under a couch we might be in trouble.

"Sure," says I. "Search wherever you want. Just leave things the way you find them. My wife blames me if anything gets out of place."

The DC stood up. Then so did the kid.

"How about that bourbon, Billy," says the sheriff, a lawman of the highest order.

"And I'll join you," says I.

"You want to join us, Teddy?" says the sheriff.

"I'm with the search," he says.

"You have to accompany me, Mr. Morton," says the DC. "I don't want you to accuse me of stealing anything."

"Never entered my head, little fella," says I, "but first I'd like to help the sheriff with his drinking problem."

So I fixed me and the sheriff two stiff bourbons—he was of the highest order—and then, drink in hand, showed the DC and Teddy around the house. As we went from room to room I kept wondering where the hell FF was managing to hide. I'd told him to stay in the house because if he was spotted outside by anyone, his death might seem to have been superficial.

The DC and Teddy did a good search, opening all the kitchen cabinets, checking the oven and fridge, under the beds, in all the closets. When downstairs again, they looked under the living room couches and in drawers and cabinets. If Louie was in any of these places neither the DC, who didn't really know what he was looking for, or I, who did, saw anything that looked like it might be him.

Then we clomped down the stairs to the rec room and found Jimmy and Lucas sitting opposite each other playing chess on an old cedar chest. They looked up at us when we came down but didn't seem in the least interested. Went back to their chess game.

The DC did his thing and then looked sternly at the two boys.

"Where's your dog?" he asks.

They both looked up at the DC.

"He's dead!" Jimmy says, and damned if Jimmy's lip didn't begin to quiver and it looked as if he were gonna cry.

"We buried him at sea," says Lucas.

"Did the dog ever play at the computer?" Teddy asks.

The boys look up blankly.

"He pretended to," Lucas says finally, "he couldn't really do it."

"Some of your friends tell us you told them the dog played video games on the computer with you," says Teddy.

"Maybe," said Jimmy. "But we always beat him."

Well, no son is perfect, and Jimmy still had a bit to learn about lying.

"Isn't there more to this basement area?" the DC puts in.

So I take him next door to the garage. We got to stare at a lot of dust, dirt, about two cords of firewood, and tools so old they'd sell on the *Antiques Roadshow* for thousands.

Back in the rec room I see that Teddy is still there, looking down on the boys' chess game. The DC ignores them and marches up the stairs.

"What's in that cedar chest?" Teddy asks.

The boys look up, startled.

"Just blankets," says Lucas. "Old blankets."

"Open it," says Teddy.

I see that Lucas and Jimmy look a bit nervous. Jimmy just sits there staring at the game, but Lucas stands and carefully lifts the chess board off the thick silver-gray cover on top of the chest and puts it on the couch behind him. Then he turns back and picks up the inch-thick furry coverlet and places it on the couch next to the chess board. He then opens the cedar chest.

Blankets. Neatly folded blankets. Teddy reaches down and searches through them for a few seconds and then straightens.

Lucas then closes down the chest and turns back to the couch. He looks startled for a second, then picks up the chess board and carefully turns and puts it back on the chest.

But calm as my boy is, both Teddy and I are staring at the couch: the silver-gray coverlet has disappeared. It's as if both our heads are being controlled by the same puppeteer: we look from the couch to the chest and back to the couch in perfect sync.

"What happened to that furry cover?" asks Teddy.

Lucas looks back at Teddy blankly.

"What cover?" says Lucas.

Teddy looks at Lucas, then me, then goes to the couch and begins to fling off the seat cushions one by one. But after he tosses off the middle cushion, the last one suddenly explodes up into his face, almost knocking him over. Although Teddy is staggering from being hit by a flying cushion, I see Louie roll rapidly past Teddy and up the stairs.

"What the hell?" says Teddy, stunned. "Did you see that?"

"See what?" says I.

"That cushion just suddenly flew at me!"

"What are you talking about?" says I.

"The cushion… hit me!"

"Come off it, fella," says I. "Cushions don't fly."

"It did! It did! That creature was under there and somehow threw the cushion at me."

"Yeah. Right," says I. "A pillow-throwing Arctic dog."

Teddy then races around the room looking under and into everything. Finally, a little breathless, stopping to confront me again.

"It can change shapes," he says. "It was a beach ball, a dog, a furry coverlet and God knows what it was when it blasted that cushion at me."

"Probably a howitzer," says I.

"You saw it!"

"I saw you throwing couch pillows on the floor," says I. "What did you see, Lucas?"

"Same thing," says my boy,

"Then where's the coverlet that was underneath your chessboard?" says Teddy.

For a moment both Lucas and me are silent.

"What coverlet?" says I.

• • •

That was it. Back in the living room we found the sheriff looking very relaxed.

"I'm off, Sheriff," the DC says, looking like he'd just lost a winning lottery ticket. "I don't believe that thing is dead, but no sign of it here now."

"Sorry about that, Mr. Prickle," says the sheriff, standing. "I was really hoping to see this sea dog."

"Can we go now?" asks the DC.

"Sure? You coming, Teddy?"

"I have to interview Mr. Morton first," says Teddy.

"Well, thanks for the drink, Billy," says the sheriff. "If that beach ball bounces up on your coach roof again, you'll let us know, right?"

"Sure thing, Sheriff. I hope he does show up again. He helped me a lot with my emails."

The sheriff grinned, but the other two stayed dead.

After the sheriff and the DC had left, I offered Teddy a bourbon, and this time he accepted a beer. Normally I would have fixed myself another drink, but these days I find that I'm so mellow with just one that I worried that another might have me happily telling the truth.

Back in the living room Teddy took the couch again and I took my rocking chair.

"This creature shows up on your boat," he begins, "you take it home, have it here for four days and the neighborhood kids say it can change shape, let itself be kicked, bounce into trees and seem to use a computer. You pretend it's a dog. Today I saw it as a cover on that cedar chest and it threw a cushion at me. I'd like you to tell our readers what else you've learned this creature can do and what you think this creature is."

The kid was getting smarter and smarter, and I was liking him less and less.

"Beats me."

"The children tell me that they think the creature understands what they are saying. Do you agree with that?"

"Most all dogs understand what humans say—what's so special about that?"

"Did this creature use a computer?"

"He sat in front of it and seemed to change the stuff on the screen. Don't know if he knew what he was doing."

"The children report that they saw him reading *Penthouse*."

"Not sure he was reading. Might have been looking at the pictures. That's what most of us do."

"Why are you hiding this creature from the rest of us?"

I stood up.

"Look, kid," says I. "The creature got run over by a car and killed and I tossed it into Peconic Bay. End of story."

"Whose car?" says Teddy. "When? Any witnesses?"

"End of story."

After I'd managed to steer the kid out of the house without contaminating his reporting with any additional false statements, I walked back into the living room just as Lucas and Jimmy appeared from the rec room. We grinned at each other.

Suddenly Louie appears from under the desk, bounces up, comes softly down on my head, then bounces up against the wall, then back to Jimmy's head and finally falls to the floor. Erupts into a tall, thin egg, then back to a sphere.

Damn show-off.

FIVE

James Rabb, Chief Investigator of Unit A's Anomalous Terrorist Activity, first learned of alien creatures on Earth from Agent Michael Johnson. The first reports, from an obscure branch of British MI5, were of a strange, usually spherically-shaped creature that could morph into different forms, and could make itself invisible at will. MI5 reported that the creature seemed to manifest unusual abilities with computers and a suspicious interest in British defense policies. It was also suspicious that it had befriended an employee of a leading British defense manufacturer. On the one occasion they got close enough to attempt to question it, it bounced out a window and disappeared.

Since the creature was unlike anything ever seen before and might be super-intelligent, the British were considering whether it might be a robot cleverly disguised as a hairy beach ball. This theory of robots remotely controlled by brilliant, probably anti-Western scientists seemed reasonable to MI5. Did Al-Qaeda or other terrorists have brilliant robotic scientists? Not that anyone had ever heard of. Had the Russians created the robots?

There were also several preliminary reports coming into Unit A of other strange, non-human creatures appearing in Kenya, Brazil, and Poland. As reported in the local media these creatures seemed to assume many different shapes—

four- and six-legged creatures, snakes, only without eyes or mouths. Most of them spent much of their time entertaining and interacting with children, just as had the creature in Siberia. These creatures seemed to put on performances of various kinds—dances, acrobatics, water tricks, games with balls. Their activities seemed utterly harmless, and not that intelligent.

At first the idea that the Russians had created the robots made a lot of sense to CI Rabb, until Agent Johnson suggested that it was doubtful that the Russians would bother to create robot beach balls to play games in the slums of Kenya.

Although CI Rabb found most of the reports of these creatures a little incredible he knew that no report should be considered too stupid to follow up, especially since he had the money and manpower to do so. He assigned agents to fly to London and Brazil and try to see what was behind the reports.

A week later Unit A received a second report from "a Russian source" that the Russians were now dealing with a similar creature in St. Petersburg. There it was associating with known dissidents and in vague ways seemed to be supporting their operations. The fact that most of these spheres seemed intent on eluding the authorities was clearly *prima facie* evidence that they were up to no good.

And then came the break that CI Rabb had been waiting for. Agent Michael Johnson came barging into his office more excited than he'd ever seen him. He presented a news article in a small Long Island newspaper of some strange creature living as a pet with a local fisherman's family, crippling a neighbor's child and then eluding efforts by a sheriff and dog catcher to examine it. It too was described as spherical but with the ability to change shape. The article indicated that although the local fisherman claimed the creature was some sort of dog and had been run over by a car, the reporter was certain that the fisherman was hiding the creature. Boys in the neighborhood claimed the creature spent a lot of time on a computer. And the reporter himself indicated he had seen the creature disguised as a small rug that eventually threw a large pillow at him.

Since the article didn't seem to indicate any terrorist activity, and was on the face of it pretty far-fetched, CI Rabb didn't see why Agent Johnson was so excited. He assumed that Johnson had brought the item to him because of similarities in the description of the Long Island creature and of those in other places. But then Agent Johnson dropped his bombshell: "Now get this, Chief," Johnson said. "Three days ago, our unit monitoring cyberattacks followed up on the attack of the CIA's Special Investigations Division to try to determine the perpetrator. Late yesterday Sub-unit 3 in charge of counter-hacking reported that our Unit A was being hacked. And when I put our men in touch with that special NSA unit they reported that the signatures of the two hackers were identical, and they worked from the same computer!"

CI Rabb narrowed his eyes.

"Go on," he said carefully.

"Chief," Agent Johnson announced, "twenty minutes ago they were able to determine that the hacker was operating from a computer in Greenport, Long Island. They're narrowing it down more as we speak."

"Greenport," said CI Rabb. "Why does that ring a bell?"

"The fisherman!" said Agent Johnson. "A pet that kids said used a computer!"

"Oh, my God!"

"Exactly, sir. Exactly!"

SIX

(From Billy Morton's *MY FRIEND LOUIE*, pp. 32–40)

After Teddy finally left, I marched back into the kitchen and poured myself a good drink. I knew that Teddy was going to get something published about Louie and an avalanche would hit us. Good hider or mediocre hider, I knew Louie was in trouble.

"This isn't going to work, boys," says I when Lucas and Jimmy joined me in the kitchen, their drinks being a Yoo-hoo and a Dr. Pepper.

"What do you mean, Dad?" asks Lucas, leaning against the fridge. "Louie hid good and then managed to disappear."

"He can elude one person," says I, "but not dozens. And that's how many will be after him when that kid reporter publishes what he knows about an Arctic superdog beach ball place mat."

"We can hide him," says Lucas.

"We gotta get Louie out of here," says I. "Get him back to sea where he'll be safe."

"No," says Jimmy.

"Scratch that one, Dad," says Lucas.

Kids always put heart before head, and I felt I knew better.

"Louie and I are going to the boat," says I. "You two can come along or not."

"But, Dad," says Lucas, "FF is part of our family!"

"He's our friend, all right," says I. "And we got to keep him out of danger."

And I marched off and out the kitchen door with Louie rolling along behind, and two sad kids trailing along after me.

Out on the water headed toward the sound, the boys just sat on the port-side coaming and looked gloomy.

"Nice day out today," says I, always the brilliant conversationalist.

"Where are we going?" says Lucas.

"Gonna take FF back to his other friends," says I.

"Back to his fish friends?" says Jimmy.

"Yep," says I.

"He's got human friends," says Jimmy, looking up at me.

"It's the humans I'm worried about," says I. "When humans discover something they don't understand and they think might be important, they want to poke it, prod it, dissect it, and generally cut it up until they know everything about it, including why it died."

"But Louie won't have as much fun with fish as he has with us," says Lucas.

"Well, that may be, but the sea's gotta be his home, because humans are not going to let him live with us anymore no matter what we say or do."

Finally, a mile out into Long Island Sound, I slowed old *Vagabond* and shifted her into neutral.

"Time to play with the fishies again," says I.

"Please, Dad," begins Jimmy.

"We like you, Louie," says I. "We know you're a lot smarter than we are, so you must know that we can't protect you from the stupid things humans do with things they don't understand. You're a lot safer out here swimming with sharks than you would be back on land swimming with humans."

"No!" says Jimmy.

Well, Louie rolled off the coaming, bounced himself three or four times off the cockpit deck like that Rafael Nadal fella bouncing a tennis ball before serving, and then takes a big bounce and, showing off as usual, contorts his shape into someone making a swan dive, and plops into the sea.

The boys and I stared after him, and then Jimmy glares at me, screws up his face into something that looked like he was either about to cry or throw up, and then swings away.

I'm not big on sentimental partings so I went back to the helm, kicked up *Vagabond*'s engine and swung the boat around to head back home, not one of us saying a single word. It's the most silent me and my boys have been with each other since the boys both learned to talk. I felt like shit.

We were coming in on Plum Gut when a school of young porpoises began showing off on our starboard bow. I told the boys to take a look, but Jimmy kept to his serious snit and Lucas barely gave them a glance.

There were six of these porpoises and they were really having fun. Fact is, I'd never seen such a performance off my bow. They dove and leapt and interweaved and danced and even seemed to ride on each other's backs in a way that I couldn't take my eyes off.

Next thing I knew Jimmy was standing beside me and staring too, his little mouth open just the way mine would have been if I didn't figure it wasn't cool to let your mouth hang open, especially since at my age I'd drool.

By God, those porpoises were dancing and diving and weaving to beat the band, and I saw that Jimmy and Lucas were well out of their snits—the three of us standing there with big stupid grins on our faces watching the floor show.

Then one of the porpoises, a small one, suddenly leapt in the air, somehow spread something that looked like short wings out of its sides, and went flying along about fifteen feet just a foot or two above the water, touched down on the sea and seemed to bounce up into the air for another twenty feet, the other porpoises leaping out of the water too but not able to come close to doing what this flying acrobat was doing.

"FF!" screamed Jimmy.

"Friggin FF," I mumbled to myself, but without in the least abandoning my big stupid grin.

FF only played at being a big overweight flying fish for three jumps and then dove back beneath the surface and disappeared. The other porpoises followed him out of sight for what seemed like a full minute but then reappeared off our port bow, but missing one of their troupe—Louie.

Jimmy went from one side of the boat to the other looking, but after a while came up to me at the helm.

"He's gone," he says.

"Yep," says I.

"Not completely, Dad," says Lucas, staring aft.

Sitting on the stern of our boat was a hairy beach ball. Dripping water.

Jimmy ran up to Louie and gave him a hug, which means Jimmy pretty much disappeared into an amorphous mass of wet fur, and I found that for some reason I wasn't hot for getting back to land without Louie anymore.

SEVEN

(From Billy Morton's *MY FRIEND LOUIE*, pp. 44–51)

Now I figure some of you are beginning to wonder why I and my family didn't act like normal red-blooded Americans and ask for thirty grand for an interview with ABC to tell them a bit about Louie, and then ask fifty grand from CBS to give new juicy details we'd held back from poor ABC, and finally a hundred grand from NBC for an interview with Louie himself. And so on.

And why were we so worried about other people knowing about Louie and having the authorities come and question him? Why didn't we take him to some university and show him off? Why didn't we email experts and invite them to come examine Louie?

Because we're stupid. And because we're paranoid: we don't trust the authorities. And we don't trust experts. An expert is someone who thinks he knows so much that he becomes an asshole. Everything he examines—a stone, animal, human— to an expert is a *thing*, a child being no less a thing than a stone. If an expert had his way with Louie, within a week the expert would be sawing up Louie to find out what he's made of; stabbing him to find out if he feels pain; shooting him to see if he would die.

"And how did you get this paranoid, Mr. Morton?" some wiseass among you is asking.

By living a long time and keeping my eyes open.

Actually, it started when I volunteered to join the US Army in '65 and ended up six months later saving the Vietnamese people from communism. My pop was a good, hard-working guy who never thought too much about anything and thus believed what the TV told him. He told me that the commies were invading Vietnam, and that if we didn't stop them they'd soon be attacking Long Island. So I signed up to save Long Island from the commies.

In Vietnam the first thing I learned was that most of my buddy grunts weren't that happy saving Long Island from the commies. They said that at first they were happy to be protecting the South Vietnamese people from the enemy—until it began to seem that the South Vietnamese people were trying to kill them as much as were the North Vietnamese, who tended to stay deep in the jungles.

In any case, within six months I was smoking a lot of pot and finding it harder and harder to obey orders to go shoot some more Vietnamese. Of course when a guy shot at me I was happy enough to shoot back and try to kill him, but I hated going into villages and dragging away the women and kids and oldsters and burning down their homes. By the end of six months I was counting the days until I could leave.

Finally, even before my term of duty was over, they sent me home with a dishonorable discharge. I guess I dragged my ass too often in response to some order some ROTC officer gave me, and let my mouth get a bit loose with comments about the horror and stupidity of what we were doing. One of my buddies said that the reason they sent me home was that some of the officers were afraid I'd accidentally throw a hand grenade into the officers' mess hall. Actually, that thought never occurred to me, except now and then during the week.

Back home in '66 I became a hippy. My dad threw me out of the house both because of the dishonorable, and because of the pot smoking, and most of all because of the lazy losers I was hanging out with—my hippy friends—especially the gal I got involved with not long after I got back.

Sandy was a smart, sexy lady who was so alienated from "America" she made me look like an establishment conformist. She got antsy if a day went by without her protesting something, and those somethings were usually somethings most Americans thought were great: like drafting kids to go kill Vietnamese, bombing defenseless people, billy-clubbing war protestors, keeping women and niggers in their place, making more nuclear bombs—stuff like that. I was hooked on her, but she was hooked on everyone: there didn't seem to be a single person being persecuted by the government that she didn't think deserved at least a good lay, with her often being the provider. Sleeping around wasn't exactly unheard of in those days, but Sandy probably set some sort of record.

Well, for six years I lived the life of a hippy radical, even long after I'd given up trying to find Sandy in a bed without someone else already there. Got arrested six times, spent eight months in jails, smoked enough dope to get lung cancer, slept with enough gals to satisfy a teenager's daydreams, and somehow survived.

But when Richard Nixon buried McGovern in '72 I decided to resign from the human race. Not that Nixon was much worse than any other guy who usually gets elected, but somehow that election made me feel nothing was ever going to change. The American people seemed happy with whatever the bigwigs thought was right. I was unhappy with whatever the bigwigs thought was right.

So by my late twenties I was burned out: just wanted to be left alone. I wasn't a wild man any more. Didn't want to protest anything, didn't want to get stoned with friends, didn't want to sleep around. Just work hard, save some money, read books, watch sports on TV, and settle into what was expected of me.

I went back home to Eastern Long Island and began taking a series of dead-end jobs that kept my body sharp and my mind dull: worked in an ice plant, on a road crew, became a plumber's assistant, worked in a warehouse moving boxes the size of elephants from spot A to spot B, and finally got a job on a fishing boat that took three- and four-day trips out onto the Atlantic. My father was a working stiff and I was returning to my roots. Why was the fishing job the one that I began to stick to? Not the fish. Rather it was getting away from land, from people, from the lies I felt were smothering me. Hard, hard work away from land and television is a good way to stop worrying about what a mess humans are making of the world. And then I finally got lucky and met Carlita.

Picked her up at the side of the road. Actually her little Honda had a flat tire and I drove merrily by not planning to stop. But I happened to glance in my rear-view mirror and noticed this incredible ass sticking out as she bent over staring at the flat. I braked my pickup truck, swerved into the nearest driveway, turned around, and went back to pull in behind her. The ass was even better in close-up. The rest is history.

"Need a hand?" says I.

"As a matter of fact, I don't," she says, although all she's done so far is take out the jack. "Thanks anyway."

"Well, glad to hear it," says I, "but I can change this thing in five minutes and it'll take you fifteen. Let me do it for you."

"No, thank you."

Up close, her big, dark eyes made her cute but not beautiful. And her voice and face were as stern as a judge pronouncing the death sentence.

"Hey, all I'm actually interested in is hanging out with you a bit, and getting a chance to look at you. If you'd rather I just stood and watched I can do that, but if I'm gonna come on to you, you might as well get the tire changed."

This little speech surprised her, and she looked at me a long moment and then smiled this marvelous face-lighting smile.

"Okay, big boy, go ahead," she says. "But when you're done I'll be driving off into the sunset."

"I expect you will," says I, "but I'll have gotten to spend ten minutes with you."

"I thought you said you can do it in five."

"I can," says I, pulling the jack over near the flat and taking the tire iron to remove the nuts. "But I'm not highly motivated to do it with my usual speed."

She smiled again.

I changed the tire, chatting her up as I did.

"You look like you got some Latina in you," says I. "Where you from?"

"Born in Cuba," she says, kneeling down beside me and taking each nut as I swirled them off.

"When'd you leave?" says I.

"1982," she says. "I was ten years old."

"Family mad at Fidel?" says I, jacking up the car.

"We were very happy in Cuba and with the revolution," she says and I could feel her bristling.

I stopped my work for a second and looked at her.

"Good," says I.

"But why do you call him 'Fidel,'" she says, "and not 'Castro' like most Americans."

"Hey, I've always appreciated anybody who stands up to a colossus to try to keep their own country for their own people."

"Most Americans don't see it that way."

I went back to work. "'Course not, and at first neither did I," says I. "I was in my early teens when Fidel marched into Havana, and I believed whatever my daddy and the *New York Post* told me. Which was that Castro was a commie bastard who was stealing people's property and shooting innocent citizens." I then let out a loud grunt as I tried to pull off the damn tire.

Got it. Had to get up and go back to the trunk to get the spare. She stood up as I passed her. Watched me take out the tire and go back to crouch down to put it on. She kneeled again beside me.

"What made you change your mind?" she asks.

"A Mexican girlfriend. She kept telling me that Cubans were much better off than most people in Haiti or the Dominican Republic or Central America and forced me to read some books. Seems the *New York Post* and most Americans had it a bit wrong."

We finished the job in silence, me putting the jack and the ruined tire back in the trunk and she thanking me and offering me her hand.

"Gonna drive off into the sunset now, are you?" says I.

"Yes," she says. Gives me a long intense neutral stare and then moves away and gets into her car, giving me another look at her incredible ass and making me feel gloomy at what I was losing.

She started the car and then turned and looked back at me.

"Five one six, three two three, sixteen twenty-two."

She flashed that wonderful smile and drove away.

I rushed to my pickup, scrambled to find a pencil, then rooted around the floor for a piece of waste paper. Wrote it down: 516 323-1622.

First time in my life I was glad I'd always liked playing with numbers.

Anyway it turns out that Carlita's as paranoid as I am. Having a mom who was Cuban and a dad who was Irish meant to Americans that she was one hundred percent Latina. Her parents named her Carlita Lopez so with her last name of O'Reilly she was pretty unique even before she'd finished teething. Latinos weren't treated too nice in the Irish neighborhood in Brooklyn where her mom and dad moved when they came to the States, so from the time she was first called "greaser," "nigger," "wetback," and "Mexcrement," at the age of four, she wasn't too happy with the world she found herself in. And it didn't help with the local Cuban community that she and her family liked Fidel and most of them hated Castro. So she worked hard to escape this world, and by working thirty hours a week for six years at various jobs, she put herself through college and law school and became a lawyer.

After she passed the New York bar exam, she worked for ten years for an Hispanic non-profit organization trying to get immigration laws reformed. Lots of luck. It looked like God had programmed every Republican in the country to fear invading Mexicans more than anything in the world. The idea that a single Mexican who had come into the country illegally might be permitted to stay was as bad to those guys as letting a convicted child molester become a guidance counselor in a grade school. Carlita got so frustrated and burned out she gave up not only her job with the Hispanic Freedom Forum, but all lawyering. Said the law was an ass, the whole legal system an asshole, and she wanted nothing more to do with assholes. She became a CPA and helped poor people with their taxes for almost nothing and, to put food on the table, helped rich people with their taxes for everything she could suck out of them. She was as good at that as she'd been at lawyering and began making good money.

So Carlita is, like me, not happy with the state of the world or of American politicians. She said what made me stand out from the younger guys she was usually getting involved with was that I seemed to see all the bullshit we were wading in, while most other men thought it was green grass. 'Course, it didn't hurt matters that even in my fifties I was something of a hunk compared to most of the guys I saw her with.

Although it took me three years, I was smart enough to get her to marry me. And we're doing pretty good, mostly because early in the game I discovered the secret of a good marriage: total capitulation. I discovered arguing with Lita wasn't a smart strategy. Telling her what to do wasn't a smart strategy. What works is surrender: what Lita wants Lita gets. 'Course it helps that every time I surrender and throw myself at her mercy, Lita grants amnesty and tends to come halfway back to my position. And being a smart gal, when I begin agreeing with her and surrendering, she sometimes begins calling me a wimp, but that only leads to our laughing together.

The fact is I've learned over the years that for us humans, being right is a losing strategy. The more convinced I am that I'm right, the more unhappiness I cause others and myself. I think one reason I love to bullshit is that when I'm doing it I'm never in any danger of thinking I'm right.

So after marrying Lita I was smart enough to settle down and save enough to buy a boat instead of muscle away as a crew member. And then to have a couple of kids and become the disgruntled old geezer I am today, living happily ever after.

Yeah, right.

When Louie the Arctic dog came into our lives Lita was as happy as me and the kids, and when it looked like some authority would inevitably come and want to haul Louie away for examination, interrogation, and dissection, she and I saw eye to eye: we wanted to try to save Louie from our fellow humans.

EIGHT

(From Billy Morton's *MY FRIEND LOUIE*, pp. 52–58)

About four days after we'd decided to keep Louie, things began to fall apart. It started with a small crowd gathering outside our house. Looking out the living room window, we saw a TV crew from a local Riverhead station. A few people knocked loudly on the door, but I shouted back from inside that there was nobody home.

I didn't have to tell Louie to hide, but he was so curious about everything that he kept wandering by the living room window wearing an old floppy cowboy hat of mine, a pink towel over most of him and a big pair of dark glasses just below the rim of the hat. He looked like a pumpkin wearing a cowboy hat moving on one long stilt.

Then three state police cars arrived and, instead of busting into our house, they began shooing away the crowd and the TV crew, forcing them to the far side of the road a hundred feet back toward Greenport. Although one police car and several cops went to keep the crowds down at the end of the street, two more cars pulled in and three cops ran around to take up positions at the rear of our house.

Lita and the kids and I were talking about what the hell was going on when a third car, a nondescript Ford, pulls into the driveway. We all stood at the window and watched two men get out, talk briefly to some big-shot state policeman and then stride up to our door.

I went to the locked door and waited as one of the men outside knocked. Twice.

"We'd like to speak to Mr. Morton," a voice says loudly.

I thought about playing possum and keeping mum but my curiosity always gets the better of me.

"What about?" says I.

"It's a private matter that we can't discuss through a closed door," says the loud voice.

"And who are you?" says I.

"Agents Johnson and Wall of the National Security Agency," says the voice.

"And what do you want to see Mr. Morton about?" says I.

Silence. Maybe whispering.

"We have to come in, Mr. Morton," says the loud voice. "We can ask the police to break the door down, or you can open up on your own."

Well, Lucas was reporting that there were now four policemen at the back of the house and two on the back porch, and Carlita spotted another car pulling up in front, and these voices sounded pretty sure of themselves. So I decided that I liked our door in the shape it was in and not the shape the cops would leave it in. I opened it.

The two guys standing on the porch looked harmless enough, medium-build, good-looking in a dull sort of way, and dressed in nice suits—although all suits look nice to me so they could have been cheap. Lita came up beside me and we all stood for a few seconds staring at each other.

"Won't you come in," says Lita quietly, and she steps back to open the door wider.

"Thank you," says the loud-voiced one. "I'm Agent Johnson

and this is Agent Wall." Johnson was a round-faced, young-looking guy with rimless glasses. Looked like he might have been nice if the government hadn't got him.

Wall was a bit heavier and would probably play the bad cop to Johnson's good cop.

"Please sit down," says Lita, backing toward the living room. "Can I get you something to drink?" Jesus, was she faking it.

"That won't be necessary, ma'am," Johnson says. "But thank you."

The two agent guys followed Lita into the living room, glancing around sharply, and then, first Johnson, then Wall, sat down on the couch.

I planted my butt in my rocker, and Lita sat on the arm of the big soft TV chair. Lucas and Jimmy had come in too, and ended up standing on either side of Lita, both frowning fiercely at these guys. Where Louie had gotten to I didn't know, but I managed not to peer around for him. He would certainly want to listen so I figured he was probably disguised as a huge hat and sitting on top of my head.

"So, what's up?" says I.

"We're here about the possible misuse of a computer in your house," says Johnson.

A computer!

"Misuse of a computer, huh," says I. "Someone watching porn?"

"Mr. Morton," says Johnson. "May we please see all of the computers you have in this house?"

Computers. Not a hairy beach ball, but computers. Or maybe both Louie and computers.

"Not unless you tell me why."

Agent Johnson gave me a long neutral stare.

"We have evidence that one of your computers was used to access certain government systems. Such activity is illegal. Technically it may be terrorism. We can confirm our evidence by examining your computers. Then, of course, we will have to determine which member or members of the household were responsible for the offense."

Well. Obviously it wasn't me. I sometimes can't even get into my own email, much less get into the NSA's. Lita mostly used the computer in her Southold office. Jimmy and Lucas are awfully bright, but not that bright. It didn't take me more than two-thirds of a second to realize that good old Louie was playing games. I couldn't help feeling proud of the little guy.

"Well," says I, "I can tell you who the culprit is. It was that damn Arctic dog we found. And he's hiding right now in this house. I'll help you find him. I'm not going to protect any terrorist who messes with the National Security Agency."

Well, 'course that's not what I said. A lot of good red-blooded Americans might have said that, but not me. And not Carlita. And not the kids. What I did say was: "I'd be happy to let you examine our computers," says I, "but no one in this house has any interest in the... NSA, not even sure we know what it is."

Agent Johnson gives me another long stare.

"Mr. Morton," he says, and the stare turns to stone. "We're quite certain that you know a great deal about the National Security Agency, so please stop playing the innocent old hick. You have a record of anti-government activity that goes back fifty years. You have harbored in this house a strange creature that apparently is highly skilled with computers. Let's cut the bullshit: where is this 'Arctic dog' that you claim was killed but obviously is still very much alive?"

"You think Louie hacked your computers?" says I, stalling for time.

"Who's Louie?" asks Johnson.

"Our deceased Arctic dog," says I. "If he hacked your computers I am truly sorry, and if he should suddenly rise from the dead, I assure you I'll tell him 'bad dog!'"

Little Jimmy giggled, but Agent Johnson again went into scowl mode.

"I'm afraid, Mr. Morton," he says, "that you don't realize the gravity of the situation. Hacking into government systems is a terrorist act. Anyone aiding and abetting the individual… or creature… that committed such an act is liable under relevant sections of the Computer Fraud and Abuse Act 1986 and the Patriot Act of 2001 to the same penalties as the terrorist himself… or *it*self."

"Pretty hard to aid and abet a corpse," says I. "Especially when the corpse has been a hundred feet under water for four days."

"You're making a big mistake, Mr. Morton."

"I often do," says I.

"And you, Mrs. Morton," says Mr. Scowl. "Are you going to see your life and that of your two fine young boys ruined by hiding some strange creature you know almost nothing about?"

"We had a dog," says Lita. "It was very special, we loved it, but we lost it. If the dog hacked your computers I am very sorry, but we know nothing about it."

He gave Lita a scowl almost as mean as the one he'd been

giving me, and then turned to the other guy.

"Henry, please go with Mrs. Morton and confiscate all computers in this house. Mrs. Morton, be so kind as to take Mr. Wall to wherever you have a computer, tablet, smart phone, or other portable device. We will give you receipts for these items, and they will be returned to you when we have examined them to our satisfaction."

"Do you have a warrant?" says Lita.

"Of course we have a warrant," says Agent Johnson, and he pulls a bunch of folded papers from his breast pocket and, still sitting, holds them out to her.

"Good," says I, ignoring the offered papers. "Wouldn't want you fellas to get in trouble with some judge because you forgot to get a warrant to steal all our computers."

Agent Johnson flushed. Lita was looking through the papers.

"Mrs. Morton?"

She stood up.

"I'll take your friend to our computers," she said, "but I do so under protest."

"Go ahead, Henry."

So Lita, Lucas, Jimmy, and this Henry agent leave the room. Agent Johnson and I sit in silence for almost a minute.

"Well, Mr. Morton, are you happy?" says Agent Johnson finally, with the sort of smirk President Bush the Worst used to like to flash at people.

"Blissful," says I. "Almost coming in my pants."

Agent Johnson couldn't suppress a look of surprise.

"You're quite a character, aren't you?"

"Just a typical old fisherman down on his luck," says I.

We then sat in silence awhile, neither of us able to think of anything witty or obnoxious to say.

The other agent finally reappeared carrying the hard drive of our main computer and one of Carlita's shopping bags, probably filled with the kids' tablet from the basement and maybe some other suspicious electronic stuff.

Agent Johnson exchanged a glance with Wall and stood up.

"We're about finished here, Mr. Morton," he says.

"Not going to take a look for Louie?" says I.

"No, we're not. We have a warrant to confiscate the computers but no warrant to search for a dead dog. Maybe next time."

"Sure wish you'd make a search," says I. "Love to see people waste their time."

"Oh, we'll be back. And I can assure you it won't be a waste of our time."

"Great," says I. "Next time let's cement our new friendship—get plastered together."

Agent Johnson had taken three or four steps toward the hallway, but he stopped and turned back to me.

"You don't have the faintest idea how down on your luck you're about to be, Mr. Morton. Not the faintest."

NINE

(From *LUKE'S TRUE UNBELIEVABLE REPORT OF THE INVASION OF THE FFS*, pp. 50–55)

Intelligence agencies are trained at birth to share as little intelligence as possible with the president since they wish to avoid two problems. First, the president asking where they got their information. One assistant secretary of defense had made the mistake of answering the president with "I'm afraid, sir, that for reasons of national security, we can't tell you." After he was relieved of his burdensome duties and reassigned to the Aleutian Islands, other NSA officials decided that the president of the United States probably should be able to access top-secret material, dangerous as they all thought that might be. They determined that from henceforth the president should believe he was getting the full story even if he wasn't even getting the first sentence of the story.

The second problem of sharing intelligence with the president is that he might act on the intelligence. All agencies feared the day when they would provide the president with new intelligence and he would take decisive action based on this intelligence and blow up the world. Or worse yet, adopt a peace plan.

In the case of the strange round creatures that didn't appear to be of this earth, the problem was great indeed. How do you tell the president that you think creatures from outer space are hacking government systems? After a few days of wrestling with the problem, the head of the NSA courageously turned the difficulty over to Presidential Aide Jeff Corrigan. If a messenger was going to get shot they preferred it be Jeff rather than one of their own.

"Mr. President, we have a problem."

"Yes, Jeff, what is it?" The president of the United States was sitting behind his desk enjoying an espresso and relaxing before the long day really got going. Jeff was standing nervously in front of the desk, his face occasionally twitching.

"Sir, you're going to find this hard to believe, but our science advisor at the NSA, Dr. Paul Leggen, reports that there are… beings from outer space now appearing here on Earth."

The president was not amused.

"Get to it, Jeff," he countered. "I don't have time for jokes. Dr. Leggen isn't writing for the *National Inquirer* these days, is he?"

"Beings from outer space are now here among us, sir," Jeff continued gamely. "They're shaped like beach balls."

The president stared at Jeff. He knew his aide in charge of briefings and coffee to be a quite serious man, and not normally given to exaggerations or practical jokes.

"Earth is being invaded by beach balls," he said.

"Hairy beach balls, sir," said Jeff.

"The earth is being invaded by hairy beach balls," the president repeated quietly, staring into space.

"Not invaded, sir," Jeff said. "So far we know of only a dozen or so here in the United States and in other nations, and they show no aggressive tendencies."

"Well, that's good," said the president. "I'd hate to be attacked by a hairy beach ball."

"That's right, sir. Their... shape doesn't indicate any sort of physical threat, but I'm afraid their extremely high intelligence may be a threat to our national security."

"The beach balls are a threat to national security."

"Yes, sir. At least one of them seems to have the ability to hack into almost any government or corporate system it wants, and has been illegally transferring funds from one bank account to another."

The president sat up. "They're hacking into our banking system? Are you sure these aren't more Muslim jihadists?"

"I'm afraid not, sir."

"This is serious. There are only a few aliens from outer space presently in the US. How many spaceships?"

"None that we know of, sir."

"They've hidden their spaceships. That sounds suspicious, doesn't it?"

Jeff bit his lip, then resumed his neutral expression.

"They may have arrived here on Earth by other means."

"Other means?"

"Means that we don't know about, or perhaps can't even conceive of."

The president stood up and stared at Jeff.

"My God, Jeff, you mean there are actually creatures here that come... come from... that are actual... aliens?"

"I'm afraid so, sir."

"I thought it was all typical internet paranoia. Are we able to communicate with these... beach ba—with these creatures?"

"It might be more accurate to say that some are able to communicate with us. That is, some seem to have learned languages quite quickly."

"And do these beach balls deign to tell us why they've suddenly decided to come to our planet?"

"No, sir, they haven't."

"But they're super-intelligent and are cyber-attacking government and corporate systems and robbing banks blind. That's not too friendly, is it?"

"No, sir."

"Shit."

"Yes, sir. That's what the NSA thinks too."

ITEM IN THE NEWS

A FEW DEFINITIONS FROM THE NEW PROTEAN DICTIONARY OF AMERICAN USAGE

BRAIN: Organ sometimes used by human beings to think. But not often.

CHILDREN: Ickie-like beings before they become human beings.

CORPORATION: An entity granted by the US Supreme Court with all the rights of an individual, and none of the responsibilities of an individual.

EARTH, THE: A small planet circling a small star in a small galaxy in a tiny universe. Considered by human beings to be the center of everything.

ELECTIONS: That process by which the rich elite of a nation solidify their power by selecting from a group of millionaires which ones will be in office.

FENCE ALONG THE ENTIRE MEXICAN BORDER: A mythical construction in the religion of some Republicans. *See angels and unicorns.*

GLOBAL WARMING: An ongoing process denied by many Americans because they are able to see clearly that it is sometimes quite cold out.

IRAQ: Nation that has been continuously bombed by the United States and other countries for twenty-five years.

Not considered a favorite vacation destination. *See ISIS.*

MADNESS: Doing the same thing over and over while each time expecting a different and better result. *See US military interventions.*

MARIJUANA: A type of vegetation which often makes humans giggle when they consume it. Considered by some humans as more dangerous than guns, and for many decades outlawed as such.

MASS MEDIA, THE: That collection of television, radio, and print outlets responsible for passing on to the people whatever issues and attitudes those in power want passed on to the people.

NUCLEAR BOMB: A scientific advance developed by the human race to wipe out the human race.

RAT RACE: A quite negative state of arranging human existence. Insulting to rats.

SELF: An illusionary concept of unknown origin which results in humans separating themselves from life.

TELEVISION: The primary source of most human opinion. Originally mistaken by early Protean visitors as household altars.

TEN

(From Billy Morton's *MY FRIEND LOUIE*, pp. 59–76)

After the agents left I was a bit surprised that Louie didn't immediately turn up. Even the kids didn't know where he was. And he didn't show up that night either. I wasn't worried about him, but a bit sad that he seemed to have deserted us just because some Feds and staties came to our house to arrest him and lock him up for a century.

But the next day he made an appearance. Of a sort. Damned if he didn't send me an email. On Lucas's cheap smartphone, which we had thoughtlessly forgotten to bring to the attention of Agent Wall.

What a jerk I'd been. Obviously if Louie could type on a computer in order to surf he could type in general. And if he was smart enough to hack the NSA, he probably was smart enough to spell out a few words. The email was pretty short.

Dear Billy.
Had to disappear for a bit, but want to meet you as soon as possible. For me, the safest place to be is on the sea. So please motor out into Long Island Sound and wait. But first go to your bank and take out most of the money I've deposited there. You're now in more danger than I am, and we both need each other's help.

Louie.

Well, this little bombshell pretty much left me speechless and dumb. 'Course I'm often dumb, but rarely speechless. I just looked up at Lita who was standing beside me. Our phone rang. I answered it.

"Mr. Morton?" a voice says.

"Yep. That's me," says I.

"This is John Kinderhook from Bank of America here in Greenport."

I didn't know any John Kinderhook, although the name was vaguely familiar from seeing it featured prominently on the cast of characters running the bank. I only dealt with people in the bank earning ten dollars an hour or less.

"Hey, how's it going, John?" says I.

"It's going fine, Mr. Morton, thank you. I just wanted to check with you about the deposit we received into your account yesterday afternoon."

"Great," says I. "I was going to check to see if it had arrived."

"Then you were expecting it?"

"Oh, yes," says I, giving my lying instincts a free run. "This fella has owed me money for years. Finally got him to pay up."

"It's quite a substantial amount."

"Lot of interest built up over the years, John."

"Uh… yes."

"How much did the fella send?" says I.

"The deposit was for four hundred and twenty thousand dollars," says John.

I was speechless.

But not for long.

"That weasel," says I, "short-changing me again. Damn bastard owes me a half mil."

"I see. Well, I'm afraid he only sent the four hundred and twenty thousand."

"Typical," says I. "By the way, John, I was planning to come in this morning and pick up some of it in cash. That going to be okay?"

"Why certainly," says John. "How much would you like?"

"What's my total balance?"

A pause.

"Your total balance today," says John, "is four hundred twenty thousand, thirteen dollars and six cents."

"Yep. Well, I guess I can get by if I withdraw four hundred thousand in cash. That work for you, John?"

This time it was the bank that was speechless.

"You want to withdraw four hundred thousand in cash?"

"Got a lot of old bills to pay, John. A lot of interest and penalties. You know all about interest and penalties, right, John?"

The bank lapsed again into silence.

"We may not have that much cash in the bank this morning, Mr. Morton. Could you—"

"Well, John, you *get it* in the bank. You wouldn't want it to get around that Bank of America couldn't pay its clients the money it was holding for them, would you?"

"No, no, of course not."

"See you in about an hour, John. Be good to be taking money out of the bank rather than putting it in."

The bank didn't comment.

I got the money. Never seen the new thousand-dollar bill before—especially two hundred of them. What with the smaller bills the cash totally filled Jimmy's school backpack I'd brought along for the occasion. To pack the rest I had to ask for a free Bank of America tote bag with the logo "The Giving Bank." They were giving that bag free to those who opened new accounts with a balance of at least three hundred dollars.

"You sure you know what you're doing?" John the banker says as a teller counted out the money.

"'Course I don't, John," says I. "Never have, never will. But I figure my money is safer in my hands than it is in yours, so think I'll take it home and store it in the freezer. Don't want it to deteriorate."

I didn't put the money in the freezer but rather into the bottom of the duffel bag I use to take my clean sea clothes to the boat. I stuffed into it Jimmy's cash-filled backpack and the Bank of America tote bag. I figured if I was stopped, I'd say I didn't know how the money got there—must be Jimmy's lunch money. Although the kids and Carlita all wanted to come with me to meet Louie out on the sound, I said no. If Louie thought we were in danger, I didn't want the kids to hear what he had to say.

I worried a little bit that the Feds might have put a tail on me, but no matter how much I looked in mirrors or reflections in store windows or peeked under my smelly armpits, I never spotted anything suspicious—except maybe a babe who looked like a reincarnation of Marilyn Monroe smiling at me from the entrance of a bar. Babes haven't smiled at me from bars for a decade so I figured this one was an NSA honey trap. But they gotta do better than Marilyn—I'm a Jennifer Lopez sort of guy.

An hour later, I was five miles out on the sound and Louie

still wasn't making an appearance. In another half hour when he still wasn't there I began to feel stupid. And I felt even stupider when old Josh Hemingway motored up in his twenty-six-foot crab boat and pulled up alongside, idling his engine just four or five feet off my port side.

"What's happening, Billy?" he says. "You got motor trouble?" No self-respecting fisherman would be drifting in the middle of the Long Island Sound without a single fishing line overboard.

"No, Josh," says I. "Everything's just hunky-dory. Motor humming along as usual like a broken lawn mower with its blades hitting everything except grass."

"Just enjoying the day then, huh?" says Josh, knowing that no self-respecting fisherman out on the water has time to enjoy the day.

"No, Josh," says I. "I'm just waiting to meet a hairy beach ball from outer space who emailed me this morning to tell me to meet him here and bring the half-million dollars he'd put in my bank account."

That stopped Josh cold. It took him five or six seconds, but then he laughed.

"Yeah," he says, spitting over the side of his boat. "That damn beach ball made the same promise to me, but he never showed up. Just can't depend on hairy beach balls."

This time it was me who was a bit surprised, and then I realized that Josh was just pulling my leg the way he thought I was pulling his.

"Still, it's nice to have almost half a million dollars in cash," says I. "Might be able to afford a new anchor line."

"Maybe even some new nets," says Josh, going back to the

helm and throwing his gear into forward. "You take care, Billy."

And Josh cruises slowly away, giving me one last wave with a big smile.

Which proves the advantage of being a habitual liar. No one believes me when I tell the truth.

Finally, I gave up. I'd been on the sound for an hour, and nothing.

I goosed the engine back into life and headed back toward land.

"Hold it," said a loud, deep voice.

I turned and there on the seat at the stern nestled Louie, looking no different than when I'd first spotted him on the boat's cabin roof so long ago—ten days maybe.

"You're late," says I, pretending not to be surprised that he could talk.

"I've been checking a few things," says Louie. He sounded like a sportscaster intoning just before a Superbowl, his voice deep and meaningful. Been watching too many newscasts.

"Thanks for the money," I says. "Is someone going to be missing it?"

"Oh, yes," says Louie.

"You hacked someone's bank account," says I.

"A bank's bank account, Billy. Thus no harm done."

I put *Vagabond* in neutral, turned off the engine and went aft to sit near him on one of the few feet of seating on the port side of the stern.

"I guess, Louie, it's time you tell me what you're all about."

"Good idea," he says.

"When did you learn to talk?" I ask. "Or could you talk all

along but decided to hold back for a special occasion."

"No, I only learned how to do it a few days ago. A friend taught me."

"Human or other?"

"Other. While I was spending my first month on Earth learning to communicate with dolphins, killer whales, sea turtles, and minnows, he was in France moving among people, so he learned how to make human sounds much faster than I."

"Well, that's great. And where's your home town?" I ask.

"Ah, my home town," says Louie, a small area of hairs seeming to part and swish with the passage of air. "It's in a different universe," he answered.

"Yeah, that's what I figured. We get a lot of tourists from there in the summer and fall."

Damned if Louie didn't reach out and poke me with a foot-long projection from his belly, as if he'd appreciated my joke.

"I love your style, Billy. You don't seem to take things seriously."

"At my age, with death knocking on the door every other Tuesday, I can't afford to take things seriously."

Although we were side by side on the aft seat, swaying to and fro with the motion of the boat on a slightly lumpy sea, I couldn't tell if he was looking at me or not.

"Are you looking at me, Louie?"

"Every second, Billy, although it took me a long time after I first arrived—six or seven minutes—to reduce my sensory input so that I saw only what the porpoises see or what you humans see and not the other million wavelengths our... people see."

"Same with hearing?" I ask.

"Same with all human senses. Most of what I'm

experiencing is irrelevant to human life. Even after I've read all your encyclopedias and surfed all your nets and explored the NSA and other government systems, I'm still filled mostly with data and programs that have nothing to do with life here on Earth."

"I guess we're pretty boring, huh?"

"Not at all. Humans are the most interesting creatures on this planet and more interesting than a lot of advanced creatures we've encountered in other places."

"What makes us interesting?" says I.

"You're so intelligent and so incredibly stupid. We've never encountered a species with so much brain power that was so stupid."

"Well, we've had a lot of practice," says I.

"Yes, you have, and you're getting better and better at it, especially here in this country."

"Oh, yeah," say I, "America's the Greatest at everything. Especially stupidity."

He bounced twice about a foot off the seat, maybe his way of laughing.

"So what are you here for, Louie—on Earth I mean?"

"You mean what's my purpose?"

"Yep."

"No purpose at all, Billy. We're here to play."

"Then what's with hacking the CIA and sending money from some bank's bank account to me. And probably a dozen others."

"I've hacked into hundreds of bank and corporate accounts, Billy. Soon to be thousands."

"Why?"

"Just for the fun of it, Billy. Just for the fun of it."

"Fun, huh."

"What you have to understand is that primitive creatures need to base their lives on purpose and surviving—to find food, shelter, safety. But when creatures find their existence is no longer endangered, they can develop a second way of living: play. They begin doing things 'for the hell of it.' We see hundreds of different creatures acting in the play mode when they're young—puppies and kittens and bear cubs and human children. Children racing each other from one tree to another, but not caring who wins. As soon as a child cares if he wins, then it becomes purposeful and stops being play. And you humans took a wrong step on the evolutionary road when purpose became your primary mode and play was seen as childish. In our evolution we chose play. And see seriousness as childish."

"Wouldn't work with us."

"But you're playing all the time, Billy. What do you think all your bullshitting exaggeration is? It's play."

"Maybe."

"Remember, that though you've been evolving for a few hundred thousand years," Louie says, "in other universes creatures have been evolving for billions. Which might explain why some are a bit more developed than you are."

"You seem to—what the hell!?"

A small porpoise had leapt right over the whole boat just missing my head and plopped back into the water.

I stood up and turned to Louie.

"You see that!? In all my days at sea—"

The damn porpoise suddenly burst up from the other side,

seemed to be aimed right at my head, then just missed me on its way back to the sea.

I leaned over to see what it was doing, but it had disappeared. I shook my head and, as I turned again to Louie, heard a flapping on the coach roof.

Damned if the porpoise—but it was a porpoise with no eyes or mouth—wasn't flopping like a dying fish on the coach roof.

"Hey, how you doing?" says Louie, and when I turned to him I sensed he wasn't talking to me but to the fish.

I looked back up to the coach roof and the fish was gone and sitting there was a… midget human, legs crossed, arms raised as if in triumph. Its head had ears and a nose, but no eyes or mouth. With his body covered with the thin silver-gray hairs that were the FF's trademark, he looked less like a human than a skinny, eyeless, toothless chimpanzee.

"Pretty good, right?" says the midget.

I slowly sat back down next to Louie.

"Yep," I says. "Pretty good. The last creature that cavorted on my coach roof was just a round beach ball."

"Louie has no imagination," says the midget. "He's all brains but lacking in elasticity."

"Thanks," says Louie.

"You going to introduce me to your friend?" I says to Louie.

"This is… the friend who taught me to talk," says Louie.

"So exactly how many of you guys are there swimming around our planet?" says I.

As I spoke, the fake human shrank back into a sphere, came off the roof and bounced over to sit beside Louie.

"Hundreds," says the new FF. "And aren't we having fun?"

"Oh, yeah," says I. "You got a name?"

"My friends in Europe call me 'Molière,'" he says. "After a writer who enjoyed writing plays about human follies."

"Well, Molière, glad to meet you. You into robbing our banks too?"

"Not yet. I've been having a lot of fun playing with your absurd Homeland Security and NSA bureaucracies. We recently ordered a branch of the NSA to investigate two-thirds of the people in the CIA. At the same time we hacked into the CIA computer systems and got them to begin investigating six thousand people in other branches of the NSA."

"Jesus, they're going to love you guys when they find out."

"And we've found a whistle-blower," says Louie, "who's gotten material to the *Los Angeles Times* that shows that the NSA has terrorist files on over forty-five million Americans based on whether they have visited anti-government websites, both left and right, or communicated with people who have."

"Hey," says I. "I must be on that list!"

"Of course you are," says Louie. "Only people who have no opinions at all are safe. If you've never expressed an opinion on any serious subject then you can have sex with anyone you like, visit child porn sites, cheat on your income taxes, extort money, bribe officials, anything at all in fact, just remember not to express any opinion on anything. That makes you an upstanding American who can go about his business without the NSA giving a single damn."

"Although it will still watch every single move you make," says Molière.

"Getting that sort of stuff published doesn't seem to make

much difference," says I. "People don't seem to care if some government agency knows every time they burp."

"Of course not," says Louie. "They know they've got no control over their government so why worry about how much power it has."

"What else have you been up to?" I ask Molière.

"I've been working on getting Homeland Security to transfer eight hundred of their Certified Public Accountants to the IRS and get the head of the IRS to use them to audit big corporations. But Louie makes bank robbing sound like more fun."

"Well, I like it," says I, remembering the duffel bag of cash sitting forward in the anchor locker. "But how do you get an IRS director to do what you want?"

"We blackmail him," says Molière. "The NSA files are filled with information that they can use to blackmail hundreds of thousands of Americans. We're borrowing some of that info to get people to be more sympathetic to our requests."

"Jesus, you guys play rough, don't you?" says I.

"Just playing by the rules your society has set up," says Molière. "We've found that blackmail and extortion are as American as apple pie."

"Apple pie and blackmail," says I. "Not often you hear the two in the same sentence."

"This old one is a very superior type of human," says Louie. "One of the very few I've found. He knows he is stupid and knows nothing, and thus is at a very advanced stage for a human."

"Thanks, Louie," says I. "I always figured it would take a genius to appreciate me."

Suddenly both FFs rolled off the seat onto the floor and in under the coach roof. At first I thought it was their way of laughing together at my joke, but then I heard a distant sound that turned into a rising roar.

I stood up and saw a helicopter approaching from the Connecticut side of the sound. When I turned to tell Louie and Molière, I saw two small power boats coming at us at full speed, their wakes so high on either side I could see them a half mile away. I went forward to the helm and turned on the engine.

"Don't bother," says Louie.

"See you," says Molière, and with a single bounce he was over the side and into the water.

"Aren't you going too?" I ask Louie.

"No, I think I'll stick around."

I could barely hear Louie with the roar of the helicopter overhead, but as the two power boats came plowing up on either side of *Vagabond,* the chopper swerved and headed slowly away.

The first boat to come up was an unmarked twenty-five-foot speedboat with four men aboard, one of them my old buddy Agent Johnson. The other three were all in suits, but I didn't recognize any of them.

The second boat, a small Coast Guard speedboat about the same length as Johnson's, pulled up on the starboard side. I noticed Agent Wall trying to put a bumper down between the Coast Guard boat and *Vagabond* and almost crushing half his fingers.

I turned off the engine and went inside the cabin for a weapon. I pulled out a bottle of Jim Beam, grabbed three coffee mugs, and went back out. Carrying my armaments, I sauntered aft as coolly as I could—an old man with balance problems never actually saunters; he mainly staggers or wobbles. I sat down, crossed my legs, and poured a shot into one of the coffee mugs.

As I was doing this, Agent Johnson climbed awkwardly aboard *Vagabond*—looked like a cripple trying to get over a fence.

"You want a drink, Louie?" I says, figuring he was probably biologically a teetotaler.

"Thought you'd never ask, Billy. Thanks."

Well. I should have figured. Humans tend to drive people to drink, even those from other universes.

I poured a good shot into a second mug and held it out to Louie. He reached out a… limb, then created some fingers—three I think—and took the mug.

"Cheers," he says and knocks his mug against mine.

"Hey, how's it going, Mr. Johnson?" says I. "You like to join us in a drink?"

Agent Johnson was straightening his clothes from his fence-climbing, but when he noticed Louie his eyes widened in surprise. As he stared, Louie reached up with his "limb" and "fingers" and coffee mug, and poured all the Jim Beam on the top of his sphere. I gotta say Louie had a unique way of drinking. Agent Johnson looked frightened.

"Is this… is this the… Arctic dog?" he says.

"This is Louie," I says. "Visiting us from another universe."

The seas were just rough enough to have the boats on either side of *Vagabond* bouncing up and down almost a foot every few seconds, rubbing against each other, and I could see the other agents aboard the unmarked boat looking a little green around the gills. Agent Johnson didn't look totally chipper either.

"Come on over and have a seat," says I, picking up the last mug and pouring a double shot for the needy agent. He stood there with one arm balancing himself on the coaming and then straightened and came aft and stopped in front of Louie and me.

"You're under arrest," says Agent Johnson to Louie. Always a good way to greet a new friend.

Louie immediately sprouts five or six short limbs out of his sphere, and raises these arms straight up in surrender.

Agent Johnson doesn't bat an eyelash.

"We have evidence that you are responsible for the invasion of several government and corporate systems. Also for stealing well over three million dollars from at least five corporations."

"Actually, I've so far stolen twenty-one million five hundred and sixty thousand dollars from eight corporations and three banks."

Confession may be good for the soul, but I thought Louie's was a bit early: he hadn't even been tortured yet.

Louie shrunk down his limbs and morphed back into his sphere.

"You're admitting you are the perpetrator?" Johnson asks.

"I am."

"Then I'm taking you to Riverhead where we can formally charge you."

"I don't think so."

"We have six armed men on either side of this boat. An Apache helicopter a quarter mile off."

"Congratulations."

"We might have to shoot you."

"Violence!"

"What's going to stop us?"

"Me," says Louie.

You gotta give him credit, he had a lot of balls, or at least one big one.

Agent Johnson reached under his suit jacket and took out a gun that looked big enough to put a hole in a rhino.

"Let's go," says Agent Johnson. Then he turns to the boat he came in on.

"Graves, Backstrom," he says. "Come aboard and take this ma… creature into custody."

Well, you and I know that all Louie had to do was bounce once and he'd be in the water and fifty-foot deep before you could say "anchors away." Still, these guys had guns and Louie seemed a bit too relaxed about what he was facing. Could bullets kill him?

Two agents clambered over the coaming onto *Vagabond*, both big guys who looked like they could handle Hulk Hogan if they felt like it. They moved toward me and Louie, both of us still sitting in the stern. When they were only a couple of feet away they stopped and stood over Louie, who never batted a hair, which, considering he had about two million of them, was impressive.

Then one of them reached down to grab Louie. The next thing I knew the bruiser flew head over heels off the stern into the water. Louie had somehow grabbed him and thrown—it was so quick I don't know how he did it.

The other bruiser looked a little less confident. In fact he took a step backward. As he pulled out his own howitzer, he turned to Agent Johnson.

"What do you want me to do, Chief?" he asks.

By now two Coast Guard guys had thrown the first bruiser four or five life rings, one of them almost knocking him out cold, but they still managed to pull him aboard.

Agent Johnson came up beside the other agent.

"We're not going to shoot you…" he says.

"Louie," says I. "His name is Louie."

"We're not going to shoot you, Louie, but we'd like to be able to question you and we'd like you to stop robbing our banks and hacking our systems."

"That seems reasonable," says Louie. "At least the first part."

"What are you doing here? Why are you hacking into everything? What are your intentions?"

"To have fun."

"Robbing banks is your idea of fun?"

"One of thousands," says Louie.

"What happens if we shoot you?"

"I don't know. None of us has ever been shot."

"You don't seem too worried about it," says Agent Johnson.

"The worse that could happen," says Louie, "is that I'd return to the ocean and feed the fish."

Just then Agent Johnson's cell phone began playing "America the Beautiful," and he took it out of a suit-jacket pocket and eased away from us toward the cabin.

"That reminds me, Louie," says I. "How did you and Molière get in contact with each other when he arrived from Europe?"

"We FFs are in contact whenever we're within fifteen or twenty miles of each other. Even as I'm now talking to you, Molière and I are communicating both with each other and with another FF that's within range. Every second I know much of what Molière is thinking and he knows a lot of what I'm thinking. FFs within range of each other are not separate beings but one."

"You reading my mind too?"

"No, I can't read your mind, but I'm getting input from you every second, and from Johnson every second, and from three or four dozen fish milling about in the water around us."

"Too bad we humans can't do that," says I.

"But you can, you do. You're receiving data from other humans and other animals every second. Even plants. Unfortunately, you haven't developed the neuron capacity to absorb and process the data. Humans vaguely understand that a baby is absorbing the mood of its mother whether the mother says something or not, or whether the mother touches the baby or not. But most other signals from other humans are lost in the clutter of 'reality.'"

"I've been ordered to take you into custody," Agent Johnson broke in, striding toward us with manly determination after finishing his iPhone chat.

"I prefer boating," says Louie.

"Let's take him to our launch," says Agent Johnson, and he and his remaining muscle-bound pal began slowly approaching Louie, neither agent looking like they thought it was going to be a piece of cake.

When they were a foot away they both reached down and tried to take a hold of Louie, but suddenly it was as if Louie were all jello: their hands couldn't seem to get a grip on anything.

"I'm going," says Louie. "But I warn you—if you arrest or do any sort of harm to my friend Billy, the things I'll do to your

NSA files will end your ability to spy on even your own mother."

The two agents were still playing with the hairy jello and getting nowhere when Louie squirmed free and bounced off the stern into the sea.

Me and the two agents looked aft and saw that instead of sinking out of sight as I expected, Louie assumed the sort of human form that Molière had shown and began doing a backstroke around the sterns of the three boats. He was soon twenty feet in front of them and moving away.

"Follow that… that… that swimmer!" ordered Agent Johnson, and he and the thug clambered back into their launch.

The crews of the two launches brought in the lines attached to *Vagabond*, restarted their engines, and threw their boats into gear. The engines roared.

They sped off at zero knots nowhere. The Coast Guard launch continued to bounce up and down against *Vagabond*, but Johnson's launch began to drift away to leeward. I saw the helmsman on Johnson's boat shift back to neutral then into forward again, but nothing happened—although the engine was working perfectly. The propellers weren't spinning.

Just then a porpoise, a hairy porpoise, leapt out of the sea, sailed over Johnson's launch, dropped something into the boat as he passed, and plopped back into the water just in front of *Vagabond*.

When I quickly looked forward, Louie was still doing his modified backstroke away from us. The porpoise was Molière.

"What the fuck's happening!?" Johnson barks, fully on top of the situation.

Next thing I knew, Molière came flying up over the other launch, dropped another something—some sort of bomb?—

before sailing over *Vagabond* to plop into the sea to my leeward.

When I saw the crew of the Coast Guard launch looking with annoyed surprise down at their cockpit floor and heard no explosions, I realized that Molière must have dropped something else.

"The prop!" someone shouts from Johnson's launch

Yep.

Good old Molière had removed the props from the two boats. Then kindly returned each of them. A gentleman.

I wondered whether mine was gone too, so I ambled forward, got the engine going, threw it into forward gear and… off we chugged, good as new, if you can call anything on a forty-year-old boat new.

Well, Molière gave one more spectacular jump over Johnson's boat—just to say "sorry" I guess, then appeared up beside Louie, where he began swimming with a modified breaststroke. I knew both these FFs could swim ten times faster shaping themselves as fish. They were using human strokes just for the fun of it.

Some cowboy on Johnson's boat then shot a round at the two FFs lazing along now sixty feet away, but Johnson ordered him to cease and desist, or something like that.

Old *Vagabond* and I spent an hour towing the two boats back toward Plum Gut—until the Coast Guard arrived in a bigger boat and took over the tow.

Last I saw of Louie and Molière, they were back in porpoise shape but each with one arm, and leaping up out of the water, bumping bellies, and giving each other high fives.

ELEVEN

(From *LUKE'S TRUE UNBELIEVABLE REPORT OF THE INVASION OF THE FFS*, pp. 78-83)

Aliens from outer space or from another universe were the greatest gift God has ever given the Western media. And aliens who were somewhat of a danger but not *that* threatening was icing on the cake. Ted Brookings' story broke in the Riverhead newspaper on the same day that the *London Daily Mirror* reported a two-minute interview with a hairy sphere who British intelligence was after for spying, but who talked exclusively about modern movies. And the next day the *Los Angeles Times* published an article about two shape-changing spheres cavorting on the beaches of southern California, with two photos, one of something leaping out of the water looking like a skinny furry porpoise, and the second of several children chasing a hairy beach ball along the water's edge. They had a *video* of that one too. The *Times* reported that the spheres seemed only to talk to children and in childish voices.

That day every newspaper, blog, cable channel, network news, Facebook and Twitter feed, and every other social media outlet in the world could talk about nothing but the "invasion of aliens." Oh, it was a fun time for the whole world, or for at least those who had enough to eat and a roof over their heads, and access to the media. The possibility (at first) and then the certainty (certainty!) that actual real aliens had at last arrived on Earth went viral worldwide. Humans had been panting after aliens for hundreds of years, and now at last we of the twenty-first century were lucky enough to have them actually show up. And they weren't blasting us with ray guns! Halleluja!

At first the media was filled with speculation about where the aliens had come from and why they had come to Earth. Sightings of spaceships crashing into the Borneo jungle, Mongolian desert, and several different oceans took up a lot of space for almost a week and then disappeared when no wreckage was found. A leading professor of weather at Iowa State College advanced the theory that FFs were created by lightning strikes during Arctic vortex outbreaks. Others wrote that the FFs weren't aliens at all but creations of advanced artificial intelligence labs. Most such writers criticized the labs for creating such useless entities.

There was also much speculation about the physical characteristics of these creatures. Did they have a computer built into a very muscular body? Did they have pain sensors? Hearts? Sexual inclinations? How did they communicate with each other? Were they somehow allied with some sect of Muslim jihadists?

Since reliability is not a strong suit of modern media, it was difficult to know what was true and what was sensationalist exaggeration. The aliens were soon called Proteans by much of the media, after the Greek sea-god noted for his ability to change shape. And the Proteans seemed to be doing a lot of senseless things that made it difficult for the media to get a handle on them. Traditionally, aliens arrive on Earth determined to conquer helpless humanity, or, because they got separated from their countrymen, they just want to go home. Or they're here to do scientific research on humans by snatching them off the street and taking them up into spaceships where they do nasty things that the survivors can't quite remember.

These Proteans had so far shown no weapons, no spaceships, and no desire to conquer anyone. None of them had yet indicated any desire to go home. They were mostly doing things that seemed playful fun, but sometimes did other things that seemed threatening. Some Protean was apparently responsible for posting a doctored video on YouTube of Vladimir Putin making love to a polar bear. Everyone loved that, with the possible exception of Vladimir Putin and the polar bear. And some mischievous Protean in the US was managing to get printed in newspapers, both digital and paper, items that at first blush seemed true, but upon mature reflection—something often beyond the capacity of many good Americans—could be seen as nonsense. For example FFs often managed to get items published that appeared to originate from oil companies:

The Earth Institute for a More Pleasant Planet, partly funded (99.44%) by Russia's Gazprom and British Petroleum, announced today that they are doubling their investments in alternative fuels, from $922 a year to $1,844.

Proteans were also paying for advertisements for products that may or may not exist, but the ads themselves were clearly a joke:

Buy Powerpunchiagra!

Guaranteed to increase your potency thirty percent, length ten percent, duration fifty percent! Possible side effects: cancer, stroke, heart attack, mild indigestion, and insanity. If you get an erection lasting more than four days please notify us and let us know how you did it.

Besides this kind of playfulness several Proteans were apparently showing off their swimming and acrobatic skills in pools, rivers, lakes, and oceans in several places around the world. One appeared suddenly at a school in Indiana at recess and began playing games with the children.

On the other hand, it was claimed by an anonymous source that a Protean was behind a drone in Syria going way off course and almost hitting a navy destroyer in the Mediterranean. Another Protean allegedly hacked into a Walmart bank account and transferred all the money to the accounts of Walmart employees. One of the Walmart owners had a stroke. However, he owned three hospitals, so got reasonably good care. Most Walmart employees spent a lot of money in a very short time, but claimed they were unaware of any unusual deposits in their accounts.

One Protean apparently got kindergarten kids in Switzerland to refuse to end a recess because they were tired of school. Rumors spread that the Swiss government was considering declaring a national day of mourning.

In that first week various countries were reacting to the Proteans differently. In Great Britain the government and the right-wing media mostly described two Proteans as Muslim terrorists in disguise. Pretty deep disguise we'd say. They claimed they had video evidence that the two had entered a mosque and prostrated themselves on the floor and practiced the Muslim pushup thing that they do to honor Allah. British MI5 claimed the Proteans had erased all the data in one of their important anti-terrorist files. So some British tabloids played up the danger of these creatures.

On the other hand, there was an alien in Brighton who, after entertaining people at the beach with all sorts of water tricks, organized a mass dance-in one day and a group beer fest the next. And another in Newcastle organized a protest march favoring longer pub hours. These the tabloids loved.

In China there was one long article in the *Beijing Times Herald* proving that Proteans were robots created by the Japanese to infiltrate China, destroy its economy, and then take over four or five rocks in the South China Sea that both countries claimed as their own.

In France, the intelligence agencies saw danger at every turn—that was their job—and at first convinced themselves that the aliens were allied with the jihadists: why else would they hack into government spy agency systems? However, the media took a liking to one Protean, who they named "Pantagruel" after some mischief-maker giant in the Middle Ages. They publicized him as a cool guy always clowning around and having fun. Many Frenchmen loved him, although most were disappointed he didn't seem to like French food. And even worse, Pantagruel tended to pour any wine they gave him all over his body rather than smell it, swirl it in the glass, and hold it in its mouth for ten minutes before swallowing, as civilized people do.

And people in Latin America, Africa, and Asia seemed to find their few Protean visitors to be interesting and fun.

They never seemed to shoot anyone or blow up anything, a definite plus. Many Brazilians loved playing something they call *futbol* but more advanced nations call soccer, using one of the Proteans as the ball. And they didn't mind that the ball didn't obey the orders of the foot or head but might bounce crooked or ten feet high or roll across the entire length of the crossbar before falling into the melee of players waiting to get their heads on it. The Brazilians called this new game "Loco futbol."

In the US, the Republican and Democratic candidates who had announced they were running for president and were seeking their party's nomination for the election still a year away were miffed. They knew that the winner of their party's nomination would be the man or woman who could get on the evening newscasts and cable talk shows most often, but their brilliant speeches and sensational PR stunts were being relegated to page fifteen of most newspapers and not even making it onto the evening news. All the people wanted were new videos or still photos of some Protean doing something crazy or something threatening.

The thirty-seven Republican candidates running for the Republican nomination were the most negative. Several of them argued in one of the debates that the playfulness of some of the Proteans was only to fool people into thinking they were harmless so they and the jihadists could take over the country. It was not explained how less than two dozen known aliens and less than thirty known jihadists planned to take over the nation. Several others cited the money disappearing from corporate bank accounts as evidence that the Proteans were trying to destroy the modern capitalist system. The

Republican candidates considered that a negative.

And all the Republican candidates jumped on some new reports that indicated that some of the money the Proteans were stealing from banks ended up in the bank accounts of churches—Protestant, Catholic, Jewish, Buddhist, and Muslim. Of course, they all talked about the money being given to Muslims but neglected to mention the other churches.

The Democratic presidential candidates were more muted. They stated with firm conviction that some Proteans were good and some were bad.

The New York Times wrote that the Proteans were of "scientific interest" and that the best way to counter any "malevolent" intentions of the Proteans was to capture one and gently question it to see what made it tick. An op-ed piece *The Times* published a day later by a former CIA director suggested that if the gentle questioning didn't work, it might be necessary to turn the creature over to the CIA for more advanced interrogation. The op-ed piece did admit that waterboarding might not be too effective with a species that sometimes liked to live underwater for weeks.

ITEM IN THE NEWS

Houston, Texas, June 3rd

The American Institute for the Scientific Study of the Benefits of Climate Change, partly funded (96.24%) by Walmart Oil and the State of North Dakota, announced today that polar bears had appeared in Central Park, where they were welcomed by everyone as a wonderful new tourist attraction. Unfortunately, naturalists believe that the polar bears are actually on a long migration to Tierra Del Fuego and Antarctica, where there are still large surviving ice floes. So, New Yorkers, enjoy the bears while you can! Another gift of global warming!

And remember, we have enough coal and oil and natural gas in the ground to burn them for another sixty years! And when we start to run out, it won't matter! The planet will be so hot we'll never need to heat our homes again!

TWELVE

(From Billy Morton's *MY FRIEND LOUIE*, pp. 77–82)

Back at the old homestead in the days after I'd talked to Louie and Molière on the boat, the shit hit the fan again.

Now we have lots of fans on Long Island in the summer and fall, but normally not so much shit hitting them. And personally, I've always wondered what happens to the shit that doesn't hit the fan. Supposedly it flies on past the fan and then splatters against some wall or someone's head or clothes. Not as bad as hitting the fan, I suppose, but still pretty bad. In any case, back at the old homestead things began to go downhill.

But shouldn't the saying be "things began to go uphill"? Isn't going downhill easier than going uphill? We sure have some stupid sayings.

First thing, Johnson and his agents did a thorough search of my boat and found the three hundred grand in Jimmy's school backpack in the anchor locker. I had carelessly put the Bank of America tote bag ("The Giving Bank") in a hidden compartment in the bilge and forgot to tell them about it. I thought I made a pretty convincing case that the three hundred grand was Jimmy's lunch money, but they insisted on confiscating it. I said they had no legal right to the money, and they said "Neither do you," which pretty much shut me up.

The kid reporter's article in the Riverhead paper and other articles about FFs suddenly began appearing all over the place. This meant that me, Lita, and the boys were of interest again. We were apparently among the three or four people in the whole world who had interacted with an FF for more than a few days. We got over fifty calls from various TV channels, newspapers, and magazines for interviews. Although one television network offered me one hundred thousand dollars for an exclusive half-hour interview with me and my family, at first we turned down all offers.

But in the second week some of the media coverage about the FFs began to turn negative. A flight from New Zealand to Los Angeles had disappeared a month earlier, before anyone had even heard of the FFs, and so far no trace of the plane had been found. One of the passengers was some bigwig in the CIA.

At first, of course, the media blamed the Muslim terrorists, but then CNN gets some fella on the air who says he has evidence that a Protean had boarded the plane in a passenger's luggage and may have whisked the plane off to another dimension. CNN showed a short clip of some guy dressed in some sort of uniform telling the expert fella that when a piece of luggage accidentally fell open he noticed a strange basketball that seemed to have hair. He didn't think anything of it at the time, so he just put the ball back in the luggage.

The expert fella said that if the Protean hadn't yanked the plane into another universe, he may simply have crashed it into the Pacific Ocean and then swum away—Proteans being good swimmers.

Seemed pretty reasonable.

If you're an idiot.

Well that little interview led to a few other claims of accidents that had been purposely caused by one of the little fellows. A ferry in the Philippines had capsized when most of the passengers had panicked and rushed to one side of the boat. Some crew member now claimed that he'd seen a hairy beach ball yell "Man overboard!" and that was what caused the capsize. Fifty more innocent people killed by the FFs.

Yeah. Right.

'Course, only one section of the media went this far. When TV stations interviewed people who had seen or interacted with a Protean, most of them seemed to like them. However, in some of the sensationalist media it was clear that any human being who suddenly disappeared was a victim of the FFs. Whether those who got abducted had been killed or mailed off to the FF alternative universe was hotly debated on a couple of the cable channels. Most of the people on Fox News thought they'd been mailed off to an alternative universe to be made sex slaves. Kinda strange thing to do for creatures who seemed to have no sex life.

Because of all this nonsense about FFs that was getting aired, I thought we should take another look at our decision not to do any interviews. I gathered everyone together in the living room for one of our family conferences. Lita had come up with the idea that the kids should be in on all decisions that affected the whole family so the boys were there too; Lucas sitting on the arm of the couch near Lita, and Jimmy on the floor leaning up against the couch at Lita's legs.

"Louie and his friends aren't able to defend themselves," I says. I was in my rocker, rocking.

"Oh, they could if they wanted," Lita says, sitting on the couch and jiggling her leg nervously. "My guess is that they just haven't gotten around to it."

"But most of the people being interviewed are government types claiming the FFs are doing nasty things."

"We can't stop that," she says.

"The people who have nice things to say about them don't usually make it on TV. But because they know we've spent a lot of time with Louie, the media *will* put us on."

"They'll put us on," says Lita, "but have you thought what it would do to our lives?"

"I just think that when a friend is being attacked we've got to defend him."

"That's right," says Lucas. "I'm tired of the lies they're telling about Louie."

"Me too," says Jimmy.

"I understand that, boys," says Lita, "but these creatures don't need our help. They're a thousand times more intelligent and powerful than we can even conceive of. They're literally superhuman. They don't need our help."

"And usually our kids don't need our help, but we give it to them."

"Not the same. Louie is superhuman, Lucas and Jimmy are children."

"I want to do something," says I.

"We do too," says Lucas.

"Right," says Jimmy.

Lita reaches down with her left hand and caresses the top of Jimmy's head.

"I understand that," she says, "but I worry that we're getting into something way over our heads. I worry that we don't have the faintest idea of what he and his friends are up to. They can speak as if they are humans, but as Louie has told you, ninety-nine percent of what they're about has nothing to do with human life."

"I know."

"No matter how different they are," says Lucas, "we know they're good."

"We *think* they're good," says Lita.

"They *are!*" says Jimmy.

Lita smiled and again caressed the top of Jimmy's head. Then she stood up and came over to me at my rocker. My bald head got caressed too.

"If you go on TV and talk about what we know about Louie and Molière, our whole family will be famous. The boys' lives will be turned topsy-turvy. I like our lives the way they are."

"We've got to tell people the truth about Louie and the FFs," says Lucas.

"If you won't do it, Mom, *I'll* go on TV and talk," says Jimmy.

"Okay, okay," says I, taking Lita's hand in mine but still rocking in my chair. "Lita's right that our lives will be turned a bit upside down, but the boys are right that we want to let people know how special and good and fun the FFs really are." I turned to look up at Lita. "So do you think, sweetheart, that you could let us take the risk and let me agree to appear on television?"

She was silent a moment, then squeezed my hand and walked to sit back down on the couch.

"Yes, you can go," she said.

"Me too!" says Jimmy.

"No, not you or Lucas."

"But, Mom!"

"Billy will speak for all of us."

"Louie will think we don't care," says Lucas.

"He'll know you care," says Lita.

I stopped rocking and stared for a moment at the rug. Needed vacuuming.

"Come to think of it, Lita," I says. "Louie will know that the boys love him, but the world won't. The best thing we might do is have Lucas and Jimmy on stage with me showing that Louie never did anything except have fun with them, and that they don't have an ounce of fear of him."

"Yeah," says Lucas.

"If I were to say nice things about Louie, people could decide it's just an old fart brainwashed by the FFs, but if the kids talk about Louie, people will believe *them*."

"Please, Mom," says Jimmy.

"You're right," she says. "If we're going to do it, the boys will make better advocates than either you or I."

"Hoorah!" says Lucas.

"You come too, Mom," says Jimmy.

"No, Jimmy," says Lita. "I'd come across as a pedantic lawyer and turn people off. You and Lucas and Dad are down-home sort of people—good for TV."

"No, you should come too," says Lucas.

"I'm willing to let you guys do it," she says. "Quit while you're ahead."

"Okay," says I. "Let's see what we can do."

"Hoorah for Mom," says Jimmy.

"Amen," says I.

THIRTEEN

(From Billy Morton's *MY FRIEND LOUIE*, pp. 84–88)

The TV show was scheduled for October 31st, Halloween night. Don't you love it? I'd told the ABC guys that the interview had to be in front of a live audience. When they protested, I told them I knew they could doctor any taped interview so that the biggest jerk in the world could seem almost intelligent, and a bright and well-informed guy could seem like an ignoramus. I might be an ignoramus, but I wanted to be my own ignoramus and not one they created with a lot of tricky editing.

Two days before show time, Louie shows up with a new FF friend. We knew our house was being watched every hour of every day, so Louie had to do a bit of maneuvering to get in. He snuck in as a giant package of toilet paper inside one of Carlita's six bags of groceries.

The other FF was named Gibberish—not by any human, but by his alien brothers. Apparently he was notorious in Ickieville for doing things at random. He got his name from the FFs because he often likes to speak at random, and it comes out as what humans call "gibberish."

In fact, Louie told me that here on Earth FFs call their own universe "Ickie" or "Ickieland" because Gibberish came up with it. At random of course.

Louie and Gibberish wanted our help in trying to disguise themselves as human beings. So far no FF had managed to pass for a human being if actually looked at closely. Louie and other FFs could assume the shape and movements of a human but couldn't get rid of their fur, since these million thin hairs are their means of absorbing and communicating sensory information. And they couldn't change the color of the hairs except with dyes or paint. So they have to cover their bodies with clothing, but of course can't cover their faces without seeming strange. And they hadn't figured how to get eyes to work. They could wear dark glasses all the time, or pretend to be blind, but that would be a bit limiting. They thought of disguising themselves as Muslim women dressed in burkas wearing dark glasses, but realized it wouldn't be such a good choice for creatures sometimes suspected of being Islamic terrorists. And abandoning their dark glasses and letting only their eyes—or lack of eyes—show seemed pretty stupid when it was the eyes that they were having most trouble with.

So that afternoon down in our basement Lita, me, and the boys tried to see if we couldn't turn Louie and Gibberish into convincing human beings. After we'd gotten both Louie and "Gibbs," as the boys began to call him, to assume the short, skinny human shape that was the best they seemed able to do, we realized that the only clothes that might fit them were those scattered over Lucas's bedroom floor.

"Why can't you guys make yourselves any bigger than midgets?" I asked Louie.

"We can pump ourselves up bigger," says Louie, "but only for about ten minutes. Then we have to deflate."

"And I thought you were a super-creature," says I. "And you can't even grow to be a man for more than ten minutes."

"Ishba palla subprana gurks," says Gibberish.

By the way, you may wonder how we could tell the FFs apart. So far, the three we'd met were all about the same size and color and hair thickness, and their normal spherical shapes seemed identical. Yet me, Lita, and the boys had no trouble identifying Louie from Molière or from this new one, Gibbs. And none of us could figure how we did it. Somehow each one exuded something that identified it to us in a unique way.

It was Jimmy who solved the hairy facial appearance by rushing in with four or five masks he and Lucas had been given over the last few years. I thought Louie looked pretty good in a Dracula mask, especially with those cool teeth, but Lita liked the most neutral mask the kids had, an old one of President Bush the Worst. I don't know how one of those ancient Bush masks got into the boys' Halloween collection, but there it was.

So as an experiment, we got Louie to swell up to five feet six, quickly got him to put on pants and a long-sleeved shirt of mine, socks and shoes, some rubber skin-colored gloves, a wig that Lita dug up that she cropped to make the hair look hippy-like rather than female, and a Greek fishing cap of mine covering the wig. And the mask of George W. Bush.

When the laughter died down, we realized that this new creature didn't look so much funny as it did like a zombie. The Bush mask was eyeless. Made him scary. Maybe it *was* a Halloween mask.

Jimmy dug up two marbles and Louie stuck them in under the mask so they showed through the eye openings. Gibberish said that FFs in other places had used grapes, ping-pong balls, lemons, golf balls and even eggs as eyes, but that they put in eyes only when they were trying to look like invaders from outer space—so that humans would feel more comfortable than if they showed up as eyeless beach balls.

Louie began showing off how he could move the two marble eyes as if he were looking at things. He was beginning to look vaguely like a human.

Except the mouth. There was no opening in the Bush mask where the mouth should be, just two painted lips. Lita grabbed some scissors and carefully cut a nice slit between the two lips. Louie showed he could more or less open and close his mouth. When he spoke to us he moved his lips in a pretty convincing way.

If you were blind or an idiot.

No matter how hard we tried, without teeth there was no way this mouth could be made to seem to be talking.

It was Lucas who produced a set of some very fake-looking false teeth. A minute later they were in place behind the Bush mask and showed up when Louie opened his mouth.

How did he look?

Like a man who should have had a lot of dental work done when he was a boy.

And then, as we were standing around Louie admiring our handiwork, a horrible thing happened.

Louie shrunk. His body suddenly collapsed into that of a four-foot-tall boy rather than a normal man. Unfortunately, his clothes didn't shrink too. He now looked like a midget clown with a head twice as big as it should be and a face that made him look like a buck-toothed zombie.

Gibberish suggested it might be better if FFs settled for being either midgets or dwarfs. He then assumed the shape of a small round human being only a little over three feet high with a big head and big feet. We dug up some of Jimmy's clothes, threw them on him, and in no time at all we had Gibbs looking like a Munchkin from *The Wizard of Oz.*

Gibbs and Louie then agreed that FFs spending all their lives as dwarfs probably wouldn't accomplish anything except to make FFs easier to find.

Gibbs then suggested that FFs disguise themselves as small zombies or vampires—that way humans might keep their distance.

Lita said she didn't think it would keep most human beings at a distance.

FOURTEEN

(From Billy Morton's MY FRIEND LOUIE, pp. 90-98)

The television interview for ABC took place in one of their main studios in New York City. They produced the live audience demanded by our contract. About a third of them were media people, and the other two-thirds ABC got from an audience that had just been hired to laugh and applaud for some comedy guy who did interviews. Saved them money they said, and wasn't forbidden by our contract.

Lucas, Jimmy, and me were ushered into a neat room where they served coffee, tea, and Diet Pepsi. A very nice man who looked like he normally sold used cars came in and briefed us about how our mikes would work, and the two boys had a lot of fun putting them on and then speaking in big deep fake voices—a bit soprano still, I'm afraid. The car salesman offered me wine or beer, but I had wisely drunk some bourbon from my flask in the limo on the drive in and didn't want to contaminate the good mood I was in.

The limo ride was interesting. First time for me. Enough room for me and the kids to play ping-pong if they'd provided a table, but this was probably an economy model limo. Carlita enjoyed it too. Rode a lot smoother than our Grand Caravan, which seems to have been scientifically designed to pick up every flaw in any highway—down to the last pebble.

Lita, I should mention, was now eight months pregnant. She'd bought a lovely maternity dress and her belly stood out round and firm. And she glowed like any pregnant lady should. The baby, we knew, was neither a boy nor a girl.

It was Louie.

He said he wanted to see the show, and that was the best idea we could come up with to get him in. When we got to the studio a nice lady security guard congratulated Lita on her pregnancy, asked if she could touch her tummy, and announced that she had felt the baby's heartbeat.

Probably just Louie burping.

Except that he never burped.

Just Louie having fun.

Soon the stage was set. Jimmy, Lucas, and me were sitting in comfortable chairs, make-up carefully applied beforehand making me look at least two weeks younger. Between us and the interviewer was a low coffee table with three glasses of water and a vase with some nice white flowers in it. The interviewer was one of those smooth, good-looking guys with a great baritone voice who can make a game of tic-tac-toe seem earth-shaking. He had a great smile that would have made me trust him with my life if I hadn't known a dozen guys just like him who would put me in front of a firing squad even if I was their papa.

I looked out into the audience and saw Lita sitting in the front row, happily pregnant, and waving to the boys. They waved back and we were all happy as could be.

Very dangerous condition to be in if you're a human being about to be part of a TV show.

Bells began to ring, some little guy came out and told the audience to shut the hell up and keep their eyes peeled for signs that read "Applause" or "Stay Silent" or "Laugh Loudly." Someone then raised a sign saying "Applause" and the audience burst into thunderous appreciation. Makes you know how God must feel.

Then the little guy left, the lights on the audience dimmed, the lights on us and the interviewer got even brighter, and the interviewer—his name was David Babbitt—broke out into a big grin. Jesus, he looked happy—like a shark who's just spotted a bleeding kid in the water.

"We are here tonight," Dave intoned in his deep baritone voice, "with three individuals who are among the few on Earth who have had a Protean live in their home for more than a day or two, in this case more than a week. We have here Mr. Billy Morton, a fisherman from Long Island, and his two sons, Lucas… the older boy, and Jimmy. Let's give them a round of applause."

Applause.

"Mr. Morton, let me start with you," Dave went on. "How did you first encounter this alien?"

"Caught him in my fishing nets," says I. "And when we threw him overboard he bounced right back up into the boat. Most fish don't do that." That got me a couple of chuckles from the audience.

"When did you first realize that this… creature was special?"

"When he followed me home and began using our computer," says I. "Most fish don't do that."

Six more chuckles.

"Surfed the net faster than even Lucas here," I add.

"And what did you first think of this alien, Lucas?" asks Dave.

"I thought he was cool," says Lucas. "From the very beginning he began playing with us—soccer, tag, hide-and-seek. And he can change shapes."

"How about you, Jimmy?"

"His name is FF," says Jimmy. "Or Louie. He's not an alien, he's just someone different from us."

"Ah… yes," says Dave. "And why, Mr. Morton, do you think these aliens are causing so much death and destruction throughout the world?"

Just like that. "Why do FFs keep raping innocent children and poisoning well water?"—surprised he didn't ask that.

"Well," says I, "I've never seen a report of any FF hurting anyone that wasn't absolute bullshit. 'Course the FFs don't have drones and missiles and a thousand overseas bases so maybe that's why they haven't gotten into the killing business yet."

If ABC had a sign "Boo and Jeer" they would have pulled it out, but they were asleep at the switch. So the audience only gasped, those few who actually understood what I'd said.

I think Dave flushed, although with his fake tan I couldn't be sure.

"Do you believe the aliens were responsible for the disappearance of Flight 888?"

"Louie'd never do anything to hurt anyone," Jimmy bursts out.

I reached forward and poured my glass of water into the flower vase. Then took out my flask and poured a shot into the empty glass. Took a swig.

"Most people believe they zapped the plane back to their own universe. And people have been disappearing—" says Dave.

"All bullshit. I've been around FFs and never seen one hurt a thing, except the time Louie accidentally rolled over a fly."

"What about the young child, Donny Arkin, he crippled only three weeks ago on your property?"

"Donny's a baby. He wasn't hurt at all," says Lucas. "He's a jerk."

"You three seem to think these aliens are all just innocent fun, but there's significant evidence that they've robbed banks of millions of dollars, cyberattacked numerous government and corporate systems, and kidnapped people off the streets, possibly sending them to other universes."

"Hey, don't knock other universes," says I. "For most human beings on this planet, a different one would be a big improvement."

"Your... friend Louie has even confessed to robbing banks," Dave went on. "How do you defend such actions?"

I was about to say something brilliant, but the next thing I knew Louie, in his usual hairy beach ball shape, came bouncing up onto the stage and plopped himself into Jimmy's lap. And Lita looked like she'd just lost twenty pounds.

The audience gasped again and then, without any raised sign from ABC, burst into spontaneous applause.

Dave was a pro. He didn't bat an eyelash. Although with all that make-up, he probably couldn't bat an eyelash if he tried.

"Mr. Louie, I presume," Dave says.

"Just Louie," says Louie. "No need for formality, Dave."

He bounced off Jimmy's lap, morphed into a skinny, furry human midget, and went and sat himself tight up against Jimmy. Then he neatly crossed his legs—like any good guest.

The damn audience gasped, then laughed and again

applauded. The poor ABC guy with the signs must have been beginning to feel impotent: a god who had lost his power.

"Well, Louie," says Dave. "Why don't you answer my last question: there are reports that you, or one of your alien friends, have confessed to government authorities that you have been electronically robbing banks. How do you justify such crimes?"

"Well, Dave," says Louie, "we're just having a bit of fun. You seem to have developed an economic system here that's forgotten how to have fun. Forgotten how to play. Your sports are not play. They're all about winning and money, the same as your economic system. So shifting money from the rich to the poor seems like a good way to begin making it possible for people to begin playing again."

"You're taking money from people or companies that have earned it," says Dave, "and giving it to people who haven't earned it and don't deserve it."

"Actually, Dave," says Louie, "we're taking money from people and companies who have gotten it through a rigged system, and giving it to people who have lost it through your rigged system. You talk about an equal playing field but have tilted it at a forty-five-degree angle against most of your people. Makes for an uneven playing field and boring games, Dave."

Louie then slid back off Jimmy and shrunk back into his beach ball mode and began bouncing.

"All work and no play makes Jack a dull boy," he says, ten feet in the air and on the way down. "You Americans are mostly dull boys."

Louie was now bouncing twelve feet up in the air, then down, then up again.

"You're trying to destroy the capitalist system!" says Dave.

"Oh, Dave," says Louie, and he suddenly bounces over to Jimmy, resumes his skinny midget shape, and maneuvers himself up so he's sitting on Jimmy's shoulders piggyback style, both "legs" straddling Jimmy's head. "Who would ever want to destroy the capitalist system?"

I raised my hand.

"I would," says I.

No one noticed.

Because Louie was now standing on his head on top of Jimmy's head.

Dave stared at Louie balanced upside down on Jimmy's head and then looked down at some notes he had on his lap.

"Let's talk about what makes you tick, Louie," Dave begins. "How smart would you say you aliens are?"

"Pretty smart, Dave," says Louie, still upside down on Jimmy's head, Jimmy giggling away. "Many of us could graduate from your high schools."

He now spread his two "legs" wide so it looked like a hairy letter "T" on top of Jimmy. "Ask me a question, any question."

Dave hesitates.

"How much is five thousand eight hundred and seventy-six times six hundred and eight-eight."

"A lot, Dave. Quite a lot. How about an easier one?"

I figured Louie could have had the answer to that tough one in a millisecond, so he was just hacking around.

"How much is six times six?" asks Dave.

"Less, Dave. A lot less."

A tittering of laughter from the audience.

Dave was smart enough to know he was getting nowhere

and, after glancing at his notes again, looked up with his most serious expression.

"How do you aliens reproduce?" he asks.

Louie slid off Jimmy's head, somersaulted onto his feet in front of Jimmy, and sat again beside him in his cross-legged guest position.

"Carefully, Dave," says Louie. "We reproduce carefully."

"And when do you reproduce?"

"When we feel like it," says Louie. "When there are no interesting games going on we often feel like creating a kid to help with the fun."

"You can create a child instantaneously?" says Dave.

"Oh, no, takes three or four weeks your time," says Louie.

"And what does your... baby look like when it is born?"

"Looks like a hairy tennis ball, Dave. Or, if he's a big bugger, a hairy softball."

More titters.

"And how is this baby conceived, Louie?" asks Dave. "Does it require, as most mammalian species do, the interaction of a male member of the species with a female member?"

"Nothing that primitive," says Louie. "We FFs are bisexual you might say."

"You have both male and female characteristics?"

"We do, Dave, we do."

And at this point I noticed, and the audience began to notice, that out of Louie's crotch was now protruding a six-inch-long, inch thick... hairy penis.

Dave was speechless.

As the penis expanded further to eight inches and two inches thick, Louie's skinny chest began to expand into two tennis-ball size breasts, again, furry breasts, which kept growing too until they were getting close to softball-sized—almost as big as Louie's head.

At first the audience gasped and tittered, but as Louie's swellings grew to their final full sizes, the titters grew to laughter, and a few claps became a loud surge of applause.

Louie uncrossed his legs, stood up and took a bow, his penis and breasts bobbing nicely up and down.

More gasps drowned out by more laughter and applause.

"Having both sexes within us, Dave," Louie says. "Anyone of us can produce a little tennis ball whenever we get the urge."

Dave was recovering nicely.

"But this means," he says, "that you can create a dozen children a year, and if you live a long time, hundreds of children."

"That's right," says Louie, "but we actually only live for twelve Earth years, and most of us don't produce more than five or six kids over that time."

Dave hesitates, looks down at his notes.

"Well, tell our audience this, Louie," he says. "Why have you and your friends come to our planet?"

"To play, Dave."

"But what is your purpose?"

"To have fun. No more, no less. To play and have fun."

"But that seems to me—"

"Hey, Dave," says Louie. "You've got visitors!"

We all looked where Louie was looking, and there, marching up the central aisle, were two men all in black with visored helmets and holding some sort of big weapons.

At the same time three other men, also carrying weapons, dressed not in SWAT-team black, but in suits, appeared at the side of the stage and began approaching Louie, who was still standing in front of Jimmy. One of them was Agent Johnson.

I stood up and so did Lucas. The audience was gasping, screaming, and pointing.

Dave looked surprised, then nervous, and he too stood up. I couldn't read Louie's expression, but I noticed his pecker was shrinking, which is what usually happens when men with guns approach a stiff prick.

In fact, all of Louie began to shrink and he was now back in fighting trim: a beach ball.

Three more men in cop uniforms appeared at the other side of the stage, two of them carrying what looked like a large chain-link net.

"There are a lot of innocent people here, Louie," says Agent Johnson, stopping with his two buddies ten feet away from where Louie rested on the floor. "If you resist, some may get hurt. Please come with us peacefully."

Louie didn't answer but began bouncing in place. All the TV cameras were nodding up and down trying to keep a focus on him: looked like oil rigs pumping up the gooey stuff.

Louie kept bouncing. Everyone kept staring. Could have gone on for years except that one of the bright cops pushed forward with his two pals and threw the mesh net onto Louie, or at least where Louie had been last time they looked. The iron mesh net crashed empty to the floor. Louie took up bouncing a few feet away.

The audience began to applaud, at first tentatively, and then fully, as if they'd seen the ABC sign. Which I doubt was anywhere in sight.

Agent Johnson, his two pals, the three cops, and the two

Robocops in black—who had arrived on stage to surround Louie—all just stood and nodded their heads up and down as they watched Louie continue his bouncing. Then Louie abruptly stopped and rested a few feet in front of where I and the boys were standing. When the cops began to approach him, Jimmy ran quickly to throw himself on top of Louie so that they'd have to shoot him to get their target. The men halted.

With Jimmy still aboard, Louie again began bouncing. And then to show off in a way that I didn't like at all: he bounced high, somehow propelled Jimmy off him up higher into the air, came down and bounced on one of the SWAT guy's heads, then up again to catch Jimmy on his way down, then onto a cop's head and then back up. Again he tossed Jimmy higher and after Louie had bounced off Agent Johnson, back up to catch Jimmy, who was now giggling away to beat the band.

The audience's applause kept getting louder and louder.

Well, all good things have to come to an end—although I'm not certain why—and the next thing I knew Louie had deposited Jimmy on my shoulders, and one of the guys in a suit had shot Louie.

The sound of the gun blast silenced the crowd. Louie quickly assumed his skinny midget shape and began staggering across the stage, right past Dave and Agent Johnson, finally collapsing on the floor fifteen feet away, rolling onto his back and spreading out his arms and legs and letting his head fall limply to one side.

Screams from the audience.

Johnson motioned his men to stay back and slowly approached the prostrate Louie. Gun in hand.

"Get that net!" Johnson ordered, standing now near Louie. "Get it over here!"

"He's dead, Chief," one of the suits said.

"Bullshit! The net!"

Not sure that ABC can keep all the "bullshits" when they do reruns, but it had its intended effect: two of the cops grabbed the net and hurried toward the stricken midget.

Louie suddenly kicked out with a limb that grew an extra foot for the occasion and knocked Johnson's gun into the air. He took on his beach ball shape, eluded the mesh net, rolled off the stage, and bounced rapidly down into the audience, bouncing from one head or shoulder to another, then past the pathetic efforts to stop him from the ABC security guards at the door. Finally, out into the hallway and away. As a few of the cops chased after him, the audience laughed and cheered mightily.

Dave comes staggering up to me with a blank look on his face.

"I thought it was a pretty good show, Dave," says I. "A bit over the top at times, but the audience didn't seem to mind."

"You're under arrest," Agent Johnson says to me.

ITEM IN THE NEWS

THE REPUBLICAN NATIONAL COMMITTEE ANNOUNCED TODAY THE SIX BASIC PRINCIPLES OF ALL GOOD REPUBLICANS

Washington, D.C.

The Republican National Committee today released a document stating that they have developed the Six Basic Principles upon which all good Republicans stand. The list is detailed and bold, and represents the most comprehensive statement that any political party has ever dared make.

SIX BASIC PRINCIPLES

1. On Eternal War: We Republicans, knowing that people throughout the world will always hate us for our love of Freedom, believe that Our Beloved Nation should be eternally at war with all who resist our just interference in their nation's affairs; that this Eternal War must be offensive rather than defensive; that all killing should take place in other lands; and that there will be peace in the world only when Our Great Nation has pacified all our enemies.

2. On Corporations Avoiding Taxes: We Republicans believe that it is the God-given right of every corporation to do everything in its power to avoid paying taxes. Many of us believe that this right is part of the Bill of Rights in the

Constitution. Thus, opening an office in a closet in Bermuda or the Cayman Islands and, as a result, being a foreign corporation and becoming exempt from US taxes, is fair and reasonable and legal, as long as the closet is at least thirty square feet in area.

3. On the Israeli–Palestinian Conflict: We Republicans believe that there should be two states living side by side in peace and harmony, with borders to be determined by the Prime Minister of Israel after consulting with surviving Palestinians. Republicans also believe that additional Jewish settlements are not desirable and should be done as secretly as possible. Finally, we believe that the Israeli government should not negotiate with any Palestinian unless the official accepts the Israeli position before beginning negotiations.

4. On Gun Control: While the pussyfooting Democrats want to make it more difficult for Americans to buy a howitzer, we Republicans believe that it is the right of every citizen to have as many weapons as he chooses, and to use them as Our Nation's wonderful law enforcement agencies do, whenever anyone makes a possibly threatening move.

5. On High Pay for Corporate CEOs: We Republicans believe that it is the God-given right of every person to get all that he can get, as stated in the clause in the Declaration of Independence that enshrines "the pursuit of happiness," and that therefore there is no upper limit to what CEOs can earn except the limit on a CEO's ability to bully more out of his board members.

6. On Avoiding Facts: While Democrats are always attacking us for our indifference to factual accuracy, we Republicans have found that avoiding all facts is a winning policy, and we will not abandon it until we are able to find some facts that actually support our point of view.

FIFTEEN

(From Billy Morton's *MY FRIEND LOUIE*, pp. 99–108)

Well, after that TV spectacular, sections of which had more hits on YouTube than any video in history, our lives were never the same. We'd been living in a Happy Family sitcom for more than a dozen years and now suddenly found ourselves in a sci-fi thriller. And for a while a police procedural.

First of all, even before we could leave the ABC studio, Lita and I were called in for two hours of questioning by Agents Johnson, Wall, and two other guys I'd never seen from an agency I'd never heard of.

However, it wasn't hard at all. We told them that we didn't have the faintest idea how Louie got into the studio or why he came up on stage. We said we had no idea he would spout subversive ideas. We said he was just an over-intelligent pet that we'd adopted and who had then disappeared. When they began asking detailed questions about how often we had seen Louie at the computer and what things Louie could do, I reverted to my more natural stance with law enforcement: total ignorance. I just answered all their questions about Louie with "Beats me."

Lita was much more cooperative. She answered their questions fully: "I'm not certain," "I'm afraid I don't remember what happened then," "I wish I could help you, but I simply don't know the answer." She was a graduate of NYU Law School.

The boys were questioned too, and they bragged about all the things Louie could do. Lucas said he was sure that if

God himself had a website, Louie would be able to hack into it and totally change things around. Probably for the better. When they had more or less finished, Agent Johnson turned to Carlita.

"As you know, Mrs. Morton," he says, "you and your husband have done nothing since we've met you except feed us lies. No more. We have or will find sufficient evidence to indict you for aiding and abetting this alien creature, who is legally a terrorist. I suggest you make arrangements for the care of your children."

"I'm sorry to hear that, Mr. Johnson," says Lita. "But I'm afraid you are on shaky legal grounds."

"In what way, Mrs. Morton?"

"I'm afraid no police agency will be able to legally arrest this alien, Louie, since he is not a human being."

Agent Johnson made a facial expression that I guess was a smirk.

"Then we'll have the Suffolk County Animal Control Agency take him into custody."

"If Louie was a dog," Lita says, "that would be an excellent idea and absolutely legal. I could not object. However, as you have been arguing ever since we first met, Louie is *not* a dog, in fact, as I know you'll agree, he is not any sort of animal. He, and all the FFs, are not warm-blooded, which is the common definition of an animal or mammal, but rather most all of his characteristics—with the possible exception of his intelligence—are those of a plant. As a plant, Louie is, I concede, subject to the regulations of the Department of Agriculture, but as far as I know, Louie has not broken any plant laws. I should also add that as far as I know there is no law against aiding and abetting a plant."

Ya gotta love her. And I do. But only because I never try to argue with her.

Agent Johnson was a lot smarter than I thought. Saying not a word he turned and left the room. He was letting us go. For the time being.

When we got home the next day (ABC put us up in a hotel whose bathroom was larger than our living room) there was no sign of Louie. The media, of course, invaded our lawn and driveway and email and answering machine, begging us for interviews, to star in a new reality TV show recreating my first meeting with Louie—you name it, they'd pay us tens of thousands of dollars to do it.

Carlita and I told the boys not to say a single word. The only way we'd be rid of them was with total silence. Not even a "no comment." It took three days before the cable channels decided that no news whatsoever from the Mortons was no longer headline news.

When we got up two mornings after the great TV interview, Lita checked her computer and found an email from Louie.

Hi, Friends.

Thanks for all the fun and help you've given me and my friends. Molière says we ought to make all four of you "Honorary Ickies." But the government is following your every fart these days so it's impossible for me to renew our contact. I'm off to safer waters—whether on land or sea still not determined. As we say in Ickieland, keep on rollin'.

Your pal, Louie.

Well that pretty much ruined our day. Our week. All four of us moped. Life without Louie suddenly seemed to us to be life without life. We managed to get the boys off to school, but Lita and I decided not to do anything that day and concentrate on moping. Then, about two o'clock that afternoon Agent Johnson knocked on the door and brought us out of our mope: he told us Carlita was under arrest.

"On what charges?" she says. There were three agents: our pals Johnson and Wall, and some tall skinny guy.

"Aiding and abetting a suspected terrorist and known bank robber," says Johnson.

"And how did I do that?" asks Carlita.

"By hiding the terrorist under your maternity dress," says Johnson. Got to hand it to him, he didn't give her a "gotcha" look when he said this, just his usual "just the facts, ma'am" poker face.

"And what evidence do you have to support this charge?" says Carlita.

"Five witnesses will testify that they saw you eight months pregnant at the beginning of the show, and we know that at the end of the show you had on an extremely loose-fitting dress over a… a slender body. Two witnesses will testify they saw the alien emerge on the floor right near you before he bounced onto the stage."

"That's all you've got!?" says Carlita, acting as if the whole case against her was based on an eyewitness account by a blind man.

"You're under arrest, Mrs. Morton," said Johnson with his usual cool. "I'm afraid we'll have to handcuff you."

"Hold it," says I.

All my life—well, since my late teens anyway—I have rarely been able to like cops, even when they wear suits and are polite. All during the late sixties after I'd gotten back from 'Nam, I'd battled cops for one reason or another, and thus must have built into myself a sort of automatic reflex that still lived after another forty years. These three guys were about to drag my wife off to jail. No way, Charlie Brown.

"You guys lay a hand on Carlita and I'll level all three of you." You must realize that although I was more than seventy years old, I felt like I was still in my fifties and thus quite capable of taking on three cops.

"Don't be silly, Billy," says Lita, who had no great love of cops either, but is a lot smarter than me.

Johnson nodded at Wall, and the big man took out a pair of cuffs and went up to Carlita.

I leveled him with a roundhouse right. I really did. Hit him hard in the side of his face and sent him to the canvas. Ali couldn't have done it better. Hurt my shoulder though.

Then I turned to take out the tall skinny guy, took a step toward him with my arm cocked, and felt my jaw explode. Where the hell did that come from? You'll be proud to know that I wasn't KOed but rather staggered backwards two stumbles, righted myself, and tried to figure how someone had hit me without my seeing it.

"That's enough, Agent Rand," Johnson said. "Don't try to resist, Mr. Morton."

Wall had picked himself up off the hallway rug and came slowly at me. I gave him another roundhouse right that knocked a lot of air particles out of their normal flow but missed all of Agent Wall by about ten feet. The next thing

I knew a battering ram had slammed into my stomach and I doubled over. As I was planning my next brilliant move, I felt Wall's knee slam into my forehead and I went to the floor. Lita leapt onto Wall's back and began scratching his face, but Johnson immediately dragged her off and got her in a chokehold.

I was lying on the floor wondering what those two big black shiny blobs were only inches from my nose, but it wasn't until I awoke fifteen minutes later on my couch that I realized that the blobs were probably Wall's shiny shoes.

So we were both arrested, Carlita for aiding and abetting a terrorist and aggravated assault on a federal law enforcement official, and me for two counts of aggravated assault on federal law enforcement officials. I guess a swing and a miss is in the eyes of the law as much a crime as an Ali haymaker. I asked Lita if there wasn't a law against law authorities aggravated assault on a citizen, but she said they'd repealed that law after 9/11.

Agent Johnson's plan was simple: if Louie would come in and surrender to law enforcement, all charges against Carlita, and now me also, would be dropped. If not, Lita would be held without bail until her trial—our wonderful anti-terrorist laws making indefinite detention pretty easy.

Despite my long misdemeanor record in the sixties, I got out on bail. It would have taken my friends several days to raise the money (one of them was Sheriff Coombs), but while they were doing that, Lucas and Jimmy came by taxi to the Riverhead Court House with twenty-five thousand in cash for bail, money from that stash I'd carelessly left in the bilge of *Vagabond*. When the judge asked Lucas where he'd gotten the money he replied that both boys had been saving their allowances. Ya gotta love that kid.

'Course it was Louie who told the boys where they could find some bail money—told Jimmy actually. During his class on American history about how all the Native American Indians had suddenly died of old age, he got a note from the principal's office that he should check the bilge of *Vagabond*.

The boys and I attended Lita's bail hearing. The courtroom was packed, most all media, and they normally wouldn't have admitted nobodies like us, but being family, they did. Lita still had her license to practice law in the State of New York and so the judge allowed her to represent herself.

"Your Honor," she begins. "The most serious charge against me is aiding and abetting a terrorist. Is this correct?"

"You know it is," the judge says. "Get on with it."

"I plead guilty to bringing into the television studio under my clothing our pet Arctic retriever 'Dr. Bulge.' I admit that I did not prevent the dog from escaping from his confinement and bouncing onto the stage. However, I do not see how this constitutes an act of aiding and abetting a terrorist. I might be guilty of letting an animal loose where animals must always be on a leash, but of no more than that. And if the State argues that the alien is not a dog, but a plant, then I am only guilty of failing to take proper care of a plant."

"Mrs. Morton, don't play games with the court," says the judge. "This alien creature, who you say is your 'dog,' has confessed to robbing banks. More importantly, the prosecution has presented evidence that it illegally hacked into the National Security Agency's systems, which by the law of the land is an act of terrorism."

"That may be true, Your Honor," says Carlita, "but this alien creature is not a human being. It therefore cannot be accused under current US law of being a terrorist. And as a result, I am innocent of the charges against me."

The judge was suddenly less talkative. After a long pause, he says: "The creature hacked top-secret government systems. That is an act of terrorism."

"I'm sure it is, Your Honor," says Carlita, as polite as ever. "And my husband spanked Dr. Bulge for it. But the fact remains that the creature is not a human being and therefore not subject to human laws and, by extension, I am innocent of aiding and abetting a terrorist."

Judicial silence.

"I must respectfully ask, Your Honor," Lita goes on. "if a chimpanzee had hacked into a top-secret government database, would the government have the right to prosecute him? I suggest the answer is 'no.'"

"This creature," the judge says, his face now a bit red, "although he does not have the body of a human being, unlike a chimpanzee has intelligence, has the ability to talk, to make friends, to *steal*. It has all the attributes of a human being except shape."

"I'm afraid, Your Honor, that the law does not yet see it that way. When new technologies come along, new laws must be passed to take into account these new technologies. When the automobile replaced the horse, new laws had to be passed to control traffic and pedestrian safety. When e-tailers began selling their products online, new laws had to be passed to regulate their actions and to collect sales taxes from them. I submit that the appearance here in the United States of a creature never before encountered is identical to the appearance of a previously unknown technology. Until Congress passes new laws, the creature, as were the technologies, is outside the law."

Judicial silence.

"And if our dog, Dr. Bulge, is not a human being, then he cannot be a terrorist. And if he is not a terrorist, then I cannot be guilty of aiding and abetting a terrorist. Therefore I cannot be denied bail. I therefore respectfully request that I be granted bail for my other offense."

The judge stared a long time at Carlita.

"Sounds pretty sensible to me," says I loudly.

Cost me five hundred bucks for contempt of court.

"I am adjourning this bail hearing until tomorrow morning at this same hour," says the judge. "Court adjourned."

That evening, I'm happy to say, the people following the case were mostly for Lita. On Facebook and Twitter and those sorts of places, people thought it was a gas that she might get off because she claimed Louie was her dog and not a genius from another universe. Most people still liked Louie because of his *Cirque du Soleil* performance during the TV show. 'Course there were a lot of angry patriots who thought Lita was a traitor who was helping some commie aliens to overthrow our capitalist system.

But the public's attitude made it tough for Agent Johnson and the judge. If the judge denied her bail for "letting her dog loose" (as one tweet had it) then there might be a public outcry. Unfortunately for Johnson and the NSA, the judge was one of those who took the laws of the land seriously. His decision the next day was that until Congress passed a law defining these new aliens as human beings, the government had no right to prosecute them. And if the creature couldn't be prosecuted for acts of terrorism, then the defendant, Carlita Morton, could not be prosecuted for aiding and abetting a terrorist. He set Carlita's bail on the lesser count at twenty thousand dollars.

SIXTEEN

(From Billy Morton's *MY FRIEND LOUIE*, pp. 115-123)

For two weeks after our brief stint as TV stars, the FFs stayed out of our lives. Then one nice sunny day in mid-November I got a phone call from the sort of dull robotic voice used to tell people their prescription was ready at the pharmacy: "This is a recording. Please take Jimmy fishing in your Boston Whaler. Thank you."

And then the dial tone.

I tried for a few minutes to figure out which of my friends was playing some minor indecipherable joke on me, but came up empty.

Out on Peconic Bay in the small Boston Whaler we kept around for family outings, we'd barely dropped anchor when Louie popped up out of the water and into the boat, first going to Jimmy and giving him a hug, and then changing himself into a talking gray life preserver—in case the government had a drone someplace keeping an eye on an old geezer out fishing with his son.

"I thought you'd broken off diplomatic relations with us, Louie," says I.

"I knew the NSA would be monitoring all your emails, so I sent that note so they'd think I was done with you and your family."

"Well, you could have let *us* know that we'd see you again.

The boys have been pretty upset."

"I'm sorry," says Louie, and bounces over to Jimmy to get and give another hug.

"What's that?" says Jimmy, and I see him pointing at a softball-sized growth on one side of Louie's sphere and then on the life preserver he morphed into.

"Yeah, what's the lump, Louie?" says I. "You FFs get cancer?"

"I'm pregnant," says Louie.

"No, I mean what is it?" says I.

"I mean I'm pregnant," he says again. "Three weeks pregnant. Little guy should be born in the next week."

I frowned. I'd always thought of Louie as a male, and though he'd told us all FFs could have kids, his announcing he was pregnant made it sound like he was a female.

"What will your... uh... baby be like?" I ask.

"Well, splitting off rather than mating as mammals do, means that all FFs are somewhat alike. My baby will be a miniature me. In our universe, smart creatures like Ickies developed who reproduce by dividing, and keeping most of what each of us has learned. So in a way we all keep getting smarter and smarter. In other universes..."

"By the way, how'd you discover other universes?" I ask.

"Too complicated," he says.

"Hey, I got B pluses in algebra and geometry one week in 1963. Figuring out how to get from one universe to another can't be *that* hard."

"We discovered how to do it by accident," he says.

"Accident!"

"Creatures often discover the most important things by accident. Of course, it's only after they've been wrestling with a problem for decades or centuries that chance can provide the nudge that lets them break through."

"So how'd you do it?"

"We discovered that if for thirty-six seconds you rubbed the legs of a Kwabi—a kind of frog—against a six-inch square of the skin of a Blipgo—a kind of small elephant—while chanting the ancient FF mantra 'Loosen lighten let go' and were in an exact spherical shape, that you were suddenly transported to another universe."

"Wow!" says Jimmy.

"Unfortunately, having arrived in this other universe the FF discovered he was stuck there since neither Kwabis or Blipgos existed in the new universe."

"So... so how did the first FFs get back home?" I ask.

"It took him several years to mutate a frog-like creature into a Kwabi and an extremely fat human into a Blipgo. But finally—"

"Oh, shit, Louie, you're bullshitting us!"

Louie laughed—a laugh that was an exaggerated version of a Santa's "Ho-ho-ho." Made me think he was about to sprout a beard, pot belly, and red nose. It was a really annoying laugh.

"The actual discovery is way too complex and too long and boring to explain."

"How different is our universe from the other ones you've visited?" I ask.

"Ah, Billy, you haven't the slightest idea about how many fantastic different ways of existence there are. One reason we FFs travel so much is that new forms of life are endlessly fascinating. What's interesting about you humans is that you've developed this incredible computer power while still having brains only slightly more advanced than those of chimpanzees."

"Chimpanzees can be really bright," I says.

"And you're only the second universe in which we've found creatures that have developed the power to destroy most all life on the planet while still having such diminished intelligence that you keep thinking of using that power."

"I guess we're pretty special."

He didn't annoy me with a "ho-ho-ho," but I felt him smiling. But then Louie the life preserver bounced down to help Jimmy get a worm on the hook, then back into his life preserver.

"I could use your help, Billy," says Louie.

"What do you need me for?"

"I and other FFs can't yet become fake human beings. We need human helpers to do things for us that only humans can do—hold money in various accounts that we can use when needed, get humans in positions of power in the corporations and trusts and businesses we're acquiring or creating. We want both you and Lita to assume a few false identities and open up false accounts so we can launder money and turn our bank transfers into cash."

"How the hell do you manage to steal so much money?"

"It's called capitalism, Billy. Your economic system is based on two principles. First, to those who hath, more shall be given. Without having a brain in their heads, rich people can't avoid making money even if they don't try. Second principle of capitalism: to really make money, find ways to cheat. When you control a corporation and control the media and control the regulatory agencies, and control governments, and control the courts, then sticking faithfully to the law is rather unnecessary. In fact sticking faithfully to the law is downright immoral to the shareholders. It is a moral duty to maximize corporate profits. Therefore, it is your moral duty to c

"You don't think much of our economic system, do you?"

"I think the players at the top have done splendid work. They've created a whole raft of games that they can't avoid winning. Then they've managed to get most of the American people to believe that because the economic elite are winners, they must be talented, skilled, and deserving. The fact is, the system they've created guarantees that they and their children will be winners no matter how stupid they are—and most everyone else will be losers."

He hopped back up on the back seat in his life preserver shape.

"In addition to setting up false bank accounts, we want Lita to work with a new FF legal defense team some of our friends have already created. We may even make her the head of it. And you, Billy," he goes on, "I want to become senior vice president at American Protective Equipment."

"What's American Protective Equipment? They make hockey masks and pads, football helmets, welder's goggles, stuff like that?"

"They make armored vehicles, tanks, Humvees, things like that."

"Not my cup of tea, Louie," I says. "I think building more weapons is the most useless, senseless, and sad thing that anyone can do."

"Which is exactly why I want you to become senior vice president in the company."

Just then Jimmy's pole bent into a quivering arc and he began reeling in a fish. Even at only eight, Jimmy'd caught enough fish that he wasn't too excited, though I noticed his face was looking pretty bright.

"Got a big one, Jimmy?" I says.

"Don't think so, Dad."

He lifted the flapping fish up out of the water—a small flat fish—and wheeled it over the side to plop it down in the bottom of the boat.

"Vice president, huh?" says I to Louie as Jimmy knelt down in the bilge to unhook the fish. "Don't think I'm qualified for the top job, is that it?"

Louie reached out a protuberance to poke me—his way of saying he appreciated the joke.

"Last time I looked," I says, "a VP means that someone else is president."

"It does," says Louie. "But the CEO is in our pocket. He's been totally corrupt. We have enough evidence to actually send him to jail, something that happens to a corporate bigwig usually only once a century."

"But I don't know anything about weapons or armaments."

"And I hope you never do. We want you to help us transform American Protective Equipment into a company that makes backhoes, bulldozers, huge trucks, and any kind of heavy equipment that can be used in building things."

"Jesus."

"Think you can help us, Billy?"

"Won't the Feds be suspicious that I'm working for you if I show up at APE?"

"They will," says Louie. "But it won't much matter. For the moment they can't touch you."

"I'll tell you, Louie," I says. "I'm not sure I want to be part of this."

"What's the problem?"

"If I'm assuming a false identity and laundering your money, I'd be breaking the law. Normally that wouldn't bother me, but if I get put away for twenty-five years my kids might forget what I look like."

"We'll be behind you no matter what happens, Billy."

"But I got to say, there's one thing that's been nagging at me about this war. In this game you FFs are playing you guys have all the heavy weapons: namely your nuclear super-intelligence. And the team you're playing against, namely humans, have built their civilization on computers that you can totally control. It's seems unfair: I don't see how you can lose."

"You're right," he says, plopping down into the bilge and with a single quick motion managing to unhook the fish, then morphing back into a life preserver. "If we used all our abilities to hack and control computers we could bring down your entire civilization in a matter of weeks. Days even. We could shut down your entire electric grid, subvert every corporate computer system, shut down every email and phone system—you name it, if it's controlled by a computer, it's ours. There'd be ninety percent unemployment, starvation, riots, civil war, and deaths as far as the eye can see.

"No, Billy, I and my friends are into play, having fun, not starting a revolution that might well lead to the destructive chaos I talked about. Games are the most fun when the sides are closely matched, so we limit our superior computer power to make a better game. The immediate destruction of your rotten system would be a catastrophe for humans. We don't want that. We want to beat the humans in various games—close games that we might lose—so perhaps humans arrive at a better system than the insane one you have now."

"You're an idealist after all!" says I.

"No, no," says Louie. "We're into playing, Billy, having fun. If your system remains rotten or gets worse, well then it does—no big deal."

He suddenly morphed into a sphere, poked me gently in the stomach, gave Jimmy a quick hug and, without warning, plopped over the side and disappeared into the bay.

Jimmy dropped his hook and the worm he'd gotten to rebait it.

"Louie!" he shouts at the splash.

I then heard the sound of a helicopter, and after a few more seconds, saw a big black 'copter coming in our direction. I turned and gunned up the outboard and began moving us slowly back toward our home port. The helicopter—unmarked, but huge, and with the muzzles of weapons sticking out on two sides—came zooming down low and hovered about fifty feet away, looking us over, the wash from their blade stirring up the water and messing up my three hairs.

I slowed the boat and waved and smiled and generally tried to seem the sort of innocent guy the men aboard would be reluctant to machine gun to death. Jimmy, too young to have the healthy survival instincts of an old man, gave the helicopter the middle finger. I began to worry that if they tried to machine gun Jimmy they might accidentally hit me.

Kidding.

They didn't open fire.

Probably out of ammunition.

. . .

In another week I was at work at American Protective Equipment.

SEVENTEEN

(From Billy Morton's *MY FRIEND LOUIE*, pp. 128–135)

The CEO of APE, Harold Barnes, was actually kind of nice. Big guy, firm, warm handshake, huge smile, and really smart. He was dressed in an expensive suit and tie of course, but no one's perfect.

Harry had studied the business proposal that some of Louie's other friends had prepared. It was sixty pages long, and I only got through the first fifteen. I'm not big on facts. I did browse through the rest, but by browsing, I mean I at least turned the pages. I kept hoping for pictures.

The meeting took place in APE's office on the East Side of Manhattan, with me, the CEO Harry, a guy named Patrick Simpson who was Chief Financial Officer, and a third guy named Sam who I think was some sort of glorified secretary. Simpson was, like Harry, under the FFs control because of sins of a serious nature. I never knew if the sins involved fucking weaker companies or fucking the wrong woman or man. I didn't care. They were human. They were fools. They did stupid things.

After a bit of idle mutual bullshitting chit-chat—about how wonderful the FFs were and how proud he is to be part of this glorious new business experiment—Harry got down to business.

"You know, of course," he says, "that this restructuring is going to be a complete disaster."

"Absolutely," says I. "Can't possibly work. I sensed this, but just don't have enough business experience to know exactly why."

"How much business experience have you had?" asks CFO Patrick Simpson.

"Traded comic books as a kid," says I. "Sold pot at retail in 'Nam and back in the States for a year. Owned a fleet of fishing boats for six years."

"Really?" says Harry. "How large a fleet?"

"Two boats," says I. "I needed two 'cause one or the other of them was usually out of commission in need of repairs."

"Ahhh," says Harry, apparently not impressed with my fleet.

"So tell me, Harry," I says, "why won't it work to transform your company from a builder of weapons and armaments to one building heavy equipment for construction?"

He sighed and tipped back in his huge leather chair.

"The answer's simple, Billy," he says. "We sell all our current products to the Department of Defense or to overseas customers that the DOD brings to us. Although technically there's competition, in fact we can pretty much name our own price for everything we sell. No one in the DOD and no one in some foreign dictatorship gives a rat's tail about what the price is."

"I don't get it," says I. "Why doesn't the government care what you charge?"

"It's other people's money. Taxpayers' money. And in addition, half the people who work in the DOD used to work for one of the defense companies. It's like selling stuff to your brother when your brother doesn't have to pay a cent out of his own pocket. He doesn't drive a very hard bargain."

"And we can't do that with bulldozers and road graders?"

"Not really," says Harry. "In so far as Deere, Caterpillar, Kubota, and APE sell some of our bulldozers to the government we can all overcharge and still get a lot of business. But on sales to non-governmental companies, which would be most of our new business, we'd all be in competition. Price seems to matter to companies and people who are paying with their own money."

"Yeah, I'm beginning to see," says I.

"And we'd be runt of that litter. We'd have a hard time, actually an impossible time, competing on price with Deere and the other big corporations in the construction equipment business. We'd never make any money. Probably go bankrupt in a year."

"Good points all, Harry," says I. "I agree with everything you've said."

"Well, that's good."

"But you forget one key fact."

"What's that?"

"From now on APE will also be operating with other people's money."

He looked at me blankly.

"I don't get it," he says.

"If we begin converting most of our factories to non-military production," says I, "we'll be spending billions of dollars while our gross income goes to zero."

I paused for dramatic effect.

"Exactly," says Harry. "That's my point."

"But the FFs want to get into the construction business," I go on. "And so they'll pour an infinite amount of other people's money into APE."

"No self-respecting bank will loan them a cent for this folly," says Harry.

"No, they won't."

"So where the fuck is the money coming from?"

"Donors," I say.

"Donors! Have mentally defective people really got that much money?"

"Involuntary donors," says I. "Donors who wake up one morning and find that a few million dollars have gone missing from one of their overseas bank accounts. In some miraculous fashion it will end up—probably having been laundered six or seven times first—in one of APE's bank accounts. And APE will soldier on toward making tractors, backhoes, and wheelbarrows."

All three of the APE executives stare at me, not open-mouthed as I would have liked—they were all professionals and rarely drooled—but obviously in some awe.

"I see," says Harry.

"You'll have your work cut out for you, Pat," I says, turning to the financial officer. "Gotta find satisfactory financial explanations for where all this money is coming from."

"You're robbing other people and companies to make our new company successful," Patrick says after a pause.

"Exactly," says I. "Capitalism at work."

Harry and Pat were silent. So was the other guy, but that isn't news. They exchanged glances. Harry finally shrugged.

"Okay, so we may actually be able to have access to enough money to convert our manufacturing to construction equipment rather than, than—"

"Destructive equipment, Harry," says I. "You're presently

manufacturing destructive equipment."

"Right, but you'll never make this company profitable again," he says.

"Probably not. But the FFs feel that profits are overrated as a goal. They think making a product that is useful to Americans and useful to the world should be the first task of any company. Having happy, reasonably paid workers is the second. Satisfied customers third. Profits… sixteenth."

"That's all very nice," says Harry, "but the world doesn't work that way."

"Capitalism doesn't work that way. The FFs are trying to develop Peopleism."

"What the hell is that?"

"I don't know, Harry, but when they tell me in more detail you'll be the first to know."

"Are you maintaining the same employee compensation schedule?" asks Patrick.

"Oh, yeah, I wanted to speak to you about that, Pat. The salaries and bonuses we're paying all our executives are based on the company being hugely profitable. With the Department of Defense no longer paying us anything we ask, those salaries are way out of line. We'll have to eliminate the bonus system and cut all salaries that are over two hundred grand by a third."

Silence.

"You'll lose ninety percent of our executives," says Harry.

"We will," says I. "But those ten percent who stay must be pretty much happy with what the FFs are trying to do with the company. I look forward to meeting them."

"And can Mr. Simpson and I resign and take a better job

someplace else?" asks Harry. "Or are you going to blackmail us into staying."

This time it was me who was silent. Took me a while to collect my thoughts. Would have taken hours if I'd had that many thoughts to collect, but I've only got a few so I was ready to speak in less than eight seconds.

"Harry, from what I'm told, you are extremely intelligent and very experienced not only in getting billions out of the Federal Government but also in manufacturing things. You know about something that's called 'robotics', which sounds sinister but apparently involves efficient manufacturing. You can resign and go make twice as much money with some other company making napalm or cluster bombs or cruise missiles, or you can stay here and help us do something that hasn't been done since the end of World War Two: change a company that has been making only destructive things that we hope never get used—but usually do—into one making constructive things that we hope get used all the time, and will. And as a bonus—not monetary of course—you'll become famous as the executive who did the impossible."

"Did the impossible with money stolen by the Proteans," says Harry.

"Tell me, Harry, do you think we could find a better man to oversee this restructuring than you?"

The question startled him.

"You probably could," he says. "But not many."

"You're here, Harry. You know this company. You know manufacturing. You know how to get things done. You've been wasting your talents building things that kill people. You might just find building things that create rather than destroy a bit more satisfying."

"And will you pay me according to your high estimate of my talent?"

I smiled.

"Harry, there are some human beings who would pay *us* to be involved in a project like this."

He snorted.

"Maybe," he says. "But I'm not one of them."

"Not now, maybe, but we'll see about later."

"What about me?" says Patrick.

"The FFs tell me you're pretty good too, Pat. They say you're one of the most creative jugglers of financial books they've ever seen. They say you can turn a two billion-dollar profit into a one billion-dollar loss without breaking a sweat. And remember, the FFs looked into hundreds of companies before they chose APE. You can lie and cheat with the best of them. The FFs say you're our sort of guy."

A longish silence.

Harry tips forward in his chair and stands. He comes around his huge desk—took him fifteen minutes—to stand in front of me.

"I don't get it," he says. "The FFs have been saying bad things about all the cheating they find in capitalism, but you're interested in keeping Patrick here on because he's a good cheater."

"Nothing wrong with lying or cheating, Harry," says I. "Just depends on what you're doing it for. If you're doing it for selfish reasons, it's bad, but if you're doing it to help other people or to prevent people from getting killed than it's jim-dandy."

He thought about that for a long time.

"The FFs are starting a revolution," he finally says.

"No, no," says I. "They're just hacking around."

"Might be interesting," he says.

"Yep."

"I'm in too," says Patrick. "I'd love to cheat for a good cause."

"Yep."

"What about me?" suddenly asks the third guy who had been silent since 1913.

"You're fired," Harry, Pat, and I all say at once.

EIGHTEEN

(From *THE OFFICIAL HISTORY OF THE ALIEN INVASION, Volume 1*, pp. 372–378. Being the abridged rendition of the meeting on Nov. 22nd, 20-- of the President's National Security Council. In attendance: the President; Presidential Aide Jeff Corrigan; FBI Chief Brandon Cake; Secretary of Defense Joe McKain; Head of the NSA Jason Epstein; Chief Investigator James Rabb; Agent Michael Johnson; CIA Director Hilly Klington; and the Chairman of the Joint Chiefs of Staff, General Pete "Blast'em" Denture.)

PRESIDENT: First of all what's this I hear about Admiral Scott being forbidden to fly from Chicago to Washington because he's on the terrorist list? And Tom Hanks being interrogated for half an hour at LAX?

UNDETERMINED: Well, sir—

PRESIDENT: And some woman who is apparently the head of the Girl Scouts of America being strip-searched?

CI RABB: Our no-fly list of terrorists has been compromised, Mr. President.

PRESIDENT: Compromised! It's been totally polluted. It's useless!

CI RABB: Yes, sir. It has become so, sir. The alien terrorists hacked into it and replaced a third of the names with the names of upstanding citizens—generals, CEOs, clergymen, star athletes, popular singers, people we're fairly certain are not terrorists.

PRESIDENT: Can't you reconstitute the list?

CI RABB: We tried that, sir, but no sooner had we finished, than three hours later the list had again been changed— another third of the real terrorists disappearing and being replaced by nuns, six-year-olds, and senile grandmothers.

PRESIDENT: Good God.

CI RABB: Yes, sir. We've decided that for the moment we must abandon our no-fly list.

PRESIDENT: You mean that right now any terrorist can board a plane whenever he feels like it?

CI RABB: Yes, sir. But he won't be permitted to bring a weapon or bomb aboard.

PRESIDENT: Well, thank the Lord for little things.

CI RABB: Yes, sir.

PRESIDENT: Now tell me, Mr. Rabb, what else are these… aliens up to?

CI RABB: I'm afraid, sir, that they've been up to quite a bit. Especially invading internet media and publishing false and damaging material linked to certain people and institutions.

PRESIDENT: Exactly what are you referring to?

CI RABB: Well, sir, to name one example, the terrorists have appropriated the NSA Twitter and Facebook accounts and are using them to publish whatever they want—stuff that is harmful to our public image.

PRESIDENT: What are you talking about?

CI RABB: Well, sir, thanks to the terrorists the NSA Twitter account posted:

"We are now able to monitor all internet and phone communications of every American. No terrorist will ever bother you without our knowing it"

PRESIDENT: Are we doing that?

CI RABB: Well, yes, but since that is technically illegal we don't wish to advertise it.

President: What else?

CI Rabb: Well, sir, I'm afraid your own Twitter account has been compromised.

President: No.

CI Rabb: Yes, sir. I have three of your recent tweets right here: "*Sorry I and my team are lying to you all the time. That's just the way our system works. I'm sure you understand.*" "*If you really knew what your government does you'd refuse to pay taxes and vote to throw us out of office. Very undesirable.*" "*We'd love to build schools and hospitals, but our first priority is billion-dollar fighter bombers to protect you from terrorists.*"

President: Can't you stop this?

CI Rabb: Well, yes, sir, and we have. We've closed down your Twitter account, along with all government systems that have been invaded and undermined.

President: They've made us do this!?

CI Rabb: And major companies are having to close down their social media accounts.

President: Same sort of thing?

CI Rabb: Yes, sir. Here's a press release that was taken to be real by most all Americans who read it:

EXXON ANNOUNCES HUGE ALTERNATIVE ENERGY PROJECT.

Dallas, Texas.

Exxon announced today that it was investing over nine hundred dollars in a new alternative energy project. This new solar energy project will involve pulling up the shades on over fifty of their south-facing windows, thus saving over $23 a month on their heating bills.

MINOR OFFICIAL: *(Snickered.)*

EVERYONE ELSE: *(Silence.)*

PRESIDENT: And what about the rest of the world, Mr. Rabb? What are these ingenious Proteans up to there?

CI RABB: Actually, sir, in terms of governmental and economic institutions, most of the damage seems to be being done here, and in the UK.

PRESIDENT: What are the Proteans doing in other countries?

CI RABB: It's hard to describe. In Russia they seem to be doing things that help the dissidents and are causing the Russian spy agencies a lot of frustration. Except for that, the aliens mostly seem to be… well, playing, intermingling with the local people in a friendly way.

PRESIDENT: Playing… There's that damn word "playing" again.

CI RABB: Yes, sir. They're not just playing with children but also getting adults to play games with them: creating events where people gather and dance or sing or drink or play games or go rushing off to invade some office or Times Square or a park and do silly things. They get people to do things for the hell of it.

PRESIDENT: Ah, that's what the *Forthehelluvit* movement is all about, then.

CI RABB: Yes, sir.

PRESIDENT: But what about the reports of the aliens abducting people or causing accidents? Do you think it's possible the Proteans took down Delta Flight 888 as some have claimed?

CI RABB: Of course it's possible, sir, but there's really no firm evidence to confirm or deny it. That baggage handler who claimed he saw a hairy basketball in a suitcase turned out to be a pretty unreliable witness.

PRESIDENT: So most nations are not having any real trouble from the aliens, is that right?

CI RABB: That's right, sir.

PRESIDENT: All right then... Now, Joe [the President is referring to Secretary of Defense Joe McKain], what is your present assessment of the danger to our country represented by these aliens?

SENATOR McKAIN: I believe the danger is substantial, Mr. President. I think the alien terrorists have the power to destroy our civilization as we know it. Any day now we may wake up and find that all the data the NSA and our other intelligence agencies have collected over two decades has disappeared. Their ability to hack into bank and corporate accounts means they can, if they choose to do so, ruin our banking system and our economy. The danger is mortal, Mr. President.

(A long silence in the room.)

PRESIDENT: Well then, apparently they can destroy our nation. I guess the next question is this: is that their purpose?

(Another long silence.)

AGENT JOHNSON: Mr. President?

PRESIDENT: Yes? Excuse me, remind me of who you are, young man.

AGENT JOHNSON: I'm Agent Michael Johnson, the Special Agent of Unit A in charge of the investigation of the

Protean named "Alien 6," or more popularly "Louie."

PRESIDENT: Ah, that's the Protean we believe is most responsible for the hacking of our databases and banking system.

AGENT JOHNSON: That's right, sir.

PRESIDENT: And as I recall now, you have actually talked with this creature.

AGENT JOHNSON: I have, and that's why I'd like to say a few things about the FFs, ah, the Proteans.

PRESIDENT: Go ahead.

AGENT JOHNSON: Well, first of all, I don't think we're dealing with an invasion of aliens who have a shared goal or purpose. We have no firm evidence that the Proteans around the world are communicating with each other or are colluding in any way. This Louie is working with two or three other aliens, but we have no evidence that he's communicated with any alien outside of his Long Island operating area.

My point is this, Mr. President, I think the danger to the United States comes solely from this Louie and a few other Proteans who may be working with him.

PRESIDENT: I see. Senator McKain?

SENATOR MCKAIN: I see no evidence that this Louie has only a few helpers. For all we know he could have fifty. And he could be in contact with every other Protean in the world and we might not know it.

PRESIDENT: Mr. Johnson?

AGENT JOHNSON: The senator is quite right, Mr. President. That's possible. But so far all the damage done to us seems to have come from this Louie. Until there is firm evidence otherwise, I believe we should concentrate our forces on him.

PRESIDENT: And what's his purpose?

AGENT JOHNSON: He may *have* no purpose. I know this doesn't make much sense, but he may be playing—play that may be destructive to us—but playing and only having fun nevertheless.

SENATOR MCKAIN: Utter nonsense.

AGENT JOHNSON: Most all the other... non-destructive or non-threatening FFs, ah, Proteans, seem to spend most of their time playing, hacking around, doing things for fun, and trying to get human beings to do things for fun. It's possible that Alien 6 is doing the same thing, only on a larger scale.

SENATOR MCKAIN: You shouldn't listen to this, Mr. President. When someone is doing destructive things, his purpose is to destroy. Let's cut this crap about play and fun. If we don't stop these aliens we'll be drowning in their fun and games.

(Silence)

PRESIDENT: Well, in either case it seems to me that we should try to capture and interrogate this Louie and his companions.

AGENT JOHNSON: Yes, sir.

SENATOR MCKAIN: And wipe them from the face of the earth.

NINETEEN

(From Billy Morton's *MY FRIEND LOUIE*, pp. 138–144)

After my first stint as Vice President of Operations at APE I was demoted to laundry man. Lita too. Louie and Molière had arranged for Lita to assume her own false identity and fly separately down to the Caymans to help them launder money. I was to go with a rat's-fur toupee as Robert T. Walton. They wanted us to open a lot of bank accounts that could receive money without the bankers tracing the flow of cash. And we'd also be opening bank, stock, and bond accounts in the US under false names. I was looking forward to an adventure until I remembered that looking forward to anything is always a mistake.

I was right to be doubtful. The trip to the Caymans to begin building a financial empire around me and Lita didn't begin too well. Lita and the boys were taking a flight from JFK on one day, and me from Newark on the next. They were traveling under the false identities of Leah Klein, widow of wealthy sweatshirt magnate Abraham Klein, and her two sons, Noah and Joel. The boys got to wear skull caps, which they thought was pretty cool. They each spent a lot of time trying to steal the other's cap. After they'd flown off on a Monday, the next day I went to catch my flight out of Newark Airport. Everything was going as smooth as ice until I went through the metal detector. I was acting cool and calm and very businessman-like when I sauntered through the detector, but when the thing began bleeping as if I was carrying an atomic bomb in my belly, I lost a bit of my cool. I got stopped as someone possibly carrying a hidden weapon, taken aside and felt up by a guy who acted as if he didn't like sexually molesting me any more than I liked being sexually molested.

This bit of trouble was happening because there were two little oversights on the part of my genius FF friends. First, I'd had a hip replacement back in '06 that had metal in it. And since I hadn't flown in an airplane since 9/11, I didn't realize that people with artificial hips were usually terrorists. So when I tried to pass through the airport's metal detector and it began bleeping away, and the sexual molester couldn't find what was causing it, within seconds I was surrounded by four security men. I was too stupid to know that I had metal in my hip so I just blustered away that I didn't know why their machine was bleeping away, maybe it was a cheap model and needed replacing.

They seemed unconvinced by that answer and took me to a small room off the main terminal that had blood on the walls and long chains hanging from hooks. Well, not exactly, but I can assure you that the chair they gave me was extremely uncomfortable.

But before that, they brought in a guy to do a thorough body search. "Body Search" is a synonym for rape: it means that no matter what your sex is you're getting penetrated. Gals have two holes down there so when body searched they get double raped.

Well, I'd had docs' fingers up my ass a few times in the army, and in more recent years during a colonoscopy, but at least with a colonoscopy they give you a huge dose of Valium so you barely feel the rape. And if you do, you feel so good you want to say "Yes! Yes!" In fact the last time I had a colonoscopy I got so stoned on the Valium that on the way home I insisted that Lita stop at a garden shop so I could look around. Now I have never bought a plant in my life—Lita is the gardener in our family—but that day I bought a $300 river birch tree. Lita was too stunned to stop me. It's in our backyard to this day; we call it the Colonoscopy Tree.

But this guy looking for nuclear bombs didn't give me any Valium, and he poked and prodded with a long tube as though if he found something he'd get a huge prize. All he found was a lot of shit.

Meanwhile, since I was now under serious suspicion, someone entered my name into additional sections of their computer, and within twenty minutes they had discovered that back in the sixties I had belonged to Students for a Democratic Society and the NAACP, and in the eighties had voted once against Ronald Reagan, and had visited the Soviet Union for more than a month just before it collapsed into being just Russia, and in 2006 and 2008 had visited both Pakistan and Iran. Twice. They clearly had me nailed.

Now you realize that the old geezer Billy Morton had never been to any foreign nation in his life except Vietnam in '65, and that had cured him of any desire to visit any other. This record they had dug up on me was actually that of Robert T. Walton, who my brilliant FF friends had found to be my new identity. They had picked Bobby because he was a successful businessman, although why he didn't vote for Ronald Reagan the first time is a mystery to this day. Since he was a successful businessman we figured he'd be right at home opening hidden bank accounts in the Cayman Islands. The FFs didn't bother to see if he had a checkered past filled with joining the NAACP and taking business trips to Russia, Pakistan, and Iran. Of course, Bobby had also gone to Jordan, Saudi Arabia, Egypt, Israel, and the island of Bali, countries not quite radical enough to arouse my questioners' attention.

My first instinct when they pushed me into their torture room (four walls, one table, six chairs, no whips or chains, but a suspicious box against one wall that I *knew* must contain razors, pliers, and whips), was to play it cool. But as they began firing questions at me, and I realized that they'd soon catch me in more lies than I even knew I was telling, I adopted a new tactic: I began to play the role of doddering senile old fool. It's a role that I have to admit was becoming increasingly natural to me in recent years.

"Is it true you voted for Jimmy Carter in the 1980 presidential election?" one guy says to me.

"1980…" says I. "When was that?"

That slowed him down a bit, but then he barks: "Why did you spend two weeks in Karachi and Islamabad in 2006?"

I blink blankly for five or ten minutes and then say: "Karachi? Is that near Kalamazoo?"

"Pakistan. Why did you visit Pakistan?"

"That's outside the United States, right?" says I.

"You fucking well know where it is, wise guy. Why did you go there?"

"Does it have nice resorts?" I ask.

"It has nothing of interest to Americans except Muslims and terrorists. Who did you meet there?"

I blinked for another six minutes and then tried: "Tourist agents?"

Imagine trying to interview a terrorist who has an advanced case of Alzheimer's. He might or might not remember a bomb he set off twenty years ago, but as for the names of terrorist friends and associates and passwords and hideouts, you'd be lucky if he came up with the name of his own mother. As the four tough guys shot question after question at me, my Alzeimer's got worse and worse, until by the end I was replying to everything they asked with "Can you please repeat the question," or "Who are you guys did you say?" After two hours they had to send in a new team because three of the four guys on the starting squad were close to killing me or themselves.

The new team talked to the first team and they had a long discussion about whether to airmail me to Egypt to be tortured—the Egyptians having better torture facilities than the poor CIA and thus could more quickly find out which buildings or airplanes I was planning to blow up. But after a bit, they decided that if I answered the Egyptians' questions the same way I was answering theirs, the Egyptians would strangle me to death after less than an hour.

Finally they sorted it all out. They concluded that the likelihood of a seventy-two-year-old American businessman, who was as senile as Methuselah in his late hundred and forties, being an effective terrorist was somewhat low. They concluded that they'd much rather have me fly out to the Caymans than have to ask me a single additional question. And hear the answer.

When they marched out, not one of them said "Have a safe

trip." I think the lead guy was planning to look into planting a bomb on my plane.

As we left, I saw two security guards hustling a man in the white collar of a priest or minister toward the room I'd just left.

"But I'm Cardinal Richelieu of Chicago!" the man was shouting. "You must have the wrong man! I swear I'm not a terrorist!"

Yeah. Right. As they manhandled him into the torture room I thought how thankful I should be that our country was being kept safe from people like him and me.

ITEM IN THE NEWS

THE NRA PROPOSES LAW REQUIRING ALL AMERICANS TO BE ARMED

Fairfax, Virginia. Dec. 12th

Saying it was "time to take action against the rising gun violence in America," the National Rifle Association issued a statement today proposing new legislation requiring all citizens to be armed before being admitted into movie theaters, schools, malls, or churches.

The NRA's official spokesman, Horace Bloom, said that the NRA had taken this extraordinary step because it "could not stand idly by and watch loonies shoot innocent unarmed Americans. Had there been several NRA members in that audience in Aurora or at that school in Newton or at that Springfield massacre the killers would have been nailed before they'd even raised one of their guns."

The law, although not yet written, has already been sponsored by 210 Republican congressmen, seventy-four Democratic congressmen and forty-seven senators.

"With a law requiring all Americans to be armed at all times, no mass murders will ever again occur in our wonderful country," declared Congressman Matt Petershot (R. Indiana).

"I firmly believe that this law will essentially eliminate crime," said Senator Orin Bash of Wyoming. "With a fully armed citizenry, which was clearly what the writers of our great Constitution had in mind, no criminal will dare undertake any violent crime. Mass murderers will be gunned down as soon as they open fire. Our movie theaters and restaurants and high schools will be safe again."

A spokesman reported that the President, although in general supporting such legislation, felt that the law should limit weapons to citizens who had reached the age of fourteen.

However children's rights advocate Jill Fortress immediately indicated that her organization would fight this limitation. "Children are at even more risk of gun violence than adults," she declared. "Allowing them to have guns would let them protect themselves against physically stronger adults. Think how many child abductions would have been avoided had those poor children been packing."

TWENTY

(From Billy Morton's *MY FRIEND LOUIE*, pp. 145–149)

The flight to the Cayman Islands was uneventful. What I remember of it. Flying first class, I was offered all the free drinks I wanted. Though I usually don't have more than a couple of drinks on any given day, some pretty lady convinced me otherwise. She was wearing a uniform that had shrunk so badly the skirt barely covered her upper thighs, and on two occasions her breasts spilled out of her blouse and I had to help her put them back in. Well, not exactly, but she did keep smilingly offering me one drink after another, and I never like to disappoint a pretty lady.

I don't remember a thing after being served my fourth bourbon, but I'm told they needed a wheelchair to get me off the plane. I'm not the man I used to be.

I guess a hotel driver met me at the airport and drove me to my hotel, but my next memory after smiling at the pretty stewardess handing me my fourth drink was waking up in bed with Louie poking me in my belly with one of his limbs. Let's call it an arm although it emerged suspiciously low on his body. In any case he woke me up, insisted on my having a drink with him, which I did. When I saw it, I hoped it was vodka, but all the evidence is that it was a hundred percent water.

Then he got me going on my assignment of being a major financial criminal.

• • •

Unfortunately, being a major financial criminal isn't all it's cracked up to be. It's a lot of work and no play. James Bond seems to save the world from super-masterminds, who have thousands of hit men, by winning money at casinos, sleeping with a lot of beautiful women, and drinking especially dry martinis. In four days in the Caymans I achieved only the last. And only one.

First of all, I missed Lita, Jimmy, and Lucas. Because we were now famous from the TV show and the YouTube reruns, Louie had told us that we could never be seen in public as a foursome. Even in our disguises, a wizened old man with two young kids and a wife with a memorable ass might grab people's attention.

Most of that first day Lita and I were busy opening bank accounts. Separately. Only after eight of the most boring hours I've ever lived through did we manage to have a drink together and go up to her room where I could see the kids. When we got to her room, the two boys paid not the slightest attention to our entrance. They were too busy on the floor playing with… Louie! He broke away from the kids and came up and bounced off my chest and then off Lita's hip, his new way of greeting us I guess. When he settled back on the rug I saw that the bump on his side had gotten even bigger and was attached by only a short inch-long, inch-wide sort of tube.

Jimmy announced that Louie was about to give birth to a new FF. I turned to Louie, who blushed modestly and gave me an "ah shucks" grin. Of course, he didn't literally do this, but I'd begun to notice over the weeks that he was somehow communicating his feelings to me in some non-physical way.

"I'm afraid we're in a bit of trouble," Louie said, bouncing up onto the big double bed, the boys bouncing up there too.

"What's up?" says I.

"I flew here inside a suitcase. Unfortunately, when the owner opened the suitcase in his room at the Cayman Hilton he began suspiciously fingering the wooly silver-gray sweater he didn't remember owning. So I formed my sphere, bounced away to his patio, took a swan dive into the hotel pool, and escaped. Since he reported the incident first to the hotel management and then to the local authorities, I'm sure the American government spy agencies know there's an FF in the Caymans. And they know this is one of the places we might try to move our money. We've now learned that they're sending three more agents here from the States to look at all recent arrivals to the Caymans. Pretty soon they'll look at Robert Walton and Leah Klein and her two sons. We're in trouble."

"So what can we do about it?" asks Lita.

"Well, as soon as I can split off junior here," says Louie, growing a limb to point to his tennis-ball growth, "I'm going to join Molière playing games on the beach—like the FFs in California. Maybe get the government to think we are harmless FFs rather than the thieving kind."

"But it sounds like it's already too late," says Lita.

"It probably is, because something else happened that has upset the government. Molière monkeyed with their list of known terrorist organizations and added the Red Cross, both Republican and Democratic national committees, and the National Rifle Association. For the last several days all members of these organizations have been on the no-fly list and gotten stuck at airports."

I laughed.

"That's neat," says Lucas.

"So what do we do now?" says I, always coming up with a question when answers were what were needed.

"You and Lita have to change identities again. Tomorrow morning I want you to check out of your hotels and become Jose Rodriguez and Maria Gomez, successful dope smugglers. We'll get you the documents and appropriate clothing. The Feds aren't interested in dope smugglers laundering money in the Caymans, they want FFs and the humans that are helping us."

"I get to be Latino!" says I. "Lita always wanted me to be a Latino."

"What about us!?" says Jimmy.

"We'll sneak you and Lucas into a safe house we have here. I'm afraid two boys about eight and eleven in the Caymans is now a red flag."

"Is the safe house on a beach?" says Lucas.

From outside there was suddenly a thunderous BOOM! and an incredible flash of light filled the room then disappeared. Lita and the boys rushed to the window to look out, and I wobbled over to join them. Nothing. Everything calm as could be.

"Was it thunder?" says Jimmy.

"Here he is," says Louie.

We all turned and saw that the small soft ball attached to Louie's side had split away and was plopped down on the bedspread beside him.

"Wow!" says Jimmy.

"About time," says Louie, and reaches out with a limb and lightly touches the new FF.

Which rolls up the limb and presses itself against Louie's midsection.

"Louie had a baby!" says Lucas.

"Is he a boy or girl?" asks Jimmy.

"Both!" says Lucas. "Remember, FFs are always both."

The furry softball then leaps off Louie and rolls up into Lucas's arms. Lucas has the biggest grin I've ever seen on him and gently pets the little fella's head.

"What's his name?" Lita asks Louie.

"It's about two hundred words long in our Ickie language. You people will have to name him the same way you did me."

"It's Louie Junior," says Lucas.

"Or Louie the Second," says I.

Neither seemed quite right, and neither Louie nor the little fella moved an inch. There was a silence.

"He's Louie-Twoie!" says Jimmy, and the newborn rolls off Lucas and goes immediately to Jimmy, bounces up to tap his face and settles into his lap.

"Louie-Twoie," says I. "What do you think, Louie?"

"I'm honored," says Louie, "and you should know that every FF born is ninety percent the same as his parent, so your name, Jimmy, is quite appropriate. Although since Louie-Twoie is actually my fourteenth split-off, technically he's Louie the Fourteenth, or 'Louie Quatorze' as Molière has been referring to him."

A silence. Lita looked at me and then the two boys.

"It's Louie-Twoie, I think," she says. "Names don't have to stick to the facts."

"Hooray for Louie-Twoie!" says Lucas.

TWENTY-ONE

(From *LUKE'S TRUE UNBELIEVABLE REPORT OF THE INVASION OF THE FFS*, pp. 108–111)

The United States defense establishment had decided that any alien not spending all its time cavorting in the water or on a beach or otherwise entertaining the public was probably a terrorist. They knew too that the aliens were using humans to help them, especially setting up bank accounts to launder their stolen billions. They had sent a special task force to the Caymans to monitor bank transactions and all alien activity. Their goal was simple: capture an alien terrorist.

Louie and Molière knew all this because they'd had Louie-Twoie sneak into the main suite rented by the agents, first disguised as a large mouse, then as a dirty gray sock lying under a bed. LT did a good job considering he'd been born only a day earlier.

Billy and Lita were doing their morning chores of opening more bank accounts as Jose Rodriguez and Maria Gomez. At the same time two FFs took turns on the beach entertaining the crowd with acrobatic tricks, playing gentle games with the children, and generally trying to pretend they were the harmless kind of FFs rather than the terrorist money-laundering sort. A young woman had joined the FF out in the water, and together they began to do amazing tricks, some even better than the two FFs working by themselves. It helped that the woman had real breasts, whereas FFs didn't.

Billy and Lita celebrated their becoming the proud owners

of millions of dollars by late in the afternoon retreating to their hotel room for some marital bliss, or as much bliss as the elderly Billy could manage. Billy maintains that he hadn't needed any Viagra—that Lita's lovemaking could erect an Eiffel Tower on a corpse.

But when Billy and Lita were making love, and Lucas, Jimmy, and LT—back from his first surveillance assignment—were playing baseball at the safe house Louie had set up for them, there was more important action taking place on the beach.

Late that afternoon, while Molière and his female partner were fifty feet off the beach doing acrobatics, Louie was entertaining the tourists too—playing games with some of the children. A vendor pushing a large ice-cream cart through the sand approached. Louie paused in his play when the cart first arrived, but when children began leaving it with ice-cream cones, he resumed, entering immediately into a triple cartwheel somersault flying fish into a sandcastle. The kids shrieked with joy and a half-dozen people applauded.

Then a spray of sticky, hot, glue-like tar began hitting Louie and the sandcastle. The ice-cream cart had sprouted a thick hose, and a white-uniformed man was blasting away at Louie, who rolled away, the splotch of sticky glue-tar that had already hit him picking up gobs of sand that slowed him. When he expanded himself to protect a child who happened to be in the path of the flow, he was hit again. When he tried to roll himself into the water, he was hit again.

Suddenly Molière burst out of the shallow water and rolled like lightning to the man with the hose and knocked him down, the hose spraying the goo up into the air like an eruption of "Old Faithful." Almost immediately another man appeared and began shooting at Molière, who rolled at warp speed back into the water. A small drone flew up carrying a giant mesh net—ten times as big as a butterfly net—hovered over the struggling Louie covered with goo, and dropped it down over him.

Some of the onlookers began applauding again, assuming this was part of the show, but then some of them saw that a small boy at the sandcastle had been hit in both legs with the hot goo and was crying. His mother began to scream. Then several women discovered goo in their hair and began to scream. Another child began to yell and cry. Another mommy screamed, although whether for her hair or her child has never been determined.

The onlookers stopped applauding. As another big man appeared and began dragging Louie away from the beach, some people began to move angrily after them. The hose man aimed the hose at anyone who threatened to get too close. Another man waved his semi-automatic pistol threateningly. It wasn't a dignified retreat—three men with a tar cannon and a gun holding off five or six people armed only with bathing suits, a rubber duck, and two badminton rackets. But it was a successful retreat. When they got to the road, two other men appeared in a pickup truck, hoisted Louie and the ice-cream cart and hose into the back of it, and sped away.

The American government had captured an FF.

TWENTY-TWO

(From *THE OFFICIAL HISTORY OF THE ALIEN INVASION, Volume 1*, pp. 434–446. Being the report of Agent Michael Johnson on the interrogation of the alien terrorist and the subsequent response to the raid on the safe house.)

When agents of the CIA captured a Protean on a beach in the Caymans they had no idea which Protean they had snared. It could have been just another harmless, playful Protean like the SuperSurfers in California, or it could be Alien 6, Louie, one of the masterminds behind the attacks on networks, bank accounts, and social media. As soon as the Protean was in custody I was notified, I being considered one of the primary "experts" on Proteans.

I flew into the Caymans within four hours and was driven immediately to the estate the CIA used as a safe house. The estate covered seven acres on the water, a huge stucco mansion and two guest cottages.

Inside I was greeted by CIA Agent Adolf Agua who was in charge of the team. He knew Unit A was at the top of the chain of command in relation to the Protean terrorists and he seemed to welcome my appearance. We both knew that a decision would have to be made as to what to do with this alien, and I think Agent Agua was happy that it would be me or my Unit A that would have to make it.

I was led to a wing off to one side of the mansion and dug partly down into the earth. Cellars are not feasible on most of the Caymans because of high water tables, but the CIA had dug down as far as they dared to create a windowless room twenty feet wide and forty feet long: in effect a giant cell. We entered through the only door to the room, a steel monstrosity more than three inches thick.

Inside there was only one agent, who greeted us nervously. The door was locked behind us. The alien was in the middle of the room, locked in a cubical glass cage about four by four by four. A hatch on top seemed to provide the only access. Otherwise the room was totally empty.

"He hasn't said a word so far," Agent Agua said as we approached. "As you can see, we've removed most but not all of the polymacatine that we sprayed on him during the capture."

I walked to within a few feet of the cage and stopped and stared at the hairy sphere, splotched on one side with some sort of black coating.

"I don't see how anyone can identify one Protean from another," Agent Agua continued. "They all look the same even when they look different—I mean even when they change shapes."

"Hi, Louie," I said.

"Hi," the alien replied. "How they hanging?"

Agent Agua looked stunned.

"You're able to recognize this one!?" he said.

"I think so," I answered. "Although I'm smart enough to know that a Protean not Louie might find it to his advantage to pretend to be Louie, so there's a possibility I'm being tricked."

"Jesus," said Agent Agua.

"What do you think, Louie?" I said to the Protean. "Are you a fake Louie or a real Louie?"

"I'm not sure," said the Protean. "This goo that they covered me with has affected the fine receptors of my computer system. I may be this entity you call 'Louie' but quite honestly, I'm not sure."

"Bullshit," I said neutrally. "One alien or another, you know precisely who you are."

"In any case I don't intend to say anything more until I'm out of this cage, in a bath, and have had the rest of this black goo cleaned off me."

"Get someone in here with a tub of water and any solvent you need to get rid of the rest of the polymacatine," I said to Agua. "And the key to unlock this cage."

Agent Agua went into action and within a half hour Louie had been released from his cage, had the polymacatine cleaned off, and was enjoying a soak in the large metal tub.

"Well, Louie, shall we have a chat?" I asked.

"Who's this Louie you keep talking to?" it answered. "Am I supposed to be named Louie?"

Now, on one level I was certain that this alien was Louie, but on another I knew that Proteans *might* have the ability to give off false signals about who they are, that they could convince humans that they were some other Protean that the humans thought they knew. On the one hand, I *knew* this was Louie. On the other hand, I knew I'd be a fool to trust a word of what this alien said to me, whether it was Louie or not. And even worse, I knew that if this was another Protean he probably had communicated with Louie, might even this very moment be communicating with Louie, and thus could quite easily fool me.

"So, Mr. X," I said to the alien lolling in the bathtub. "Can you please tell me what you're doing in the Caymans?"

Agent Agua and I were standing side by side three feet from the tub.

"Enjoying the waters, Mike," it replied.

"There are plenty of waters around Long Island," I said. "Why come here?"

"To see one of my old buddies."

"And when were you planning to return to Long Island?"

"Who says I come from Long Island?"

I should note that the voice of this alien was not the same as the voice of the Louie on Billy Morton's boat, and it was different too from the voice that Louie had used during his television performance. But all three voices were definitely similar.

"Where *do* you come from then?"

"Ickieland."

"We'll never get anything out of this thing this way," said Agent Agua. "He's playing with us."

"Agent Agua believes being nice won't work, Louie," I said. "I think he wants to revert to more traditional CIA methods of interrogation."

"Oh, no, please, not that, not that, I'll tell you anything you want to know!"

"Good," I said, fully aware that he was mocking us. "Please give us the names of the humans you're using to open dummy accounts here in the Caymans."

"Smith, Brown, Johnson and Agua."

"Fuck you, asshole."

This was Agent Agua's contribution. Without another word he turned and strode back to the door, motioning to one of the video monitors that he wanted to leave. After several seconds the door opened and he left.

"Impetuous sort of gentleman," said Louie.

"If the CIA threatens to kill you unless you tell us the names of your human helpers here in the Caymans and elsewhere, what will you do?" I asked him.

"What do you think?"

"If you're the Louie who befriended the Mortons then I don't think you'll help us."

"Choose death rather than dishonor?"

"It's all a game, Louie," I said. "And I imagine the rules of the game that you follow demand that you not betray a teammate."

"Hey, you're catching on!"

"So you'll die."

"Beginning to look that way."

Twenty minutes later Agent Agua returned and ordered all of us out, leaving Louie alone—except for the four video cameras and several wall lights.

Agent Agua led me to the control room where we watched Louie bouncing around the room like a ballet dancer doing practice leaps. Then he hit a switch and all the lights in the room went out. The video screens were now all black. The only thing being transmitted were the soft sounds of something like a very flexible beach ball hitting various surfaces at random intervals. Louie was to be denied light and water until he talked.

However, the next day Agent Agua indicated that he'd received orders from CIA high command to try a certain technique that might make the alien talk before he died from lack of light and water. The technique was not exactly high-tech: it involved using a chainsaw to cut off small parts of the alien until he either talked or died.

I immediately protested and took my protest to CI Rabb, my chief at Unit A. He consulted with someone higher up in the NSA and then reported to me that the CIA was to be in charge of the interrogation for the time being. He indicated that if the Protean died without talking, it was the best we could hope for; since if he didn't talk he would be permanently out of circulation. I was not amused by the NSA's new euphemism, "out of circulation." It used to be called "dead."

Agent Agua and his men found that the chainsaw tended to hit the steel wire they had used to hold the alien in place even more than it cut into the alien. So they then tried a large, extremely sharp carving knife. This they could plunge into the restrained alien but could not easily use to carve out a piece of his body. It apparently took the agents another two hours of dedicated hard work, but they finally managed to cut out two pieces of the alien; one a chunk about the size of a small fuzzy football and the other about half that size. An agent took the two pieces away to a makeshift lab they had set up to examine these alien fragments.

Louie was not giving them useful information. As he was being first chainsawed and then carved up, he simply made jokes.

"Ouch."

"Careful, you're getting near my penis."

"Wow, that feels great! Do some more of that."

"Hey, you just took away my memory of a one-night stand I had with Florence Nightingale back in Ickieland."

Eventually, Agent Agua ordered a temporary suspension of activities. He retreated back into the mansion. He was even kind enough to consult with me about what other techniques we might try the next day. One of his men had come up with the idea of planting large fire-crackers into the alien and exploding them. The alien might realize that this was worse than death by a thousand cuts and finally tell us something.

It was an interesting idea, but we never got to see if it might work.

The safe house compound was well defended. There were over fifty motion sensors planted around the grounds, twenty floodlights, and another twenty video cameras mounted strategically throughout. In addition there were the seven CIA agents and four additional security guards hired from a private contractor. There were three separate goo guns ready for use. And all the traditional human weaponry associated with killing people.

Agent Agua was awakened at midnight: something had activated two of the motion sensors near the sea. When the floodlights came on, the agents saw a sphere-shaped alien fifty feet from the water rolling toward the mansion. Even as Agent Agua was ordering a full alert, all the lights on the grounds and in the mansion flickered and went out. In another few seconds most of them came on again, powered by a diesel generator that automatically kicked in.

The monitors in the control room now picked up two other Protean spheres rolling rapidly toward the mansion, one from the surrounding mangroves and another from near the gate. The security man on duty on the flat roof of Louie's prison opened fire on one of the Proteans, continuing to shoot until it disappeared up close to one side of the mansion. Another guard saw the other Protean rolling rapidly in from the front gate, but it disappeared close to the house before he could get off any shots.

Agent Agua and I both arrived at the control room at the same time, and he radioed to inform all the agents of the locations of the various aliens. But then the video cameras watching the sides of the house began to go out one by one. Three of the floodlights also went out. All three of the invading aliens had disappeared.

Agent Agua ordered two of his men and one of the goo guns to the room housing the generators. He ordered two more men to take up defensive positions near the entrance to the prison room—also with a goo gun.

Although the mansion had barred windows on the ground floor, the second-floor windows had been left as they'd originally been built. Within three or four minutes of the first alarm, an agent reported that a Protean was in the upper hallway and had rolled down the stairs to the main floor.

In another minute, we heard gunshots and could see on one of our remaining monitors that a Protean had broken through the locked door to the generator room. The agents there began firing at the Protean, but it bounced from floor to wall to floor so rapidly it was difficult to hit it.

Then came four or five shots just outside the control room. Something slammed into the wooden door. Then silence. There were four of us in the room: Agua, myself, and two other agents.

An alien exploded through the door, knocked Agent Agua's feet out from under him, then knocked over a second agent the same way. I and the other agent fired at the sphere, but it was moving so rapidly in such random directions that we both missed. The alien bounced off a wall into the agent's head and knocked him out. He bounced again and hit the agent he'd spilled earlier as he tried to rise, appearing to knock him out too. I was firing at him as he bounced from wall to head to wall and this time managed to hit him twice. Then the alien smashed into the tower of the main computer, bounced off a wall to hit it hard again, and then bounced to the hole it had made in the door and away.

None of the monitors in the control room were now working: the main computer had been damaged. We could no longer see what was happening. Agent Agua recovered quickly from the attack. He and I knew that it was Louie that they were after; the control room and generator room were only sideshows.

We raced through two rooms and two hallways of the mansion to get to the prison door, hearing shouts and gunfire as we approached. Three aliens were bouncing from wall to floor to agents in attack and retreat, gunfire and black goo following their every bounce. They managed to level two of the guards, but when Agua and I entered and began shooting, they all three bounced and rolled past us and out into the main part of the mansion. We chased them, but in another few seconds they had escaped from the house and were away.

We had wounded all three aliens and totally thwarted their efforts to free Louie. We had triumphed.

TWENTY-THREE

(From *LUKE'S TRUE UNBELIEVABLE REPORT OF THE INVASION OF THE FFS*, pp. 119–123)

After the failed raid, all four FFs returned to the safe house. Molière, Gibberish, and an FF named Baloney had been hit by bullets and were feeling a bit "under the weather": their computer and "muscle" powers were reduced by as much as a third. LT had escaped unhurt.

Baloney had gotten his name because "baloney" was his response to any comment made by a human and to most of what Louie and Molière said. Baloney somehow said it in a way that meant that what you'd said was baloney but was nevertheless acceptable because in this flawed world, baloney was about as high as we could aspire to. Even after he himself said something that was actually pretty smart, he'd always add, "Baloney, of course." Louie told Billy that Baloney was even worse when he talked in Ickian since his saying the equivalent of "baloney" in the Ickie language usually took fifty or sixty pages.

The wounded warriors were soon joined by two new small FFs, pieces of the carved-up Louie. Because they were unprepared split-offs rather than the result of intentional birthing, they had limited skills and intelligence compared to Louie-Twoie. In effect, they were "born" with major birth defects, and would be limited for the rest of their lives. But that didn't stop the FFs from including them as part of their family. The smaller of the two—not much bigger than a golf ball—became a sort of pet of LT's. Compared to the elastic

LT, WeeWee—that being the name LT gave him—couldn't do much of anything in terms of changing shape, but he loved to ride around with LT, often becoming an "eye" in the middle of any head that LT momentarily created. "Chubby," the larger fragment, was more independent.

Louie-Twoie, Molière, and Baloney now devised a plan to make a second attempt to free Louie. The plan gave LT and Chubby the most important roles. Louie-Twoie had shown his usefulness in the initial raid by rolling into the estate after the three larger FFs had attacked, and himself destroying several floodlights and video cameras. He'd also stayed after the wounded FFs had fled and used his tiny size to get into the mansion to listen to the agents make their new plan, one that involved Johnson and his men sending a two-car motorcade to the airport at eight A.M. the next morning, and then flying Louie from there to "a place of no return"—a CIA site in the Poconos of New Jersey. Once the terrorist was there they were confident he would not leave alive.

Molière gave the most important job to LT and Chubby because they were the only ones small enough to do it. The new rescue attempt would be very low-tech. It could have been pulled off by a couple of teenagers—if the teenagers had been able to reduce themselves to the size of soft balls.

At dawn the next morning LT and Chubby snuck in close to the CIA house. The FFs knew the agents were using two vehicles to take Louie to the airport. When men emerged from the mansion, with Louie in some sort of two-foot-square cage, LT waited to see which car they were putting Louie in, and which they were using as a guard car. Then he guided Chubby to roll under the guard car sedan, and then rolled himself under the sedan containing Louie. He then bounced up into the engine. Within a minute the two cars drove off.

Molière was giving LT and Chubby instructions, informing them that the guard car was taking the lead, presumably to look out for an FF ambush. When Molière finally gave the order, LT used the razor-knife he'd brought along to cut the spark plug wires. The car sputtered, slowed and stopped. LT leapt down from inside the engine and slipped into the grass of the nearby ditch.

When the lead car was radioed and told what was happening, it made a U-turn to go back the mile or so to the car holding Louie. But that's when Chubby attacked the spark plug wires with the tiny pair of scissors he'd been given.

While the agents were still inside trying to restart the car containing Louie, LT punctured a hole in the right rear tire. He'd barely finished and hidden again in the grass when Billy drove up and parked behind the agents' car.

"Can I help you fellas?" Billy asked as he got out.

Agent Agua leapt out from the driver's door and approached Billy.

"We don't need any help, old man," he said. "Move on."

"Just being a good neighbor," said Billy, standing between the two cars.

"Get out of here," said a second agent, getting out the passenger door and drawing his gun.

"Okay," said Billy. "But you sure you don't need help with your flat tire?"

Both agents looked startled, noticed where Billy was looking, and came up beside him to stare at the flat tire.

"Shit," Agent Agua said.

"That helps," said Billy, "but you still got to change the tire."

"Scram!" Agent Agua drew his gun.

"No need to kill me," said Billy. "I'm not that hot to change a flat tire."

Billy walked slowly back to his car, got in and drove off.

Molière and Gibberish had jumped out of the open passenger window while the agents were distracted. They joined LT in the high grass. When the two agents holstered their weapons and knelt down to look at the flat tire, Molière and Gibberish bounced up and bopped the two agents from behind. "Bopping" is the closest English word to an FF's throwing out part of his body to strike at high speed.

A gunshot exploded from the inside of the car: the last agent began shooting at Molière and Gibberish, who both hopped immediately onto the car's roof. LT rolled out of the grass in through the open passenger door and, before the agent knew LT existed, LT knocked the gun out of the agent's hand. Molière was immediately inside the car bopping the poor man's head.

Billy appeared again with his rental car and, within a minute, Molière, Gibberish, LT and the caged Louie were away, leaving three moaning, mostly unconscious agents lying beside the road. As they were leaving, the guard car came sputtering along, barely making five miles per hour.

Billy waved jauntily at them as the two cars passed.

TWENTY-FOUR

(From Billy Morton's *MY FRIEND LOUIE*, pp. 172–176)

Four hours later they were out at sea in a sleek thirty-seven-foot Carver cruiser Molière had arranged to buy the day before when he felt certain we'd have a need for it. With the help of a human friend, he'd bought it from a local drug dealer down on his luck and impressed with the cash being offered.

Splitting with Lita and Jimmy was the hardest thing to do, but Molière and Louie convinced us it was necessary. If she traveled with both kids there was a fair chance they'd be identified. And the FFs wanted me to pilot the Carver. They'd bought it both to escape the pursuit of the CIA, and to get the millions in cash off the island.

Lita and I said our goodbyes standing near the rental car Lita and Jimmy were driving to the airport. Lucas would come with me. The boat was at a dock fifty feet away.

"What have we gotten ourselves into?" says Lita. She was dressed in a frowsy dress, with padding around her waist and a blonde wig. She looked like a fifty-year-old nanny. Her new name was Isabella Cola.

"Into trouble, sweetheart."

"All of Louie's plans seemed to involve danger. This is no life for the boys."

"I know."

"Since that time on Long Island getting prepared for coming here our family hasn't been together for more than a few minutes. Now Jimmy and I have to go back alone while you and Lucas sail off into more trouble."

"Sail *away* from trouble we hope."

"This has got to stop, Billy."

"Yep. Like to know how."

"One way or another, when we're back in New York, we've got to figure out a way."

We hugged and kissed and kissed again, and then had to go our separate ways.

Gibberish, Baloney, and the two new little Louie fragments, WeeWee and now Chubby, who'd made it back, were not coming with us for reasons the FFs neglected to tell me. But when Lucas, Louie, Molière, LT, and I boarded the boat that evening I discovered we had another human crew member. She was a twenty-eight-year-old gal named Karen Bell that Molière had met two days earlier while cavorting in the sea. She had let him toss her into the air and ride piggyback on his porpoise shape and generally become part of the act. The crowd loved it. And so did Karen.

She'd worked for almost two years with a *Cirque du Soleil* traveling company as an acrobat. She was a tall, six-foot blonde, with not much fat, and what little she had was distributed exactly where if I were God I would have put it. I could see why humans might drool over her, but I assumed Molière's only interest was in having her become a trusted crew member. She was between shows and was the sort of adventurous young gal who was free at the drop of a hat to do something stupid—namely become a crew member of a boat run by three alien creatures from another universe, and with the supposed captain an old man who at first glance looked like he'd have to spend the whole voyage being helped down into his bunk. And a kid aboard too.

Our primary purpose was to escape from the Caymans and the CIA. We figured they might suspect we'd try the sea, but since all FFs were able to swim for days underwater at pretty good speeds they didn't really figure they'd need a boat. Our final destination was a lonely beach off the east side of Key Largo, just fifty miles south of Miami. Our ETA, assuming we didn't blow a gasket, run up onto a reef, or get zapped by a drone: twenty hours later.

You should know that Louie seemed to be his old self. He took his usual sphere shape and looked the same except perhaps a little bit smaller. He complained to me after having lost several cubic inches that he'd lost a lot of his intelligence. His IQ was down to 660,777. I figure here on Earth that he would still get by.

I was expecting Louie and Molière to try and keep my and Lucas's identities secret from Karen, but they didn't. In fact, they seemed to accept Karen as being as trustworthy as yours truly. Which annoyed me a bit. I'd proven myself a friend of the FFs a hundred times, but as far as I could see this gal had done nothing except let Molière play some tricks with her in the water. And not only did they tell her up front who Lucas and I were, but when they began telling me about some of the things FFs were up to around the world and the sorts of games they were playing, they let Karen listen too. Pretty lousy spy-craft it seemed to me. And even worse for my ego.

After a couple of hours of motoring we were all sitting—if FFs can be said to sit—in the aft section of the Carver. There was no one at the helm since we had the boat on automatic pilot. I didn't bother to hop up every minute or so to make sure we weren't about to impale ourselves on an oil tanker, because I sensed that Louie and Molière had radar that looked right through the Carver's superstructure and could probably pick up a toy rubber duck twenty miles away. Our big cruiser, named *Who Cares?*, zoomed along at thirty knots west-northwest without a human hand touching her wheel. The boat was planing, something old *Vagabond* probably did as a youngster but hadn't done more than once since I'd owned her.

The problem was that though I love being on a boat out on the ocean, I like to *hear* the water splashing around the boat, hear the seagulls crying, see what's happening around me. At anchor or hove this is possible. Even at fourteen knots—*Vagabond*'s supreme speed—it was possible. But at thirty or forty knots you could only concentrate on what was right in front of you, and that was at best a distant blur of sea. Speed may be fine for some things, but out on the water it's a waste.

Anyway, me, Lucas, Karen, and the three FFs were all on the cushioned seats, sometimes bouncing a bit as *Who Cares?* surged from one wave to the next. Louie-Twoie was throwing himself from one side of the cockpit to the other—like a puppy dashing senselessly back and forth in a living room. Occasionally, Lucas would leap up to intercept him, usually missing. It was late afternoon and I was having my first drink.

Louie was on his third drink, and I'm afraid I couldn't help getting annoyed every time he poured a mug of bourbon over his top. I couldn't see that he was actually enjoying it or that booze ever had the slightest effect on him, so it seemed to me a waste. Still, the guy had just given me several million dollars in various accounts, so I was a little reluctant to complain that he was wasting four or five bucks worth of my booze.

That's when Louie and Molière began to talk to us in more detail about what they were up to. Louie'd always told me that he really enjoyed human beings, found us the most interesting creatures he'd come across since the one-legged Pepperjacks he'd visited two years before—creatures that were brainy as hell but spent most all their time trying to mate with each other and create little Pepperjacks that they would pawn off on the mothers. Apparently they were creatures with a lot of pleasure centers. Pepperjacks were brainy and stupid, he said, just like humans.

I knew Louie seemed to see our planet as a huge garden that had been doing fine until one of the plants, namely humans, started getting bigger and bigger and killing off or making life miserable for a lot of the other animals and plants—including ourselves. He thought we were a bit insane: working day after day to make life miserable for ourselves and a lot of the rest of life on Earth.

"Your civilization is organized around two purposes," says Louie that afternoon. "Greed and power—which are completely inconsistent with human happiness.

"Think about it: you could be organizing your society so that humans try to live in harmony with each other and with the creatures around you. I've been to three or four societies in other universes that do that. You could organize your society around the purpose of making sure that all humans have what they need in terms of food and shelter. Most societies in other universes do that. Instead you in America have created a society where you encourage everyone to want to have more money and more things and more power, and to not give a damn about other people, especially people in the rest of the world. And only rarely to give a damn about all the other creatures and plants on Earth."

"It's insanity," says Molière. "Almost all of the people who buy into the system are doomed to feel themselves losers. The only happy people are the winners."

"Hey," says I. "I'm now a millionaire. I must be a winner! I must be happy!"

"You were happy long before we came along," says Louie.

"But your civilization is insane," says Molière, pouring a glass of water over his head (he's a teetotaler). "Western therapists can't cure this since therapists are as insane as everyone else. Insanity is built into your system."

"And worst of all," says Louie, "unless someone or something intervenes, humans are doomed. You can't change your system because the people who control it have no interest in changing it. And they've got the power to prevent everyone else from even tinkering with it a bit, much less throwing it over and trying some new purposes, some new systems. Your civilization has become a cancer, eating away at the health of your planet."

Molière and Louie suddenly bounced off each other and back to their same places.

"That's why we're interested in playing games that kill off some of the cancerous cells," says Molière, pouring himself another drink. "Games that end the dictatorships that create the cancer cells."

"What dictatorship?" says I. "We had a president for eight

years who wasn't able to do a damn thing. He couldn't even dictate to Congress, much less the American people. And this president is just as helpless."

"Dictatorships, not a dictator," says Molière. "All the power in the country lies with dictators, and there are dozens of these dictators, who together run the country for their collective benefit."

"Who are these guys?" says I.

"They're the men who run your corporations," says Louie, "and your corporations control most all of the economic and political life of your country—they run the world."

"And corporations are dictatorships," Molière says. "All the power is at the top. Does an employee get to have any say at all on the policies of the corporation? Do the customers? Governments are supposed to have a say, but in the last few decades corporations have convinced most people that government regulations are harmful to the economy. They've made the regulatory agencies so weak and so packed with people indirectly being paid by the corporations they're supposed to regulate, that governments have almost no real control."

"Here comes a boat," says LT.

Karen and I stood up to see what was approaching, but the FFs stayed where they were, probably because they didn't need a line of sight to "see" the boat that was approaching. I soon saw it was a big Coast Guard cutter. Maybe we hadn't escaped the Caymans and the CIA after all.

TWENTY-FIVE

(From Billy Morton's *MY FRIEND LOUIE*, pp. 180–187)

We'd wondered whether the CIA would think we might try to leave the Caymans by sea, but when nothing had happened in the first four hours we'd gotten cocky. Thought we could sit in the cockpit and discuss the nature of the universes.

"Turn the boat toward them," says Louie as he and Molière disappeared below.

At the helm, I took her off autopilot, slowed her a bit, and turned her in an arc toward the approaching Coast Guard.

Louie and Molière emerged from the cabin each dragging four of the waterproof bags they'd stashed our cash in.

"Stay here," Louie says to Louie-Twoie, and then bounced over the coaming and into the sea. Molière followed—they had both taken the waterproof bags with them. LT morphed into a small rat and scurried below.

As we neared the Coast Guard cutter, I slowed the boat. They slowed too, and soon the boats were tied alongside each other. In another minute the Coast Guard chief honcho stood in front of me, a nice-looking guy, though a bit overweight. Behind him, also aboard *Who Cares?*, were two crew, each with holstered guns.

Lucas sat on the port side glaring at the Coast Guard honcho. Like his old man he has a tendency to glare at most authorities. Karen stood beside me glaring too.

"Are you carrying any arms, contraband, or more than ten thousand dollars in cash?" asks the chief honcho.

"Not any more," says I. "Threw all that stuff overboard a half hour ago. But if you find any leftover cash, let me know. I can use some."

"Do you have the right to board this boat without a warrant?" asks Karen.

"Can I see some identification and the title to the boat?" asks the officer, ignoring Karen.

"Sure," says I. "I'm Jose Rodriguez and this is Karen Bell. The boat title is below."

"I want to see passports too," says the officer. "And search your boat."

"Great," says I. "Let us know what you find. We threw all the corpses overboard yesterday."

The honcho gave me a scowling look and then watched his two men follow Karen into the main cabin.

After Karen had found our passports and the boat's title, the Coast Guard captain looked them over, then gave all three documents to one of his crewmen. The guy then hopped from one boat to the other and disappeared into the main cabin of the Coast Guard cutter. How I envied him his ability to hop. I haven't hopped in years.

The captain went to the stairs leading into our main cabin, looked in, and then went below.

"Is he going to arrest us?" asks Lucas.

"Probably not," says I.

"Was it legal for them to search our boat like that?" asks Karen.

"Anything's legal if you've got the weapons," says I.

"Where do you think Louie and Molière went?" Lucas whispers.

"Some day we'll find out," says I. "I hope."

As I sat down, Karen went over to port and began chatting up a young guy who looked, uniform or no uniform, even younger than the kid reporter. With Karen being friendly, his face glowed like he'd just won a lottery.

About three minutes later the captain emerges from our main cabin.

"You've got rats," he says.

"Yep," says I. "Damn thing's been aboard since I bought her."

"And you're traveling rather light, aren't you?" he says.

"Always travel light," says I. "Don't like material possessions."

"Like this little two-hundred-grand cruiser," says the captain.

The young kid who'd taken our documents emerged from the Coast Guard cutter cabin and hopped back onto our boat. He gave our passports and boat title to the captain along with a two-page computer printout.

The captain handed me back the documents and went over and sat down and began reading the printout.

"You are Jose Rodriguez?" he asks, finally looking up.

"You got it," I says. "Joe himself in the flesh."

"You don't speak with a Spanish accent."

"I dropped it after I became an American citizen," says I.

"You have a record as a drug dealer spanning forty years."

"Yep. Outstanding record. Retired now though. Two years ago. Straight as an arrow ever since."

"And where are you going with this high-powered boat?" he asks.

"Fishing," says I.

"Where? Where's your next port of call?"

"Not sure. Planning to go for marlin off the north coast of Cuba."

"I should warn you the Cubans can confiscate an American boat that enters their territorial waters without proper visas."

"Really? Will they take good care of it?"

"And what are you doing aboard this boat, Miss… Bell?"

"I bait the hooks," says Karen.

I was beginning to like her.

He stared at her a long time. Then looked down at his printout.

"You're an acrobat?"

"Part-time," says Karen. "Mostly I bait hooks."

"Why are you feeding me this bullshit, Miss Bell?"

"Not her fault, Captain," says I. "She catches it from me."

"Why are you both feeding me this bullshit? What the fuck are you two doing off the west end of Cuba with one fishing pole that would probably break in two if it hooked a minnow, two lures, and not even a fishing chair?"

Karen and I look at each other.

"We're having an affair," she announces. "And we don't want anyone to know."

Yeah. Right. Even I couldn't believe that one.

"And where is your actual destination?" the Coast Guard asks.

"Miami. Our next port of call is Miami."

"And what do you plan to do there?"

"Make mad passionate love," says Karen.

She could use a new scriptwriter.

The Coast Guard looks at her, then at me, and sighs. I figure he's trying to decide which is more likely, that she's a professional hook baiter or that we could make mad passionate love.

"You're presently not wanted by any law enforcement agency, Rodriguez, so though this whole business smells fishier than a gutted marlin, I have nothing to cite you for except improper placement of life preservers. My bosun will write out a ticket.

"As for you, Miss Bell, you also have no outstanding warrants. The only thing I might charge you with is lying, but in the United States that's never been a crime."

He stood up. He looked at Karen and he looked at me.

"I don't suppose you have any hidden Proteans aboard," he says neutrally.

"We had a whole boatful," says I, "but they got sea sick and ordered a spaceship to come pick them up. Didn't even thank us for the boat ride."

The Coast Guard guy just stares at me.

"Some day drop me a line and let me know what you were up to today," he says quietly and there's even a hint of a smile. "Because I sure as hell can't make head nor tail of a boat with nothing on it but an old bullshitter and a young bullshitter, and the boy you've never introduced me to who spends all his time glaring at me. No dope, no money, absolutely nothing suspicious except that nothing makes any sense, which makes everything suspicious."

"Give me your card," says I, "and I promise to write. You won't believe what I tell you, but it'll make a great story to tell your kids."

It took him a second or two, but he soon realizes that I'm serious.

"I'd appreciate that," he says. And he reaches into his pants, pulls out a wallet and then from it a card. He hands it to me. "Kelly McGuire" says the card. "Captain, US Coast Guard."

I offered him my hand.

"I'll get you the story," I says as we shake. "If I live long enough."

"You do that. Let's go, boys," he adds to his two men.

"And thanks, Captain," says I. "You're a decent guy. Sorry we can't tell our story yet."

"I am too," he says and is over the coaming and back aboard his boat.

ITEM IN THE NEWS

A FEW MORE DEFINITIONS FROM THE NEW PROTEAN DICTIONARY OF AMERICAN USAGE

ADVERTISING: The center of modern civilization, now with a new formula and fifty percent off. It enables humans to replace the old excrement they didn't need with new excrement they don't need.

BLACK LIVES MATTER: A movement among black Americans to get white Americans to change their minds on the subject of whether skin pigmentation ought to affect the constitutional right not to be killed for offenses such as running away, jaywalking, and selling illegal cigarettes.

BUDDHISM: A human institution based on the notion that human institutions are always a source of suffering. Un-American.

CAPITALISM: That economic arrangement whereby corporations and the extremely wealthy arrange the system so that they control the media, the politicians, and all branches of the government, and thereby guarantee that the bank accounts of the wealthy, by the wealthy, and for the wealthy shall not perish from the earth.

COMPROMISE: A quaint method of political interaction recently made archaic by the Republican Party.

DEATH: Life's transition to a less active state. Considered by most of Earth's life forms to be as natural and agreeable as birth, but perceived by humans to be a fate worse than death.

GAZA: An open-air penal colony on the Mediterranean where most all are serving life sentences, and prison riots against the wardens are punished severely.

HUMAN-INDUCED CLIMATE CHANGE: An ongoing process denied by many Americans because they know that God alone controls the weather, and accepted by most other Americans with a bored shrug.

IMPERIALISM: That process by which wealthy Western nations for three centuries dominated, terrorized, and impoverished much of the rest of the world. Not mentioned in American dictionaries.

LOVE: That feeling of joy and oneness that transports a human being from his or her usual sad illusions to a state of wonderful illusions.

MEN: The dominant group among humans. Major cultural error.

MILITARY DRONES: A weapon developed to kill people in far away lands that permits the killers not to miss karaoke night at their favorite bar.

MORAL SYSTEMS: Humankind's effort to control the natural.

MUSIC and DANCE: Humankind's most wonderful inventions.

NETWORK NIGHTLY NEWS: A half-hour TV program during which lengthy and important commercials are interrupted by occasional discussions of trivial recent events.

RACIAL PREJUDICE: The human attitude of members of a ruling race toward those they dominate and oppress.

RICH MAN: It is harder for a rich man to get into heaven than a camel through the eye of a needle—but the rich man snickers: he can *buy* heaven, and shrink camels.

TERRORIST: Anyone who perpetrates an act of violence against unarmed human beings. In American usage, does not include actions by members of the American, European, or Israeli police forces or military.

TIME: A human concept based on their inability to see all life in the present tense.

TWENTY-SIX

(From the *OFFICIAL HISTORY OF THE ALIEN INVASION, Volume 1,* pp. 256–259. From the Presidential Tapes, Dec 9, 20--. Present: the President; Senate Majority Leader Angelo Portobello (who is also a Republican candidate running in the presidential primaries).)

PORTOBELLO: Your new legislation making Proteans legally human beings is totally unacceptable, Mr. President. It doesn't stand a chance in either the Senate or the House.

PRESIDENT: And what amendments do you and your followers plan to take to the floor?

PORTOBELLO: Not just my followers—most Republicans want a law making Proteans legally human beings only to make it easier for the government to prosecute and imprison them. Your suggested legislation doesn't do that. It makes them human beings in almost the same way as real human beings. It would let them compete as equals and thus they would dominate Wall Street, the corporate world, sports—everything. Our plan is to define Proteans as human beings with special qualifications—as non-mammal human beings whose rights are limited. We want to be able to prosecute them as humans for hacking computer systems, robbing banks, revealing government secrets, speeding more than fifteen miles an hour—but *not* human beings for other purposes—like competing on a level playing field in entertainment, sports, money management, stock trading, and things like that. We want a law that will define the Proteans as citizens, but as second-class citizens.

PRESIDENT: I don't like that.

PORTOBELLO: From the very beginning our Constitution divided human beings into different classes—property-owning human beings, male and female human beings, and slave human beings. Our Founding Fathers put many limits on non-property holders, women and slaves, and our proposed law making the Proteans second-class citizens has a long and honorable American history.

PRESIDENT: A history we should be ashamed of.

PORTOBELLO: In any case, this new law will divide human beings into two *new* classes: traditional human beings, and non-mammal human beings. Under our legislation the Proteans will become *non-mammal human beings.* However, the law will make it illegal for non-mammal human beings to operate a computer or handle money without the written permission of the Director for the Maintenance of Proteans. Moreover, it will be illegal for them to bounce more than five feet high, speed at more than fifteen miles per hour, stay under water for more than five minutes, pour alcohol over themselves, and so on. They will be second-class human beings, like women and slaves used to be.

PRESIDENT: You know I'll veto the bill, Angelo.

PORTOBELLO: And we have the votes to override it.

PRESIDENT: But why have you created all these trivial crimes like bouncing more than five feet high? They make your proposed legislation almost comical. Why the hell are you insisting on keeping them in?

PORTOBELLO: Because those trivial crimes make it easier to arrest Proteans. It will be difficult to convict a Protean of hacking computer systems or transferring funds from hacked bank accounts, but we can always find witnesses that agree that a Protean sped at more than sixteen miles per hour, or bounced more than five feet high or poured a bottle of beer over its head. For these trivial crimes we can arrest and convict them, and lock them up. This is essentially how our marijuana laws worked for almost a hundred years. Smoking or owning a small amount of pot was a federal crime, but in the long history of the law very few middle-class white people have been sent to jail under the law. But literally hundreds of thousands of black and Hispanic folks were arrested and easily sent to jail whenever a policeman or prosecutor felt like it. Nations have always created laws to permit them to jail people they're trying to keep as second-class citizens.

PRESIDENT: No, Angelo, I don't like it. What will the penalty be for bouncing over five feet or pouring beer on a head?

PORTOBELLO: Two weeks in solitary confinement.

PRESIDENT: Solitary confinement?

PORTOBELLO: It's brilliant, Mr. President. The CIA discovered in working closely with a Protean captive in Egypt that Proteans need regular sunlight and regular water. When locked in a solid cell and denied light and water the Protean captive usually dies in about a week. So the Anti-Terrorist Task Force suggested we make all Protean crimes punishable by two weeks in solitary confinement. By keeping them in a light-free cell without water, we can wipe the terrorists out.

PRESIDENT: Good God. Is that your plan? You want to wipe out *all* the Proteans!?

PORTOBELLO: Well perhaps not all. But they have the potential to wipe us out, so most of my party want to strike first, and our proposed legislation will do that.

PRESIDENT: This is madness. We should be trying to get the Proteans to be on our side, work to use their supreme computer powers to help us, rather than robbing us blind. I will veto your law and convince enough Democrats to block your trying to override it. No death sentences for bouncing over five feet high.

PORTOBELLO: You'll lose, Mr. President.

PRESIDENT: Then we'll all lose.

ITEM IN THE NEWS

(Being the op-ed piece in *The New York Times* written by the Protean terrorist Louie, published December 10th, 20--)

There is nothing you have to do.

There is nowhere you have to go.

There is no one you have to be.

Roll on.

The sun rises in the morning whether you want it to or not.

The sun sets in the evening no matter how you feel about it.

Sometimes it rains. Your opinion on the matter is not relevant.

Sometimes someone dies. Every second someone dies. Your grief or rage do not produce a resurrection.

Your car fails to start. Engines do not respond to obscenities.

You have discovered your soulmate. The universe yawns.

Your leader does something particularly thoughtless and stupid. Your snarls do not change his mind.

After hours or years of effort you win the big race or big promotion. Within a few days everyone but you seems to have forgotten.

You met someone important to you and know that you

made a terrific impression. Too bad. Now you will have to live up to that impression for the rest of your life.

You met someone important to you and know that you made a horrible impression. Good. You can try something different next time.

You feel that no one pays any attention to you. You are lucky. If only other humans would stop paying attention, you could let go and at any moment be whoever you feel like being. But when you notice someone paying attention then you have to narrow your act to perform for that someone. The role you might really have wanted to play gets stuffed in the costume trunk.

A straight line is the best way to travel between two points, and the worst way for humans to travel through life.

All you do is build mole hills that you imagine are mountains. The first strong wind will blow away all that you thought was eternal.

Nothing lasts. Thank your Buddha, nothing lasts. All life is cursed and blessed by this simple truth: nothing lasts. The paradox you humans struggle to close your eyes to is that if anything were eternal it would be unimportant. Only change is interesting. All life is change. The being you are at the beginning of this sentence has changed forever before you reach the period that ends it.

And we thank God it is so. Nothing lasts.

But humans fight change and thus fight life. Most human misery lies in the effort to preserve something—someone's love, wealth, a new sofa, a child's charm, a talent that is fading. Let them go, let them go. Every effort to preserve something blocks the arrival of something new that might enrich you.

Humans dream of a perfect life, and miss the perfection of life.

TWENTY-SEVEN

(From Billy Morton's *MY FRIEND LOUIE*, pp. 198–204)

"How'd you get involved with Molière and the FFs?" I says to Karen after we'd settled down in the cockpit, Karen sitting opposite me on the port cockpit settee. I'd set our course for Key Largo, speed down to twenty knots: didn't want Louie and Molière to get out of breath trying to get back to us. Lucas was below playing with a small rat.

"Simple," she says. "I was swimming about fifty feet off shore and Molière comes along and says, 'Want a ride?' And I said 'yes.'"

"Weren't you a bit afraid?"

"Of Molière?" she says. "I'd seen that TV show where Louie talked and performed. That made me like FFs. When Molière first offered me a lift I thought he might even be Louie. I hadn't gotten to know both and be able to distinguish them as I can now."

"That's strange, isn't it? I mean if you took photos of them side by side I couldn't in a million years tell which was which, but when you're with them you know immediately."

"By means we don't know about, they somehow radiate their individual personalities."

I stood up and went forward to make sure we weren't approaching an iceberg. Nope.

"How'd you end up becoming a lowly crew member on this boat?"

"I'm not a lowly crew member," she says, smiling. "I'm first mate."

"Whatever," says I. "Did Molière ask you?"

"Yeah, he did. He said he liked me and hoped I'd join your cruise."

"Think he was hitting on you?"

"Maybe."

"How about you? You attracted to hairy beach balls?"

She laughed.

"No. But I'm attracted to Molière. I like him a lot."

"Well, lots of luck," says I. "Molière and Louie are so much smarter than we are, they probably look at us the way we look at… turtles, say. We might find a turtle cute, but we don't usually plan a long-term relationship."

Karen laughed again.

"And do you figure Molière is more on the male side or the female side?" I ask.

"Doesn't make any difference. He's simply a creature I like. His sex doesn't matter."

Next thing we knew Louie had surged up onto the stern coaming and bounced into the cockpit, his four bags of cash splashing down in a mess onto the cockpit floor. A few seconds later, Molière was there too. He hopped down into the cockpit and gently placed his four bags in a neat row. Lucas and the small rat, hearing the commotion, came up out of the main cabin.

We were a family again.

Later that night, Louie and I sat in the cockpit and talked. Karen and Lucas had gone to bed, and Molière was down below in the main cabin looking at an app that told him about every pebble between where we were and Key Largo. Louie-Twoie was keeping watch from the counter forward of the wheel. For some reason he'd shaped himself as letter U, his two "arms" raised. Lack of stability made him wobble a bit.

"Things are getting a little hairier than I figured when I agreed to help you, Louie," I says. "I didn't know I'd signed up for breaking prisoners free from the Feds and a lot of flying bullets."

"We never meant to involve you this way, Billy. Of course, we also never intended for me to get captured."

"I might enjoy it if I weren't married, but this seems to be involving Lita and the boys in a way that worries me."

"We'll try to get you out of it, Billy. In fact Molière, Gibberish, and I have been talking about what happened in the last few days and decided to draw back from our more aggressive ploys against governments and corporations. Things have gotten too hot for our taste too."

"Getting chopped up and shot not that much fun, huh?" says I.

"It isn't. I've lost about fifteen percent of my capacity and Molière and Gibberish have lost about the same. Baloney got hit three times and has lost closer to twenty-five percent. He's had to cut back on a quarter of his 'baloneys.'"

"Does getting carved up and shot hurt?"

"There's no pain involved in quite the human sense, but we all feel... *down* I guess you'd say. It affects our spirits."

"So you're going to withdraw a bit from your game against the dictators," says I.

"We're going to change the focus," says Louie. "Our aggressive actions against banks, corporations, and your security agencies don't communicate to humans that we're into play. We want to try to make human beings stop taking everything so seriously—including the injustice of the economic system they're stuck with—and get into doing things for the hell of it."

"Lots of luck."

"You're right, of course. We'll be trying to change a culture that has dominated your human life for centuries. Everyone believes that having a serious purpose is the key to being a good human. We FFs believe that being able to play is the key to being a good human. We probably won't make a dent in your culture, but it's the game we now want to concentrate on."

"Not a single dent," says I. "Humans can't be changed."

"We'll see."

I was pooped, so I said goodnight to Louie and LT and went into the main cabin and then down to my berth, which was forward at the forepeak. Molière had deserted his app and, as I was passing the master cabin, I heard Karen emit a low scream. I turned back to the cabin door.

"You okay?" I says.

There was only silence. So I knocked on the door and pushed it open.

There was only a dim nightlight at the head of the bed and the light from the boat's main hallway, but I saw Karen's blond hair spread out on one end of the bed and her bare feet and her long legs at the other. The main part of her body was covered—by Molière.

He was about three and a half feet long, with one end of his body over Karen's... pelvis let's call it—and the other over her face. His whole body was pressing into her, and it didn't take me long to realize that he was humping her. I heard Karen moaning.

I backed up a step, closed the door behind me, went forward to my berth in the forepeak, and with a groan lay back on the foam bed.

First inter-universe sex in the history of mankind. Or is it intra-universe sex? Have to look it up. The way Molière was going at it, maybe it wasn't the first. In fact, giving it some thought for three or four seconds, I concluded that any creatures that could change shape like our FFs were probably capable of mating with a few million different creatures. Jesus. Talk about polymorphous perversity: Molière and Louie could set some sort of inter-universe record. Or is it intra-universe?

And I knew from Louie's performance on the TV show that an FF could assume a female shape as easily as that of a male. Hell, an FF could create five or six sexy holes all around his body at the drop of a hat. Wouldn't even have to drop the hat. And a male could take his pick. And an FF could come up with four or five breasts if he wanted, big nipples too. Breasts any size you want.

Jesus, this is ridiculous. Get a hold of yourself, Billy.

TWENTY-EIGHT

(From Billy Morton's *MY FRIEND LOUIE*, pp. 205–211)

"You folks have a good time last night?" I ask Karen and Molière, who were sitting side by side with Louie across from me in the boat's cockpit. That morning we were off Taverna Key and only twenty miles from our destination in Key Largo.

Karen laughed and I felt Molière smile.

"I told you I liked Molière," says Karen.

"You hop into bed with everyone you like?"

"Don't be a human being," Louie says to me.

'Course I then realized what a jerk I was being. Two people, well two *creatures* that I liked a lot had just become lovers. I should be celebrating, not acting like a stupid old… human being.

"Sorry about that," says I. "I'm about ninety-nine and forty-four hundredths asshole and it occasionally shows."

I got up to walk over to Karen.

"You're a gem, Karen," I says. "And you and Molière make a great couple."

Karen stood up and gave me a big hug. It was pretty nice to hold a lovely new woman in my arms and, if I weren't trying to be noble, I'm sure my pecker would have raised his head.

"You're a wonderful man," says Karen and after squeezing me hard moves her face forward and gives me a long, soft kiss right next to my mouth. My pecker forgot all about nobility.

"I'm a jerk," I says, "But I tend to get over my jerkiness pretty quick."

I turned to Molière.

"How'd you get so lucky to pick out such a winner on your first try?"

Molière laughed.

"I've looked at tens of thousands of humans since I first landed here," he says, "and I knew what I wanted and I found her."

"Don't want to complain, Molière, but you sound like an ad for an online dating service."

Karen laughs, but Molière, Louie, and LT become absolutely still.

"Trouble coming," says Molière.

"Take us toward shore, Billy," says Louie.

"Full speed," adds Molière.

Although not hearing anything, I rushed to the helm, took her off autopilot, and swung west at close to forty knots toward the barely visible shore of the Keys about five miles away. Over the roar of the engines and the smashing through the sea, I still couldn't hear or see anything suspicious, but then heard Karen shout: "There they are!"

'Course I wanted to take a look, but I was stuck to the helm. I was vaguely aware of Louie and Molière rushing past me to go down below, and of Lucas coming up beside me.

"Get your life preserver on," I says to Lucas. "And bring one for me too. And Karen." He disappeared.

Louie and Molière emerged from below with their four bags each of cash, though they stayed under the cockpit roof.

"If they begin to shoot at us, Billy," says Louie, "you, Lucas, and Karen jump into the water. Put the boat on autopilot to keep going at this speed toward shore."

"She'll crash aground," I says.

"Better the boat be destroyed than you."

I put her on auto and finally walked out of the cockpit to take a look at what was happening. A helicopter, obviously military, with two guns showing.

The 'copter fired a round that hit in the water ahead of us—probably not a miss but a warning to stop. We were now less than two miles from shore. I went back to the helm and slowed the boat down to twenty-five knots, hoping that would make them think we were surrendering.

"The water shoals to five feet about a half mile from shore," says Molière. "We'll be aground in less than three minutes."

"What happens then?" I ask as I snapped on my life preserver and made certain Lucas had secured his.

"Get in the water and swim toward shore."

"Great. I should be able to make it in less than a month. If they don't hit me with at least twenty rounds in less than a minute, I'll lose all my faith in the US military."

"They're after us, not you," says Louie. "They want you humans alive."

"Glad to hear it," says I.

A round of machine-gun fire now swept across our bow, the teak decking pockmarked with exploding splinters. We were now a mile from shore and a half mile from running aground.

I slowed the boat down to fifteen knots, but a few seconds later another round of gunfire swept across the bow.

Louie and Molière, dragging their bags of loot, left the cover of the cockpit roof, bounced into the sea, and disappeared underwater. Louie-Twoie, shaped for the first time in days as a normal sphere, stayed on the cockpit shelf next to the helm. Karen was standing behind Lucas with her arms around him. I slowed the Carver to six knots.

Suddenly all three of us were slammed against the control panel: our faithful cruiser had hit the shoaling water.

I turned off the engine and walked out of the cockpit to the port side.

"Let's go," I says, and climbed awkwardly up on the coaming and jumped into the sea.

I'm a pretty lousy swimmer for a guy who's worked on boats half his life, but I windmilled clumsily toward shore, Karen with Lucas alongside me.

The helicopter surged up and hovered overhead. A guy at the gun mount shouted something to us. Couldn't hear a word.

I raised my hands in surrender and then felt something strange: I was being dragged toward shore by the scruff of my neck five times as fast as I could swim. Louie or Molière must be dragging me.

The guy at the gun mount stared down at the strange apparition: an old geezer moving at five or six knots toward shore with both arms in the air.

My legs touched bottom and I realized we were all now near the mangroves at the edge of the southwestern tip of Key Largo. Mangroves are the most useless growths the Good Lord has ever come up with, unless you're about to be shot and killed by gung-ho guys in an unfriendly helicopter.

Suddenly me and Karen and Lucas were in among the low trees and tough to see from above. But just as I was beginning to feel safe I saw four armed men running along the beach toward us only fifty feet away. Jesus. I immediately felt myself being dragged pretty fast through mangroves.

The men on the beach stopped running and began shooting at us, the bullets crackling through the mangroves like angry bees. Whether to kill us or to get us to stop I don't know, but we can find out after they declassify the CIA account of the operation in 2121.

The rest is anticlimax. The helicopter never did shoot at us. We didn't drown. We didn't get separated. We eluded the guys on the beach who'd continued chasing us, probably because Louie gave me a ride on his porpoise-shaped back and we moved at fifteen knots instead of five. Karen and Lucas rode on Molière's back just behind us. When we were finally sure the military had given up chasing us, we waded ashore and found an old van parked near a vacant cottage. Louie-Twoie hot-wired it, and soon we were off to less exciting places.

Thank the Lord. I hadn't been shot at since 'Nam, and I found I didn't like it today any more than I did then.

TWENTY-NINE

(From *LUKE'S TRUE UNBELIEVABLE REPORT OF THE INVASION OF THE FFS*, pp. 139–142. Being Molière's memoir about his writing of his play *Love Has No Boundaries*.)

Back on Long Island after getting shot up in the Caymans I decided it was time for a change of games. I was losing my enthusiasm for taking on the most powerful government in the history of the earth and having to fiddle around with boring banking and exciting rescue attempts. I decided to write a play.

Playwriting comes easily to FFs. It's our natural way of being. At home in what Billy charmingly calls "Ickieville" we are playing a variety of roles all the time, the roles often depending on what games we participate in on any given day. We have no "plays" as humans do because they would be redundant. We are acting in plays every moment of every day.

On Earth now we do the same. I, for example, played a French intellectual for three weeks after my arrival, could quote all of Jean-Paul Sartre backwards and forwards, and did a brilliant critique of Emmanuel Carrère's latest. When I heard from an FF who'd arrived from America about what Louie was doing, I decided to go join the game. But now I was getting a bit bored with stealing money and blackmailing helpless but deserving humans, so decided I wanted to become a Broadway star. Or rather an off-Broadway star, since it takes too long to mount a Broadway play. All I needed was actors and a script, which I would whip off in a few minutes. Money was not a problem.

It actually took longer. Writing always involves first determining one's audience, and I realized that I was stuck writing this play for humans. I had to limit myself considerably. Like a human writing a play to entertain pets.

The first problem was in using FFs as characters. The only way they could be "real" for a human audience was by their seeming to be human. To work, my play would have to pretend that FFs had human emotions—could love, hate, be jealous, greedy, angry. Well, all play involves pretending so I would create human FFs.

Then there was the problem of the appearance of the FFs in the play. I realized that for humans the changing shapes of FFs was fun. My FFs would have to be continually changing their shapes and apparent beings, and often appear in various mostly human shapes.

Next there was the genre. Since we FFs consider all human beings to be fools, there was really only one genre available for my play: farce. And how appropriate: my French friends had given me the name 'Molière' and here I was suddenly deciding to write a farce!

Finally, there was the story. All good human plays stick to the basics: love, hate, rivalry, jealousy, lust, and greed. I'd have to fill the play with all the most powerful human emotions. What I'd do is create a few characters, some human, some FFs, throw them into a dramatic situation, and let nature take its course—human nature of course.

And thus we would have a farce.

THIRTY

(From Billy Morton's *MY FRIEND LOUIE*, pp. 215–222)

I got to tell you folks, I'd never lived in a spy-thriller before, and I wasn't certain I was cut out for it. At more than seventy, leaping over tall buildings in a single bound or overpowering six uzi-armed villains with my bare hands was a bit beyond me. In the Caymans the FFs somehow managed to see to it that not a single bullet was fired too close to me and that my major contribution consisted of telling the bad guys that they had a flat tire, running an expensive boat onto some shoals, and watching a few mangroves get chewed up by bullets that scared me… considerably. (Lita has asked me to cut down on the foul language in this book.)

Of course, back in the sixties I lived for a few years in an anti-war war movie with the good guys getting killed and the bad guys getting promoted. And then for a while I lived in a seventies type of film about my lost soul looking for a purpose in life while I protested and got stoned, drunk, and laid, and became more and more disillusioned with protesting, getting stoned, drunk, and laid. That movie ended, as all the good movies did back then, in unhappy anticlimax.

I didn't find another starring role until I met Carlita, got married, and we had Lucas and Jimmy. Then we played the Happy Family show: nothing really important happening but all of us having a pretty good time, with no problem greater than "Lucas stole my cupcake."

Then Louie and the FFs entered our lives. Now I was starring in a spy-thriller, and I was beginning to feel this was a film I'd rather not be cast in.

It was a full two days until Lita, me, and the boys managed to be together again in our old farmhouse outside Greenport. That night in our bedroom Lita and I talked it out. Side by side in the king-sized bed, both of us leaning back against the headboard, she told me we had to break from Louie and the FFs.

"We can't go on like this," she says. "I won't let my sons go through what poor Lucas had to endure down there in the Keys."

"Actually, I think he enjoyed it," I says.

"I don't care if he thought it was the greatest time in his life," Lita shoots back. "He could have been killed. You could have been killed. No more."

"Got ya, sweetheart."

"You'd better get me, and don't 'sweetheart' me when I'm mad as hell."

"Got it, Mrs. Morton."

"That's better." She smiled. I leaned over and put my arm around her. She stiffened.

"Next time Louie or LT get in touch, you tell them 'no more.'"

I removed my arm.

"Got it, Mrs. Morton."

But they didn't get in touch with us. There was no sign of Louie or Molière. No message. Nothing. And LT had disappeared without telling me a thing about what he was up to. It didn't help that LT still hadn't mastered talking yet so when he tried to explain his plans it came out something like "isboo protatiti barotin sis ooper." We figured that our house was undoubtedly bugged, our phones tapped, and our emails being read. Louie would probably not want to endanger us by trying to get a message to us or put himself in danger by trying to sneak into our house. Despite her concerns about the danger the FFs put us in, Lita was as curious as any of us to know what was happening to Louie and the other FFs, so she suggested I take Lucas and Jimmy out on *Vagabond* and see if Louie didn't get in contact.

So that's what I did. Me and the boys spent a while losing bait to the most intelligent fishies I'd ever had to deal with. I figured they'd probably been taking lessons from the FFs. They ate so much of our bait I imagined a lot of them would die of obesity. In any case, no Louie, and after three hours we gave up and motored home.

Lita had begun working in New York City five days a week for the Protean Defense League, so I was having to bachelor it. The boys were back in school.

Almost a week after we'd gotten back from our Cayman adventures I was ordered to take the laundry to the local laundromat—too much had accumulated from our Cayman trip. I waited until the boys were out of school and got Jimmy to join me. He loved putting the coins in the slots, something I was happy to subcontract. I was enjoying sitting on one of the reasonably nice chairs when the last bunch of laundry in the basket waiting to be washed began talking to me. Actually, it seemed that it was my dirty sweatshirt hoody that was talking—the one with the logo "Old Age Sucks"—but when I looked closer it seemed to be my underwear.

"Not too happy, are you, Billy?" says a voice I knew was Louie's.

"I hate doing laundry," says I.

"You know what I mean," says Louie. "We've got you and Lita and the boys into a mess and we want to get you out of it."

I looked around the room. Two people were busy sorting their dried clothes while the third was reading an exciting article about detergents in the *Reader's Digest*. Jimmy was at the front of the room staring out the window at something. The machines were making a pretty good racket so I figured my whispers either wouldn't be heard or would be interpreted as the muttering of a senile old man. Old age has its advantages.

"And how do you plan to do that?" I ask.

"I think, Billy," came the smothered voice, "that the only solution is to have you killed."

Louie sure was bringing excitement into my life.

"We've learned that the Coast Guard boat that boarded us reported to the NSA what they'd found, and the NSA realized that it was you and Lucas. That's why that helicopter and those military guys showed up off Key Largo. And the men on that 'copter would be able to identify you and Lucas too. And Karen. The NSA knows that you probably helped us escape from the Caymans. They probably realize now that it was you who stopped to help the agents with their flat tire. The only reason they haven't called you in for questioning is that they still hope they can use you to capture me."

"Think I could plea bargain by telling them where you live?" I says.

"Probably. If you knew where I lived. No, Billy, I'm afraid the only solution is to kill you. Molière and I think the best plan is to blow up you and your family in your boat. That will free you from worry about the Feds."

"Yep," says I. "Death frees people from a lot of worries."

Louie let out one of his annoying "Ho-ho-hos." Shook the laundry basket.

"I'd like to rewrite this script a bit," says I. "Maybe try a plot development that doesn't involve me and Carlita and the boys getting blown up."

"No, no," says Louie. "Getting blown up is just what is needed. We FFs know everything the NSA knows, so we've got easy access to people who produce the best false papers in the world. But before you can use them, we've got to kill you, blow you and your boat up with a big bomb."

"Couldn't you settle for a really small bomb or a few fire crackers," says I. "And make it seem like the boat blew up without it actually happening? Isn't that what making movies is all about?"

"Need a big bomb, Billy," says Louie. "One that will blow all four of your bodies to such small smithereens not even the NSA can find any trace of you—make them decide the fish ate all your remains."

As I said, I'm not sure I'm cut out for this kind of movie. I'd been hoping I'd live long enough to get to the scenes when I get to win big money at a casino with a luscious babe oohing and aahing beside me and the crowd gasping at my brilliance and the way I handle an Aston Martin. But beginning the movie with my getting blown up didn't seem too promising.

That night in our kitchen Lita and I talked it out again. She was having a herbal tea while I was drinking a big mug of hot chocolate laced nicely with a coffee brandy. I told her why Louie thought it might be useful if we got killed.

"He thinks we've got to have new identities because the

government will be monitoring our every move for the rest of our lives," I says, "or at least as long as there are any FFs around. And they also may threaten to hurt us if Louie and his friends don't give themselves up. It will help both us and Louie if we take on new identities."

"Oh, Christ, Billy, this is a mess. I don't want to give up our present lives."

"I don't either," I says. "But we've already lost them. Spending half our time dodging bullets or in courtrooms is not the way we're used to living."

"I just want Louie and his friends to let us live without them," says Lita. "He wants us to pretend to get killed and then take on new identities. Where would we live?"

"Louie thinks he can relocate us any place we want."

"Damn it, there isn't any other place I want. Only here. I don't think we should do this."

I pushed myself over near her and took her in my arms.

"Then we won't do it," I says.

"Thank you," she says. As if the decision were only mine to make.

"Getting blown up isn't my thing anyway," I says.

"I'm glad."

"And much as I like Louie, I'm beginning to think that every time he has a brilliant new idea, I end up almost getting killed."

ITEM IN THE NEWS

Vancouver, British Columbia. March 30th

The World Institute for a Warmer Planet, partly funded (99.44%) by Peabody Energy and the Canadian Natural Gas Pipeline, Ltd., announced today that the people of the island of Tsonga in the South Pacific have been successfully relocated to the island of Wali-Wali only nine hundred miles away. All Tsongaese agreed that Wali-Wali is a lovely island, almost exactly the way Tsonga had been thirty years ago. Wali-Wali, being almost four feet above sea level, will remain an island for at least another twenty years, giving this generation of Tsongaese a happy life until their next migration or possible extinction.

THIRTY-ONE

(From Billy Morton's *MY FRIEND LOUIE*, pp. 225–231)

Before we went to see his play, Molière told us it had taken him six minutes to write it—seventy pages and an eighty-minute play. It must be nice to have a brain so powerful you could write a four-hundred-page novel between lunch and dinner. Or between your main course and dessert. It takes me a day to get out two or three pages on this book. 'Course it would help if I could type quicker than six words a week.

Molière had a theater—off-Broadway—and a cast of six. And of course he was his own chief "angel." So a little less than two weeks after he'd come up with his new idea, *Love Has No Boundaries* opened at the Markham Theater in the East Village. Lita and I decided to go. When the boys learned that Louie-Twoie was part of the play we had to take them too.

First play I'd seen in forty years. Lita had seen a few—mostly protest plays written by grape pickers or illegal immigrants or abused lesbians about picking grapes, being illegal, and getting abused. I figured Molière was more into fun, and I could survive the evening. The fact that the play was advertised as *Molière's Love Has No Boundaries* may have helped sales.

Actually it probably hurt them. Not many red-blooded Americans have even heard of Molière, but he sounded French, which was a big negative.

The curtain rose on a giant swimming pool taking up

more than half the stage. It was surrounded by a sandy beach with a dozen bathers.

Suddenly Molière comes shooting up out of the water, does a triple somersault and ends with a swan dive back into the pool. He does two or three more tricks like this and the beach-goers laugh and applaud. Then this beautiful young woman in a bikini so small that if it shrunk even a tiny bit it would disappear from the universe, walks up to the side of the pool and dives in. For a few seconds nothing happens. Then Karen shoots ten feet into the air, does her own somersault and swan dive and plops back into the water. Then she again shoots ten feet up this time followed by Molière; they do simultaneous somersaults and coordinated swan dives. More applause.

Well, no sense in my trying to describe all the tricks they did—you've probably seen them on YouTube. Fact is, they were pretty amazing. I laughed and applauded along with everyone else.

Then the lights went out, we heard a grinding noise that went on and on, and then when the lights came back up the scene was a big living room with four or five humans and two FFs, both in their usual hairy beach ball shapes. They were partying. The scene had a lot of clever dialogue that indicated that Molière was attracted to the Karen gal, but the other FF, who was supposedly Molière's dad, was pretty down on Molière having anything to do with a human being: humans being low-life. According to the dad, Molière's thinking her special was like Einstein being attracted to a raccoon. And a big, good-looking human being was telling Karen she was a fool to be attracted to Molière, who was ugly, shapeless, and an intellectual snob. There were confrontations, slamming doors, and longing looks from Karen toward a hairy beach ball. Molière didn't produce any longing looks, in fact he didn't produce any looks at all, but he did say a few nice things to her.

In the third scene Karen and Molière in his usual beach ball shape enter a hotel room. Karen sits in a big easy chair and they talk awhile, showing that they like each other. Then Molière rolls a bit and hops up into her lap. She puts her arms around him. Molière then sprouts a head and two arms and some lips. He hugs her and they kiss. After a long kiss—the audience throwing in a few gasps and a few giggles—Molière sprouts two thick legs, hops to the floor, and, in a wobbly fashion, picks up Karen and staggers with her over to the bed where, with a mighty effort, he throws her up onto it. Then hops up beside her.

And sprouts a pecker. A good stiff one.

The audience gasps and giggles, many of the gals gasping, and the few kids in the audience, including Jimmy and Lucas, giggling.

Then Molière kneels down on the bed beside her and sprouts two more arms and begins ripping off all of Karen's clothing. Well, having once or twice tried undressing a woman, I can tell you that having four arms instead of only two is a big advantage. Like a windmill at full throttle Molière whisks away all of Karen's clothing before you could say "What the fuck?!"

Then he lies down on top of her and goes to work, clearly engaging in an act that once a century is called "fornication." When he first starts humping her the audience is strangely quiet. I'm not sure whether most were fascinated or shocked or straining to get a better look. I myself was just grinning.

Then the audience did a strange thing: a few people began to boo, but were almost immediately overwhelmed by others applauding, then more and more, and some started cheering.

The curtain fell. And the applause died down and there was laughter and chatting. And some wise guy shouts: "Encore!"

The next scene was of Karen lying in a hospital bed in a white hospital gown and giving birth. Molière was propped up as a beach ball on a bedside table looking worried. Actually of course he wasn't looking anything at all, his acting talent being somewhat limited by his not having a face or eyes. In fact, now that I come to think of it, Molière's acting ability was limited to his changing shapes. And his talking.

Karen finally gave birth.

To a hairy baby softball played by Louie-Twoie, who had compressed his normal size for the role. He popped out from between Karen's legs and bounced around the room a bit and then went to his mom and snaked his way under her gown to bury himself on her chest, probably to get a milk delivery. More gasps, giggles, and applause.

The last scene of the play was a little uneven, boring at first, better at the end. It took place in a nice middle-class living room with all the traditional bourgeois stuff. Sitting in an easy chair, Molière was shaped like a small human being wearing jeans and a T-shirt and reading *The New York Times*. Karen and her two children—a soccer-ball-sized LT and a four-year-old human kid—were watching television. It was a thriller program about Muslim high school kids using the chemistry lab to make a poison gas to wipe out people on a subway train. Of course the stars of the show were the cool federal agents who were going to catch them before they could earn an "A" in chemistry and wipe out dozens of American commuters.

Karen and the boys and Molière exchanged about a dozen bits of dialogue showing that they had become solid, stolid, upstanding, normal middle-class American citizens. The scene was so boring and banal that I personally began to hope the high school kids would release the poison gas in the damn living room and put us all out of our misery.

Just when the audience was getting ready to throw rotten tomatoes at the actors, Louie-Twoie begins bouncing around the room like a berserk soccer ball.

"Leb's eff shom fun!"

And the little four-year-old human suddenly leaps off the couch and does two cartwheels and a somersault, and Molière surges up out of his easy chair as a beach ball and begins bouncing around the room, Karen leaps up and throws off her long skirt and sweatshirt and, dressed in bra and panties, begins choreographing her gymnastics with Molière's and LT's.

As they cavorted around the room, Louie shattered the TV set, the boy smashed several lamps, Karen wrecked the rocking chair and Louie-Twoie smashed the glass in a nice china closet. Smashed a bit of the china too. They were trashing the bourgeois life that I'd thought they'd sunk into.

Then all four of them left the stage and began dancing or bouncing or doing cartwheels in the aisles among the audience. Some members of the audience joined them and soon a conga line of twenty or thirty people led by Louie-Twoie was snaking up onto the stage and then back down off it.

A good time was had by all.

Molière, Karen, LT, and the boy led the audience out of the theater into the Village where they sucked up a few more conga dancers and disappeared into the night.

The reviews of the play the next day were mixed. "Lowbrow porn," said the *New York Post*. "A provocative look at inter-universe relations," said *The Times*. "What the fuck was that?" wondered the *Village Voice*. "I'm speechless," said *The New Yorker*, as part of a two-thousand-word review.

The next night's performance was even more sensational. And shorter. In scene three, the moment Molière sprouted his pecker and rolled on top of Karen on the bed, a dozen policemen appeared and half of them went on stage and threw a blanket over the obscene couple. For a moment some of the audience thought that this was part of the play, but most realized that the cops were real and began to boo and hiss.

In any case, the play came to an end. Karen and Molière were arrested, and LT and the boy actor taken off to social services to see how traumatized they'd been by being forced to act in an obscene play.

Naturally, Carlita was called in to defend them and managed to get them out on reasonable bail. In a brief press conference afterwards, she pointed out there was nothing obscene about Molière's having two limbs, or three limbs or four limbs, and where his limbs sprouted from was irrelevant. FFs did not have peckers, she argued (I think she used a different word), and therefore couldn't act obscenely if they tried.

As for Karen, at no time was any of her pubic area (Lita's phrase, not mine) visible to the audience. Moreover, her bare breasts were visible for only a short time, and bare breasts had been a staple on stage and screen for centuries. Carlita announced that she was confident she would win the case.

But the play was closed by court order, and none of us good guys had any desire to spend time trying to get it open again right away. We suspected that the play had been closed not for being obscene but because it showed humans and FFs loving each other. The Powers that Be didn't like that.

Molière's team had made videos of both the opening night performance and the police-raid performance and began posting parts of them on YouTube. College and community theaters all over the world began clamoring for Molière and his team to stage their play in their theaters.

'Course it wasn't all wine and roses. There was a lot of toilet water and poison ivy too. Some Christian churchmen, Jewish rabbis, Muslim imams, and Southern atheists were unenthusiastic about the mixing of the races, and saw intercourse between a human woman and a member of an unknown and hostile terrorist species as even worse than if she'd given herself to an ape or an ostrich. Some of us thought the idea of an ostrich was a good one and Molière ought to incorporate it into his rewrite of the play.

People were split down the middle about *Love Has No Boundaries*. Those who sort of liked FFs thought the play (or rather the YouTube videos) fun, while those who hated or feared the FFs thought it was simply a further horrible attack on our human way of life. Many of the naysayers were more upset about Karen giving birth to an alien softball than they were the simulated sex.

"The idea that our species may become contaminated by a race of hairy balls is too frightening to contemplate," said the

Reverend Peter O. Platt, and then spent an hour and a half contemplating it. He concluded he was against it.

The New York Times was more reserved: "There is no evidence that penetration by any part of the body of a Protean into a human female can result in conception."

In response, Gibberish wrote a letter to *The Times'* editor which included the following provocative sentences: "You'd be surprised what miracles we FFs can perform. Watch your wives, my friends, watch your wives."

The letter didn't improve the FFs' PR very much. In fact it was soon the main quotation used to attack them for threatening to take over the world.

Still, some people stayed sane. The *Presbyterian Science Monitor* wrote: "Since only the least intelligent and most promiscuous women would ever be tempted to give themselves to an alien, we can be confident that any offspring of the coupling will be of a distinctly inferior quality."

Right. If you mate a creature with an IQ of two million with another creature with an IQ of seventy, you'll get on average an inferior creature with an IQ of only one million.

Oh, what a falling off there would be.

THIRTY-TWO

(From *LUKE'S TRUE UNBELIEVABLE REPORT OF THE INVASION OF THE FFS*, pp. 150–154)

The gigantic explosion rocked the North Shore west of Mattituck Inlet not quite enough to wake the dead, but enough to disturb the sleep of many of the living. It got hundreds of citizens out of their beds, wondering if finally we'd stumbled into a nuclear war.

There were actually four witnesses to the explosion, two having a late-night drink on their patio overlooking the sound and two others lying on the beach and making love. They all reported an explosion. It was loud.

There was no boat on fire as an aftermath. The boat had disappeared. There was a small burning of gas or oil on the surface of the water but it quickly died out. A few minutes after the explosion there was only darkness and silence.

Several people called 911 to report the explosion. Both county and state police rushed to the scene. So did Sheriff Coombs. So did five fire engines.

The Coast Guard sent two boats to investigate. Sheriff Coombs, when he saw that in the darkness there was nothing to see from the shore, drove to a Mattituck Marina, commandeered a high-powered cruiser from a friend, and zoomed out of Mattituck Inlet to see what he could see on the water itself.

The Coast Guard and Sheriff Coombs discovered very little. There was some floating wooden debris, an oil and gas slick, but no sign of any bodies—in fact nothing of any significant size remained. The Sheriff had seen the results of two or three boats destroyed by gasoline explosions, and there had been a lot more debris. This explosion must have been beyond anything he'd ever seen or read about.

By dawn, several witnesses had reported that they had seen a thirty-six-foot fishing boat motoring west from Plum Gut that evening, and one witness said that the fishing boat anchored about where the explosion occurred. In another half hour Sheriff Coombs had learned enough to be pretty sure that the boat was Billy Morton's. With two phone calls he verified that Billy's boat was not at its Greenport pier, that at least one person had seen Billy and his family motoring out of the marina late that afternoon, and that there was no one at home at the Mortons' North Road home. Neither their boat nor they were anywhere to be seen.

The question was whether Billy and his family were all on the boat when it blew up. And why—or who—blew it up.

Sheriff Coombs had no answers. But he made up for it by having plenty of questions.

The NSA knew immediately that the Mortons had been on board when the explosion occurred, and that they had all been killed. The NSA had planted a bug on the boat, a very sophisticated one that they were able to monitor from one of their satellites. Nothing is ever too expensive for a government bureaucracy, especially if it's to save the nation from its many enemies. Like the Mortons.

The bug made the Mortons' last hours very vivid. After the family had eaten dinner and the sun had set, Mr. and Mrs.

Morton began drinking and chatting in the cockpit, and the two boys began playing a noisy game of speed chess down below. This lasted until ten twenty-seven P.M. Then the family prepared for bed. There was much idle talk and the sounds of drawers being opened and closed. After some rustling of people shifting in their beds, there was fifteen minutes of silence, only broken by a cough from one of the boys. Then there was the sound of someone stirring in a bunk, the sound of something striking something, and then a long burst of "foul language" from Billy Morton, mostly attacking his berth's low ceiling but also complaining about God. Mrs. Morton was heard to say, "Shut up, you old fool, you'll wake the boys."

After the swearing bit there was silence for exactly three minutes, then a loud *bang* immediately cut off by total silence. The tape ended at the exact moment of the reported time of the explosion. The NSA's expensive bug was no more. So too, concluded all those who heard the recording, were the Mortons.

ITEM IN THE NEWS

NEW GIRLS' SPORTS CHEER GOES VIRAL

Troy, NY. Nov. 20th

A cheer created for the College of Saint Rose's Girls' Basketball and Field Hockey Teams has gone viral, being tweeted over five hundred thousand times and posted on Facebook almost the same. The cheer was apparently created by a Protean alien whom the girls call "Boo-Boo." It had been playing with both teams for more than a week during practice sessions.

God is good, God is great,
Who do we appreciate?
God, God, God.

THIRTY-THREE

(From Billy Morton's *MY FRIEND LOUIE*, pp. 240–246)

Our survival wasn't exactly a miracle. What happened was that me, Carlita, and the boys packed up a big picnic lunch and a lot of other stuff, and went down to *Vagabond*. I motored us out of the harbor and east out to Plum Gut and into the Long Island Sound. Louie had wanted to blow us up in Coecles Harbor, but I said I didn't want to pollute that small body of water with the debris of my boat and the diesel fuel. I thought that was pretty thoughtful, and even Lita gave me a peck on the cheek. Louie relented. We decided to blow up off a lonely stretch of beach east of Mattituck Inlet. The Long Island Sound had been absorbing tons of junk for four hundred years.

However, before we blew up the boat, Louie suggested that we first all get off it. I approved this idea. So after the sun had set, we all began putting on a performance for the bug that Louie said was aboard. We started by having a couple of hefty belts in the cockpit, the boys noisily arguing down below. But while we were doing this we were all getting into the scuba gear Louie had provided us with. When we were geared up and ready to abandon ship, I turned on the tape we'd prepared earlier of the family talking to each other as we supposedly undressed and got into our berths. And then trying to go to sleep, and my banging my head on the ceiling and loudly indicating my displeasure. It was a great tape. It was my first official acting role, and if you ever get to hear the NSA recording you'll be impressed by how convincingly I swear. Had a lot of practice.

After my swearing spree, there was another few minutes of silence and then a gigantic BOOM! The boat blew up.

We, of course, were gone. A half hour earlier we'd slipped into the sound and swum underwater the hundred yards to shore. When we got there in the pitch darkness, we took off our scuba gear and then climbed some steps to the land above, and to a car that conveniently drove up and offered us a lift.

If I'd been directing the film we would have stayed to watch the big explosion, but Louie said we should be well away before people began to rush to the shore to see what had happened and noticed us in the car. I tried to convince him that he didn't have to worry about being realistic in a thriller, but he pretended he didn't know what I was talking about. So then, car lights off, we left.

If you've never seen an FF drive a car you don't know what you're missing. Turned our thriller into a farce in less time than it takes to burp. Louie drove in the shape of a one-legged sphere with no head. After two minutes of watching this headless apparition apparently steering the car with his belly button, I insisted Carlita take over.

We were out on the North Road three miles from the sound when we heard a distant explosion, sort of a vague *pfoom*. The guy in charge of sound effects clearly didn't know what he was doing.

But even that little *pfoom* made me feel suddenly tired and sad. I thought we were supposed to be having fun. I'd just blown up a boat I'd owned and loved for more than twenty years.

And I began complaining to Louie. Now that me and my whole family were dead, our house and all our personal possessions would go to some distant relative we hadn't seen since before World War I. Louie told me to relax, that since all four of us were now nothing but smithereens, we weren't legally dead, that it would take years of haggling before that distant relative could ever manage to get us declared legally dead, and by that time the world might be a very different place. And we could keep the house as it was for years, and if we ever got the urge, we could get someone to break in and steal all the personal possessions we wanted and take them to our hideout in Antarctica or the eastern Congo or some other place the governments of the world hadn't yet gotten around to bugging.

"What about my boat?" I complained. "You blew up my boat. I'll never be able to steal that back."

Louie just laughed. "I bet you got sick of that boat years ago."

'Course when Louie said I had gotten sick of the boat years ago, I sputtered and fumed, but Louie just let out another "Ho-ho-ho." Pretty irritating, I can tell you.

But after a few minutes I got to thinking. Sailors say that there are two 'specially happy moments in a sailor's life: the day he first buys his boat, and the day he finally gets rid of it. So actually, after another few minutes, I began to alternate between grumpy complaining and occasional giggles. Lita and the boys might have thought I'd finally lost all my marbles, except they already knew I'd lost all I had to lose.

We didn't drive home and have supper. In fact, I figured we'd never drive home and have supper in that house again. Or go out on the boat together.

Bummer.

. . .

Louie had Carlita drive us to a place on the North Shore of Long Island near New York City. I can't give you the name of the town since it's an FF military secret, but we holed up in a big mansion hidden away in some woods. The FFs had taken control of the security system, so the security company monitoring the cameras set around the house and grounds were fed a steady diet of empty lawns and empty rooms while we frolicked, and conspired to overthrow the world. Or at least watched TV.

Because for the next two or three days, it was big news that the famous TV stars and alien lovers Billy Morton and his two sons, and the brilliant lawyer Carlita Morton who had singlehandedly gotten the US Congress to actually begin passing a law they could all agree upon, had been blown up. And their remains eaten by seagulls.

We Mortons were again TV stars. Although no longer on live TV. Only in reruns. Scenes of small pieces of wreckage from my boat drifting up on Long Island beaches, and then scenes from our ABC TV appearance, or of Carlita talking to the press after her release on bail, were played over and over again, often to funeral music. It would have been medium-size news even if we were the total nobodies we'd been before Louie plopped into our lives, but because we were friends of Louie and other FFs—alien criminals and terrorists—we were important. And the big question that the cable TV channels kept asking their experts and scholars and retired corporals was: why did the terrorists murder the poor Mortons?

Yep, that's how they played it. The FBI almost immediately announced that the explosion was caused not by propane or gasoline but by dynamite. And everyone agreed that the Mortons would never have any use for dynamite. They were murdered. By Louie and his pals.

And, of course, they were right—Louie was our murderer. In any case, the questions that Americans were asked to consider for the next several days were:

Why did the FFs murder the Mortons?

What did the Mortons know that forced the FFs to silence them?

Were all Americans who made the error of befriending an FF in danger of being blown up?

When would the FFs begin blowing up Americans who hadn't made the mistake of befriending them?

Day after day, night after night, the same questions were asked, and the same experts gave the same pretty ridiculous answers. No one ever said he wasn't sure. No expert in the history of the universe (our universe anyway) has ever answered a question on TV with "beats me." They're paid to answer questions even when they don't know anything. So answers came flooding onto our TV sets, Twitter feeds, blogs, Facebook pages, and newspaper op-eds. Everyone had an answer. And the answers were real doozies. Various guys and gals said: The FFs used the same type of bomb they'd used to bring down Delta Flight 888 over the Pacific.

Poor Jimmy Morton had become so loved by one of the FFs that he'd been told about the *single thing* that could kill an FF. That made him a threat. Nice kid, but *Boom!*

The FFs had special suicide FFs who could go anywhere and, when they felt like it, explode. It was an FF suicide bomber who had taken out the Mortons.

Lucas Morton was a child prodigy computer genius who knew the trick the FFs used to hack government systems and had developed a way to block it. Smart kid, but *Boom!*

The FFs were anxious to test out their new remote-control explosive device, one they could hide in things as small as a golf ball, and the Mortons were the first victims.

Carlita had managed to access from one of the FFs' computers their master plan for taking over the world, and though she had no written record of it, she knew everything. Nice looking broad, but *Boom!*

The *Vagabond* was the very boat on which Louie had made his first contact with human beings and, unbeknownst to humans, there were important traces on the boat that would reveal secrets about the FFs that had to be kept buried. *Boom!* Buried.

Billy Morton (hey, that's me!) had been told the secret formula to get from one universe to another, and although Morton (still me) couldn't make head nor tail of the formula, if it fell into the hands of an intelligent human being (not me), humans might be able to strike back at the FFs. Nice old guy, but *Boom!*

So, Carlita, me, and the kids spent half of our day laughing at the TV, and the other half being fitted for clothes that would be part of our new identities. The kids and Carlita loved trying on new things, while I snarled and snapped. I wasn't interested in wearing a tuxedo or expensive boots or having my hair done in a new way. With only three hairs total, the styling options were limited. The hairpieces they tried to shroud me in looked like hairpieces. At best they made a seventy-two-year-old man look like he was seventy-one and three quarters. I was old and bald and wrinkled and I loved life and I loved myself just as I was. But somehow they had to create a Billy that was not easily recognizable. Lots of luck.

We lived in the west wing of the mansion. There were a few other human beings in the east wing working under the instructions of Baloney. Apparently they were the ones who'd set up a lot of bank and brokerage accounts on Long Island, Brooklyn, and Manhattan for us and other friendly humans. They were also making sure our false identity papers were in good shape and getting us written biographies of who we were supposed to be, biographies that we could study and memorize and forget all about as soon as we began to be questioned. The people in the east wing had no idea who they were creating these false identities for, nor that the famous Morton family had actually risen from the dead and were living in the west wing of the mansion only thirty feet away. It was important that the only people who knew the Mortons were still alive were us and the FFs.

The plan was for us to be a rich retired couple living in a Brooklyn condo. Lita and I both preferred to live in the country, but Louie said small towns or suburbia were out: Lucas and Jimmy would be identified in a second. In cities people didn't bother to look at each other. I was to be a retired Wall Street exec. Yeah. Right.

The second night we were there, I stayed up after Lita and the boys had gone to bed and had a couple of drinks with Louie and Gibberish, who began discussing some of the ways they hoped to get people to enjoy *Forthehelluvit* events and some of the big ones they were working on. They kept talking about playing and games and fun. I appreciated their communicating in English for my benefit, but frankly I wasn't much into fun and games these days and told them so.

"I'm stuck being a human being with two boys I love, and I don't see much fun in trying to create a new life when you keep telling me that they're easily recognizable when seen together and so can't be seen together. What kind of fun is that for them?"

"It's a challenge," says Louie. "And you should see it as a sudden shift in a game that means you have to develop new strategies. But you and the boys should have fun doing it."

I thought about this awhile, got up and poured another drink on top of Louie's "head," and then sat back down and took a sip of my own. Gibberish had told me that he only drank on alternate Tuesdays. Except during leap years.

"Well, I can't say I'm having much fun these days," I says. "Boat gone, house gone, getting ready to pretend to be the sort of rich business asshole I've never wanted to be in my life—not exactly my definition of a barrel of laughs."

Louie sat there on the couch for a bit and then jumps down and rolls over and bounces up into my lap.

"Billy, I'm sorry," he says. "We *are* being unfair to you. It may have been a mistake to have killed you and Carlita and your wonderful boys. Molière and I were talking just yesterday about how we should have figured out a different way to do it. I'm really sorry."

"You should be," says Gibberish. "Your best human friend and you may have ruined his life."

Well maybe that was an exaggeration, but I still felt that

living a new life wasn't going to work out.

"I'm sorry, Billy," says Louie.

"Yep," says I.

THIRTY-FOUR

(From Billy Morton's *MY FRIEND LOUIE*, pp. 258–263)

I don't think Louie has any sense of what it means for a human being to get old. He doesn't seem to realize that for me to have to travel for five or six hours on buses and planes as I did on the Cayman Islands trip is like a young man running a marathon. Now he was asking me to go with him on a quick four-day trip to Iraq on a mission that needed him to have a human companion. A fifteen-hour journey. I told him I figured he had plenty of other human friends, so why pick on me?

"Most of my other human friends, and I only have a few, I've kept out of my games that involve illegal enterprises, but from the moment you let me in your kitchen door, you've become so deeply involved in my games that another crime won't make a bit of difference. Just add a year or two onto your ninety-year sentence."

Louie wasn't too good at sugar-coating.

"What makes you think they won't recognize me going through security?" I ask.

"You're dead, remember? And my other human friends are alive and known. No Fed is looking for a terrorist corpse."

"So what crime am I going to commit now?" says I.

"Aiding and abetting me to get to the Middle East where I will aid and abet the alien terrorists who are doing damage to American planes and drones and intelligence operations."

"So you guys have come down on the side of the Arabs, have you?" says I.

"Oh, no, we're also messing with Al Qaeda, ISIL, and most of the other twenty-six Arab and Persian groups fighting the Americans. Actually, we're a bit like the American military itself, getting involved in civil wars that should really be none of our business and ending up, just like the Americans, fighting against both sides. Your American Air Force was the first air force in history to end up in Syria bombing both sides in a civil war. When the Iranians moved in some 'volunteers' to fight ISIL in Iraq, the Americans bombed them and the Arab terrorists with the same planes on the same day. That's efficiency. It does make bombing easier when you don't have to worry about good guys and bad guys, because you've decided both sides are bad."

"You going to be involved over there for some time then?" says I.

"Oh, no," says Louie. "I'm just going over to give a few tutorials."

"Tutorials!"

"The FFs in the area are trying to get everyone to stop fighting. But they have relatively limited skills in computer hacking. They need help. They've managed to reprogram drones to blow up where people won't get killed, and they've totally messed up ISIL's communication systems. Takes them days now to plan how to chop off a new head. But our FFs can't stop the US fighter-bombers and cruise missiles sent from aircraft carriers in the Mediterranean and Persian Gulf over Iraq and Syria that kill some Arab men and the usual bunch of women and children."

"Couldn't you email them instructions?"

"Ho-ho-ho. If I tried to communicate with them in English it would take about six *Encyclopedia Britannicas* to give them some hints about how to proceed to hack the aircraft carriers and their missiles and planes. In person I can teach them in twenty minutes."

"Aren't there other genius hackers like you they could use?"

"Probably. But I'm the one they've asked for help."

"And I'm the one that you've asked for help."

"Yep."

First time Louie had used my favorite word.

Actually, I'd noticed that all FFs tend to modify the way they talk depending on who they're talking to. When talking to kids, they talked like a kid. When talking to an uneducated lout like me they talked everyday American, but when talking to Carlita they talked like brainy nerds. Louie told me once that it was just natural for them to speak in the language of the creature they were speaking to.

Lita agreed that she could handle looking for tutors for the boys and the condo hunting in Brooklyn. 'Course at first she resisted, but I guess she concluded that since I was dead I couldn't get any deader. She didn't see how I could be of much help to Louie and the FFs, but if they requested it, and it didn't involve the boys, then she wouldn't veto it.

The flight to Paris and then on to Cairo and finally to Baghdad was not as bad as I thought it would be. I was disguised as a rich socialite, I guess because that was about as far as the FFs could get from the roughneck fisherman I usually was. I was wearing an expensive toupee that was so good I thought I'd grown a head of hair overnight. I was also wearing under my suit jacket a really great furry vest. Only problem with it was that every now and then it would sprout a limb and begin tickling me.

Molière and Karen and LT were on the plane too, but I couldn't sit with them or talk to them. Even in my disguise it would be a mistake for me to be seen with FFs. Molière and LT were allowed to travel without too much hassle because they'd become famous actors, what with their off-Broadway hit play. In fact, it was that success that had gotten them invited by some renegade general (who hadn't gotten the memo about all FFs being terrorists) to entertain our boots on the ground in Iraq.

'Course we didn't actually *have* any boots on the ground in Iraq; our soldiers were all wearing sneakers. Or if they wore boots, they made sure they stayed inside or, when traveling, went directly from steps to a Humvee or attack helicopter without letting their boots touch the ground. When desperate, they took off their boots and fought barefoot.

Molière had told me that they hoped to entertain more than four thousand soldiers and contractors during their four-day stay. Which was pretty good, since there were supposedly less than two thousand American military in the whole country. Apparently in their new shorter version of the play, Louie-Twoie was going to get to dance as a centipede, a chipmunk, a giant bumblebee, a six-inch cockroach, and a platypus. Not sure how interested our boys would be in dancing cockroaches, especially with Karen hanging around somewhere, but you never can tell.

Going through customs and security at the Baghdad

Airport was the easiest I'd ever heard of. Apparently the Iraqis figured that everyone who wanted to kill people was already *in* Iraq, and there was no sense in wasting time on screening latecomers.

We went straight to a fancy hotel in the heart of the city somewhere now called the Purple Zone, only a block from the American Embassy. It used to be called the Green Zone but had seen so much blood in the last couple of years it was now Purple.

If you've never seen the American Embassy in Iraq you should know that it makes the Kremlin look like a summer cottage. It's so big that it's said that more than fifty people have gotten lost in it and never been seen again. They're always finding corpses in some obscure room no one has entered in years. Only cost a billion dollars, and we got it finished just in time for all the American troops and most of the other security guys to leave the country. 'Course lately they've been coming in again.

I slept for thirteen hours. Would have slept longer but Karen came into my hotel room and sat on my bed and began gently caressing my face. Not a bad way to wake up.

During our stay Louie sometimes disguised himself as Molière. That is, whenever he wanted to go some place he went with Karen, or Karen and me, so that everyone assumed he was Molière. 'Course Karen and I and anyone who knew either of them could tell the difference, but almost no one in Iraq knew them. And the CIA agents who were usually following us couldn't tell the difference between them either. We figured they were following Molière because he was with Karen. He was thought to be a harmless clown, the lucky winner of a hot human babe, but not a threat to anyone unless they were homophobic and scared by someone who could have five stiff peckers at the drop of a skirt.

It was on the third day of our visit that Karen, Molière, and LT were supposed to give their first performance at the American Embassy. It was sold out—2,500 tickets, to both Americans and Iraqis, the Iraqis naturally all having to wear straitjackets when in the company of a large group of Americans. But less than six hours before the show was to go on, the commanding general ordered the performance canceled. I guess the bigger guys back in the Pentagon suddenly realized that in Iraq, with soldiers having their computers seriously fouled up by FFs, it wasn't too hot an idea to have a performance celebrating a union between a human and a terrorist, all FFs being, in the Pentagon's eyes, terrorists.

Actually I wouldn't have been able to see it anyway since I was going with Louie and a new Iraqi acquaintance of Louie's to tour a famous historical site outside the city. Big ruins. Famous for being old. And ruined.

I was wearing Louie as a sort of fleece vest again under my suit jacket. The Iraqi who was acting as my guide was named Khalid, and he spoke a lot better English than me. We'd managed to throw off the two guys who'd begun following us that morning, so were alone in a pretty deserted place with nothing much around us except three zillion grains of sand.

We had our big meeting in the men's room of the little museum that was part of the ancient site. Present on this historic occasion besides me and Khalid, were Louie and two other FFs named Abe and Oops. Oops got his name from his tendency to knock things over and say as he rolled happily away, "Oops." He'd spent a lot of time in the States, but the last three months had been here in Iraq. What he'd been doing in Iraq I was never told.

Abe was not named for our great president, but for Abraham, the grand old man of the Old Testament. Abe knew more about the Bible, Christianity, Judaism, and Islam than any creature in our world's history. He could quote word for word the Old Testament backwards or forwards at the drop of a hat. In Hebrew. Same with the Koran in Arabic. Fortunately, none of us were wearing hats, so couldn't drop one even if we'd wanted to, and were thus spared a recital.

The three FFs were all in their fighting trim—round— while I was in my non-fighting trim, sitting on a toilet—the only seat available. I missed my rocker.

"Excuse us, Billy and Khalid," says Louie, and for the next four or five minutes no one speaks a word in any human language. The three FFs move around the bathroom a bit, seemingly at random. Nothing in their shape or their hairs indicates that anything in the least is going on. But presumably they're exchanging an amount of info that would take three humans a century to communicate.

"Wow," says Oops after about ten minutes. "It's really easy, isn't it?"

Nice of him to speak in English when he didn't have to.

"The wrath of the Lord shall fall upon them," says Abe. Not sure what he was talking about, but I have that reaction to most preachers.

But then they all went again into conference in their own computer language, and Khalid and I were left to our own devices. Which, this being a two-seater, two-urinal, two-sink bathroom, were not much. Khalid had been standing near the door all this time smoking cigarettes. He was about fifty years old and looked a bit on the morose side. I decided maybe it was my moral duty to try to improve US–Iraqi relations by talking to him. 'Course, it's not easy to improve relations with natives of a country that you've been bombing for more than twenty-five years, but at least I could be polite.

"So, Khalid," I says. "What do you do when you're not helping the FFs?"

"Who are the FFs?" he asks.

"The Protean terrorists," says I.

"Ah, yes, the *Jibawli*."

"*Jibawli*?" says I.

"It is an Iraqi slang word meaning something like 'the funny ones.'"

"Funny ones, huh," says I. "Not much fun in Iraq the last thirty years."

"No. Not much fun."

"So how'd they get that name?"

"Because in the middle of suffering and death, they still manage to be funny and have fun."

I thought about that. Yeah, Louie, Molière, and Gibberish were like that. Never saw either of them stop being... light. And Louie-Twoie, Jesus, he'd probably invent a new dance to perform on his dad's grave.

"Whose side are you on in all these wars going on around here?"

"I am on the *Jibawli*'s side," he says. "They try to stop the killing by all sides." He pauses. "They will not succeed."

The FFs were miracle workers, but I had to agree that

bringing peace to this place was beyond anyone's capacity.

"Are you a Sunni or a Shiite?" I ask.

Again he pauses, lets smoke drift up past his face toward the ceiling.

"I am nothing," he says.

"Safest thing to be in Iraq these days," says I.

"Yes," he says.

Not for a single moment had he smiled or looked anything but gloomy.

The conference seemed to be at an end when the three FFs began bouncing around the bathroom like kids at recess. Off walls, off toilets, off me and Khalid, off each other—it was a dance of a sort, but a comic dance, a frolic. No sounds, just enthusiastic bouncing. And I was surprised to see that Louie was on the slow side compared to the other two. More of an intellectual than an athlete I guess. Or maybe having bits of his body carved away really had affected him.

Finally they stopped.

"Good meeting, guys," says Oops.

"We shall smite them until the very timbers of their buildings shake with fear," says Abe. Not a small talk sort of guy.

THIRTY-FIVE

(From *LUKE'S TRUE UNBELIEVABLE REPORT OF THE INVASION OF THE FFS*,
pp. 165–170. Being an excerpt from an unpublished memoir by
Carlita Morton.)

It took me only a few days with my husband away in Iraq to
realize that when he got back our new lives were not going
to be what we'd hoped for. First of all, I missed working at
the Protean Defense League. The two weeks I'd worked
there had been wonderful. For one thing the PDL bosses
weren't all white males. We like to think that women have
made tremendous strides in achieving job equality, but I
can remember only two years ago Billy and I walked into an
insurance company office in Riverhead to look into getting
a new policy, and there, prominently displayed on the wall,
was a photo of the bosses of the company: nine white men
and one woman. After seeing this photo, I turned and looked
into the open office area: about a dozen women and two men.
Incredible. At the PDL the human bosses included an equal
number of men and women.

I felt our job at the PDL was important. We were
monitoring what was happening to FFs throughout the world
and were trying to free them whenever one was dragged
into the legal system. I had been surprised to find that in
the "civilized," "advanced" nations, the authorities often
seemed more disturbed by the *Forthehelluvit* actions that
the FFs inspired than the cyberattacks on their banks and
government agencies. Any FF seen at some sing-in, dance-in,

drink-in, etc., was considered guilty of having fomented the event and, if captured, charged with conspiracy to incite riotous behavior. They should actually call it "conspiracy to incite people to have fun."

Our problem was that the established "justice" systems were rigged to enable the authorities to dictate what was considered justice. Whenever an FF was captured and jailed, they would argue that no bail should be granted since an FF was a clear threat to flee and, once free, almost impossible to re-apprehend. Judges usually accepted this argument. Then the government authorities would begin the process of drawing out all proceedings as long as possible, since their goal, the incarceration of the FF, had already been achieved.

However, governments have one major problem: there are no measurable differences that humans can detect among various FFs, no "fingerprints" so to speak. It means that the only FFs getting jailed are those who are actually caught in the act of committing something defined as a crime. Louie is the most wanted "man" in the world, but how can they find him when almost every FF in the world looks just like him? Identifying FFs isn't made easier by FFs loving to assume different shapes.

The authorities have developed a special X-ray machine which shows that the internal images of FFs vary considerably and can be used to identify an FF. The X-ray becomes in effect a fingerprint or DNA ID. The Department of Health and Human Services has issued an edict that every FF come to a hospital and be X-rayed, but turnout has been low. Currently this method of identification seems pretty useless. If an agent sees an FF committing a crime, bouncing high in the air for example, but fails to capture him right then and there, he has no way of knowing which FF was the culprit. Unless, of course, he's carrying an X-ray machine at the time and the FF stays still long enough to be X-rayed. But Baloney told me recently that in monitoring the NSA, FFs have learned that the government is working on a handheld X-ray machine that will solve that very problem.

Not only was I having to give up a job that I loved, but our whole family was having to give up the house and area we loved. In three days I looked at almost a dozen condos. They were all modern, immaculate, filled with the latest gadgets that would monitor everything from your toast to your coffee to the temperature in your closet. I couldn't see our family being happy in a single one of them.

Billy and the boys are messy. They rarely wipe their feet when entering our house and seem always to neatly place their clothing on the floor. Over the years I'd adjusted and no longer noticed rugs that needed to be vacuumed or floors that needed to be mopped. I've become as happy with messiness as my men folk. I don't know which thing depressed me more: that in any immaculate apartment the messiness would *look* messy, or that living in the city, Billy and the boys would no longer be traipsing in with sand, mud, leaves, or grass cuttings on their shoes. The nearest sand, mud, leaves, or grass cuttings to any of the condos was usually many blocks away.

And what would Billy do in our new life? He'd still read, of course, but lost forever would be having a couple of drinks with his old buddies, spending several days out on the water, walking through the woods down to the sound.

Every family and each individual has their own needs, and I couldn't see any of our basic needs being fulfilled in the rich new life Louie thought he was setting up for us. I'm depressed. And I see no way out.

THIRTY-SIX

(From Billy Morton's *MY FRIEND LOUIE*, pp. 263–266)

That night we partied. In Baghdad in those days that meant you went someplace where you weren't going to be shot at or blown up.

We went to the nightclub in the basement of the US Embassy. It was a big place built to entertain seven or eight hundred people, but there were only about a hundred there the night we went, only twenty or so soldiers. It was Abe, Molière, Karen, LT, Khalid, and me. Louie was there wound around my chest, making me sweat even more than the desert heat, despite the air con.

Two other young women were also there that either Karen or Molière had found to join us, whether as female company for me and Khalid I didn't know. Felt sorry for the two gals though: neither Khalid nor I paid them much attention. I was being faithful to Lita. Khalid was being morose. Of the hundred other people in the nightclub, I figured only half of them were agents, although I may have erred on the low side. Probably the two gals at our table were agents too.

In any case we partied.

Kind of boring actually. The entertainment was a rock band that might have been big back in the last century, but was kind of small now. We drank of course, me having to pour stuff down under my sweatshirt to let my Louie vest join in. Molière was, as I've said, a teetotaler and only poured water over himself. Perrier actually. The American Embassy didn't serve straight water. Twenty-three bottles of Perrier.

Karen drank mostly wine with a few sips of champagne. Khalid drank vodka. I sipped at a couple of bourbons.

Louie-Twoie, you'll be surprised to know, was a big drinker. Like any young kid trying his wings, he sampled every drink on the menu. His favorite seemed to be Scotch and prune juice. Kid's got a bit to learn.

There was dancing too. Although there was only one woman for every four men, the gals that got out on the dance floor were worth watching. Might have been nice except for the music. Neither Karen nor Molière felt like dancing, LT was too small, I was too old, and Khalid too morose, so all but Abe stayed put. Abe did ask one of the two gals with us to dance and he managed to grow two legs and two arms but forgot a head so looked a little strange.

It didn't work out too well. The gal came back and told us Abe had called her a whore. Abe had abandoned her and was lecturing a group of GIs at a table not far from ours on the virtue of turning the other cheek. I figured it wouldn't take more than five or six minutes for them to shoot him.

Things only got interesting when Jake Manningham, First Secretary at the Embassy, joined us. He was a good-looking guy in his late forties who I'd noticed earlier at a table nearby with two gals almost as nice looking as Karen. They all seemed to be putting drinks away at a good clip, but none of them seemed very cheery. Finally, he'd stood up, said something to the gals, and sauntered over. He asked if we'd mind if he joined us for a bit. We all said "fine"—except Khalid, of course, who just looked morose.

When he introduced himself he casually said that although his title was First Secretary, he was of course primarily an intelligence agent working for the CIA. He'd worked in Iraq from 2008 until 2010 and had returned a year ago.

"So, you having a good time?" says I, when he paused.

"No one has a good time in Iraq," he says, not morosely like Khalid would say it, but soberly, factually.

"Spying not that much fun?" says I.

"More fun than pretending to train Iraqi soldiers or policemen, or pretending to try to get their electric grid together," he says. "I get to meet more interesting people."

"Met any Proteans?" asks Molière.

"Until tonight, just one," he says quietly.

"What was he like?" Molière asks.

Jake takes a small sip of his Scotch.

"Dead," he says.

Awkward silence.

"Tough to get intelligence from a corpse," says Karen.

"That was my position," says Jake.

"You didn't get to question the Protean?" asks Molière.

"I was there for one of the interrogations," he says. "Strangest thing I've ever been at."

"How so?" says I.

"All the guy did—the Protean—was make jokes."

"Jokes…" says I.

"No matter what someone asked, he'd find a way to give an answer that, if we didn't feel we were there on serious national security business, would have been funny. Usually he was in the normal spherical shape but every time he made a jokey answer he'd change his shape to that of a two-foot-wide smiling mouth. Even when we began… forceful means, he still found things to joke about."

"Yeah, we Proteans can be pretty annoying that way," says Molière.

"I think that's why they put him in solitary and cut off his supply of water and light," says Jake quietly. "Took almost three weeks, but they managed to kill him. Didn't get a single piece of useful information."

I wondered how Louie and Molière and LT would take this. For a moment all of us were quiet.

"How many of us have you killed?" asks Molière.

"That's the only one I know of that died at our hands," says Jake. "I think our A-15s have killed a few with missiles."

"Why were they shooting at them?"

"We think the Proteans are behind our drones being reprogrammed to miss their targets. Officially every Protean in Iraq is an enemy. I actually don't know how you guys are here."

"You think all Proteans are terrorists?" asks Molière.

"Whichever one of you two is Molière," says Jake looking from Molière to Abe, "is a visiting VIP. So is the small one here named Louie-Twoie. Whichever one of you isn't Molière is not a visiting VIP and therefore is clearly an alien terrorist."

"I am the Voice of Truth that speaks from the heart of the universe," says Abe.

Jake stares at him a long moment.

"Whatever," he says.

I couldn't figure out what this guy was up to. He was saying things to us that no self-respecting intelligence agent would say to a party that included his agency's enemies.

"When are you resigning?" asks Molière out of the blue.

For the first time, Jake looks a little startled.

"What makes you think I'm resigning?" he asks.

"Because you obviously have no interest in holding on to your job," says Molière.

Jake looks from one FF to another, then picks up his glass and finishes his drink.

"No one in his right mind would want to hold on to my job," he says quietly.

Since no one else asks the obvious, I do.

"Why not?" says I.

"All we do is turn shit into bigger shit," he says. "Everything we do to try to stop radical Muslim terrorists just makes them stronger, makes it easier for them to recruit even more terrorists. We've spent two trillion dollars fighting the war on terror. What have we achieved? On nine-eleven two-thousand-one there were maybe a thousand anti-American radical Muslim terrorists around the world. After fighting three or four wars against them and spending trillions, there are now millions of terrorists wanting to kill Americans. Every time we drop a bomb and kill twenty Arabs, some of them usually women or kids, two hundred become radicalized and want to join up. It's madness."

"Sorry to hear that," says Molière.

"You know, there's a solution, Jake," says Louie from my chest, but imitating my voice.

"And what's that? Drop a dozen nukes throughout the Middle East and eliminate half the Muslims?"

"Games, Jake, games," Molière answers. "If you humans would just see all your struggles as games and your opponents as your fellow humans—as your *brothers*, as your *friends*—

you'd eliminate two-thirds of the misery you're creating for yourselves and the world."

"Yeah," says I, from deep in my chest. "Imagine if your bosses suddenly began thinking of those resisting you as 'rebels' or 'resisters' or 'freedom-fighters' rather than terrorists. Or those resisting the dictators our government props up around the world as 'rebels' or 'resisters' or 'freedom-fighters.' That would change everything. As soon as we call anyone a 'terrorist' he ceases to be a human being and he and his family and anyone standing anywhere near him can be tortured or bombed or killed. That's pretty sick."

Glad Jake was staring into his drink as my chest delivered this speech, since the movement of my lips had absolutely nothing to do with the words coming out of my chest. It was Louie speaking.

"And so you create more and more terrorists," says Molière.

Jake looked from me to Molière and then reached over and took my glass and with a nod to me, took a big swig. He'd emptied his.

"We should get out of this hellhole and let the damn Arabs settle their differences among themselves," he says.

Silence.

"No offense, Khalid," he adds.

"I will be happy to see you go," says Khalid. Morosely.

"Not as happy as I will be to leave," says Jake.

THIRTY-SEVEN

(From *THE OFFICIAL HISTORY OF THE ALIEN INVASION, Volume 1*, pp. 366–369. Being Agent Michael Johnson's informal notes on his meeting with Chief Investigator Rabb of Unit A.)

I asked for a special meeting with CI Rabb and finally he gave it to me.

"Chief," I said. "I think Billy Morton is still alive."

"Oh?"

"Roger Cayle brought to my attention the video and audio from the flight that the Proteans Molière and Louie-Twoie took from New York to Paris to Iraq. I'm convinced that they show Billy Morton aboard the flight, sitting five rows behind the two Proteans and the woman Karen Bell."

"What… what video are you talking about?" the chief asked.

"Remember, the CIA ordered special video and audio monitors mounted on the plane carrying Molière to Iraq. They wanted to examine all the other passengers, especially those that interacted with either of the two Proteans or Karen, to see if any of them could be identified as humans suspected of aiding and abetting the Protean terrorists."

"Ah, yes, that video."

"There are three things that made me conclude that the elderly man sitting five rows behind Molière is in fact Billy Morton in disguise."

"Although we know for a fact that Mr. Morton was blown up on his boat."

"We *thought* that Billy Morton was blown up on his boat. Until I saw the video and listened to the audio tape."

"Did this Morton apparition ever approach or talk to the Proteans or to this Karen Bell?"

"No, but as I say, three things indicate it was in fact Billy Morton."

"What three things?"

"First, the elderly man is wearing a toupee, and a suit, but otherwise fits the description of Billy Morton. He *looks* like Billy."

"But never bothers to talk to his friends five seats ahead."

"No, but there is the second thing: at one point Karen Bell gets out of her seat and walks down the aisle. As she passes the man I think is Billy, she winks at him. And keeps going."

"She winks at him. What does the Morton ghost do?"

"Well, not much—he smiles a bit."

"A wink."

"A wink directed at the passenger I'm convinced is Billy Morton."

"What's the third thing?"

"The audio."

"The audio."

"It picks up this passenger appearing to talk to himself."

"Oh, well," the chief said. "There you have it. It must have been the senile Mr. Morton."

"The audio was cluttered with other voices and the sounds of the plane. At first there appeared to be nothing to it but an old man muttering to himself."

"Exactly."

"But after I'd seen the videotape I insisted that our experts work on the audio and see if they could determine much more precisely what the passenger was muttering."

"Okay, that's good."

"They claimed they couldn't get anything that made sense, but I insisted they let me hear the best version they'd been able to recreate. At first it all seemed gibberish to me too, but suddenly I thought I got it. The audio voice seemed to be saying, "Hammetui, stopicklingme.""

"Hammetui, stopicklingme," echoed CI Rabb.

"I've become certain that what the passenger was actually saying was 'Damn it, Louie, stop tickling me.'"

Chief Rabb only stared at me.

"Stop tickling me…" he repeated.

"Billy Morton was wearing Louie as a sort of sweater or vest. And Louie was tickling him."

Chief Rabb stared at me for several more moments.

"Tell me, Michael," he finally said. "When did you last take a vacation?"

ITEM IN THE NEWS

DEMOCRATIC CONGRESSMAN INTRODUCES LEGISLATION OUTLAWING THINKING

Washington, D.C.

In what most observers consider a political masterstroke, Rep. Jon John (D-MN) today introduced legislation making thinking by Democrats illegal.

"We Americans believe in a level playing field," the congressman said. "And this legislation will do just that. For the last decade we Democrats have been operating at a severe political disadvantage: gathering facts and thinking about our nation's problems, while Republicans have been proceeding totally without facts and thought and have thus gained an enormous political advantage. This must end. Democrats must stop thinking. My legislation will achieve this."

When asked to comment, Republican House Speaker John Ruan said, "No."

"No, what?" asked the reporter.

"Just 'no,'" said Speaker Ruan.

"But to what are you saying 'no,' Mr. Speaker?"

"Everything," said Mr. Ruan.

THIRTY-EIGHT

(From Billy Morton's *MY FRIEND LOUIE*, pp. 276-282)

Back in New York it didn't take Lita and me more than a half hour to know that we'd never be able to create as good a life as we'd had before our "deaths." I was exhausted from my Iraq trip, and when an old man is overtired he's always depressed. Even if Louie had plopped me down in the middle of Eden I'd have probably begged for an old farmhouse on a half acre. Lita wasn't tired, but she was even more certain than me that we were doomed to be miserable in our new lives. No matter how expensive the condo, it was still a small group of rooms in a huge building in the middle of hundreds of other huge buildings. You usually had to walk half a dozen blocks to see a tree. Growing out of concrete.

Not our style.

As soon as I realized how miserable Lita was, I felt a lot better. We were on the same page. The boys weren't miserable yet, but they were clearly working on it. We were sure they would be when they realized they could never be Jimmy and Lucas again.

So Lita and I arranged to meet Louie in our temporary hotel room in Queens. The room was a bit shabby for a guy who'd recently spent time setting up a half-dozen multi-million-dollar bank accounts, but I didn't notice; I'm a shabby sort of guy.

I was sitting up against the headboard of the king-sized

bed, with Lucas beside me. Lita was in one of the two easy chairs and Louie on top of the dresser. Louie-Twoie was there too, spending his time trying to shape himself into new giant bugs, mostly a ten-legged centipede sort of thing with a bulbous head. Louie-Twoie still hadn't learned to talk clearly yet, and Louie worried he might be a little slow. Jimmy sat at the foot of the bed, when he wasn't running after a centipede.

"This won't work, Louie," says Lita, as usual getting right to the point. "A life away from the water is just not natural to Billy or the boys. And the boys always enjoyed school. Tutoring is already a drag and they've been at it for less than a week."

"I understand," says Louie.

"And I don't want any life that takes me away from the kids and Lita," says I. "Even if it's just for a week."

"You've got to find some way we can be ourselves," says Lita. "Be near the water, near forests, and have a house where we can look out the window and see trees and flowers instead of gray walls and crowded streets."

"Be yourselves…" says Louie.

"We have to have lives that are almost identical to what we had as the Mortons," she says.

"Actually," says Louie, "Molière and I have created several identities that would have you be a happily married couple with two kids in a country environment."

"So you've done it!" says I.

"We have," says Louie.

"Well?"

"It won't work."

"Why not?" says Lita.

"Because your faces are too well known," says Louie. "We can change you with wigs and make-up and the way you dress, and we might be able to make Billy look a few years younger, but we can't disguise the boys. Just not possible. They've been seen by millions of people on the YouTube reruns of that television interview and now, with your sensational deaths, you're being seen a million times all over again. They'd be recognized the moment they entered school."

"The boys weren't recognized in the Caymans," says Lita.

"Yes, they were," says Louie.

"They were!?" says I.

"That's why we insisted they go to a safe house. Someone had reported seeing them to the local police and the NSA got wind of it, and then of course we did too. And this was before you became famous all over again by getting blown up."

"Shit," says I.

"Isn't there anything we can do?" says Lita.

"Well, Gibberish came up with an idea, but his solution could possibly be worse than the problem."

"The solution can't be any worse," says Lita. "What have you got?"

Louie hopped off the dresser and squashed a strange two-legged bug that had three four-inch antennae sticking up out of its body, and a tiny elephant trunk at his front. Then he bounced back on the dresser. It took Louie-Twoie about ten seconds to puff himself back into bug shape, but then he was missing his trunk and one of his antennae.

"Molière and I killed you," Louie said. "We were thinking of un-killing you."

"How?" says I.

"Resurrection," says Louie. "We thought we'd try resurrection."

"That would put us in pretty elite company," says I.

"It would. We're afraid it would make you more famous than ever, and it wouldn't change the fact that you're both still accused of felonies, and that they might be tempted to use you to get at us."

"But how'd we do this?" says I.

"We haven't yet quite figured that out," says Louie.

"Great," says I. "You guys are the most super-intelligent creatures our whole universe has ever known, and you can't solve a simple problem like resurrecting me and my family. Jesus did it with Lazarus and didn't break a sweat."

"We have to reappear again as the alive Mortons," says Lita, "and have a plausible story about what happened since the night the boat blew up. A story that doesn't get us into more trouble than we're already in."

"That's about it," says Louie.

"I know!" says Lucas.

We all turn to stare at him.

"We were abducted by aliens!" he shouts.

I laughed.

"We were!" says Jimmy.

The sober-minded and intelligent adults in the room were strangely silent.

"Abducted by aliens," says I. "What American wouldn't believe that?"

"Excellent idea, Lucas," says Louie.

"But which aliens abducted us?" says Lita. "Was it Louie and Molière?"

"And where did the aliens take us?" says I. "What did they do with us?"

"They took us to their universe!" says Lucas.

We all began mulling that.

"That could get complicated," says Lita.

"I don't remember a thing," says I. "None of us remembers a thing."

They all look at me.

"One moment we were on the boat going to bed, and the next we woke up in our old home two weeks later."

Not bad for an old guy who doesn't read much science fiction.

"And the four of us won't get our stories confused," says I, "because we won't have a single story to tell."

"You're a genius, Billy," says Louie.

"Yep. Once every half-century."

THIRTY-NINE

(From Billy Morton's *MY FRIEND LOUIE*, pp. 290–295)

Well, let me tell you, waking up in my own bed after two weeks of pretending to be so many other people was one of the great moments of my life. And this despite the fact that we had no electricity in the house, no water, and toilets that couldn't flush and were soon filled with poop. We had arrived after midnight in a car driven by Molière. I was finally getting used to being driven by a long skinny something with only one leg, no head, and steering with his belly button. By getting used to it, I mean I no longer screamed every time we were within two miles of another car.

Lita had a new smartphone, so first thing in the morning, after we'd breakfasted on a dozen doughnuts we'd bought on the drive out from New York, we began making phone calls.

The first was to the electric company to turn the electricity back on. Sheriff Coombs had had it turned off after we'd been dead for about a week. When the electricity guy asked who I was I said I was the homeowner, William Morton.

"Right," says the Con Ed man. "And I'm Thomas Edison. We need to note the name requesting the renewal of service."

"William Geronimo Morton," says I. I love to give myself interesting middle names since my parents gave me Henry.

"I thought you were dead," says Con Ed.

"I was," says I. "But I got better."

The next call was to Sheriff Coombs to let him know we'd been resurrected.

"Jesus Christ, Billy," he says. "Is this really you?"

"It is, Jerry, it is."

"No way you could have survived that explosion," says he. "What the hell happened?"

"Don't have the faintest idea," says I. "One moment we were asleep on the boat and the next, just an hour or two ago, we wake up here in our house. Gotta tell you, it was a surprise."

"Jesus Christ."

"There's no electricity here so we don't even know what day it is," says I. "Could you fill us in on the date?"

"It's December twenty-second, Billy."

"Holy moly! We've been asleep for almost two weeks!"

I'm sure the sheriff wanted to explode out another "Jesus Christ," but he restrained himself.

"That's right. Your boat blew up just about two weeks ago."

"My boat blew up!? What are you talking about!?"

There was a silence while the sheriff processed this data.

"Billy, I think maybe you and I had better have a talk," he says. "A lot has happened since you fell asleep."

"Well, you'll have to come here, Jerry. Our car seems to be missing."

"It's still down at the marina where you took it the day that… that your boat blew up."

"I don't know what you're talking about, Jerry."

"I know," he says. "That's why I'll be right over."

Lita said she'd bicycle to the marina and get the car and then do some grocery shopping. Lucas and Jimmy wanted to go tell their friends that they were still alive. At first I vetoed it. I reminded them that it was a school day and their friends would still be in classes.

"We'll go to school," says Jimmy.

"Yeah, Dad," says Lucas. "It's the last day before Christmas vacation, and we don't want to be truants. We're not sick."

"You may not be sick," says I, "but you're dead."

"We've got to come back to life sometime," says Lucas.

"School, school, school!" says Jimmy.

Well, they had to see their friends sometime. That's why we'd resurrected ourselves, so they could be back with the people they know.

"Okay," says I, "but remember, you don't remember a thing. You didn't even know two weeks had passed until you checked the news on Mom's smartphone."

"Okay, Dad," says Jimmy.

"But we already know a lot of that stuff from watching TV in that place we went to right after we blew up," says Lucas.

"Well, see what's been written since then, but don't forget, you don't remember a thing. You went to sleep on the boat and you woke up here this morning."

"We were abducted by aliens," says Jimmy.

"No, you weren't," says I. "Let *them* reach that conclusion. All we know is that we don't remember a thing."

"The aliens erased our memories," says Lucas.

"I'm sure they did, but let other people figure that out," says I. "Our safety lies in our stupidity. Believe me, as soon as people find out we're really alive, they'll *know* we were abducted by the FFs. They thought the FFs had blown us up, so they'll think they abducted us, dissected us, brainwashed us, and erased all memory of what they did to us. Remember, most people have read a lot more *National Enquirer* stories than we have."

When Lita got back with the car and some groceries, I drove the kids to school. They were three hours late so I had to take them to some special office before they could get to class. The lady behind the desk took one look at us and fainted.

So they had to find a substitute for her. It was the principal himself. He was sharp as a tack.

"I thought you were dead," he said.

"We were," says I, "but we're back. And the kids don't want to miss any more school."

He had about 2,506,000 other questions he wanted to ask, but he had a school to run.

"I'll get the papers you have to sign," he says. "Miss Mellon, take Lucas and Jimmy to their classes."

Cool guy, especially for a principal.

Sheriff Coombs was a cool guy too, especially for a cop. He was there when I got back from the school, sitting on our couch drinking a big glass of orange juice Lita had given him. She whispered to me as I was passing that she hadn't said much of anything to the Sheriff—he'd just arrived.

"So what's the story, Billy?"

"No story, Jerry," says I, sitting in my favorite rocker. "We just lost two weeks of our lives, that's all."

"And you don't remember a thing about your boat blowing up?"

"Nope. I've been reading about it this morning though. Seems that the FFs murdered us."

"That's what the papers mostly say," says Jerry.

"Did you think it was them?" I ask.

"I didn't know what to think," he says. "Just as I don't know what to think now. Something smelled fishy then, something smells fishy now."

Ah, I'd forgotten that Sheriff Coombs had a brain.

"Smells fishy to me too, Jerry. Makes no sense whatsoever."

"Not to me anyway."

"Do you think the Feds will keep after us even though we were dead for a while?" I ask.

"You were never dead," says Jerry. "Just missing. Now you're found. I think you two had a court date last week, so you'd better get in touch with your lawyer."

"Shouldn't be too hard since I sleep with her every night."

"No one's going to believe you don't remember a thing," says Jerry.

"I don't either," says I.

Jerry looked at me long and hard. He knew I must be hiding something, but he hadn't had time yet to figure out any of the things it might be. He liked me, and I don't think if I told him the truth he'd betray me, but it wasn't an option I wanted to test.

"Your death was a local police matter, Billy," he says finally, "so I guess your returning to life is too. I'll have to make a formal report. Probably ask you to make a statement about your disappearance. Any problem with that?"

"'Course not, Jerry."

"I guess I got one more question."

"What's that?"

"Why did you take your family out for an overnight the day the boat ended up being blown apart?"

The question worried me at first, and then I got a brainstorm. I get one every decade or so and I never know where they come from.

"Come to think of it," I say after a long pause. "Louie told me to go out there so he could meet me."

"I see."

"And he never showed up."

"You think he had you… blown up?"

I went into a brooding silence.

"I can't believe Louie would do that."

Sheriff Coombs stands up.

"A lot of unanswered questions, Billy," he says.

"Anything you need just let me know. You're a friend."

"Yeah, a friend," he says. "Not sure how close a friend."

Close enough so that we both knew that I knew a lot more than I was telling, and that he knew a lot more than I dared think about.

But Lita, Lucas, Jimmy, and I were together once more and we were home. Our normal lives could begin again.

Yeah.

Right.

FORTY

(From Billy Morton's *MY FRIEND LOUIE*, pp. 300–305)

I've got news for you, my fellow Americans: it's no fun being rich and famous. Lita and I had gotten Louie to return us to our home in Greenport, but not even superhuman Louie could return us to our previous lives. We'd been famous before, but it would have been a pretty brief fame if we hadn't been abducted by aliens and had two full weeks of our lives erased from our memories. Being with Louie on the TV show on Halloween night seemed to have given us our fifteen minutes of fame, but being resurrected from the dead after being abducted by aliens for two weeks—that represented at least a decade of fame.

Americans had been lusting for almost a hundred years for genuine proof of alien abductions, and now they had it. Who could be more trustworthy than Billy Morton and his two cute boys. Americans were a little suspicious of Lita because she was so smart and educated and some sort of agitator, but me and the boys were genuine uneducated Americans: the salt of the earth. Who could doubt our truthfulness?

Anyone who knew us is who. I was known all over the North Fork of Long Island as one of the biggest bullshitters of all time, but when it came to my saying we went to bed on the boat and woke up two weeks later in our beds at home, not a single one of my friends had the slightest doubt that I was telling the truth. Except maybe Sheriff Coombs.

The reason, of course, was that it was such a *dull* lie, hardly worthy of the Billy Morton they knew and loved. If I were making up what happened after the boat explosion I would have come up with a really interesting whopper.

For example, that the explosion had killed us all, and we'd gone to heaven. Saint Peter had at first rejected me for being the big liar I am, but Jimmy had pleaded that if Dad was going to the Other Place, Jimmy wanted to go with him, so St. Pete relented and let us in. We were there for two weeks meeting old friends and dozens of famous people from all of human history. I was a bit surprised to see that Hugh Hefner made it, Elvis of course, and even George the Worst Bush. Guess Jesus can save people after all.

I had a long talk with Ronald Reagan, who is a lot duller than I thought. At the end of two weeks, some other angel comes up and tells us there's been a Divine Glitch and Divine Rewrite and we're headed back to Earth again. But since two weeks have passed, they'll have to send us back on December 22nd rather than on the day we died. And the angel tells us to tell people that we'd blanked out about what had happened and that the Lord would forgive that sin of lying because it was the result of the Lord's Divine Glitch.

I got so enthusiastic about some of the lies I was coming up with that I asked Louie if we couldn't please change our story about not remembering a thing to one of my creative stories. But he said no.

As a result of my dull lie, all my friends, except for Sheriff Coombs, thought I really didn't remember a thing. With me being uncreative, the media took over for me and began to produce the biggest load of… far-fetched nonsense since the last time I really got rolling.

The media didn't actually learn of our resurrection until three days after we'd returned and a few papers and commentators thought it was noteworthy that we were resurrected almost on Christmas Day. First confirmed resurrection in more than two thousand years and it occurs at Christmas! But after a couple of days people began to notice that the Mortons never went to church except to see their friends get married or buried, and Mr. Morton (me) had a reputation as being untruthful and had a criminal record back in the sixties for which he had never repented. The media dropped the Christmas resurrection angle within two days.

One Republican candidate for president declared in one of their endless debates that we were abducted so that the FFs could go into our brains and remove all the info we knew about FFs so we could never tell it to the authorities. He suggested we might want to be loyal to the FFs, but might not be able to endure "enhanced interrogation".

Another candidate declared that one of his investigators had concluded that we were taken to the Ickie universe and put in a circus where for two weeks crowds of FFs came to toss us bananas and laugh and point. He argued that it was another example of the cruelty of the aliens.

The *New York Post* had an op-ed piece claiming we'd been taken to a laboratory on a secret part of Plum Island where our bodies were totally gutted and FF computer parts and programs were inserted into all sorts of bodily places. We were now essentially robots totally under the control of the aliens. It was claimed that we now shit data sheets rather than poop.

You couldn't turn on a cable TV channel or even a nightly network newscast without some candidate or some expert with an AA degree from a community college throwing out some new explanation.

And of course fame meant uncontrollable media lust: they offered us huge amounts of money if we'd just agree to burp on TV. But we didn't need their money any more—Louie had set us up for life with more money than I could store in our whole freezer.

And the government was not actively prosecuting us, probably because they thought they were using us as bait to trap Louie. So two weeks after we'd resurrected ourselves in our Greenport home we felt we were again leading a sweet normal life.

Almost. I managed to go back to work at APE and found that I'd barely been missed. It was all my secretary's fault. Althea Riggs was a big black woman—weighed close to a hundred-eighty pounds—and had as oversized a mind and heart as she did a body. She hadn't trusted me at first—actually a very healthy instinct—but when she saw behind my rough uncouth exterior an inner being equally rough and uncouth, she'd grown to like me. She'd been a big help when me and Louie and Molière had drawn up a profit-sharing arrangement for everyone who worked in the company. And also with our putting in a by-law that the board of trustees of the company had to have at least fifty percent women and fifty percent employees earning less than a hundred grand a year. And when I was dead for two weeks she took over for me and stood up to Harry Barnes and the other capitalists like the good union person she was. And made me feel redundant when I went back to work.

Trouble is, I realized, normal life is never normal. It's always filled with strange things happening that are in some way normal but still weird. Louie-Twoie had adopted us and, as he became a large part of our kids' lives, Lucas and Jimmy began to change. Whereas when we first got back the boys seemed to be comfortably part of our family, now their focus seemed to be… elsewhere—with LT actually. I used to think that the boys listened to me as if I were God, but after LT had been around for two or three weeks, it seemed they listened to me like I was a deodorant commercial.

We first got a sniff of the change when Lita got a phone call from the school. They wondered if Jimmy and Lucas were sick. They'd missed the previous two days of school.

Well, I got nothing against skipping school. My old high school ordered a major celebration every time I actually showed up. But Jimmy and Lucas were sort of nerds about studying and doing well in school—mostly the evil influence of Lita, who'd been a straight-A student since she'd finished teething. As far as I knew, neither of the boys had missed a day of school except when one of them was dying or dead.

So the night after we got the phone call from the school Lita and I called the boys into my study—the living room—for a serious discussion of *Responsibility*. Louie-Twoie was there too. LT alternated between being a chipmunk with a bushy tail and a six-inch-long two-by-four that did slow somersaults. I think Lita and I had gotten so used to LT's being continually improvising and never sitting still that we barely noticed him.

"We understand you didn't go to school yesterday or today," Lita began. She's the scholar and lecturer of our family,

I'm the sit-down comic (I never stand these days if there's a chair within a mile and a half). "Can you tell us why you didn't go to school?"

Lucas and Jimmy exchanged a single long glance. They were sitting side by side on the couch. Lita was standing—that's what all authorities like to do—while I was in my rocking chair.

"We didn't feel like it," says Lucas.

Now think about that, folks. "We didn't feel like it": if that isn't one of the most revolutionary statements known to mankind, I don't know what is. Jimmy then followed it up with an even more revolutionary statement: "We wanted to have some fun," he says.

"Tell me, Sgt. Peters, why didn't you join that attack on the fortified hill?" asks authority. "I didn't feel like it," says Sgt. Peters.

"Tell me, Miss Welles, why did you and Miss Peoples suddenly disappear and take the afternoon off?" asks authority. "We wanted to have some fun," says Miss Welles.

If human beings started using those two sentences on a regular basis, civilization as we know it would collapse.

I wondered how Lita would handle these insurrectionary statements.

"Why didn't you tell us this yesterday when you pretended to come back from school?" Lita asks in her soft, terrifying, prosecutorial voice.

Both boys looked down at the rug. Nothing there but a furry centipede.

"We should have," says Lucas. "I'm sorry, Mom."

"Me too," says Jimmy.

"What did you do yesterday?" asks the prosecutor.

"We took a long walk along Orient Beach," says Lucas.

"Found a baby octopus!" says Jimmy.

"It was a big starfish," says Lucas.

"What else did you do?" soft voice, mind of steel.

Lucas seemed to have to think about it.

"We broke into a summer cottage and ate a can of ravioli," he finally says, eyes on the centipede.

"You broke into a summer cottage and stole a can of ravioli," says the prosecutor, in her mind debating between misdemeanor and felony charges.

"It was fun!" says Jimmy.

Revolution! If crimes are "fun," then the center will not hold!

"And today we took the bus to Riverhead, and pretended we were orphans and asked people for money because we hadn't eaten a thing in two days," says Lucas, who seemed to want to get all their crimes out at once to avoid serial prosecution over several days.

"We got enough dollars to buy ice cream and cookies and still pay for the bus back to Greenport!" says Jimmy. The kid has no sense of morality. A chip off the male block.

"You cadged money off people under false pretenses," says the prosecutor, probably knowing exactly under what statute this was a crime.

"I'm sorry, Mom," says Lucas.

Amoral Jimmy doesn't say a word.

"And did LT aid and abet you in these escapades?" Lita asks. If she'd been asking as a prosecutor she'd have referred to "crimes" instead of "escapades," but she was beginning to soften back into Mom.

"It was his idea!" says Jimmy, proud of LT.

"LT," says Lita. "What do you have to say for yourself?" 'Course he hadn't said a coherent word since he'd been born so the question was a bit rhetorical.

Louie-Twoie assumed the shape of a soccer ball and sat motionless on the rug.

"Urf… iggle… susorra… immypoosis," he says.

Lita and me stared at him blankly.

"He says he's sorry," says Jimmy. "He wanted us to have more fun."

Lita kept her prosecutor face in place. With difficulty.

"Life is not always about having fun," she says.

"Issaillysootbe," says Louie-Twoie.

"He says it should be," says Lucas.

Lita looked even more stern.

"Maybe for FFs," she said. "Not for humans."

"Issailllysootbe," says LT again.

Lita hesitated a long moment and then walked over to the couch and gave both Lucas and Jimmy gentle kisses on the top of their heads.

"Please don't skip school again," she says, still standing close to them.

Silence.

Even I had expected them both to say "Okay, Mom," but neither said a word.

"Is that understood?" asks Mom.

"School isn't all it's cracked up to be," says Lucas. Heresy.

"I want you to promise me you won't skip school again," says Mom.

Silence.

"I promise never to skip school again without telling you," says Lucas.

Wow. In this household this is major rebellion. If we had a dungeon, Lucas would be in it within five seconds.

Mom moved away from her two boys and stood next to me and my rocker.

"I hope you won't skip school again," she says softly.

"Okay!" says Jimmy, and he jumps off the couch and begins chasing LT, now a big-eared, no-eyed rabbit, out of the room.

Lucas slowly stands up, hesitates, and then goes up and buries his head in his mother's chest and throws his arms around her in a big hug.

You gotta love kids.

ITEM IN THE NEWS

ATTORNEY GENERAL INVESTIGATING DECLINING XMAS SALES

From Robert Dolt at *The Wall Street Journal*.
Jan. 12th. New York City

After the Commerce Department reported that sales at major retail outlets for the Xmas shopping season showed a sharp decrease from the previous year, the attorney general called upon the Justice Department to investigate.

"With the nation still enmeshed in its patriotic war against Muslim terrorists throughout the world," he said, "it is clearly the duty of every American to do his bit for the war effort by supporting our economy and shopping."

He indicated that the people's failure to do their duty over those Xmas weeks needed to be investigated. The AG suggested that it was possible that terrorists had infiltrated major retail outlets and sabotaged their promotional activities. It was also possible that such terrorists had been hacking into computers and blocking internet spam from reaching millions of intended recipients. Low-paid postal workers may also have been infiltrated by mid-Eastern moles leading to them dumping thousands of sales catalogs destined for the mailboxes of upstanding Americans eager to do their duty. He suggested that it was possible that ISIS and Al-Qaeda operatives in the

US were now eschewing "big scene" terrorist activities for small-scale operations that undermine our economy in just as malicious a manner as demolishing the Twin Towers or shooting up a luxury hotel. And the suffering of Americans, although spread more widely, would be equally great. Corporations, their sales and profits down, would have to cut jobs, bonuses and dividends, and ship more jobs overseas. America's rich, the backbone of our nation, would get richer at a slower pace, with untold psychological suffering.

The AG has ordered the NSA to access the banking, credit card, and online shopping information of all Americans. He seems determined that by next Xmas we will be able to determine who is and who is not doing their best during Xmas shopping season.

"No more will American citizens get away with going to a mall and wandering around in and out of stores but buying no more than a Coke or a Mars Bar. His credit card records will tell the tale: he did not spend as he should at Xmas."

"For almost a century now," he concluded, "it has been clear that Christ was born and died so that retail sales would go up in the fourth quarter. This is why we think of ourselves as a Christian nation."

FORTY-ONE

(From *LUKE'S TRUE UNBELIEVABLE REPORT OF THE INVASION OF THE FFS*, pp. 189–194)

Unfortunately, Louie-Twoie's evil influence on the innocent Morton boys wasn't limited to inciting them to commit individual crimes. Typing into Lucas's iPad or getting out sentences that the boys could understand, LT soon had the boys moving onto bigger things. He began preaching the value of doing things for the hell of it, and the two boys took to it like salmon to an uphill stream.

The boys actually claimed that it was the weather that made them do it. They'd been going to school for more than six winter weeks when in mid-February there was suddenly a warm day. After eight days of cloudy and cold, the sun was out and temperatures in the spring-like high sixties. Lucas claimed that if it had been cloudy and cold again it might never have happened.

At about two o'clock when Jimmy's teacher was taking her usual afternoon break, Jimmy's third-grade class, following the plan Jimmy had whispered to most of them earlier, got up and left the room. They marched next door and invaded the fourth-grade classroom. Jimmy told the fourth-graders and their teacher that there was a school-wide meeting about to take place out on the front lawn. The teacher was unsure what to do, but her students weren't. They followed Jimmy and the third-graders out of the room and down the hall. There they met Lucas's sixth-grade class pouring out of their room past a frantic middle-aged woman trying to stop them. When Lucas and his classmates met half of the eighth-grade class on their way to a science lab, Lucas told them that everyone was taking a spring break and they should join them. Most of them did.

Within five minutes, five different classes, more than a hundred and thirty kids, were out of the school and heading across the lawn toward the main road into town, with a lot of them shouting and waving at the students still in their classrooms to join them. Those that saw them go decided to take a recess too.

Of course the teachers and principal, trained in the art of keeping students in line, tried to stop the mass exodus, but there were hundreds of children and not many teachers. Worse they hadn't been given permission to carry guns and thus weren't able to shoot at the escaping students. Of course many US schools now let their teachers carry guns, but the Greenport School was clearly behind the times.

Close to two hundred students crossed Route 25—backing up traffic in both directions for five minutes or so—and then headed down 6th Street toward the water. Some teachers were hurrying along beside them trying to get their charges to go back to school, but the kids didn't seem to notice. When people came out onto their porches to look at them, the students urged them to join up. A lot of them did, and, of course, more responsible adults called 911.

The school recess finally reached the public beach that lies on Peconic Bay, which was almost deserted when they arrived. The crowd had now more than doubled—it was the largest crowd in the beach's history. In February.

When Jimmy and Lucas came to the water's edge, their

classmates clustered around them. The two brothers looked at each other, smiled uncertainly, and then waded out into the water. Both boys said later the water was so cold they wanted to turn and run back, but they pretended it was fine and kept walking. Within a few seconds, with Jimmy and Lucas wading steadily out into the water, a whole bunch of boys and girls abruptly raced into the water, five or six of them splashing past Jimmy and Lucas and throwing themselves into the bay and swimming. Jimmy, laughing, threw himself into the bay and began swimming too. Lucas screamed and dove into the water. Other kids were screaming too. And laughing.

A few of them turned and waded quickly back onto the dry beach, but most of them buried themselves in the water or splashed some of the newcomers. Some settled for just screaming. Some teachers tried to pull a few of their students out, but since they had to wade into the water to get to them, it looked to some people like the teachers were joining the swim-in. Several of the adults that had joined the parade happily decided to join the party. Most of them took off their shoes and socks and any nice shirts or pants before wading in. Probably that's how the idea of going into the water in just underwear got started.

In an article in the Riverhead paper the next day it said that more than two hundred kids and adults went swimming in the month of February in Peconic Bay, a few of them only in their underwear. And another couple of hundred were watching, most of them laughing or applauding. And most everyone had fun. Two or three had MP3 players and boomed out loud rock music. A lot of people began dancing, most all of them with clothes on.

Everyone seemed to be having a good time. Even Principal Coughlan was laughing with one of the teachers. The police cars and fire engine and ambulance that showed up didn't seem to know what to do, so a few members of the fire department joined the dancing and the chief himself took a swan dive off the end of the dock. He got a lot of cheers. The policemen however kept their cool: they stood around looking stern. Although Sheriff Coombs spent most of his time laughing with one of the pretty teachers.

The only member of the public the ambulance crew found to take care of was Mrs. Blugg, a first-grade teacher, who was in her sixties. She collapsed after swimming and doing a lot of dancing. The Riverhead newspaper said that when they got her to the Eastern Long Island Hospital, she was pronounced alive at arrival. She didn't die in the hospital and was released the next day, claiming temporary insanity.

There was a lot of that going around that day. "Mass hysteria," was the way the newspaper described it. The next day over the school PA system the principal announced that it had been "contagious mass hysteria," and warned the students that if they did it again they would be suspended and would have to spend their time at the beach.

But when Jimmy and Lucas were being interviewed by the reporter, Jimmy said what most of those who had participated thought: "It was fun."

Jimmy and Lucas were both suspended from school for two weeks, but didn't seem to mind. The authorities knew both boys had been hanging around with Louie-Twoie, and witnesses claimed they saw at least two small FFs at the beach that day. Since a game of dodgeball was played in the water with one of the FFs as the ball, it was pretty clear that FFs were involved. The Suffolk County Police ordered that all local FFs were to be rounded up, X-rayed, and interrogated, and they would have been if any had been successfully chased down. The closest the cops got to catching one of them was when an FF—Jimmy claims it was LT—leapt into a patrol car in the shape of a raccoon or skunk and kissed the patrolman on the lips. The cop got off four shots, but the skunk got away.

FORTY-TWO

(From Billy Morton's *MY FRIEND LOUIE*, pp. 311–317)

As the weeks went by, I was loving all the fun and funny things the FFs were coming up with throughout the world. Every day Lucas and Jimmy told me stories about how the FFs were becoming big hits among humans. An FF rock band named Three Blind Mice had produced a hit that had reached number three in the charts, whatever that means. In any case, it was popular. The song was called "Love Me, Baby, I'm Not Anyone." Seems the FFs were pretending to long for a human friend. A million teenage girls indicated they were ready to be friendly.

And FFs were becoming hits in other areas too. One of them had become a basketball star, with rubber legs, incredible speed, a vertical jump of twenty feet, and ninety percent shooting accuracy—scouts thought he sometimes missed on purpose. His name was Boomerang and he started in the spring as a star in the Italian league. But when NBA scouts heard about a player who averaged ninety percent of his team's points and was leading them to an unbeaten season, they were desperate to sign him up. A few owners worried that since he was an alien it might be illegal for them to play him, but others knew that if the league had come to accept blacks, the civil rights laws would force them to accept aliens. In two pre-season games against LeBron James and the Cavaliers, Boomerang scored 130 points, held LeBron to a total of nine points in the two games and stole the ball from him twenty times.

That was it. The owners recognized a losing development when they saw one: it was decreed that no non-mammalian human could play in the NBA. For similar reasons, all professional sports began to ban the FFs.

Which is a shame. You should have seen an FF named Wow leap up thirty feet at Fenway Park and take a home run away from some great player I'd never heard of.

But the FFs were doing a lot of other stuff that was upsetting the big shots even more. For one thing, they seemed to be concentrating their stealing on lobbyists, shutting many of them down. An unpaid lobbyist doesn't tend to work too hard. For another, often when a corporation gave bonuses to its execs, the FFs would steal it from the exec's account before the poor exec had bought a single new yacht. And even worse they gave all the money to soup kitchens, free clinics, church charities, and other subversive sorts of organizations.

And they were even having an effect on our Eternal War in the Middle East. Our military seemed to be getting to the point that our war-making policies had been aimed at for almost twenty years: we were now fighting just about everyone: Sunnis, Shiites, Alamites, Druzes, Turks, Iranians, Iraqis, Syrians, Lebanese. Even the Israelis were getting nervous. There was no longer any concern about collateral damage since *everyone* on the ground was our enemy. But the FFs were making American drones useless. It seems the drones were blowing up a lot more sand than Arabs. A couple of American warships had lost their propellers. And the cruise missiles fired from our warships were killing a lot of sea life rather than Arabs. Only a few of our aircraft seemed to have had their computers hacked, so the poor US military wasn't exactly unarmed. But it felt that way to the generals.

But the stuff I liked best of all were the *Forthehelluvit* events that the FFs were inspiring, described by the media as "spontaneous combustions," "infantile rebellions," "group insurrections," and "Protean-induced hallucinations," and by Lucas and Jimmy as "freaky fun-times." Although our local Greenport Freaky Fun-Time Swim-In only got publicity in the local North Fork papers, other such events began to get national press.

All over the world people suddenly left their homes, places of work, schools, and occupations, and, as a group, did something seemingly purposeless: began to play music, danced, hiked, swam, went bar-hopping, had "kiss-ins" or "hug-ins" or "write-ins," invented games, invaded schools, government offices, banks, hotels, restaurants, football stadiums, and acted in ridiculous ways that disrupted normal life. The biggest of these spontaneous combustions was the "Jones Beach Happening" where a hundred fifty thousand people had fun at rock concerts, dance-ins, kiss-ins, demolition derbies in the parking lot, nude volleyball, and a half-dozen other activities that annoyed everyone except those involved.

The group insurrection that received even more publicity was the "Battery Park Swim-In and Rock Concert" that attracted only twenty thousand people but most all of them worked on Wall Street and had taken off with the markets still open—a major crime in the financial world. However, my favorite was the "Walmart Rebellion" in which more than a hundred thousand employees at hundreds of stores abandoned their positions and began partying in the parking lots. The bosses naturally thought of firing everyone, but thought better of it when they heard several employees say that "Being fired would be a promotion."

Of course, the candidates still running for president in March had trouble handling this issue. A lot of people seemed to like the *Forthehelluvit* events, but most of the candidates, especially the Republicans, were against both the aliens and fun. They were the party of law and order and discipline and hard work. And they felt they had to be against the *Forthehelluvit* events because the candidates that the Proteans were supporting, all independents, were all in favor of them. In fact many of the political rallies of the Proteanistas turned into spontaneous street parties. Their first candidate for president, a former mayor of Utica, New York, insisted that booze was served at all his rallies and that they all ended with music and dancing. Speeches by candidates were limited to ten minutes and hecklers were limited to three.

Watching all this I was happy as a lark.

But how do we know larks are happy? Just because they sing? But most all birds sing. Have you ever seen a lark smile? Or laugh? I bet they have their problems just like you and me.

So let's say instead that all that spring I was happy as a me.

Until I got arrested and thrown in jail.

In late March my driver picked me up at our old farmhouse to take me into APE headquarters for my two-day stint turning swords into ploughshares. Or anyway Humvees into dump trucks. I had turned down Harry Barnes' offer of a limo and instead was being driven into Manhattan by my happy-go-lucky Mexican driver in a Ford Focus. Didn't want my friends on the North Fork to think I was getting a big head.

I never got there.

I knew something was up when a state police car pulled up beside us lights flashing, and signaled my driver to pull over to the side of the road. Ever since I'd known him my driver had broken all records for slow driving on the L I Expressway. I hadn't the faintest idea what was happening. We were actually pulled over onto the only really wide shoulder on the entire expressway.

The state trooper pulled in behind us, and, as they always do, took two weeks to get out of his car and come up and say "hello."

Finally, he climbed out of his vehicle and moved with the deliberation of a walking mountain toward our little Focus. He stopped at the driver's side and raised a gun and pointed it in at me.

It suddenly occurred to me that I was about to be assassinated. I felt a bolt of fear I hadn't experienced since the last time a Vietnamese peasant had tried to kill me.

Just then there was a screech of brakes and a car swept in to stop in front of us. Three men surged out of the car and ran up to my side of the Focus. They were all dressed in neat suits and looked to me like either Feds or insurance salesman. The biggest one, a guy of at least six foot six and weighing in at two hundred and eighty pounds, banged on my passenger-side window. I lowered it.

"You're under arrest, Mr. Morton," the giant says.

Nope. Not an insurance salesman.

"Me!?" says I, filled with moral outrage at being discovered to have committed crimes, and filled with relief that I wasn't about to be assassinated but was only going to be sent to prison for fifty years.

"What have I done wrong? I've been an upstanding citizen ever since I got married. I can't think of a single crime I've committed." Actually, I could think of sixty-seven, but I'm not big on confessing.

"You're under arrest for impersonating a drug dealer," says Hulk Hogan, "for money laundering, for aiding and abetting an alien terrorist getting into and out of Iraq, for insider trading in your trading account with Ameritrade, for destroying shareholder value in American Protective Equipment, for faking death and initiating a false insurance claim, for aiding and abetting a known bank robber, and child neglect."

"Is that all you've got!?"

"The Government means to prosecute you to the full extent of the law."

"I'd expect no less from the Government," says I. "But what's this about child neglect?"

"Your two boys were seen unaccompanied by any adult at the Jones Beach *For-the-Hell-of-it Be-in*. There were two hundred thousand people there."

"And five thousand of them were unaccompanied kids!"

"The fact that other parents were negligent does not mean that you can avoid responsibility for your own failure as a parent. Our government is gravely concerned for all children."

"Yeah, except for those who live in Arab lands and Africa."

"Will you come peacefully, Mr. Morton?"

"Sure. Got nothing important on my agenda today. Where we going?"

"To Manhattan Police Headquarters."

"Hey, that's great," says I, opening the passenger-side door and struggling to get up and out. "The last time I visited there was back in sixty-eight. Got me for assaulting a police officer. I was running away with a hundred other hippies and was going so fast I ran up the back of some overweight cop and knocked him down. The police station was nice enough, but the cops broke two of my ribs when I fell down some stairs. Hope they've improved the banister."

"Put him in cuffs, Jim," the mammoth says to one of the other suits.

"Gentle. I'm a helpless old man."

"Careful not to break both his arms, Jim."

Actually, the police station was not the same as back in sixty-eight. And it was different too from the one I stayed at in the fall of sixty-six. And from the one in the fall of sixty-seven. On the other hand, one booking is pretty much the same as the next. I was fingerprinted and had some perp photos taken that made me look seventy-two years old.

They took me before a judge who knew what he was going to do before I even showed up. He convicted me on all counts, and sentenced me to 2,800 years in solitary confinement at Guantanamo. Well, not quite that, but he ordered me held without bail. The bail hearing was to be in four days with the DA asking bail to be set at a million dollars.

They let me make a phone call, and I got to talk for three minutes with Lita. Told her I'd had a wonderful drive down the Long Island Expressway and met a nice man who made the Incredible Hulk look like Bambi, and I was in jail with bail set at a million dollars—high for child neglect, but children are our most precious assets. She managed to get my general drift and arranged to see me the next day.

But that evening, after midnight actually, I had two visitors to my cell. One was Agent Johnson and the other a man who Johnson said was his boss, a guy named Rabb, who was a short spark plug sort of guy who looked like he thought he'd never made a mistake in his life. The door clanged behind them and the guard, not bothering to lock the door, walked noisily away. My cell seemed to be isolated from all the others.

"As I guess you now know, Billy," Johnson says, "we've accumulated a lot of evidence that you've been helping your Protean friends in illegal activities. We are certain that we can easily convict you of aiding and abetting terrorists."

"Don't doubt it," I says.

"Unless you can get your friend Louie to surrender to us," says the fireplug, "you'll be spending the rest of your life in prison."

"And your wife too, Billy," says Johnson. "We now have evidence that she imitated a Jewish widow and was deeply involved in money laundering in both the Caymans and New York."

"Been busy, have you?" says I.

"This is not fun and games, Billy," says Johnson. "Unless Louie gives himself up, you and Carlita will never see your children again, except from inside a prison."

"That's it, is it?" says I.

"That's it. We won't be going to court for another four days.

We won't let anyone know the charges we're holding you on until then. If Louie surrenders before that, then we'll only charge you with hiring an illegal immigrant as your driver and specifically clear you on all other counts. If Louie isn't in our custody by Monday morning we'll throw the book at you."

As I sat on my cot in that cell and listened to what Agent Johnson was saying I felt more and more depressed. If it were only me they had in their clutches I'd tell Louie to stay free, although I doubt he'd listen. But if they were going to jail Lita too…

"Well," I finally says. "I guess we'll just have to wait and see what happens."

"Yes, we will," says Agent Johnson.

Rabb sniffed and sneered and then marched to the door, swung it open and marched noisily down the hall.

Agent Johnson and I looked at each other. Then he reached inside his suit jacket and pulled out a silver flask.

"Want to share a drink, Billy?" he says quietly.

Jail's not all it's cracked up to be. My description of my arrest and getting locked up with huge bail may make it seem as though I wasn't bothered in the least, but that's just me trying to be cool. The fact is I was scared. I was scared when that trooper pointed his gun at me, scared when the Incredible Hulk banged on the car window, and scared when I was alone in jail.

I'm too old for this shit. Too stuck in my ways. When I was in jail almost fifty years earlier it was actually interesting. I was young and confident and rebellious and stupid and didn't know what I was doing. Now I was old and uncertain and, though still rebellious in theory, in practice I was a sitter. In my rocking chair I have all sorts of rebellious thoughts. And they stay thoughts.

When I got a visit from Lita I could see she was worried too. Worried mostly about me, but also about Jimmy and Lucas. What would happen to them if both their parents ended up in jail? Not too good. She had relatives who could look after them, but that was just saying horrible would only be semi-horrible. After talking it over, she told me she thought we ought to bring the boys to Manhattan, where we were now stuck, so the family could be closer. I pointed out that Louie might turn himself in, but she shook her head.

"We aren't that important to the FFs."

FORTY-THREE

(From *LUKE'S TRUE UNBELIEVABLE REPORT OF THE INVASION OF THE FFS*, pp. 203–208)

As far as we can reconstruct it, Louie called the number that the NSA had posted for Proteans to dial in case they wanted to turn themselves in and be locked up for life. He announced to the NSA that he would surrender the next day, Saturday, at about noon, in Central Park. Where in Central Park he neglected to say.

However, the next day a small crowd began to gather in the park around the statue of Alice in Wonderland, a triptych in bronze of Alice, the Mad Hatter, and the March Hare. The NSA managed to determine that the people, including a few reporters, were being invited there via social media, which said that the famous FF Louie was going to appear and make a speech. By eleven o'clock a hundred people had gathered, and by noon almost five hundred. There were also two dozen NYPD officers, and six neatly dressed men who might be insurance salesmen. One of the men was very very very big.

As the minutes passed a few people in the crowd began a low chant of "Louie! Louie! Louie!" and after a while the whole crowd, with a few exceptions, joined in.

And lo and behold, a Protean finally made an appearance, bouncing down a pathway and then from head to head across the top of the crowd to the statue itself, where he settled on Alice's bronze head. Most of the crowd applauded enthusiastically, although those in uniform and the six suits could only manage frowns. The six insurance salesmen went into a huddle, presumably to plan what sort of exceptionally high insurance premium they would recommend.

Louie, for it was indeed he, arrived as his usual sphere, but soon turned into a large human head supported by four six-inch "legs." He'd stuffed into his face two lemons as eyes with a small black circle painted on each. Out of nowhere he plopped on his head a stovepipe top hat out of the nineteenth century: Abe Lincoln from outer space.

"Friends, Romans, countrymen," Louie proclaimed in a booming voice that reached easily across the crowd. "Lend me your ears."

This was clearly plagiarism, and even worse was to come.

"I come here today not to praise the great non-warrior Louie, but to bury him. For I have come to surrender to the all-powerful authorities who rule you humans and your lives. You see them now around you ready to take me into custody."

Some in the crowd booed.

"However, they have granted me permission before my incarceration to make a few remarks.

"First of all, we should never forget that 'Tweedledum and Tweedledee agreed to have a battle, For Tweedledum said Tweedledee had spoiled his nice new rattle.' That pretty much sums up the Protean position on war.

"Secondly, I must remind you that 'T'was brillig, and the slithy toves, Did gyre and gimble in the wabe: All mimsy were the borogoves, And the mome raths outgrabe.' I know all of you have given this famous quotation much thought over the years, but an FF named Gibberish has said that it is too profound for humans to understand. He tried to simplify its wisdom for his human friends by saying 'T'wasn't brillig but dumdum that the stilthy rovens did gore and bimble in the coatree: All mumsy were the boringtoves, And the momme ratsies grayedout.'

"Unfortunately, neither his human friends nor we FFs could make any more sense of Gibberish's profundity than we could of the original, so I will get to my concluding remarks, which are much more in tune with a traditional oration.

"It is a far far better thing that I do today than I have ever done before. Give me liberty or give me death. I have not only grown gray but almost blind in the service of my country. That government of the people, by the people, for the people, shall not perish from the earth. And we must fight the malefactors of great wealth. We have nothing to fear but fear itself. We must guard against the acquisition of unwarranted influence, whether sought or unsought, by the military–industrial complex. Ask not what your country can do for you, but what you can do for your country. I have a dream… Tear down that wall!

"And let me conclude with this: I am not a crook. We don't want the smoking gun to be a mushroom cloud. I was against the war before I was for it. I did not have sexual relations with that woman."

Louie paused, swung his two lemon eyes in an arc over the crowd.

"And finally," he says, "let me say, 'so long.'"

He then bounced down off Alice's head, rolled and bounced across the top of the crowd's heads and outstretched arms and finally into the unsuspecting arms of the Incredible Hulk. Louie placed his stovepipe hat on the agent's head.

"I surrender," he says.

ITEM IN THE NEWS

LEADING REPUBLICAN PRESIDENTIAL CANDIDATE ENDORSES MONEY

Riyad, Saudi Arabia. July 28th

In Saudi Arabia today, the leading Republican candidate for president of the United States reiterated strongly his belief in money.

"Our great nation is in trouble today," he stated in a speech before the Saudi Conference for Petroleum and Profits, "because our president has failed to understand and believe in that which has made America great: money."

The charismatic Republican went on to explain that unless people were motivated solely by money, modern American capitalism would not work.

"From Adam Smith to Ronald Reagan to Rush Limbaugh, great thinkers have known that everyone following his own economic self-interest—money—is what makes capitalism work. If before following their own economic self-interest our citizens and corporations begin doing what some radical Democrats are advocating, like worrying about workers, communities, the environment, or inequalities of wealth, the system would break down and our nation become second rate."

When challenged during the Q&A period about whether it was fair to lower taxes for the rich while cutting programs to alleviate the suffering of the poor, the wealthy candidate spoke eloquently of how it was the wealth of the successful that would ultimately relieve suffering.

"It is only because of the high taxes and other restraints on the hard-working rich that we have poverty in our nation," he said. "My heart goes out to the suffering of the poor. That is why I have spent my entire life trying to earn as much money as I can—which, I should remind you, is the duty of every American—so that others will benefit indirectly and in the long run from my efforts to become rich."

"It's all right," he went on, "for social workers or charities and other well-meaning entities to do things that help the poor, but only as long they are getting well paid for doing so. Anyone helping another human being without being economically rewarded is undermining our free enterprise way of life. They will destroy our nation."

FORTY-FOUR

(From Billy Morton's *MY FRIEND LOUIE*, pp. 331–337)

Louie had given himself up so I could go free.

I felt terrible.

The Feds kept their promise. I pleaded guilty to employing an undocumented worker and paid a stiff fine. All the other charges were swept under the table. 'Course, at any time they wanted, the authorities could bend over, reach under the table, pick up all the charges, and bring them with a big grin to a judge. I was about as secure as a turtle on the point of a needle.

And over the next week we learned that the FFs were sitting on the same needle. Since we knew that conversations in jail were bugged, Louie wasn't able to tell Lita anything when she went to visit him, but he could communicate with Molière sitting in the jail waiting room.

Molière reported that the FFs were beginning to lose the game, or as the humans saw it, the war. The NSA had suddenly gotten smart: they seemed to have developed a series of defensive measures that had cut into the FF's ability to hack into whatever they wanted. The first setback came when all the pages containing data that incriminated various establishment big shots suddenly disappeared from the NSA systems. All the potential blackmail material was no longer available.

In addition, the FBI, the CIA, and the SEC were on to most of the bank and stock-trading accounts that the FFs had set up with money stolen from banks and corporations. Including all of mine.

"How come the NSA's suddenly gotten so smart?" I ask Molière.

"It's not the NSA," says Molière.

"Then who is it?"

"Machiavelli and Gibberish," he says.

"Gibberish! He's on our side!"

"He was. Now he's on their side."

"No!"

"He's thinking of running for president in the Republican primaries and he decided that if he wanted any voter support it might be a good move to work *with* the government instead of against it."

"That's horrible! He's a traitor!"

"Oh, no," Molière says. "FFs often end up on opposite sides in games we're playing. Just as Louie and I enjoy playing games against the dominant people of a planet, Machiavelli likes to take the opposite side in a game against FFs he thinks are very strong—which in this case is Louie and me. So Gibberish changing sides is no surprise. Besides, both running for president and changing sides were probably random decisions on his part."

"What do you mean?"

"Gibberish thinks FFs should always be wary of unthinkingly slipping into having a purpose rather than playing, so he sometimes starts making decisions randomly."

"But all this means that all over the world, you FFs are playing not only with each other but *against* each other!?"

"Of course," says Molière. "Back home in Ickie most all our

games are against each other. One reason FFs like to travel is they get a bit bored playing the same opponents over and over."

I was silent. It was a bit of a blow to realize that all FFs weren't on my side. Made me feel a bit smaller than I usually feel. The FFs were playing with us: to them we were no more than pawns in their supersized chess game.

But I was still worried about Louie. He was still in prison, a place where FFs sometimes die of suicide. And Machiavelli and Gibberish were making it more difficult for his side to win the game they were playing. FFs were all about fun, but I was beginning to wonder where in all this anyone was supposed to find fun.

FORTY-FIVE

(From *LUKE'S TRUE UNBELIEVABLE REPORT OF THE INVASION OF THE FFS*, pp. 222–228)

The effort by Gibberish to become president of the United States might have seemed like a long shot. For one thing it was late in the primary season to announce a candidacy, and he hadn't done the paperwork to enter most of the remaining primaries. However, as soon as he announced his candidacy for the Republican nomination in March, polls showed that thirty-five percent of the American people favored him over the human candidates, and twenty-five percent of Republicans favored him.

At first his candidacy went well. His rallies consisted not of a long speech but of people playing games, or having a dance-in, hug-in, or kiss-in. Sometimes the whole gathering would leave the hall or stadium they were in and march through the streets trying playfully to get bystanders to join the march and support Gibberish for President.

The Gibb's supporters loved it. So did the media. A Gibb rally was much more fun than those of the other candidates. His favorability rating in the polls began to go up.

Then Gibberish and his team made a catastrophic mistake: he began making long speeches and releasing position papers. Experienced politicians had long ago learned that position papers were a waste of time—no one looked at them—and sometimes dangerous—when people read them and realized the candidate had ideas that they disagreed with. Gibberish's ideas were, unfortunately, not ideas that many Americans agreed with.

First of all, he wanted to bring all American troops back from foreign countries and put them to work building bridges, schools, highways, and hospitals. Instead of bombing bridges, schools, highways, and hospitals in foreign countries.

Most Americans were appalled. They thought that building a thousand bases in foreign lands and sending tens of thousands of soldiers to operate out of them must be required by the Constitution, so natural did it seem and so long had it gone on.

And Gibberish announced that he would propose an inheritance tax of ninety-five percent on all accumulated wealth of over one million dollars. He claimed it would let the children and grandchildren of the very rich begin at the same level as that of the poor and middle class.

The rich did not want their children and grandchildren to begin at the same level as that of the poor and middle class. They wanted their heirs to begin at the top and never have a chance to plunge to the depths of the bottom ninety percent. The newspapers, TV stations, and sponsored think tanks (all owned by the rich) began yelling at the top of their voices that this was cruel and unfair to the rich who through pluck and luck and having inherited millions from their own dads, had accumulated wealth.

And Gibberish advocated turning all hospitals, clinics, pharmaceutical companies, and health insurance companies into non-profit entities, and to provide free health care for the entire American population, the government paying for everything. This was clearly socialism if not communism. And it was part of the American catechism that socialism and communism were evil.

So these ideas were outrageous. It clearly infringed on a rich American's right to take his loot to the grave, or at least give every cent of it to his kids or girlfriend. The ideas infringed on an American's right choose his own health care. It infringed on the rich person's right to have much better health care than the non-rich. It infringed on an American's God-given right to die because of a lack of health care.

Within three weeks of his outlining a clear, specific program, Gibberish's campaign for the presidency was in deep trouble. The Republican state party apparatus in every state in which Gibberish was trying to get on the ballot put so many legal blocks in his way that he was soon spending two-thirds of his campaign money on hiring lawyers.

His poll numbers began to collapse. In three weeks the thirty-five percent who had favored him among the general population had dropped to twenty percent. The percentage of Republicans who supported him had dropped to ten percent, and it was widely suspected that they were all Democrats in disguise.

Because his polling had gotten so low, the Republicans changed their debate format so that no candidate could be in a debate unless he was averaging at least eleven percent support in the Republican primary polls.

Finally, Gibberish's candidacy for the Republican nomination for president of the United States came crashing to a halt when he gave a speech at the annual Freedom Summit of the Ohio Republican Conference of Great Men—"great men" referring to the Republicans they invited to speak at the conference. They invited Gibberish for the publicity it would bring them. Having invited him, they decided they had to let him speak.

The rest is history.

"My friends [Gibberish began to the assembled Republicans], I come before you today to announce that I am abandoning all my efforts to bring immediate equality to the nation through my various socialist programs. [A few cheers from audience.]

"Instead, I will now be running for president of the United States for one reason only: I would like to update your whole democratic system of elections so that we can have people serving throughout the nation who are truly representative of the people. After I have been elected and completed my task, I shall resign. [A few more cheers.]

"My friends, the idea that free elections are the essence of representative government is, as I'm sure you know, utter nonsense. Free elections today mean *un*-representative governments.

"Those who are elected by the minority that bother to vote are inevitably from a narrow class of people—overwhelmingly male, wealthy, and Caucasian. In fact, your elected officials are a lot like you people in this room. [Cheers.] Our present elections guarantee that no poor people will reach public office, and many fewer women, blacks, Asians, Muslims, and Hispanics than are in your population at large. Elections are structured to guarantee that rich whites will dominate, no matter what their party or platform.

"I humbly ask you today this simple question: What

would happen if we substituted a lottery system, where all citizens can sign up to 'run' for a specific office, whether it be councilman, congressman, governor, or president, and the winner for each office would be chosen not by other citizens, but by *chance* from the list of candidates who had signed up?

"With such a system you would immediately see what real representative governments would be like. If women chose to run for office in the same numbers as men, then women would soon constitute half (or more) of all government office holders, local, state, and national. All minorities, if they chose to run, would be represented proportionally. Even rich upper-class males would be represented in all governmental offices in proportion to their numbers in the general population. Of course, this would be perhaps ten percent of all office holders instead of eighty percent, but I think most Americans would feel they could live with this. [Loud booing from the audience.]

"Except you people in the ten percent. [More booing.]

"A second great advantage is that a lottery would do away with all competitive elections for governmental offices. No more elections! No more political ads! No more hypocritical lying speeches! No more dirty tricks! No more billionaires spending millions promoting candidates and ideas that represent only their own interests! No more will your government officials have to spend half their time trying to raise money, a quarter of their time on electioneering, and only a quarter of their time on the job that in theory they were elected to do!

"A third great advantage of choosing office holders by lot would be the doing away with the two party system... [More boos.] An historical accident that has cast a pall of hypocrisy and stagnation across American lives. No longer will elections involve only a choice between Tweedledum and Tweedledee—called for some reason, Republicans and Democrats.

"All the problems facing, or more often *created by*, present governments, instead of being dealt with by men and women with close ties to the large banks, military contractors, big media, pharmaceutical and health insurance corporations, whose interests are hardly those of most citizens, would be dealt with by a genuine cross-section of citizens, most of whom would be able to speak for their own interests for the first time in their lives.

"In present governments almost no one speaks for the interests of average citizens. The vast majority of your elected officials tell the average American that he will gain from tax cuts for corporations or stock holders or the very rich, the idea being that these riches will miraculously 'trickle down' and 'create jobs,' for those in the middle and lower income groups. Strange that few elected officials ever talk about a 'trickle up' theory—where the government gives tax breaks and subsidies to the poor and middle classes, who will then spend money and create demand and new jobs and thus eventually more profits for corporations and more money for the rich. 'Trickle up' theories never seem to catch on with the governing elite.

"Americans have been told that you need to spend hundreds of billions on missile defense systems, slightly faster jet bombers, more nuclear subs, more bombs and missiles, more bases and troops overseas, more bombing of Arabs wherever you can find them, but you can't afford a national health care system that would cover all; that you can't afford to create an educational system where students attend for free, and graduates go to work when they graduate rather than into something like a debtors' prison. How often have the American people actually been asked whether they would rather have universal health care and free college education for all instead of new fighter planes, subs, and upgraded nuclear weapons? Never.

"In a new, randomly selected representative government, the decision about how much is spent on what would no longer be made by those who are beholden to companies who directly benefit from such decisions, but rather by ordinary citizens."

Voice from audience: "Ridiculous!" [Cheers from audience.]

"Ordinary citizens. Aye, there's the rub. Some of you are undoubtedly thinking that ordinary citizens are not smart enough, educated enough, experienced enough to make these decisions, that you—the smart, the educated, the Harvard grads, and the already elected—are the ones who know best what is good for them. But compared to those who are now elected officials in Congress, most ordinary citizens will look like geniuses. And even the stupid uneducated ones who chance chooses for office would know one thing that the rich who presently rule our nation will never know: what might work to make their lives better.

"Although the very first great democracy, that of Ancient Greece, chose its officials by lot, this idea is for Americans appalling, ridiculous, 'undemocratic,' and doesn't even rise to the level of possibility—or so the elite pundits will assure us."

"Right!" from the crowd.

"However, as long as your nation has its present election system, controlled by your 'free' mass media—free to be dominated and controlled by the corporations—then you will have unrepresentative governments *of* the rich, *by* the rich, and *for* the rich, governments that find dominating both its own citizens and the rest of the world is in their own narrow interest."

Cheers from audience, shouts of "Yes, Yes!"

"My friends, it should be clear: Better a roulette wheel."

Rising chorus of boos makes Gibberish raise his voice.

"And also, never forget this: Booblepoop nicoburp sartosis… tinglewitt… marshmel…"

The boos drown him out.

FORTY-SIX

(From *THE OFFICIAL HISTORY OF THE ALIEN INVASION, Volume 1,* pp. 432–438)

It was in February that the head of the NSA, Jason Epstein, sent the famous memorandum to all three hundred and six sub-agencies within his jurisdiction. The memo decreed that the United States should consider itself at war with the Proteans.

He outlined in detail the Protean activities that made clear their threat to the American government and businesses:

1. Protean terrorists have fatally compromised both American and Russian nuclear missile sites. They have redirected almost thirty Russian and over a hundred US missiles. Some are now reprogrammed to be inoperable, others to blow up in the underground silo. In at least three nuclear submarines the missiles have been reprogrammed to blow up in the submarine. This reprogramming has crippled the American nuclear deterrent and makes it dangerous to launch nuclear devices against deserving foes such as Iran, Russia, North Korea, and Muslim terrorists.

2. Through their hacking of the NSA databases, Protean terrorists have gained information about public officials, corporate leaders, and employees of the NSA that implicate such people in various crimes or scandals. They have been using this knowledge to blackmail congressmen, CEOs, other high-ranking government and corporate officials, and even some of our own employees. Including blackmailing more than six congressmen into proposing a law cutting defense and homeland security budgets and closing down twenty of our spy agencies, leaving us with only sixty. The bill would also eliminate spending on all new American planes and warships for five years. They are trying to pretty up their bill by transferring all the money saved to building or repairing American hospitals, roads, bridges, schools, universities, water systems, and electricity infrastructure, but the effect on our national defense would be negative.

3. In early December of last year the Proteans distributed more than five million dollars to various people in the Miami Dade County area. Some distributions were made using helicopter and Cessna flights over the poorer neighborhoods of the city and county. But their other less dramatic distributions were far more insidious. People in the employ of or under the influence of the Protean terrorists went door to door to hundreds of small businesses and gave them tens of thousands of dollars either to save or expand their businesses. Many of these people used the money to buy personal luxury items, but others used it to expand their businesses, hire new employees, or pay their existing employees higher wages, all of which may constitute unfair competition against the big box stores like Walmart and Target.

4. Beginning early this year there have been at least a hundred reported "For-the-Hell-of-It" events around the world, and undoubtedly thousands of unreported smaller ones. Even though most large corporations have fired employees who engage in such events, the popularity of

For-the-Hell-of-It events seems to be growing, and with it, in some duped minds, the popularity of the terrorists.

5. The Proteans are befriending other species on our planet and turning them against us. On at least three occasions Proteans, or their human henchmen, have entered chicken, duck, or pig factories, disabled all the employees by somehow putting them to sleep, then released the animals into the wild. This is clearly cruelty to animals. Chickens, ducks, and pigs that had been given all the food they wanted—even more—and were totally safe from predators, found themselves back in the wild where they had to fend for themselves. We are publicizing that many have been eaten by predators.

In several stockyards, cattle that for centuries have gone blissfully to slaughter have begun to rebel and kick and attack with their horns and, when possible, run away from the slaughter. On at least two occasions Protean terrorists have been seen in the vicinity. In addition, ocean-going Protean terrorists have been warning fish and whales and dolphins of approaching fishing boats. Over a dozen factory-fishing boats have mysteriously had their propellers fall off. The NSA and our military have enough enemies in the world without having dozens of our animal species turning against us.

As a result of these considerations, this Agency has reached the conclusion that we should cease to differentiate between Proteans who appear to be engaged in only harmless activities and those we know are engaged in subversive activities. We must consider ourselves at war with *all* Proteans.

Although a few Proteans may indeed be innocent of anti-government activities, they are reproducing little Proteans, some of whom undoubtedly *will* become part of the Protean anti-government, anti-corporation movement. In fact, we have asked the Government to introduce a law that ensures the off-shoots of any Proteans being prosecuted for a crime are prosecuted for the same crime, since they were a part of the entity that committed the crime. Protean children are not like human children: they are in fact only sub-units of the original Protean. We are asking Congress to pass a law that will treat them as such.

Finally, *every* Protean, no matter how innocent it may appear, could at any time be recruited by the terrorists for terrorist activities. The NSA and NSA agencies must *all* act under the assumption that there are no innocent Proteans.

All Proteans are guilty until proven innocent.

FORTY-SEVEN

(From *THE OFFICIAL HISTORY OF THE ALIEN INVASION*, Volume II, pp. 76-81.
Being the transcript of the interrogation of Alien 6, alias "Louie," by Agent
Michael Johnson, which took place in a special cell of the jail that Federal
authorities had created for Protean terrorists. Agent Johnson reported that
the alien terrorist bounced around his cell, altered his appearance, or rested
on the floor of the cell in the shape of a foot mat.)

AGENT JOHNSON: I'm authorized to negotiate with you for your possible release and the dropping or lessening of charges against the six other Proteans currently held by us.

TERRORIST LOUIE: Sounds good.

AGENT JOHNSON: Unfortunately, we can't trust any assurances that you may give us that you'll keep to any agreements we reach. Can you think of any reason we should trust you?

TERRORIST LOUIE: I can. If I and my friends could hack into the NSA's systems then we could have destroyed those systems. We can hack into the systems that control your electric grid, foul them up, and shut down the power throughout the entire country. If we were stealing billions from your bank and corporate accounts we could, if we chose to, shut down your financial system. Haven't you ever wondered why we haven't?

AGENT JOHNSON: Tell me.

TERRORIST LOUIE: For you and your government, your interaction with Proteans is a war. For us it's a game. You and your fellow humans think the purpose of a game is to win. We think a game has no purpose except itself. We play it to play, not to win. If we sense a game is getting lopsided and that one side has too much power, we usually change the rules of the game to give the weaker side more strength. Or good players change sides from the winning team to the weaker team.

AGENT JOHNSON: What's this got to do with our being able to believe that you might keep your promises?

TERRORIST LOUIE: Because if I promise something that will keep the game going on a mostly even level, you can expect, based on the limitations we've been imposing on our playing, that I'll keep that promise.

AGENT JOHNSON: What's this game you think you're playing?

TERRORIST LOUIE: It's a game to wake you human beings up to the mess that you've been making of life on Earth for the last fifty years. If humans begin changing things so they become less destructive of most life on this planet, and reduce the suffering that their civilization is imposing on most other humans, then we win. The vast majority of human beings also win. Of course, the few millions who benefit from your sick way of doing things will be losers: their power and wealth will be diminished. Since your world's governments are controlled by the few who benefit, your governments are all fighting us with everything they can think of.

(A silence of several seconds.)

AGENT JOHNSON: So tell me, if we agree to free you and the other Protean terrorists under our control, what can you promise us in return?

TERRORIST LOUIE: I can promise to continue the game with the same limitations and restraints we've been showing. We will use no power other than what we've already demonstrated.

AGENT JOHNSON: That's not nearly enough. We want you to promise to cease your hacking, your stealing, and your disruption of our military operations.

TERRORIST LOUIE: We might promise to stop most of our hacking of government systems and reduce our stealing, but your military establishment and its operations are at the heart of what makes your civilization sick. If we can't continue playing against it, then from our point of view, the game isn't worth playing.

AGENT JOHNSON: What if we threaten to kill all the Proteans in our custody and arrange to have your friend Billy commit suicide? I think you might be a little more generous in your terms, don't you?

TERRORIST LOUIE: No, Mike, we wouldn't. We know that governments kill their enemies: that's part of the game we've chosen to play.

Do you realize that when I started playing this game I had only two other FFs helping me? In the rest of the world, last fall perhaps, there were another dozen FFs who were into playing games against governments, corporations, and the military. Today? Today there are almost a thousand FFs in tune with us and playing our game against you—the exact figure is of course classified in our files as "somewhat secret," our highest category of secrecy. FFs who last fall were happy playing little games have been drawn by your killing of our brothers into playing our big game. Congratulations.

AGENT JOHNSON: So essentially you'll reduce some hacking and some stealing in return for the release of six Proteans and our promise not to harm the Mortons.

TERRORIST LOUIE: Your government has kidnapped those FFs and we're willing to pay a ransom to free them.

AGENT JOHNSON: There is one other non-negotiable item that our government is demanding in return for freeing Proteans: you must stop dismantling our nuclear bombs and their delivery systems. They are basic to our national security.

TERRORIST LOUIE: Don't be silly, Mike. The nuclear weapons you humans have developed are at the core of your insanity. They greatly increase your *in*security. Think about it: you're still spending hundreds of billions of dollars every year to maintain and increase your ability to destroy the planet. Other countries are guilty of doing the same, but on such a small scale compared to the United States that it hardly matters—although FFs are working to disarm the Russian, Chinese, and Israeli nuclear arsenals as we speak.

AGENT JOHNSON: We will not agree to commit national suicide.

TERRORIST LOUIE: You're already committing national suicide. That's what your nuclear weapons arsenal and your invading half the countries in the world with your military bases is all about. You're in the process of destroying your country and the world. If that isn't suicide I don't know what is.

(A long silence)

AGENT JOHNSON: Then there won't be a deal.

TERRORIST LOUIE: Seems that way.

AGENT JOHNSON: I might as well add that there are other conditions my government has asked me to put to you. We will not have our democracy undermined. You must cease destroying the nation's PACs and other democratic entities formed to express the opinions of their founders and to support candidates of their choosing.

TERRORIST LOUIE: Come on, Mike, even *you* know that's ridiculous. It's the massive fundraising political entities that are undermining your democracy. In fact, they've so undermined it already that democracy in your country ceased to exist a decade ago.

AGENT JOHNSON: Well... maybe.... I guess we'll have to agree to disagree.

TERRORIST LOUIE: We'll pay up front five billion dollars each for the six Proteans and your leaving my Morton friends alone. We'll stop all our hacking except for Homeland Security and the Department of Defense. We'll reduce our stealing to a half billion dollars a month. Finally, we'll agree that no FF will ever again within the sight of humans bounce more than six feet high.

AGENT JOHNSON: I'll forward your proposal to my government, which we both know will reject it.

TERRORIST LOUIE: So I go to trial.

AGENT JOHNSON: You will, Louie, and I wish it weren't so. I really do.

TERRORIST LOUIE: You ought to consider changing sides, Mike. We're in a bit of trouble these days and could use a good player like you.

AGENT JOHNSON: In America we call that treason.

TERRORIST LOUIE: In Ickie we call it changing sides.

FORTY-EIGHT

(From *THE OFFICIAL HISTORY OF THE ALIEN INVASION, Volume II*, pp. 176–182. Being the transcript of the meeting between the President of the United States and Alien 32, alias "Molière," on July 27th.)

(Before the meeting, the president's personal security team disabled the six video and audio recording devices installed in the Oval Office by various spy agencies. However, we have footage of the event because the president's security team left their own device in place. In any case, unbeknownst to the security team, the CIA made sure that a listening device was installed in the president's belt buckle each morning, so in effect every word the president spoke in his years in office was known to the CIA, except when he left his pants and belt at a distance from a bed.)

The president stands beside his desk when a door opens and the Protean Alien 32 known as Molière rolls into the room. He rolls up to the president, assumes a more or less human shape and extends a limb and hand. The two shake hands.

PRESIDENT: Thanks so much for coming, Mr... Molière.
MOLIÈRE: My pleasure, Mr. President.
PRESIDENT: I'm going to sit in this rocking chair. Please make yourself comfortable wherever or... however you like.
MOLIÈRE: Thank you, sir. If you don't mind I'll just sort of wander about as we talk. When I sit still I usually fall asleep.
PRESIDENT: I understand you're quite a celebrity.

MOLIÈRE: *Was* quite a celebrity. But authorities around the country are forbidding or closing any new performances of the play. They're also trying to get the videos removed from YouTube and other sites. My fame is receding pretty fast.

PRESIDENT: The NSA was very disappointed when they heard that the… Protean who was to visit me was you. They told me they didn't feel it would be politically wise to arrest and torture you until after your fifteen minutes of fame were over.

MOLIÈRE: A sense of humor!

PRESIDENT: Only when I'm alone—at least from human beings.

MOLIÈRE: That's sad. It's when you're with other humans that you most need a sense of humor.

PRESIDENT: I'm afraid we're getting a bit away from the important matters I'd hoped we might discuss.

MOLIÈRE: No, Mr. President, a sense of humor is the most important thing we could possibly discuss. You humans always think that if you talk seriously about serious problems that you can find serious solutions. But most of the problems you think are serious are so minor that the deaths of five fleas would match in seriousness what you spend years trying to deal with.

(The president stares at Alien 32, who in his sphere shape is momentarily settled on the couch.)

PRESIDENT: I'm afraid I can't conceive of what you're talking about.

MOLIÈRE: Probably not. So let's try it your way. Let's play at being serious.

(Alien 32 assumes his more or less human form, sitting on the couch and crossing his legs. He produces a couple of ping-pong balls and stuffs them into his "head" as eyes.)

PRESIDENT: I think that's best. Your Protean friends are destroying our nation, and we have no choice but to fight you in every way we can. Will you and your people consider stopping your subversive activities?

MOLIÈRE: Exactly what do you have in mind?

PRESIDENT: Well, to begin with, stop interfering in our efforts to stop the Muslim terrorists.

MOLIÈRE: Agreed. We will work to stop *some* of those you call terrorists.

PRESIDENT: You will?

MOLIÈRE: We already are. We're blocking their military efforts whenever and wherever we can. Of course, you and your papers and television shows call half the world terrorists, so we can't promise to try to stop all of them.

PRESIDENT: That's true, but you're blocking *our* military efforts even more.

MOLIÈRE: And that too will help you stop the terrorists.

PRESIDENT: How?

MOLIÈRE: For every five terrorists you kill you create ten. At your present rate of bombing and killing, our computers indicate that in another five years you'll have converted the entire Muslim population of the earth to wanting to fight against you.

(The president stops rocking.)

PRESIDENT: I fear you and I are not on the same wavelength, Mr. M.

MOLIÈRE: What if you declared next month "National Celebrate the Aliens Month"?

PRESIDENT: I'd probably be impeached.

MOLIÈRE: By half your population. The other half would cheer.

PRESIDENT: Half our population might cheer perhaps, but ninety percent of the House and Senate wouldn't. I'd be impeached.

MOLIÈRE: Ah, well, your House and Senate have embraced a policy of Eternal War for two decades now. By adopting that policy your governments are always looking for military solutions, and have spent fifteen years with your bombing and invasions creating hundreds of millions of Arabs and others who hate you and will resist you. And now with your aggressive actions against us you're turning most of us against you. Do you think your government will ever question the wisdom of the disastrous policies you've been following for so long?

(The president sighs.)

PRESIDENT: I doubt it.

FORTY-NINE

(From *LUKE'S TRUE UNBELIEVABLE REPORT OF THE INVASION OF THE FFS*, pp. 229–236)

CI Rabb was happy when he was notified that his limo had arrived to take him to the NSA Unit Leaders Meeting. He walked down the steps of his Washington town house, happy to let the driver open the limo door, and happy to slide into his seat and let the door softly shut after him.

Then he noticed another man was already in the car. He turned and saw that the man was dressed exactly as he was. Even more amazing, he looked absolutely identical to CI Rabb. The only difference was that this twin was wearing gray suede gloves.

"We're late," the man said.

"Who… who… are you?"

"I'm Chief Investigator Rabb of Unit A," he answered. "I assume that's who you think you are too?"

"Stop the car!" CI Rabb shouted.

The car simply drove on, and when the driver turned around to smile at him, Rabb was horrified to see that the driver was new and although he was dressed in a chauffeur's uniform, his face looked exactly like Rabb's too.

"What… what's going on!?" he asked the man in the back seat.

"One of us is due at the eleven o'clock Unit Leaders Meeting. Do you want to handle it, or shall I?" The man's voice sounded exactly like Rabb's own.

Rabb reached over to claw at the other man's face, but his arm was easily clutched and held. With his other hand the new Rabb took a needle out of his suit jacket breast pocket and jabbed it into Rabb's arm.

"What are you doing!?" Rabb shouted.

"Gentlemen," CI Rabb began at the meeting that morning. "Today I'm going to give you a different report from the ones I've been giving you over the last half year. I'm sure some of you will be upset with what I'm going to say, but I have to say it.

"I believe that our policies in relation to the aliens are failing. I believe that our aggressive rounding up of the Proteans on any charges we think we can use, and kidnapping Proteans and taking them to black sites when we have no charges, have been turning hundreds of Proteans against us. I believe it's a major mistake that we've neglected to bring more Proteans into our corporations and government agencies to work *for* us rather than against us. As far as I know, there are presently only five such Proteans, one working in the Department of Human Services, one with Ben & Jerry's Ice Cream, one with an NSA unit in charge of cyber security, one with Google, and one with the National Council of Churches. We use as a reason for this neglect that no Protean can be trusted, but in each of the five cases where an agency or company has used a Protean he has been of great service.

"We know that these creatures use a computer more powerful than humankind can ever conceive of, and yet we've made minimum effort to get them working *for* us rather than against us.

"We must acknowledge that most of the original aliens

who arrived here on our planet had no interest in playing games that would damage our economic or military systems. That the vast majority of them were really here just to *play*, that most—"

"Oh, come on, Mr. Rabb," said the FBI director. "Let's not hear anything more about their damn play."

"You must admit that in the last few months getting people to play seems to be what most Proteans are trying to do."

"And those *Forthehelluvit* events are almost as destructive of our systems as their cyberattacks are on our agencies," said the FBI director.

"Nevertheless, most of the increase in the number of our Protean enemies has been created by our aggressive actions against the few who from the first were doing things that damaged us.

"Therefore I propose that the US Government declare an amnesty for all Proteans for anything they have done—"

"Oh, for God's sake," said someone.

"And invite all Proteans to come and work for our government in any way that they think they can be of service."

"Invite the foxes into the hen house!" said CIA Director Hilly Klington.

"The Proteans are not all foxes," said CI Rabb. "We'll find that most of them are chickens, and if we invite them in we may find they will roost and begin to lay eggs that will help feed our population."

"We'll convert Protean terrorists into chicks!" said Director Klington. "Maybe you can also tell us how we can convert Muslim terrorists into chipmunks!"

"The point is," said CI Rabb, "that we can't know if they

will work within our system rather than against it unless we invite them to do so!"

"It's too late!" said the FBI director.

"You're suggesting surrender," said Hilly Klington.

"I… I…" Suddenly CI Rabb stood up.

"I'm afraid I'm feeling unwell," he said. "You'll have to excuse me."

And CI Rabb ran on his short stubby legs from the room, seeming to shrink with every step he took.

A brief silence.

"Fire him immediately," said the FBI director.

FIFTY

(From *LUKE'S TRUE UNBELIEVABLE REPORT OF THE INVASION OF THE FFS*, pp. 237–240)

Agent Johnson arrived at work at his usual time of eight-thirty A.M. At nine A.M. CI Rabb arrived, greeted people along the hallway in his usual fashion and entered his office. He had Johnson summoned, and the two went over the latest worldwide developments. CI Rabb gave Johnson some minor new assignments. Agent Johnson found absolutely nothing out of the ordinary.

However, at nine-thirty CI Rabb unexpectedly and without explanation left the building.

A half hour later CI Rabb returned, coming in the door dressed exactly as he had been when he left, but with his tie and hair askew.

"I've been kidnapped!" he shouted, looking bewildered, and staggering down the hall as if drunk. "I've been kidnapped!"

Two women warily approached him to try to calm him down.

"What happened?" one of them asked.

"I was kidnapped!"

"But when?" asked the other. "You've only been gone from the office for thirty minutes."

Mr. Rabb stared wild-eyed at the woman.

"No, no, I haven't been free since yesterday morning. I was kidnapped!"

Agent Johnson heard the commotion and now approached his chief.

"But you and I met half an hour ago, Jim."

"No, no, that wasn't me! I'm me!"

"But yesterday... Exactly when were you kidnapped?" asked Rabb's administrative assistant, Carlo Minelli.

"On my way to work! There was another me in the car!"

"You didn't attend the Leaders Meeting?" Johnson asked.

"No, no, I was in a black hole with champagne and jelly beans!"

"You didn't make the presentation yesterday morning at the NSA meeting?" Agent Johnson persisted.

"No, no, that was him. I'm me!"

A crowd of more than a dozen had clustered around the seemingly deranged chief investigator, and Agent Johnson realized that this hallway meeting had to end.

"Into your office, Jim," he said. "We'll talk there."

"Call the FBI!" shouted Rabb. "I was kidnapped!"

Johnson took Rabb by the arm and walked him rapidly toward his office. Three others, including Carlo Minelli, followed the two men inside, the last one closing the door.

Johnson waited until CI Rabb had collapsed onto the couch and then turned to the others.

"Out!" he said. "Everyone out except Carlo and me. Now!"

Two of the men hesitated and then left the room.

"Lock the door, Carlo," Johnson said.

As Rabb's assistant locked the door, Johnson went to the big desk, pulled out a drawer and disabled the automatic tape-recording machine.

"The FBI!" Rabb shouted. "They still haven't been informed. Call Cake!"

"Get a sedative," Johnson said to Carlo, who quickly

moved to the bathroom off the office.

Johnson then walked slowly over and knelt down in front of CI Rabb.

"Take it easy, Chief. Everything's going to be all right. I've told Mrs. Argyle to call the FBI. You're safe here."

"He kidnapped me! Only caviar and jelly beans!"

"I know, Jim, I know. It must have been horrible."

"He was polite! Just like me. But *I'm* the real me!"

"You are, Jim, you are."

Carlo came up with a glass of water and a bottle of pills. Johnson took the bottle, checked what it was, poured out three pills and told CI Rabb to take them.

"They'll improve your memory," he explained.

"I remember everything!" Chief Rabb shouted. "I was kidnapped!"

"The pills will counteract the drug that the… the other you must have gotten you to drink."

"The champagne! It was poisoned!" He grabbed the pills, stuffed them into his mouth and took two big swigs from the glass of water.

"You'll be all right, Jim. You can relax now."

After ten minutes Chief Investigator Jim Rabb calmed down and told Johnson and Carlo what had happened. Perhaps.

He told about getting in the limo, seeing his twin and being jabbed with a needle. When he awoke, he was in a dark room with only a mattress on the floor and a small sink and toilet. His watch said it was ten o'clock at night. Lying next to the mattress was a small tray. In the dim light from the single bulb overhead, Rabb saw that on the tray was an open bottle of champagne, an elegant, thin long-stemmed glass holding something bubbly that looked like the champagne, a large plate containing crackers and caviar, and a huge plastic cup heaped with jelly beans.

It wasn't until nine the next morning that Rabb was disturbed. His cell door was opened and there was again the man who looked exactly like him.

"Hi," the man said. "Hope you slept well."

"I barely slept at all," said Rabb, whose speech was somewhat slurred from having drunk most of the bottle of champagne between seven and eight that morning.

"Well, we'd better get going. You're already more than an hour late."

"You're coming too?"

"No, only one of us should show up. Probably this time, it best be you."

When Rabb had finished his story of the kidnapping, Carlo asked, "Did you come into the office as usual this morning, Chief? At nine?"

"That wasn't me! I'm me!"

"Of course you are," said Johnson, then handed him the glass of Scotch and water that he'd gotten Carlo to make. Then both men went off to the far side of the office.

"We've got to warn everyone that the aliens can imitate humans," said Carlo excitedly. "We no longer can be certain of anyone!"

Johnson stood looking out the window.

"We've got to sound the alarm!" Carlo persisted.

"No."

"What do you mean 'no!?' We've got to act!"

"No."

"What are you saying!?"

"Think about it, Carlo. What will happen if everyone in every spy agency thinks that the aliens can pass as any human being they want."

"It's a disaster! They can totally manipulate us!"

"Exactly. But what if this imitation Rabb is a one-off. What if it is very difficult for the Proteans to convincingly become human beings. This fake Rabb spent only half an hour at the NSA meeting, then pleaded illness and fled. He spent less than half an hour this morning in our offices faking Rabb, then made an excuse to leave. For some reason he apparently can't maintain a role for more than a short time."

"But they can do it! The terrorists can do it!"

"Also, why did the Protean Rabb bring the real Rabb to the office this morning? He thus let us realize that he had imitated the real Rabb. He *wants* us to sound a warning. He *wants* to create a panic."

Carlo was silent.

"If most Proteans can easily pretend to be an actual human being then there's little we can do about it. That way lies madness. We've got to bury this. Tell people that CI Rabb had a breakdown—is having a breakdown. He's insane. Of *course* there's no second CI Rabb. Of *course* he wasn't kidnapped."

Carlo remained silent.

Abruptly, Chief Investigator Rabb appeared and took Johnson by the collar of his suit jacket.

"I'm me, right?" he said pleadingly.

FIFTY-ONE

Louie's trial began with great visuals. The courtroom was packed. Six burly security men wheeled in a five-foot-square glass box with a tiny hatch on top. The glass was three inches thick. The hatch had a padlock on it so big it could have been used as an anchor for the *Queen Elizabeth*. The box was placed next to where Lita was sitting with her team of two defense attorneys. Inside the box was Louie.

A few people in the audience began to applaud, but whether they were applauding the security guys' great work on the cage or the appearance of Louie wasn't clear. The judge gaveled the people back to silence.

Lita rose and objected to this primitive and humiliating enclosure the prosecution was forcing her innocent client to endure. The judge ruled that the enclosure was necessary. Lita objected. The judge noted the objection.

After a few more legal technicalities were dealt with, the judge asked the prosecutor to make his opening statement. The prosecutor was a tall, emaciated guy with a huge mop of dark hair and dark, piercing eyes. He rose and ambled over to the jury.

The jury, which had taken two weeks to empanel, consisted of twelve typical American citizens—meaning a quarter of them thought Jesus would be coming soon, that Iraq had taken out the Twin Towers, that Donald Trump was an intellectual giant, and that the Protean invaders were the Antichrists. Another third believed that there was nothing wrong with America that sealing off all our borders and getting rid of all liberals and black people wouldn't cure. The rest were too miscellaneous to describe.

"Ladies and gentlemen of the jury," says the prosecutor in a deep booming voice that would have made any prophet proud, "the prosecution's case is simple—"

"Point of order, Your Honor."

Lita stands and faces the judge.

"Mrs. Morton, the prosecutor has just begun his opening statement. What possible point of order can you have at this stage?"

"I'm sorry, Your Honor," Lita begins with that wonderful soft steely voice that turns me on even when she's discussing baked beans and sauerkraut. "I probably should have made my point of order before Mr. Davis began, but listening to his opening words made me realize that we are wasting our time unless and until we settle a very basic point. May I approach the bench?"

The judge scowls.

"All right," he says finally.

Lita and the chief prosecutor come up close to the judge.

"So what is this important point?" asks the judge.

"Is the person locked up in the glass cube here the same man that Agent Johnson heard confess when he first accosted the defendant on Mr. Morton's boat on the Long Island Sound? Is the wrong alien being tried here?"

"This is ridiculous," whispers the prosecutor.

"This trial cannot proceed further," Lita continues serenely, "unless and until the prosecution can prove that the accused sitting in this glass monstrosity is indeed the alien named 'Louie' who is accused of the crimes cited in the indictment."

"Mrs. Morton," says the judge in a low voice, "the accused has been in custody for almost six weeks. This is the first time the court is aware of that you have questioned the identity of your client."

"Your Honor," says Lita, not quite whispering but in a soft voice. "In trying an alien, now defined as a non-mammalian human being, we are in uncharted waters. Normal human beings all look different from one another, and we often have either multiple witnesses to the identity of an accused, and/or we have fingerprint or DNA evidence associating an accused with a crime.

"In this case, we have nothing except the testimony of a single witness, Agent Michael Johnson, to the effect that the accused is in fact the same alien as the one who he alleges confessed to him on the boat. At no time did Mr. Johnson pick the defendant out of a line-up as the one who had confessed to him. He simply declares, 'Yes, that's the guy.' However, we all know that humans are usually unable to distinguish one alien from another. Before this trial can proceed, the court must hear evidence that the defendant is indeed who the prosecution claims he is."

"And how do you propose the court do this, Mrs. Morton?"

"With a traditional police line-up, Your Honor. Line up ten FFs—ten aliens—and let Mr. Johnson identify the one who confessed to him. That alien can then be tried."

"This is ridiculous, Your Honor," says the prosecutor. "We can't at this late date question who the defendant is. He's the hairy sphere locked up in the cube at the defense table. Let's move on."

Well, you didn't have to be a mind reader to see that the judge was a little uncertain what to do about this unique objection being raised by the defense. After a bit more give and take between Lita and the prosecutor, the judge sent them back to their seats and announced to the jury and to the courtroom that he was adjourning the trial to the next morning while he researched this pretty unique legal challenge.

Well, that night and the next day the press and the TV guys had a lot of fun with this.

"Who's Who?" headlined the *New York Post*.

"If Louie isn't Louie," questioned the *Washington Post*, "then who is he?"

A TV talking head wondered whether the Proteans could change their soul—who they were—as easily as they could change their shape. This would make prosecution of any single alien impossible. It was cheating.

The next morning, the judge ruled that before the trial could proceed, one or more witnesses must identify the defendant who confessed to Agent Johnson from a line-up of six aliens, the line-up to take place Monday morning at ten A.M.

Wow. The media had another field day: "Will The Real Louie Please Stand Up," headlined *The Post*.

A Republican candidate for president created a sensation when he declared in a major speech that all Proteans were in fact identical, and that unlike snowflakes, each of which is apparently unique, Proteans are all essentially clones—

identical in every way. There was no need to prosecute one that pretended to call himself Louie. The country wouldn't be safe until they were all wiped out.

FIFTY-TWO

(From *LUKE'S TRUE UNBELIEVABLE REPORT OF THE INVASION OF THE FFS*, pp. 242–247. Based on the tapes of the National Security Team Meeting on August 20th, obtained by a cyberattack made by Louie and shared with his friends. Those in attendance included the president, Defense Secretary Joe McKain, FBI Director Brandon Cake, Head of the NSA Jason Epstein, and CIA Director Hilly Klington. There were also six others. Agent Johnson wasn't present.)

"Thus, more than fifty of our men were killed, and hundreds wounded," concluded Secretary McKain.

"And it's the Protean terrorists who have caused, directly or indirectly, these deaths," said Hilly Klington.

"But weren't men working on the ship's computer systems to undo the Protean's hacking?" said the president. "Isn't it possible that some error made by these men caused the explosion?"

"Mr. President," Secretary McKain said, "we will come up with evidence that Protean terrorists were to blame for the explosion—just give us another day or two."

The door to the room burst open, and former Chief Investigator James Rabb and his assistant, Carlo Minelli, rushed into the room closely followed by five Secret Service men.

"Mr. President!" shouted CI Rabb. "This is *me*!"

"What is this!?" Secretary McKain exploded. "What are these men doing here!?"

Carlo Minelli rushed toward the president until he was grabbed by two Secret Service men.

"Mr. President," he shouted. "You must know that in this

very room right now there may be alien terrorists pretending to be human beings!"

Secretary McKain was silenced only for half a millisecond. "Nonsense!" he said loudly. "Get these men out of here!"

"Hold it," the president said. "I want to hear what they have to say."

Rabb, also being held by two Secret Service men, struggled toward the president.

"I'm me, Mr. President! But two weeks ago I was *not* me! An alien terrorist who looked like my twin kidnapped me and poisoned me with champagne and jelly beans and took my place at the meeting of the National Security Council. And since then Agent Johnson has tried to make people think I've gone crazy. But I'm not crazy! I'm me!"

This statement by Rabb affirming his sanity was met by a bit of healthy skepticism by most present.

"This man has been in a Walter Reed psychiatric clinic for the last ten days, sir," said Hilly Klington. "He is not himself."

"I *am* me! I am!"

"He's not insane!" said Carlo, still being held firmly by the Secret Service. "I went along with Agent Johnson, but I now know it's my duty to warn you that the Proteans can *become human beings*. We know they fooled us into thinking one of them was Mr. Rabb here, so we can be certain they can imitate other human beings. There may be a Protean terrorist here right now pretending to be one of us."

This little bombshell from Carlo stunned everyone. A few began looking at one other warily.

"You're saying, Mr. Minelli," said the president, "that you are convinced that some... alien was able to impersonate Mr.

Rabb and gave that strange talk to this group two weeks ago?"

"Yes, yes. There were two Mr. Rabbs that day. I know it!"

"What does Agent Johnson have to say about this?" said Jason Epstein.

"I didn't dare tell him about what I was going to do," said Carlo. "But he knows that what I'm saying is true."

"Then why did he tell us that Mr. Rabb had had a breakdown?"

"Because he was afraid that all of us would then look at everyone else as a possible Protean terrorist rather than a real human. He was afraid we'd all become paranoid."

Most in the room began to look uneasy. Suspicious. Paranoid.

It was rumored that one prominent member later admitted that he'd wanted to shout "Arrest everyone in this room!" but thought better of it when he realized that the five members of the Secret Service might actually be hidden Protean terrorists.

FIFTY-THREE

(From *LUKE'S TRUE UNBELIEVABLE REPORT OF THE INVASION OF THE FFS*, pp. 260–264)

The judge, prosecutor, and defense teams, the ten security men, Agents Johnson, Wall, and Kerry, and three pool reporters, all turned to watch as policemen carried a huge cubical cell with six FFs inside into the courtroom, and set it down on the floor near Judge Agassi's bench. Without hesitation, the judge asked Agent Johnson to approach and identify Alien 6, Louie.

Johnson walked toward the cube, but when six feet away began to frown. The six FFs were all in their spherical shape and all looked alike. Moreover, they weren't standing still but were milling around, weaving about as if in a slow-motion square dance. Lita later reported that even she couldn't be certain who was who.

"I can't identify Louie through the glass," Agent Johnson said, "especially with them all moving around."

The judge then called up the attorneys, and they had a long squabble about whether the aliens had to be let out of the glass cage to have a proper lineup. Even with ten security men in the room the prosecutor was uncomfortable with letting them out of the cage, but knew that his case depended on Johnson identifying Louie. While Carlita argued that Johnson should be able to ID them *in* the cage, the prosecutor found himself arguing that they must be let loose and forced to stand in a traditional straight line. The judge consulted with the head of security in the room, a Captain McCullough, and then decided in favor of the prosecution.

After all the security men had taken out their guns, and the tar hoses were ready and aimed, the six FFs were let out of the cage and ordered to stand in a straight line. Each took its place, and soon the six FFs were quietly lined up on the floor in front of Johnson: six identical hairy beach balls. Johnson looked at each briefly and then turned to the judge.

"The Louie I've known now for almost ten months," he said, "is the second alien from the left."

Just as most everyone in the courtroom began to squint at the second FF from the left, the six FFs rolled and milled around in utter confusion and then formed a new line.

"Alien 6, alias Louie," Johnson said calmly, "is now the FF on the far right."

The judge banged his gavel.

"If any of you Proteans moves from his present position," he said, "I will cite you with contempt of court and you will be held without bail. Stay where you are."

The six FFs stopped milling.

"Captain McCullough, please mark the defendant," said the judge.

The top security man quickly went up to the FF on the far right and zapped him with the handheld X-ray machine.

"Your Honor," said McCullough after examining the readout. "This Protean is the same as the one that I X-rayed in his cell yesterday."

"Of course he is," Johnson said triumphantly.

"Thank you, gentlemen," said Judge Agassi. "Captain McCullough, have your men put Alien 6 back in his glass cube. You other aliens are dismissed."

"Yippee!" said one of the six.

"Your testicles shall feed the fishes through all eternity," said another.

"Order in the court!" shouted the judge. "Mrs. Morton," he continued more calmly. "The prosecution witness has twice identified this Protean as the one who confessed to him on the boat. Captain McCullough has indicated that the Protean Agent Johnson identified is the same one who has been in our jails for almost a month. I conclude that the defendant has been adequately identified and the case may resume. Captain McCullough, please—"

"Stop!" came a booming voice.

Everyone turned to see two short uniformed security men and a man dressed nicely in a blue suit entering the courtroom.

"This man is a fraud!" barked the blue suit loudly.

"Order in the court!" shouted the judge. "What is the meaning of this!?"

The blue suit marched toward Johnson, his two security men with him.

"This man is not who he claims to be, Your Honor," he said. "He's actually an alien pretending to be Agent Johnson. He has purposely identified the wrong Protean."

Everyone looked at Johnson.

"Identify yourself, sir," said the judge to the newcomer.

"I am FBI Agent Arthur Whirl in charge of counterterrorism actions against Proteans."

The two short security men who had come in with Agent Whirl aggressively pushed and shoved the six FFs up against a wall, the FFs being amazingly passive.

"Check this gentleman's identification," said the judge to McCullough.

McCullough did so.

"It seems in order, Your Honor."

"This is ridiculous," said Johnson. "Ten people in this room can verify who I am."

"Proteans have the ability to duplicate themselves perfectly in the form of any human being they want," Agent Whirl addressed the room. "And we've intercepted messages that make it clear a Protean is imitating Agent Johnson in this courtroom." He turned to Johnson. "You are an alien terrorist in disguise."

"This man is a fraud," said Johnson. "I don't know why he's doing this, but he's a fraud. In fact… in fact… it's possible he himself is an alien pretending to be a human."

"Baloney," said one of Whirl's security men.

Johnson and Whirl stared at each other and everyone else stared at them.

"Tell me, Whirl," said Johnson. "Who can we call to verify that you're here at the orders of some superior?"

"You can call Director Klington herself," said Whirl aggressively. "And other agents are on their way here."

Johnson walked slowly toward Whirl and stopped only two feet away. He carefully examined the other man's face.

"My God, you *are* a Protean!" he said, and lunged at Whirl. He was shunted aside and staggered past him.

"Grab him!" Johnson shouted to Wall and Kerry.

The two agents rushed up to take hold of Whirl, who spun away. As they turned to continue their attack, the two short security men who had come in with Whirl dived in, and soon all six men were wrestling, smashing into desks, breaking a wooden railing, toppling chairs. Two of the men fell to the ground in a wrestling embrace. The other security people rushed to the melee, but couldn't decide whose side to be on. Nevertheless three of them pitched in anyway, feeling it to be their duty.

BLAM!

A loud explosion was followed by debris flying from the wall about three feet below the ceiling. Then another BLAM! and more debris.

The fight broke up as all the men struggled up from the floor and looked to see a hole in the outside courtroom wall almost a foot wide.

"Yippee!" shouted one of the FFs.

Three of them began bouncing up and down, at first only four or five feet high, but then higher and higher, up almost to the twenty-foot-high ceiling. All of them began to sing "So long, it's been good to know ya…"

Louie and the other two FFs began to bounce too. One of the FFs disappeared through the hole in the wall. Two other FFs did the same, singing "So Long" as they went. One of the hot tar teams opened fire at the bouncing FFs, but Abe bounced himself off the wall and slammed into the man holding the hose sending him to the floor, the hose flying.

Louie was having trouble reaching the sixteen-foot-high level of the hole in the wall, but Molière gave him a boost and Louie made it to the edge.

"Love ya!" Louie shouted and disappeared.

Abe attacked the second hose holder but when he bounced away suffered a direct hit from the third team, sending him to the floor. He tried once to bounce, rose only three feet and was hit by another stream of tar. In another few seconds he was immobile on the floor. Just before the tar covered all of him Abe managed to shout something mostly intelligible but which ended with:

"…be all buried in shit higher than Everest…"

For a long moment everyone was speechless. Several police rushed to the door, others began speaking into radio transmitters attached to their noses or other body parts. Four cops tried to corral Abe, who was attempting to roll or hop but only looked like he was burping. Several security men uttered oaths that we won't repeat here.

Judge Agassi never lost his dignity. After about a half minute, he rose, his black robe swirling nicely around his legs.

"Because the defendant is no longer present in the courtroom," he announced with great dignity, "court is adjourned."

FIFTY-FOUR

(From Billy Morton's *MY FRIEND LOUIE*, pp. 377–382)

Well, the mass media noticed the escape. For most of the next week. Although their stories didn't always have much to do with reality.

It seems that the hole in the wall was caused by two FFs in a pickup truck fifty feet from the back of the building shooting two gray bowling balls with a powerful slingshot. You gotta hand it to the FFs: here are the most brilliant creatures in the history of our universe and what do they use to free some of their captured friends? A slingshot, with the ammo being a bowling ball. From the back of a ten-year-old Ford pickup.

Actually, Louie told me that the FFs had decided never to use any weapon against humans that we use to kill other humans. So they couldn't use grenades or artillery or any of the million weapons humans have developed to kill each other, and had to settle for a slingshot.

Where were the three cops stationed at the back of the building when the FFs shot their bowling balls? Working on a different case. It seems three drunks had staggered off the street toward the courthouse wall. Two of them were gals whose not extensive clothing was in disarray and the other a big guy who claimed the gals were molesting him. The gals claimed he was trying to take off their clothes, which, based on torn blouses and bras half-off, seemed a reasonable accusation.

The three cops worked to handle the situation. One of

them made a call for backup to come and get these drunks off their hands while the other two tried to hustle all three of them away from the courthouse wall. But all three seemed to want to stay near the courthouse—no matter how much the cops pulled at their arms or breasts.

The arrival of the pickup was not noticed. The two FFs in the back of the pickup, pulling back on a huge rubber band more than six feet long and five inches wide were not noticed. The flinging of a bowling ball at terrific speed toward the courthouse was not noticed.

However, the sound of the balls hitting the courthouse wall, and the falling of debris down on the cops and the drunks *was* noticed. The cops turned and saw the two FFs in the pickup truck and immediately pulled their guns and ran toward them, one of them beginning to blast away. The FFs flattened themselves in the truck as it quickly pulled away, all three cops now firing at it.

Behind them, at the courthouse, the FFs bounced down from the hole in the wall and rolled quickly away in different directions. The three drunks, suddenly sober, ran quickly into an alley and disappeared.

'Course my version of the escape, based on what Louie and Molière told me two days afterward, was not too similar to the one the authorities came up with. The official version, and the one that made it into the media, said nothing about three fake drunks distracting the cops and nothing about a slingshot and bowling balls. A "squad" of "Protean terrorists" had blasted the courthouse with an advanced bazooka-type weapon and escaped in a sophisticated eight-foot-long drone they'd made just for the occasion. The message was clear:

these Protean terrorists are capable of anything. Therefore, every red-blooded American, and even those with only pinkish blood, should be scared shitless.

Exciting as the "official" description of the escape was, the media are never satisfied with just one exciting version when other exciting versions are possible too. One candidate for president claimed that the hole in the courthouse wall was caused by a lightning bolt, which, since it was sunny and clear that day, had clearly come from the Ickie universe. The Protean terrorists could even hit us from their own universe. How could we possibly stop them!?

A more sober candidate suggested that Muslim terrorists, angry at the ways the FFs in the Middle East were thwarting their activities, had tried to blow up the whole building but had managed only a one-foot hole in one wall.

The citizens of our great nation were divided on what to think about the Great Courtroom Disappearing Act. Those who still liked the FFs thought their disappearance was a gas. Those who were frightened of the FFs which, thanks to the hard work of the NSA propaganda campaign, and to the media's love of promoting fear, was now more than half the country, were just frightened: the FFs couldn't seem to be stopped.

Two days after the Great Courtroom Disappearing Act, Louie-Twoie snuck into our house disguised as the end of a wet mop held by our cleaning lady, who was coming to do her once a decade cleaning. LT had at last mastered the art of speaking and he told us that things were getting interesting. Unfortunately, he had fine-tuned his English by watching Bugs Bunny cartoons for hours on end and had adopted that voice as his own. I kept expecting him to say "What's up, doc?"

Unlike with us humans, where things getting "interesting" means big trouble, for the FFs things getting interesting was the highest praise. After LT had told us everything, I think maybe "big trouble" is more accurate.

Louie of course was again freed, but Abe had been captured and no one knew where they had taken him. Molière, Gibberish, Baloney, and Oops had now been added to the FBI's ten most wanted list. That list was now so filled with FFs that American criminals were petitioning the FBI for a separate list just for normal red-blooded American crooks and murderers. They were feeling left out.

It was only from LT that we learned that the FFs had had two plans to free Louie, a backup in case the bowling balls didn't work.

It was Gibberish disguised as Agent Whirl, and Baloney and Oops disguised as the two short security men he brought with him. They had hoped to convince the judge that Johnson was an FF in disguise and take Louie into custody themselves. When the bowling balls worked they simply disappeared out the door during all the chaos of everyone trying to stop the bouncing FFs.

FIFTY-FIVE

(From Billy Morton's *MY FRIEND LOUIE*, pp. 383–386)

But though Louie was free, more than fifty FFs were locked up around the world. As a result, Louie had contacted Machiavelli for a meeting with Agent Johnson and the head of the NSA, a guy named Epstein. The meeting would include himself, Molière, LT, Machiavelli, and Gibberish. The meeting took place in the middle of New York Harbor less than a quarter mile from the Statue of Liberty, on a yacht owned by bad old Harry Barnes. Harry had apparently come to realize how much he was enjoying his new life being blackmailed by the FFs and getting less wealthy every day. Rumor had it that his personal fortune was down to two hundred million.

Here's LT's account of that meeting:

"We're here to talk about changing some of the game rules," says Molière to Machiavelli and Gibberish and to Johnson and Epstein. "Too many FFs are in the penalty box. Our games aren't advancing. We want to talk about a re-deal."

"Ah, you wish to surrender, is that it?" says Machiavelli.

"Not exactly," says Louie. "What we propose is to take a few of our players out of the game before they get killed. Let them go back to Ickie."

"Ahh."

Louie turns to Johnson and Epstein.

"We propose that every FF in some sort of imprisonment

be freed under the condition that he return to Ickieland."

"No way," says Epstein.

"Your side gets rid of the trouble of trying to imprison us and having to give us public trials."

"These creatures have committed crimes and must pay."

"These trials will hurt your side as much as ours. We will get to explain and defend our actions, giving us massive propaganda power. If you find one of us guilty all you achieve is keeping them off the streets until they die of natural causes. Or of suicide in your jails, an act you claim whenever an FF dies in your custody. Our proposal will let you get rid of them now—within a week or two."

"And besides," adds Gibberish, "it's a long American tradition to try to get rid of undesirables by sending them back to where they came from. A hundred and seventy years ago your people were red hot to send all the blacks back to Africa. Just consider us as particularly obnoxious blacks."

"That was back then," says Epstein. "But this is the twenty-first century. Times have changed."

"So I notice," says Louie. "Now you shoot blacks or lock them up."

"A bit like what you're doing to us," says Gibberish.

"Damn it, we—"

"In exchange for their freedom," says Louie, "all imprisoned FFs will agree to go back to our Liberia: Ickieland."

"We should consider this proposal," says Johnson to Epstein.

"Why should we free *any* prisoners?" says Epstein. "We're beginning to win this war. And besides, the only Protean who's escaped in the last half year is this Louie here. All our

Protean prisoners are effectively out of this war—or 'game' as you call it—whether they're in your Ickieland or in jail."

"No, they're not," says Molière. "They can talk to the press, they can communicate with hundreds of other FFs even when they're locked up in jail. As long as they're here on Earth they're in the game and powerful players in the game."

"And what do you FFs gain by having fifty or sixty of your friends return to Ickieland?" asks Agent Johnson.

"We'd know that friends whose lives are now in danger are safe," says Louie. "They'll live to play other games."

"But I'm sure you must think that somehow it also helps your side in its efforts to destroy our civilization," says Epstein.

"Not at all," says Louie. "And besides, we don't want to destroy your civilization. If we'd wanted to do that we could have done it in a couple of hours a year ago. Relax, we're on the side of life on Earth—even human life."

The next thing LT told us made us realize how serious Louie must think things were getting. In FF lingo "serious" is the worst things can be. LT told us that the FFs were planning the first great worldwide conference of FFs to take place since they'd arrived a year ago. FFs from all over the world were to gather in the ocean off the East Coast of the United States to decide if any of their games should be abandoned, or have their rules changed, and what new games various FFs wanted other FFs to join. Many would swim to the meeting place, while others planned to buy, rent, or hijack seaplanes or high-powered sea-going yachts. The business portion of the conference would take about thirteen minutes our time, but then most of the FFs would want to hack around and play a bit with their ocean friends. Then, in less than a day, it would be back to playing around the world.

When we asked LT how many FFs would be there, he said he wasn't sure since FFs were creating little FFs all the time and their population was exploding, but his best estimate was about 2,207. Some FFs didn't want to abandon the games they were playing and thus couldn't make it. When Lucas asked if it wasn't dangerous to gather so many FFs in one place and whether they worried about the Government finding out and trying to kill them, LT said: "Well, FFs never worry, Lucas, but we're aware of possible countermoves."

"You'd better be," says Lita.

ITEM IN THE NEWS

A FEW MORE DEFINITIONS FROM THE NEW PROTEAN DICTIONARY OF AMERICAN USAGE

ALI, MUHAMMAD: Black American boxer who changed the culture of sport and was wise enough to see through the lies of the nation he was born in and stand up against them. A one in a million human being.

ANOTHER IDEA: What the universe generates whenever a human being comes up with a plan.

BELIEFS: Organized systems of thought whereby humans fool themselves into thinking they know something.

BITCH: Female dog. Also female human having a bad day. *See asshole.*

BULLSHIT: Term used by human beings to describe most human discourse. *See baloney.*

CONSUMER: A human being in an advanced civilization.

COPS: Uniformed officials of the state used to keep the poor in their place—usually jail.

GOD: An imaginary entity given different attributes by every human being. Considered by many to have created man in his own image. Yet few blame him for this.

HUMAN BEINGS: The planet's way of committing suicide.

ICKIES: Intelligent creatures from Universe 699B-234 (Boodle Map). Very full of themselves and not to be trusted.

INHERITANCE TAXES: Taxes encoded in law to distribute some of the excessive wealth of the rich to the general population and to give the people a slightly fairer chance to play in the money game. Currently being dismantled by the wealthy and their representatives so that the people won't have a slightly fairer chance to play in the money game.

KING, MARTIN LUTHER: Civil rights activist who opposed American military invasions of other countries, opposed the inequalities of wealth, opposed suppression of labor, and opposed his society's efforts to keep black people as second-class citizens. Remembered only for the last.

KISSING: One of the better human inventions.

LEGAL SYSTEM: A complex system of laws designed to keep in place the established system of government and financial dealings. Like all systems in modern capitalist nations the system works for people with money but not for those without money. As a result people are prosecuted for breaking trivial laws involving very little money, but rarely prosecuted for crimes involving millions of dollars.

MILITARY–INDUSTRIAL COMPLEX: Those corporations, defense department agencies, congressmen, generals, admirals, mercenaries that work assiduously together to increase the power of these corporations, defense department agencies, congressmen, generals, admirals, and mercenaries so that the nation may continue its journey toward self-destruction. A famous Republican president warned the nation about the growing power of this military–industrial complex. All that is now remembered of him is that his name was Ike.

MONEY: The be-all and end-all of modern civilization.

OLD AGE: State reached at different ages by different people. Considered by some humans as pretty much a disaster and others as a mellow old time full of fun. Brains don't remember, arms don't lift, feet don't run, penises don't rise, sounds don't register, food doesn't taste, friends all die, but otherwise a mellow old time full of fun.

PENIS AND BALLS: Human organs noted for acting independently of the brain. Leading determinate of male behavior.

PRIMITIVE MAN: A human being who is not a consumer.

PROFESSIONAL FOOTBALL: The sport that legalizes black men hitting white men as hard as they want. Favorite sport of black men.

SAUDI ARABIA: The country that contributed fifteen of its citizens to killing more than two thousand people at the World Trade Center, that suppresses most women's rights, that beheads people on a regular basis, that contributes money to support Sunni terrorists like ISIS, that bombed Yemen back into the Stone Age, and has been America's favorite nation among Arab countries for more than seventy years.

SLEEP: State in which human consciousness rests. Often not distinguishable from waking state.

TEENAGER: Human between the ages of thirteen and nineteen. Noted for doing things which human beings over the age of thirty desperately wish they could still do.

TWITTER: An internet site that permits human beings to share profound thoughts and serious philosophies in two sentences or less.

UNITED KINGDOM: US aircraft carrier lying off the coast of Europe, used for bombing Arabs in various places in the Middle East and Africa.

WALMART: Famous for shifting hundreds of thousands of jobs overseas, paying its employees low wages, driving thousands of small companies out of business, and making members of the Walmart family billionaires. Consistently voted by the Chamber of Commerce Corporation of the Year.

ZEN: An Eastern mode of thought that appears to be strikingly similar to Ickian non-thought.

FIFTY-SIX

(From *THE OFFICIAL HISTORY OF THE ALIEN INVASION, Volume II*, pp. 279–282. Notes from the second half of the meeting on August 2nd of the National Security Team after the removal of Rabb and Minelli. Some of the material has been redacted for the purposes of national security, but will be released in three centuries' time.)

SECRETARY McKAIN: There you have it, Mr. President. We know now that Protean terrorists can impersonate human beings. They are thus even more dangerous to us than we had realized. But even without this latest outrage of our brave sailors being murdered in the Persian Gulf, we know the Proteans are every day destroying our economy and our way of life. Their seducing of so many of our citizens into their *Forthehelluvit* activities has made normal business life difficult, if not impossible. The stock market is down more than forty percent. More than a dozen companies have gone into bankruptcy. Unemployment has soared to a level not seen since the last big recession in '08. We are losing our power to suppress the Sunni and Shiite terrorists in the Middle East. Our nuclear deterrence has become compromised. If we don't eliminate the Protean terrorists we're doomed.

PRESIDENT: We are not doomed, sir.

SECRETARY McKAIN: Doomed. Another year like this and our economy and military forces will be a complete shambles, rather than the mostly shambles they are now.

PRESIDENT: And what are you proposing that we do now that we're not already doing?

(Sounds of whispering among some of the participants.)

HILLIE KLINGTON: Mr. President, we have reason to believe that the Protean terrorists are planning to xxxxxxxxxxxx xxxxxxxxxxxxxxxxxxxxxxxxxxxxxxxxxxxxxxxxxxxxxxxxx xxxxxxxxxxxxxxxxxxxxxxxxxxxxxxxxxxxxxxxxxxxxxxxxx. We feel that this event will give us a unique once-in-a-lifetime opportunity to take down their leadership. What we propose is that we xxxxxxxxxxxxxxxxxxxxxxxxxxxxx xxxxxxxxxxxxxxxxxxxxxxxxxxxxxxxxxxxxxxxxxxxxxxxxx xxxxxxxxxxxxxxxxxxxxxxxxxxxxxxxxxxxxxxxxxxxxxxxxx xxxxxxxxxxxxxxxxxxxxxxxxxxxxxxxxxxxxxxxxxxxxxxxxx xxxxxxxxxxxxxxxxxxxxxxxxxxxxxxxxxxxxxxxxxxxxxxxxx xxxxxxxxxxxxxxxxxxxxxxxxxxxxxxxxxxxxxxxxxxxxxxxxx and thus eliminate much of the danger facing us.

(A long silence.)

PRESIDENT: That's outrageous.
SECRETARY McKAIN: But absolutely necessary.

(Long silence.)

PRESIDENT: I'll take it under consideration.

FIFTY-SEVEN

(From Billy Morton's *MY FRIEND LOUIE*, pp. 390–393)

"We've decided to organize the biggest *Fun-In* in human history," says Molière from the top of a file cabinet.

We were all in Lita's office at the Protean Defense League: Molière, Louie, LT, Baloney, and Gibberish, who had apparently rejoined the good guys for reasons no one would explain to me. Karen was at the meeting too, along with six other human friends of the FFs, including Harry Barnes.

"The *Forthehelluvit* event to end all *Forthehelluvit* events," adds Gibberish.

"Baloney," says Baloney.

"And present our plan to the big FF convention coming up in two days out in the Atlantic," says Louie. "We hope to get many FFs from around the world to join us."

"Exactly what do you have in mind?" asks Lita. She's at her desk, I'm in the only comfortable chair in the room, and Jimmy and Lucas are sitting on two extremely hard chairs normally intended for visiting lawyers or Feds. Four of the other humans, including Karen, are crowded onto a settee. Harry Barnes is standing in the middle of the room looking like he's ready to take over the meeting.

LT has assumed the shape of an owl, with two beautiful walnut eyes, painted white and brown. Can't fly though, so he just sits on a windowsill looking wise. Never seen him so inactive.

"This Labor Day," says Molière, "we plan to get every group we can find and seduce them to march—for the hell of it."

"We think we can get more than a hundred different groups, unions, churches, leagues, the Boy Scouts and Girl Scouts, leftist and rightest organizations, governmental agencies, brokerage house employees, high school bands, office workers—you name it—we're trying to get them to join us on the first Saturday in September."

"The NYPD know about this?" says I.

"We've invited the Patrolmen's Benevolent Association of New York, but so far they've given us no firm commitment other than that they'll hassle us to the best of their ability."

"You trying to get *them* to join the march?" I ask.

"We're also trying to get government workers from six different agencies, including the Department of Defense and the CIA."

"Jesus."

"We're arguing that they can monitor what's happening better if they're marching with us than any other way," says Molière.

"Baloney," says Baloney.

"The plan is to have groups start out from all five boroughs of New York and march until they all converge on Central Park."

"And then what?" asks Lita.

"Then we all settle into the park and have fun."

"And what's it all supposed to prove?" she asks.

"Absolutely nothing," says Gibberish. "No creature in its right mind ever tries to prove anything."

"Baloney."

"And how long will people stay in Central Park?" I ask.

"Ahh, interesting question," says Louie.

"Until we all march out of the park and take over Manhattan," says Gibberish.

"And what's taking over Manhattan involve?" asks Lita.

"Ahh, interesting question," says Molière.

"We shall see what we shall see," says Gibberish.

"Profound," says Baloney.

"What did you say?" says Gibbs, startled.

"Baloney."

"To accommodate the half million or so you hope to have march into the park," Harry says from the middle of the room, "we're going to have to do a lot of advanced planning—food, shelter, porta-potties, blankets, tarps. Have you done any planning yet for contingencies?"

"A lot of planning," says Molière. "And we'll need a lot of help from every human in this room, you especially, Harry. And the dozens of other humans we're working with on this."

"You can't pull off a big event like this," says Harry, "without a lot of planning."

"And a lot of money," says Karen.

"Exactly," says Harry.

"We've begun to run short on our stolen loot," says Louie, "so we may have to tap you, HB, for a few million. That work for you?"

"*Mi moola es su moola,*" says Harry.

"But whatever we do, we've got to keep it light," says Gibberish. "We're not trying to overthrow Western civilization, only have fun and let a few humans have fun too."

"Can't we do both?" I ask.

"Ah, Billy," says Louie, "you still haven't got it."

"What's that mean?"

"It means that the answer is no." Louie says. "You won't get far if you pursue with seriousness the overthrow of the system. Only when you learn to play will your civilization change. If you fight it, the forces of the system will absorb every blow and leave you feeling you're fighting a war buried in molasses. Change the way you live. Learn to play. Make fun of the dictators, don't fight them. Only then will the system slowly change."

"All of life is a great mystery," suddenly comes from the owl on the windowsill. "Only fools try to figure it out."

We all stared at LT, whose walnut eyes were slowly revolving as if he were drunk.

"Baloney," says Baloney.

FIFTY-EIGHT

(From Billy Morton's *MY FRIEND LOUIE*, pp. 398–403)

When Louie invited me and Lita to go out onto the Atlantic on Harry Barnes' big yacht and see the earth's first great gathering of the FFs I was naturally gung-ho to do it. I loved being with FFs and I loved being out on the ocean.

Naturally Lita vetoed it. Even Louie admitted that they'd learned that the government had asked some sort of special operations unit to look into ways they could kill as many FFs as possible on this wonderful occasion. Louie tried to assure her that their computer hacking was keeping them pretty much up to date on the government's plans, but Lita said that "pretty much" was not the same as second-by-second knowledge of what the military was up to. Lita assured me that it wasn't that she minded my getting killed so much as that the kids might get upset. That gave us a laugh, but it still left me feeling frustrated: I really wanted to go.

But as you know, arguing with Lita is like arguing with a blizzard—no matter what I say, I get snowed under.

So I did what every red-blooded man has to do every now and then—I decided to ignore her and sneak out to sea without her permission. And with any luck I'd get blown up or drowned and not have to face the consequences with Lita.

I wanted to take the boys too, but there are limits to my stupidity.

Out on the Atlantic on Harry's yacht *Big Bucks* I had just as great a time as I thought I would. We were surging along at forty knots, heading to a rendezvous point about halfway between New York Harbor—from where we left—and Bermuda.

At first there were a dozen FFs, half that I already knew, and two dozen human beings, most that I didn't know—Harry, Karen, and my secretary, Althea, being the ones that I did. The humans were drinking a lot of Harry's high-priced booze, and the FFs were bouncing around the boat and diving into the ocean or surging up out of the ocean shaped like long fish and then landing on deck as spheres. Although I wasn't sure, it seemed as though the whole first day and night dozens of new FFs were popping up onto the boat, spending ten or fifteen minutes with us, and then diving back into the ocean. LT told us that they could swim as fast or faster than our yacht was going so didn't really need a ride.

Meeting new humans who had made friends with the FFs was fun. We traded our tall tales about how we'd met our FF or FFs and what we were doing with them—or rather what they were doing with us.

One gal told me that she met her FF when she and her boyfriend were making love at a campsite in the woods. She suddenly noticed past her guy's shoulder a round beach ball rolling slowly around them. She knew what an alien terrorist looked like, so she screamed, figuring she was about to be murdered or raped. But the beach ball began talking to her and her guy, and told them he was just passing by and enjoyed seeing human beings enjoying life. It took about three hours but this FF—she named him "Peeping Tom"—managed to convince her that FFs were not terrorists. He wanted her help in getting her Christian sect to assist the FFs in getting money and food to some pretty hard up people in her town of Newburgh. Which she and her guy ended up doing.

When I figured we must be getting close to the meeting site, about four P.M. on the second afternoon, we began to see a lot of porpoises swimming along in our direction, and a few FFs among them bursting out of the water in all variety of fish shapes. At first there were only fifty or sixty, but as we continued to move east the fleet grew. Soon there were hundreds on each side of our boat doing leaps and somersaults that made Marine World look like a kid's fishbowl with a few goldfish.

Our ship began to slow, dropping to fifteen knots, so soon the FFs and the porpoises, and now at least two dozen orcas were swimming in circles around us, and around two other large boats that were now within a quarter mile of us. FFs were again surging up onto the boat and then seconds or minutes later diving back into the ocean.

Normally I like being out on the sea because there's no one else around, but this day I stood stupidly smiling for half an hour at this incredible jubilee of play: thousands of FFs and sea creatures swimming and diving and dancing among a fleet of about ten ships. This planet had never seen before and probably never will again such a gathering.

The *Big Bucks* and most of the other boats stopped moving and we all wallowed in the gentle swell. Gibberish, Louie, and LT had plopped up onto our deck and soon they and five or six of us humans got into a pretty interesting chat. It began when Althea asked if FFs had personalities or characters.

"We have acts," says Gibberish. "Many acts. You people might call them personalities, but we call them 'acts' or, more accurately, 'adoptive temporary lunacy.'"

Karen and I and a couple of others laughed.

"What's that mean?" Althea asks.

"It means," says Gibbs, "that everything we do is an act, is pretending, is play, and because our actions are never necessarily related to reason, we think of it as temporary lunacies."

"Great," says I. "Makes me feel real important."

"You know that feeling important is at the heart of the human sickness," says Louie. "If humans could just let go of the feeling that you as an individual and humans as a species are important, you'd be cured. You'd begin to live at one with each other and with all the life around you, as the creatures we're watching are doing. Instead, somehow over the last three or four thousand years you've come to feel you're God's chosen people, the only beings who count."

"And what a disaster that's making of things on Earth," says Gibbs.

"Don't all creatures naturally feel they're the center of the universe?" says Karen. "Isn't that what each life form needs for its survival."

"Other forms of life have no sense of importance at all," says Gibbs.

"We know," says LT. "We've talked to hundreds of thousands of them."

'Course, none of us humans had lately had a good chat with a tulip, bumblebee or amoeba, and that pretty much undercut any rebuttal one of us might want to make.

Nevertheless, I was about to say something witty or clever, when Louie and Gibberish suddenly leapt over the ship's railing and into the sea. LT bounced toward the rail and then back again.

"They're going to drop a nuclear bomb on us, and we don't think we can stop them," he says.

All but one or two of the FFs leapt into the sea. I turned and headed up to the bridge. LT came with me and so did Karen. Even as I climbed the stairs I could feel our yacht accelerating and turning.

Harry Barnes was on the bridge with the captain, and Harry looked more worried than I'd ever seen him. The captain stood next to the crewman who was at the helm and had turned us back west at full throttle.

In the sea around us I could no longer see a single creature, not even a seagull.

"Anyone know when the big bang is coming?" I ask, more to break the silence than because I wanted an answer.

Harry Barnes shook his head and the others were silent.

We all waited. It wasn't good for my digestion to be creeping along at forty knots expecting to be blown up any second, so I swallowed a shot of Harry's expensive bourbon. Didn't help.

I was about to try a second drink when Baloney appeared and told us that Louie, Molière, and an FF named Brain were back on our boat trying to defuse the bomb or mess with the evil bomber's computer system to prevent it from reaching the right location. I went down to the master cabin where they were working.

The three FFs and two crewmen were working from two computers. One could never tell from its bearing whether an FF was happy or scared or gloomy, but the fact that all three of them were totally motionless except for their numerous digits was not a good sign. I can only relax when I see FFs bouncing.

"Five more minutes," says Louie.

"Five more minutes for what?" I ask.

"Until the plane is over its intended target."

"Aren't all the FFs like us scooting away at full speed?"

"Yes. But they were only warned twelve minutes ago. Even at a mile a minute a lot of them are still going to be within range of any blast."

"Can't you guys just dive down half a mile and escape damage that way?"

"We're like porpoises: we can't go deeper than five or six hundred feet."

After a bit, "Four minutes," says Molière.

A lot of unintelligible stuff was happening on both computers, and I knew both Louie and Molière were focused on trying to save everyone. Talking to us took only a millionth of their attention so I didn't feel guilty nagging them with questions.

"Are we going to die?" I ask.

"Yes," says Molière. "You're going to die."

"In that case anyone got any candy or bourbon?"

"You'll die," says Louie, "although perhaps not today."

Perhaps: not exactly the most reassuring word in the history of the world.

I didn't want to die inside—even with some friends in a fancy master stateroom—so I left and went back up on deck. The sun was shining, the sea had a nice gentle swell and a few pretty white caps, and everything was hunky-dory. Nothing to fear but fear itself. And a nuclear explosion.

I saw the crew had gotten the ship's two lifeboats loose from their davits and sitting on deck. And a big rubber dinghy too.

The ship's first mate was ordering a crewman aboard each.

The two crewmen who'd been with the FFs at the computers suddenly came hurrying out onto the deck. I didn't have to ask them if the FFs had succeeded or failed: their frightened faces said it all.

So I rushed back up to the bridge. I wanted to have the best view possible if I was to get converted into smithereens.

When I arrived, only the man at the wheel was staring forward—LT, the captain, Harry, Karen, and two new crewmen were all staring aft. I joined them. I was just about to ask where the bourbon bottle had gone when the beautiful blue noonday sky behind us to the east exploded. The brilliant flash blinded me. As I waited with my eyes not seeing much and braced myself against the aft wall, I was suddenly slammed hard and flat against the aft part of the bridge, and then, as I struggled to clear my woozy head, thrown sideways to the floor. Someone tumbled on top of me and rolled away.

As I lay there stunned, I found myself sliding sideways up against and then onto the port side of the bridge cabin. Half-blind and still woozy from slamming my head, I wasn't thinking with my usual brilliant clarity and vaguely wondered why I seemed to be lying on the side wall of the bridge instead of the floor. And then I wondered why the water that was beginning to fill the bridge cabin was rising around me and not on the floor where it belonged.

My vision was still blurred, but I struggled to sit up to keep my head above the rising water, vaguely thinking how clever I was to sit up and thus not drown.

Then someone grabbed my arm. The water was at my chest.

"Get up!"

It was Harry Barnes. With his help I managed to get to my feet. I still couldn't see anything clearly, but the next thing I knew we were both tumbled again and were splashing in the water—on the ceiling. I finally realized that the *Big Bucks* had been knocked first on her side and now had totally turned turtle. Those of us still in the bridge cabin were twenty feet beneath sea level, and in another couple of minutes would be ten thousand feet below sea level.

I was now scared shitless. Not literally—I still have good poop control—but my entire life flashed before me, which was actually a bit boring since without a remote I couldn't slow it down—so it was just a blur of color and time.

When you get to my age and have to choose between taking things easy and dying, or doing something strenuous to survive, the first option has a lot of appeal. But suddenly I was gripped again by one shoulder and dragged toward the opening where the sea was surging in. I couldn't tell who it was, but a moment later someone grabbed my other arm and we pressed forward against the rush of incoming sea, me taking a mouthful of salt water before I wised up and held my breath.

And then we were outside the boat and rising. In only a few more seconds we burst up out of the wonderful Atlantic Ocean. And I breathed again.

Neither my eyesight nor my brain was functioning very well, but I finally realized that one of my rescuers was Karen. She was still with me, kicking with her legs and swimming hard with one arm away from the sinking yacht, pulling me behind her. My other rescuer had disappeared. I finally unwoozied enough to remember that I could swim, and began kicking my legs and freeing my arms to do my version of the crawl, which in my case means a crawl.

I was following close to Karen and couldn't see anything but the rise and fall of the swells that we were swimming through. If we were planning to swim back to New York City I doubted I'd make it. But after less than thirty seconds I saw Karen suddenly grasp the side of one of the fibreglass lifeboats, and a few seconds later we were both hauled up and into it. I would live to die another day.

It was LT who with Karen had gotten me out of that bridge coffin-in-the-making, and it was him or maybe another FF who'd gotten the lifeboat to come pick us up. The other lifeboat had capsized when thrown from the *Big Bucks*, but two crewmen were clinging to it and a third was swimming toward it. They all had lifejackets on, which made me wonder why none of the smart guys on the bridge had thought of putting one on. There were four of us in the lifeboat and we were motoring over to pick up the three men clinging to the overturned lifeboat.

I sat down in the bow of our boat holding firm to the port coaming, and wondering why my teeth were chattering and my whole body going into a long tremble. I guess the Atlantic water is cold. I looked to my right as we approached the capsized boat and then to the left. Then I suddenly saw Harry Barnes, waving a desperate arm at me from forty feet away. He was floundering.

"Get Harry first!" I shouted at the guy at the helm of our boat and pointed off to where Harry's wave was becoming more of a flailing grope. The guy looked at his buddies clinging to the boat and then to Harry flailing and sinking, and swerved away and picked up speed to save Harry.

We got him into the boat and looked around for any others that were alone in the water but saw none. We did sight the rubber dinghy with several people aboard it, one of them Althea. We sped back to pick up the men at the capsized lifeboat.

Harry knelt in the bottom of our boat, Karen hitting him on the back as he spat up seawater.

For half a minute, he gasped and shuddered and stared at the swishing water in the bilge. Finally he looked up at me sort of blankly. Then a vague smile came over his face.

"I insured the damn boat for almost fifty percent more than it's worth," he said.

"Holy Christ!"

As one of our crewmen helped his buddies up into our boat, he was staring off to the east, so I looked too.

A mountain range had suddenly grown up in the middle of the ocean, and it seemed to be making its not so leisurely way toward us. Not a mountain maybe, but a long hill twenty times higher than any wave I'd ever seen in fifty years at sea. It didn't really seem to be moving but rather simply growing taller and taller.

We were all of us mesmerized. We couldn't figure exactly how we were going to die, but I doubt that any of us were making plans for the next day.

The mountain grew and grew, and suddenly it was here and we were climbing it. The guy at the helm must have really known his business because he'd turned our tail toward the mountain just before it arrived, so that though the mountain was moving at thirty knots, we were moving at twenty-five in the same direction when it hit, so the mountain's impact was barely felt. And he slowed the boat as soon as we were in it, and we had the strange sensation of looking down the side of the mountain at the relatively calm ocean we'd just been on and feeling ourselves rising upwards at what seemed incredible speed. We kept rising and rising until the mountain peak suddenly passed under us and we saw it speeding away to the west, and we slowly began to descend its backside.

Holy Christ indeed. If someone could package what we'd just been through for a Coney Island ride, that someone would soon be richer than Harry. In less than a minute it seemed we were down in a valley and the helmsman had turned us back east and we were seeing a bunch of much smaller hills heading our way.

Not one of us had said a word during the entire experience.

"You all right?" Karen finally asked quietly.

I looked up at her in something of a daze and finally nodded.

"Sure," says I. "It'll take more than a nuclear bomb and a tsunami to do in old Billy Morton."

She didn't smile. Neither did I.

ITEM IN THE NEWS

(Being tweets from August 23rd)

@JLoBoy: I'm flying in from London and we just saw an incredible flash in the sky! Our plane went sideways!

@DumpyHumpy: Wow! Incredible flash above the water way off behind our boat! Big explosion? Big lightning storm?

@CannibusKim: Our plane is sinking! I think we're going to die!

@JLoBoy: We're still flying and no more flash in the sky. Scary.

@DumpyHumpy: We've been hit by a tidal wave! Our ship almost tipped over. Dining room a mess. Babs bloody nose.

@CannibusKim: We're still alive. Don't know how. Pilot says it was some sort of explosion but we're okay.

@maXimumLucy: Tsunami! Houses gone people washed to sea. Can't believe it!

@DumpyHumpy: Lot of people hurt. Big waves still coming but not like first. Babs very frightened.

@bermudacoastguard: Tsunami alert. Tsunami alert. Tsunami alert.

@maXimum Lucy: They're dead, they're all dead!

@uscoastguard: Possible tsunami approaching East Coast. All ships on high alert.

@maXimumLucy: Hundreds! No one to help. The whole North Point has disappeared under water.

@Peteyboy12: Just heard from @DumpyHumpy that his ship hit by big wave. May be on way here. Better check with weather bureau.

@GregsterEggster: Holy shit! The ocean is sinking. I can see beach now out half a mile. Sudden big leak?

@HappymanJunior: We've been hit by a monster wave! Half the village wiped out. Carry's house hit!

@uscoastguard: Emergency. Emergency. Emergency. Tsunami hitting Long Island, Cape Cod, Jersey coast. Full alert.

@GregsterEggster: Get out! Get out! Get to higher ground!

@Peteyboy12: Hit by tidal wave. Damage to some homes. All right here except for garbage cans.

@maXimumLucy: Our whole village is gone! All of Bermuda must be lost!

@HappymanJunior: We're still alive. House flooded to four feet but still standing. Carry's house gone. But she can swim.

@uscoastguard: All citizens on East Coast should take precautions against large waves.

@GregsterEggster: Finally, think we're safe. Jane and Kiki crying. Oh my God.

@HappymanJunior: House going! Outta Here!!!

@uscoastguard: Tsunami warning for now and next hour. Move to higher ground.

@GregsterEggster: So many bodies. So many bodies.

FIFTY-NINE

(From *LUKE'S TRUE UNBELIEVABLE REPORT OF THE INVASION OF THE FFS*, pp. 278–282)

The nuclear explosion five hundred miles northeast of Bermuda resulted in tsunamis that caused much destruction and over two thousand deaths. More than a hundred human friends of the FFs who'd been on boats in the area were killed and more than fifteen hundred people on the island of Bermuda. There was also widespread property damage and more than thirty deaths on the US East Coast. If the death and destruction had been limited to Bermuda, our government would not have suffered much bad publicity. Our killing hundreds if not thousands of Protean terrorists would justify some suffering on the part of the population of Bermuda, which was more than two-thirds black and multi-racial. However, the destruction or damage to thousands of homes along the East Coast, many owned by wealthy people with political power, was more difficult to justify.

Initially no official said a word about trying to destroy the aliens. The NSA had planned to release a story stating that there had been a tragic accident on a nuclear-powered submarine. A nuclear accident seemed the obvious best way to explain this tragic event, but before they released this explanation, an agent of the CIA suggested that they have an "anonymous source" release to a few key media sources a "reliable report" that the aliens had stolen a nuclear bomb and were transporting it to the United States when, either accidentally or on purpose, it exploded.

Wow! All the bureaucracies agreed that this CIA version was a masterstroke: it changed an accident on our part into a violent act of terrorism by our enemies. The Powers That Be pushed this version of events to every media outlet they had influence over, which was essentially all of them.

Unfortunately, enemies of the Powers That Be began to release their own version. Leftist blogs, news outlets, and social media sites all over the world reported that there was a giant gathering of aliens in the Atlantic, and that the American military had tried to wipe them out by dropping a nuclear bomb. Dozens of humans and FFs who had survived were interviewed and backed up this account.

At first, the Powers That Be had their media friends fight this version of events, pointing out that it had been created by the lying alien terrorists and by leftist intellectuals who were always seeing government conspiracies where there were none. Our leaders would never endanger American lives and property by such an act.

Unfortunately, the idea of an alien terrorist accident worked against the Powers That Be's year-long campaign portraying all aliens as super-bright beings capable of incredible things. How could they be so stupid as to have a bomb accidentally explode in the middle of a big family reunion when less intelligent human beings over a period of eighty years had never had such an accident? This was a bit difficult for an intelligent human being to accept.

Fortunately for the Powers That Be, most human beings are not intelligent and are totally under the influence of the mass media. Thus, the Powers That Be version of an alien-caused explosion was winning out, at least in the United States. The rest of the world was much more suspicious, and most media outlets went with the alien version that the US military had dropped a bomb on them.

Only the US Navy was permitted to have access to the site of the explosion. The Powers That Be were unable, however, to come up with any fake evidence that would back up their version of events over the aliens' version of events. The investigators found the remains of many porpoises and other sea-going creatures, along with the remains of Proteans and humans, but nothing to indicate who had dropped the bomb. The relatively few fragments of dead Protean terrorists made the authorities worry that they may not have killed as many of them as they'd hoped. Or had the surviving Proteans zapped the fragments back to their home universe for proper burial?

The experts aboard the Navy ships soon concluded that the nuclear explosion had occurred just above the water and not in it. They reported this to the Powers That Be, who requested that the Navy classify this information as Triple Top Secret, not to be opened until the year 4666. Unfortunately for the Powers That Be, many airline and ship passengers reported seeing a bright flash in the sky, a flash not normally seen with underwater blasts. Enemies of the Powers That Be also had experts who began to present arguments that the tsunamis created by the explosion were of a type that could only have been made by an explosion above the water rather than in it. If the explosion was above the water rather than in it, then how could it be from a bomb being transported through the sea by alien terrorists?

Facts are horrible things. At least to the Powers That Be,

who immediately began working on an explanation for these inconvenient facts. They decided on a new story that they felt would be the ultimate winner: an admission of responsibility that got everyone who counted off the hook. The president of the United States was shocked to discover that rogue CIA agents, working outside the agency with a bomb the agency had control of to use in Iran or Russia, had tried to wipe out the alien terrorists by exploding it on their ocean conference. They lamented that they were unfortunate dupes of one bad apple who shouldn't have damaged so many homes along the East Coast, even if they did kill hundreds of Protean terrorists.

"We Americans always do all we can to avoid collateral damage. These rogue agents broke that basic principle. They will be punished." It is rumored that three of them had their annual vacation time reduced from four weeks to three.

In less than a week the Powers That Be had put out three different versions of how and why the explosion had occurred.

Most Americans didn't notice. As soon as the Powers That Be began to push the president's report that the explosion was the result of a patriotic rogue agent trying to save his country from the Protean terrorists, the Powers That Be were home free. Most Americans totally forgot the earlier versions.

However, the overall effect of the explosion, the tsunamis, and the public reactions afterwards, was negative. The Protean terrorists might be robbing our banks, spying on our spy agencies, and damaging our economy, but there was no proof that they'd ever used weapons to actually kill anyone. Actually, of course, many Americans believed the aliens *had* been killing people: tipping over ferries, yanking airplanes off into their own universe, and kidnapping and zapping off dozens of innocent Americans into a life of sex slavery to hairy balls.

But most Americans seemed to be concluding that the first nuclear explosion in more than seventy years that actually killed people (mostly Bermudans, fortunately), whether purposeful or by a rogue agent, just might be a bit of overkill.

SIXTY

(From Billy Morton's *MY FRIEND LOUIE*, pp. 404–407)

Things never stay the same. You can never step into the same river twice. I'm sure that's a quote from some old Greek, but I've forgotten which one. Probably because I never knew. Or if I did know, I couldn't pronounce it.

Karen, Althea, Harry and I all survived our trial at sea. Harry was even about to be a hundred thousand dollars richer from his insurance claim. When Lita and the boys first heard on TV about the nuclear explosion in the Atlantic they assumed the worst, and Lita cussed me out real good. But within less than six hours of the news, an FF showed up at her door to reassure her that I was alive and well and contrite.

I and the other survivors from the *Big Bucks* had been picked up by another FF-owned ship and taken back to New York. And LT was able to give us some bittersweet relief by telling us that his dad, Molière, Gibberish, and Baloney were all alive, but that almost a third of the FFs that had been gathering had been killed or badly damaged. "Seven hundred and sixty-two dead," said LT, FFs always having exact figures. The last-minute warning that saved most of the FFs had come from Machiavelli who had broken the code with which the agencies were hiding their plans. Mac seemed to feel that wiping out most of the other team's players was not in the spirit of fair play. He changed sides.

Some of the FFs who were killed had stayed in the area

trying to warn all the sea creatures to get away. Others had been killed hoping to try to stop the bomb from being dropped or from exploding.

When Louie and Molière showed up less than an hour after I'd returned to our farmhouse, I told them how mad I was at what the government had done in killing so many innocents.

"You ought to totally shut down all our American killing machines," I say, looking fierce and feeling fierce. "Program every missile and bomb to explode on release. End this endless killing."

"Not our way, Billy," says Louie calmly. "It's up to humans to stop their sick members from violence. If *we* did it, as soon as we disappear—as we will—things would go back to the way they are now."

"They killed dozens of your personal friends. They killed one of Molière's kids! Don't you people care at all!?"

"We care," says Molière. "Just not the way you humans do."

"Death is just life in other forms," says Louie. "Perhaps because we FFs live such brief lives—ten or twelve years—compared to many other creatures in various universes, death seems always to be just around the corner. So we find it easy to concentrate on living."

"Death is everywhere every second," says Molière. "It's so common we're seeing it all around us every day. If some all-powerful God were to give some creature eternal life, that creature would immediately become the most miserable being in the universes. Of all the silly things humans try to do, trying to extend their lives way beyond their natural limits is the silliest."

"Well, we humans seem to think that every individual life is important," says I.

"Certainly," says Louie. "Every human being *is* important—as a flea on the behind of a baboon."

"Not that important," says Molière.

"You don't feel sad losing Abe and Oops?" I ask.

"Why?" says Louie. "They enjoyed themselves most every second and then died. What's to feel sad about?"

"But weren't they your friends?"

"Do you mean will we miss them?" asks Molière.

"I guess that's what I mean."

"Abe and Oops each had three kids, each of whom is a chip off the old block."

"Right down to quoting something from some religious book," says Louie. "I bet Abe's last words were 'I am the Resurrection and the Life.'"

"And Oops' last words were 'oops,'" says Molière.

"Although in our language his last words in the last second of his life if translated into English would run to over a hundred thousand words."

"But 'oops' is not a bad, brief English translation," says Molière.

SIXTY-ONE

Labor Day: now celebrated as the last chance for Americans who still have some money to go to the beach. It had become pretty meaningless. But this year the FFs were going to try to make Labor Day a huge *Fun-In*, perhaps the largest mass gathering in human history. Americans were amazed that only two weeks after almost a fifth of their earthly population had been nuked, the FFs would want to have fun. In the media, the only ones railing against the monstrosity of what the government had done, whether as a group or because of "rogue" elements, were humans. FFs just kept making jokes and playing. They had no emotions. They were *inhuman*!

Which, of course, they were. And it soon became clear that their efforts to create a huge, joyful march and *Fun-In* were going to be successful, at least in terms of attracting huge numbers of people. But a lot of humans were angry at the killing of the FFs and were into protesting rather than fun, but the FFs were working on them to loosen up.

Tens of thousands were joining the march to show their solidarity with the FFs and to protest the government's use of a nuclear weapon against their ocean block party. And people losing faith in the economic and political system because of workers' low pay or no pay, their continuing back-breaking medical expenses, and their realization that neither political party seemed able to do anything about anything, began gathering into dozens of groups, some organized, many just linked by common resentment and anger.

The "Tea Party" had originally risen out of anger at the government for wasting money on worthless blacks and Hispanics who won't work for a living, and being too nice to Mexicans and Latinos who are strolling across wide open borders to steal jobs and welfare from hard-working Americans. But in the last year they'd begun to realize that the government wasted a lot more money on the military and corporations than they did on welfare and food stamps. Lazy Americans might rip off thousands from the stupid government, but oil companies and pharmaceutical companies and military contractors were ripping off billions. Many of the original Tea Party members had become just as angry at the government wasting money with its endless wars in the Middle East as were the progressives and peaceniks.

Actually it's only progressives. There haven't been any peaceniks in almost fifty years. They've all realized that war is the American way.

Both the established national unions and some maverick Latinos, and a third group of non-union workers who'd organized themselves to march, all welcomed the other marches, even if some of them were normally anti-worker, like the National Tea Party Federation and Republicans for Responsibility. In fact, many of the first groups to sign up for the *First National Fun-in* were groups not noted for fun: Democrats for Democracy, MoveOn, the National Rifle Association, Americans in Favor of Burning Coal, Oil and Natural Gas Forever, Citizens for a Gluten-Free Diet. The FFs had gotten some of these groups to join the march by telling them that they owed it to the world to march in protest against the FFs and the whole *Forthehelluvit* movement. By marching they could show where the hearts of Americans really lay: in the barrel of a gun or a better diet. The FFs even had hundreds of signs created for these groups: "Proteans Go Home!" "All Proteans are Muslims in Disguise!" "We Believe in Work, not Play!" "FFs aren't that Much Fun!"

However, unbeknownst to these organizations, the FFs had developed plans to infiltrate most of them with human beings a bit more into play and a bit less into preaching.

So that Labor Day more than thirty different marches started from all over the five New York City boroughs, all of them heading toward Central Park in the middle of Manhattan. In Harlem it began when a bunch of *Forthehelluvit* people doing a "march-in, dance-in, beer-in, music-in" joined the huge group called Justice for Cops: Let them Face Trial that wanted to protest police overkill. Both sides had a lot of posters: "Unarmed Black Men are not for Target Practice," "If it Ain't Fun, Don't Do It," and "Let Black Kids Live." These two groups ended up being joined by Justice Now! and Latino Lives Count, which is the group that Carlita marched with. Both those groups had joined together to protest the death of the latest unarmed teenagers. One victim was a Latino boy in Queens shot in the back by a cop defending himself from the threat of being sucked into a vortex by the speed with which the kid was running away. And only three weeks before that a black teen had been shot when he brandished a tennis racket at some nervous cops. For some reason they only wounded him. Some claim that the department later docked the policemen involved a day's pay for poor shooting.

Gathering on 125th Street, these four groups began marching down Park Avenue. The people on the march were walking and dancing and drinking and playing music and waving posters. Many were dressed in outrageous or corny costumes: everything from Shrek to Captain America to Mickey Mouse. The marchers soon filled Park Avenue. Since the majority of drivers don't really want to run over other human beings, this street-filling tended to foul traffic.

As the marchers passed businesses and offices, some of the workers decided to take the afternoon off and join the parade. Some businesses decided to close early. A liquor store owner, probably after sampling too much of his own inventory, had one of his kids send out a case of wine and some six-packs of beer to the marchers. Much cheering and thanks, and the liquor store closed, its owner and employees and customers joining the parade.

And all over the city, similar groups were soon marching north from Brooklyn and west from Queens, each heading toward midtown Manhattan and Central Park. And at two P.M., hundreds hanging out in Washington Park in Greenwich Village decided to march uptown and join the fun. Tea Party and NRA groups more than three thousand strong were heading south on Second Avenue just three blocks east of the Harlem group. The NRA members, true to their cause, were all armed: shotguns, hunting rifles, pistols, automatic rifles, and one blunderbuss. Among all the sixty or seventy groups marching the NRA members maintained the most serious and sober expressions throughout. Many times *Forthehelluvit* people tried to join them with beer, music, flowers, and dancing but they soberly marched on. One doesn't mess with the NRA.

Over on the West Side MoveOn, Beer-Lovers of America, Free Hispanics from Statelessness, and Revolutionaries for Gradual Change had begun a march down Columbus Avenue starting at Columbia University. They were joined after ten blocks by one of the many FFs Go Home groups, and People For People—some sort of radical group that believed in friendliness. All of these groups were tweeting or texting to bring in more of their friends. Primitive types even used landline phones. More primitive types tried shouting.

All over the city people began getting off buses and joining in. Subway passengers burst up out of the ground to join various actions in the street.

By four that afternoon there were half a million people spread out among many groups all heading for Central Park. Citizens Concerned about Climate Change started in Chelsea, the American Nursing Association from Belleview Hospital, Gays Against Marriage in General from the Village, and so on.

And thousands of children from every part of the city, who were normally lined up by their parents on sidewalks to watch a parade, began not to watch the parade, but to join it.

The mood of the crowds was happy. Even those who wanted to blow up the Pentagon or assassinate various elite members of the Powers That Be were swept up into the good mood and flipped the safeties on their weapons. Since people were drinking, some got drunk. Since some were smoking pot, some got stoned. Since some were thieves, some stole. Some liked to dance and danced. Some loved to play and hear music, and so you could hardly join any march at any point without hearing some band or someone blasting away. A gay time was being had by all—well, mostly all, since there were a lot of purposeful people who were simply trapped by the crowd and couldn't get where they seriously felt they ought to be.

The city, state, and national authorities were not having a good time. When they began to realize how many different marches were being organized and that they were all heading for Central Park, they tried to break up the various groups as they were getting started. That seemed like a pretty easy thing to do. Until they tried to do it.

From the first they were undermanned. They managed to break up various groups as planned, but no sooner had they radioed in their success than they received reports that the group had reformed three or four blocks away and was bigger than ever. It was like squashing a bug and, when they took their foot off, there were suddenly three bugs. It didn't help matters that people were coming in from every direction to join the various marches. The *Forthehelluvit* people didn't seem to care if they joined a march of the Police Benevolent Association or Gun Owners For Self-Defense or Flower Growers of Eastern Long Island. When confronting a huge mass of marchers, the cops realized that they could either tear gas them all or shoot them all. Tear gassing, they knew, would only make people run faster to wherever they were going. Shooting them all might have worked, but would have involved an incredible amount of paperwork. Eventually the cops ended up standing aside. It is rumored that some joined the various marches, a rumor vehemently denied by all responsible media.

But this was chaos. The authorities realized that their initial efforts to stop marches from even starting were failing. They felt they had to take a major stand. When the Powers That Be decide to crack down on somebody, the first people they look for are blacks, then Hispanics, then intellectuals. So the march they decided to stop by whatever means necessary was the one coming down Park Avenue from Harlem, some carrying nasty posters like "Let Kids Live," and the ones giving everyone the middle finger.

ITEM IN THE NEWS

LOUIE-TWOIE'S THOUGHTS

(Published in the *National High School Weekly Journal*,
August 7th edition)

"An apple a day keeps the doctor away."
Only if you throw it at him.

"A penny for your thoughts."
For humans that is a vast overpayment.

"A rising tide lifts all boats."
Not the sunken ones.

"To those who hath, more shall be given."
Spoken like a CEO.

"Sing before breakfast, cry before noon."
Still, one sang.

"The meek shall inherit the earth."
What's left of it.

"It is better to give than to receive."
Unless you're the receiver.

Human beings are fools.
A few, holy fools.

The past keeps you enslaved. Kill it.
Personal history keeps you enslaved. Kill it.
The self keeps you enslaved. Kill it.
Every day is a new dawn. You ignore it and grow old.

SIXTY-TWO

(From Billy Morton's *MY FRIEND LOUIE*, pp. 408–412)

That Saturday morning Althea had arranged that our entire office—all twenty-five of us—would march under our own banner: "APEs for a Better World." Our union guys said they were marching under "Workers Take Over!"

When I watched on Althea's iPhone the dozens of different marches starting all over the city I was both exhilarated and depressed. Marching involves walking, and these days I'm not much of a walker. If they had a motorized rocking chair I would have been blissful, but without one I felt old.

Of course I went. I could no more resist joining people marching in protest than a lemming can resist racing to jump off a cliff. Lucas and Jimmy had come to the city with me and would march with us. Karen too.

We all joined the marchers who were coming down Park Avenue from Harlem. Lita called to say she was ten blocks behind us. We were pretty impressed with the variety of handheld signs around us: "Bury all Nukes," "FFs Are Not that Smart," "Citizens for Wider Sidewalks," "Come home, America," "Cancel Government." A lot of the signs were the same: a giant middle finger being raised from a cartoon hand.

Althea, our APE friends, me, Karen, and the boys got in with the group with the "Cancel Government" sign, and I walked the first two blocks like the real stud I always unconsciously think I am. Surprised me as much as Althea and the boys. Nothing like being with a bunch of young people to give an old guy pep—young people being anyone under fifty-five.

We marched down Park Avenue for about fifteen minutes and, just as I was beginning to get so pooped I was looking around for someone to carry me, all of us came to a halt. Something was happening up ahead. Then we began to be able to ease forward again. At 80th Street we saw some of the marchers near 79th Street moving back toward us.

"Cops up ahead!" some guy shouted. Seeing the retreaters, some of our crowd began turning west toward Central Park. There was no panic. Everything still seemed matter-of-fact: we're blocked up ahead, let's head toward Central Park now rather than at 72nd Street as we'd planned.

Ever since I got out of 'Nam I've been cursed with a terrible flaw: when I know cops and protestors are face to face some place I have to be one of the faces. Karen felt the same way. So I got Althea to help me and the boys through the retreating marchers toward where the action was.

Soon we got close enough to see about a hundred NYPD cops lined up two deep all the way across Park Avenue. The marchers were blocked. A guy with a bullhorn was ordering us to disperse. Dressed in black, the cops looked like characters out of a sci-fi movie. They were armed with shields and guns and batons and tear gas and tar guns and water hoses. They also had a huge armored vehicle, fresh from controlling our friends in the Middle East. It had three guys on top brandishing some sort of automatic rifles. However, I'm sure they'd been ordered not to shoot unless they felt nervous.

The guys and gals in the front row nearest the police

didn't seem upset at being told to shoo. Damned if some of them didn't begin to sing "Happy Birthday" to the cops. Two or three went up and kissed a cop, or tried to. Getting past shields and glass visors to an actual pair of lips wasn't easy. A few cops did seem for some reason to adjust their visors upwards.

Another group began singing "God Bless America." Most of the others happily turned right and began marching toward Central Park on 79th Street. Althea and I stayed to listen to "God Bless America" and were able to get up to about the fifth row in front of the long line of cops. A small rock band of guys and gals in their fifties began playing The Beatles' "Why Don't We Do It in the Road" and a lot of people began singing along with them, including Lucas, Jimmy, and Karen. I can't carry a tune any better than I can carry a hippopotamus, so I spared the other marchers.

People having fun or not, the lead cop was still bullhorning for us to disperse, move, go home. Some of the cops began banging their clubs against their shields. Shock and awe I guess. The guys with automatic weapons in the armored vehicle couldn't bang their guns on their shields, so to make their own threatening noises they shot a few rounds into the air. Killed two pigeons and knocked out three panes of glass in a nice town house.

But then things began to get hairy. The crowds that had been moving west toward Central Park were suddenly surging back, and Lita and her crowd were now pushing down Park Avenue behind us from the north. An entirely new group of people, the Tea Partiers and the huge group from the NRA, were now coming in from the east on 78th and 79th Streets.

People were crowding in on us from every direction. Those of us near the line of cops couldn't go home even if we wanted to.

Things might have worked out okay—even in our universe they sometimes do—but Murphy's Ancient Law is pretty powerful; if something can go wrong, it will.

The Establishment Union marchers had arrived at 64th Street and one or two speeches had been given. They'd been joined along the way by a thousand or so people who weren't part of the labor movement but just wanted to join the parade and have fun. When all these people began to hear from their smartphones that only a quarter mile north the cops were harassing a huge crowd of marchers coming down from Harlem, they didn't like it. When one of the labor leaders interrupted a particularly dull speaker and told the crowd that thousands of marchers just a few blocks north of them needed their help, most of the crowd surged northwards.

Back where I was, the cops actually showed great restraint. Although facing a crowd of thousands made it tough for them to relax, they kept blaring away at the crowd to back up, but in fact it was they themselves who finally began to retreat. They moved a block south to 78th Street. They might have moved further south, but at that point the labor crowd was beginning to arrive from the south. More Tea Partiers and NRA guys were pressing in from the east. The cops reformed their long double line, this time with one side facing north against us and the other south against the labor guys.

About this time the NRA guys—some NRA gals too— came into the sight of the long line of cops. The poor cops had been facing thousands of protestors armed with nothing more threatening than posters, songs, and kisses, and now suddenly fifty or sixty guys and gals carrying guns and looking a bit angry show up. With more of them on the way.

If the cops had been uneasy before, they were now scared. And the poor NRA guys were even more confused than the cops. They'd marched into a situation where cops were confronting citizens, but citizens who looked like the sort of citizens who didn't like the NRA. Whose side should they be on?

I heard what sounded like a gunshot. Then two or three more gunshots. The whole line of policemen began to fire their weapons. Tear gas was shot into the crowd. The tar gun teams began hosing people with tar. The men in the armored vehicles began blasting noisily away with what was later claimed were rubber bullets, although later the bullets weren't rubber.

The NRA guys had never before confronted a situation like this, but when fired upon an NRA guy or gal does not say "Hey, what's the matter?" or "Can't we talk about this?" He shoots.

Sounded like a hundred fire crackers going off all at once.

When the cops and the NRA began shooting at each other I panicked. Actually just about everyone anywhere near the gunfire panicked. As bullets flew all around, it seemed that many people opted to lie down for a while. Or forever.

A SWAT team riding in two armored vehicles suddenly steamed in on 79th Street from the east, it later being reported that they didn't squash more than three Tea Party people on their way, although once on Park Avenue they were able to up that count. Karen and Althea were trying to drag me and the boys toward Central Park, and any macho desire I had to be a courageous stud faded completely when I saw the SWAT team guys blasting away into the crowd. Never have I been so happy to be dragged away from my stupid machismo than I was that day. I grabbed Jimmy's hand and began to run.

At my age, running is not one of my strong suits. In fact it's not even one of my suits. With a hip replacement and arthritic knees, when I go from a walk to what is intended to be a run, the pain bells go ringing in both knees and my lower back. Muscles that haven't been used for five or six years scream as loud as they can that they don't want to participate in this ridiculous project (running). After about four or five what can charitably be called "strides," my whole body grinds to a halt and I can barely walk. But that afternoon I ran. For almost an entire block. Jimmy could barely keep up.

And I claim I don't fear death.

SIXTY-THREE

(From *LUKE'S TRUE UNBELIEVABLE REPORT OF THE INVASION OF THE FFS*, pp. 316–321)

By nine o'clock that night the standoff was in place. There were close to a million people in Central Park, most of them south of 79th Street. Police, SWAT teams or National Guard units had stationed themselves on all four sides of the park. Drones and helicopters circled overhead.

Earlier, hundreds of those marchers fired on by the police had turned destructive. Most riots take place in slums or ghettos, not on Park Avenue. The Powers That Be don't really mind if some dumb Korean grocery store or Big Boys or KFC or black-owned liquor store gets robbed or burned down, but antique shops, art galleries, tea rooms, fancy dress shops, Citibank branches: now you're talking actual property. The governor called out the National Guard and declared martial law.

Harry Barnes and his human and FF friends had somehow gotten into the park thousands and thousands of tents, sleeping bags, blankets, tarps, porta-potties, and an incredible amount of food. They'd ordered over twenty thousand pizzas to be delivered to the park from more than two hundred pizza parlors. They'd ordered ten giant water trucks to come into the park. The authorities hadn't yet been able to close off all traffic into the park, although when they heard that pizza delivery trucks were causing a major traffic jam at the East 72nd Street entrance, they ordered a crackdown: no more vehicles permitted to enter. But it was more than four hours before they had enough men to enforce the order, and even then many cars and trucks continued driving into the park over lawns and through shrubbery.

Inside the park, there were over a thousand armed members of the NRA who, having seen dozens of their members shot and many killed, were not in a friendly mood. They were determined to resist the authorities should they be attacked.

However, most everyone else in the park, not having been directly involved in the Park Avenue mini-war, was concentrating on having fun. They were taking no thought for the morrow. A few people felt it might be nice to go home, but weren't too enthusiastic about having to go through a line of police whose inability to control their trigger fingers made leaving and still staying alive a bit iffy.

Nevertheless, it's estimated that twenty thousand people, mostly old folks or parents with young children, or friends or relatives of those killed or wounded, left the park that evening and night. Unfortunately for the Powers That Be, more than forty thousand people found a way to sneak into the park, people from all over the country. Groups were chartering planes to get to New York City and Central Park. Planeloads flew in from London and one from Paris that Molière had organized with his French friends.

And the world was paying attention. Almost a hundred and eighty people had been killed that afternoon, as well as fifteen policemen—although three of the police had been killed by friendly fire. As many as a thousand people were in hospital, either from gunshot wounds or from getting trampled. Fifteen of the dead were children, and another three-dozen kids were in hospital. Another thirty or so of the dead were older men and women. Two elderly women were among those squashed by armored vehicles. Almost half of those in hospital were women. All this was not good PR for the latest "I Love New York" campaign. Or for the NYPD. Or for the Powers That Be.

In eleven major cities throughout the world other *Fun-Ins* were taking place, with violence limited to heart attacks, motorcycle accidents, and severe indigestion. Most of the world thought that the *Fun-Ins* were great, that the "Manhattan Massacre" was just another example of "Only in America."

That afternoon and evening the people in Central Park began organizing themselves for survival. Tarps were set up around and under trees or up against walls. Various groups occupied several of the buildings in and around the Central Park Zoo and all the other small buildings in Central Park Nation's area of the park. The Meadow was now home to over three thousand tents, some quite large. Other open areas had more tents. Off to one side of the Meadow more than fifty people, led for some strange reason by Beer-Lovers of America, began digging latrines and erecting outhouses. These were to supplement the hundreds of porta-potties already in place. Various people opened restaurants, probably better called food distribution areas, in the several restaurants already in the Park, in three places in the Central Park Zoo buildings, and in open areas where they cooked over open fires. Several women from Sink Oil Companies, Not Oil Wells along with a gang from Gays Against Marriage in General, got together to gather all the firewood they could. There was a bit of an argument when the Gays wanted to chainsaw down a mostly dead maple tree. The environmentalists at first were absolutely against killing a still living tree, and only when the Gays agreed to plant four new trees in the same spot did they give in.

There was a lot of hot air exchanged in Central Park that night. The *Forthehelluvit* people kept trying to break up the arguments with games and music or kiss-ins or dance-ins, and in most cases it worked. The one thing most groups agreed on was to stay in Central Park as long as they could.

And all that afternoon and evening games were being played—soccer, touch football, baseball, long jump contests, races around one of the lakes, and other games made up on the spot. The biggest hit was Capture the Flag, played with more than three hundred players on each side. Ended up in total chaos.

Only a few showers were available because late that evening the Powers That Be had cut off much of the water to the park. People were forced to use the three lakes they had access to—The Pond, The Lake, and a third big pond named Conservatory Water. Only city bureaucrats could have come up with three such unimaginative names for lovely lakes. However, it could have been worse: nowadays, to earn money, the city would probably name them "Walmart Pond," "Bank of America Lake," and "Ripkin, Blatts, Funnel, and Kegs Body of Water."

It turns out that bathing to get clean often means a drastic reduction of clothing, and soon there was a lot of nude swimming and, it being dark, a lot of pleasant hanky-panky.

That night hundreds of musicians got together to play music, mostly rock, and within a half hour thousands of people were rocking and dancing and singing and generally not suffering much.

There were probably two hundred campfires around the park and at least one big bonfire, although several environmental groups succeeded in getting it put out as a waste of valuable wood. The campfires were used both for pleasure and for cooking. With pizza deliveries now on the slow side (only a hundred got through the blockade after ten P.M.), the Central Park Nationers were forced to eat several thousand hamburgers and Kentucky Fried Chicken pieces dropped from the sky that night. The Nation had also been bombed with four thousand cans of Campbell's Vegetable Soup, which at the rate people were eating it, would last into the next century.

Twenty cases of champagne and four crates of caviar had somehow been brought in by Republicans for America. The fact that these people were still part of the Nation despite being against what ninety percent of the other citizens of the Nation stood for was appreciated by all. The fact that more than a dozen women from the Nurses Association of the Northeast had befriended them probably improved their morale and their willingness to stick around and roll with the punches. And with the nurses.

Of course there was considerable sexual action that night. Not only did the Republicans of America and the Nurses Association of the Northeast find common ground (usually inside tents), but so did Tea Party members, mostly guys, and Citizens For Sound Science Against The Pollution of Our Earth, a poorly funded but militant group of mostly women.

Women for Women members, passionately interested in

equal pay for women for equal work, and for the elimination of all old bald white men from the top of all corporations, somehow hooked up with Revolutionaries for Gradual Change. They probably hoped to convert them to being Revolutionaries for a Bit Faster Change. Actually the Women for Women platform didn't call for the elimination of all old white guys from being CEOs. It only decreed that the number of old white guys as CEOs in Fortune 500 companies couldn't exceed the percentage of old white guys in the general population, which, it seems, is only eight percent. If all went well with the Women for Women platform, four hundred and sixty of the five hundred CEOS of the Fortune 500 companies would have to resign.

And there were of course orgies. You can't get close to a million people together with not much to do except drink and dance and smoke dope and write political manifestos without some creative type suggesting an orgy. So some did, and it was an idea not always dismissed.

SIXTY-FOUR

(From Billy Morton's *MY FRIEND LOUIE*, pp. 420–427)

Lita finally got to us and spent the first half hour hugging Lucas and Jimmy until Lucas threatened to join the NRA if she didn't let him breathe. We were lucky to get a tent just big enough to hold us, our boys, three FFs, and Althea and Karen. That first night it rained a bit and we ended up having ten people in our tent, our six, two gals from Sink Oil Companies, Not Oil Wells, and two guys carrying an "FFs Go Home!" poster.

Actually they were part of the Tea Party group that had been gassed and shot at and run over by armored vehicles back on Park Avenue. That, and talking with Louie-Twoie, and learning that the tents and everything had mostly been brought in by the FFs, meant that by the morning these guys had changed their sign: it now read "FFs Can Stay!"

The next morning drones and army helicopters were flying over the park. About two o'clock two larger planes appeared, and just when people began to think we were about to be bombed, the big planes began dropping huge bundles, which fell slowly to the earth when parachutes opened. The good guys had arranged another food drop.

By noon the Powers That Be seemed to have decided not to try to get us out of the park yet, probably hoping rain or boredom or fear would eventually get us to go home and watch TV.

'Course it wasn't working out that way. The people in the

park had smartphones and iPads and a dozen other kinds of doohickeys that let us know that people all over the world were looking to the Central Park Nation for guidance. Made us determined to stay.

Karen, Molière, and our two boys spent most of that afternoon playing in half a dozen games that would form, be played, and dissolve. FFs and humans played together and once or twice even formed teams playing against each other. I think the FFs usually let the humans win.

The leaders of twenty or so protest movements got together in the early evening to write a manifesto. Considering how much booze, pot, other dope and fatigue were involved in creating this document, and how little time we all had to work on it, the result turned out pretty good. We could only agree on fifteen demands of the twenty we wanted to come up with, but these were all interesting. Most were a bit too serious for my taste, but Americans don't respect anything unless it's serious.

SIXTY-FIVE

(From *LUKE'S TRUE UNBELIEVABLE REPORT OF THE INVASION OF THE FFS*, pp. 338–340. Being the first incomplete draft of the *CENTRAL PARK NATION MANIFESTO*.)

We the People of the Central Park Nation, having gathered peaceably together to have fun and to protest against our government's abuses of authority and failure to perform any actions except those that make matters worse, do hereby make the following fifteen demands:

1. Every living American over the age of eighteen shall be legally required to vote and be given every opportunity to vote. No state law shall abrogate this basic duty and right.

2. No human being and no legal entity shall be permitted to spend more than a total of ten thousand dollars in any year promoting political candidates or political messages, and all such spending shall become part of the public record.

3. The pay of all company executives shall not exceed the average pay of its workers by more than thirty times. No bonuses shall be paid to any employee unless the same percentage bonus is paid to every employee in the company.

4. All local police forces shall have a racial composition proportional to the racial composition of the community in which they serve.

5. Women shall have equal pay for equal work. No white man over the age of fifty shall be named as a CEO of a Fortune 500 company until fifty percent of the CEOs in the Fortune 500 are women.

6. Every human being in the United States not presently a citizen, whether here legally or illegally, shall have the right to apply for citizenship for him or herself and his or her children. Each shall be given a hearing within thirty days of so applying. The boards hearing these petitions for citizenship shall consist of judges and others whose racial and gender compositions reflect the racial and gender compositions of the nation as a whole.

7. Beginning immediately, the United States military shall cease building any new bases on foreign soil and shall reduce such bases by one quarter each year for the next four years until their number has been reduced from over one thousand to no more than eighty.

8. All hospitals, clinics, pharmaceutical companies, health insurance companies, drug manufacturers, and educational institutions shall by law become not-for-profit entities.

9. The Federal Government shall within two years disable and dismantle ninety-nine percent of its nuclear arsenal and shall insist that any other nation receiving any American aid disable and dismantle ninety-nine percent of their nuclear arsenals.

10. Beer shall be named the national drink of the United States of America.

11. All military action of the United States against any nation or group of people now taking place anywhere in the world must cease within thirty days and shall not resume until such action or actions receive the agreement by two-thirds majorities of both the House and Senate.

12. All subsidies to American oil and coal companies shall cease, and a tax of ten percent levied on every well head, every truckload of coal, and every barrel of oil sold.

13. The Federal Government shall immediately develop plans to reduce within two years by at least one trillion dollars expenditures for the departments of Defense, Homeland Security, the National Security Agency, and the CIA, and shall transfer the funds thus saved to building hospitals, clinics, and schools, repairing and building roads, railroads, bridges, water systems, electric grids, and for paying for free education for all through four years of college.

14. The minimum wage in every company doing business in the United States shall be three percent of the highest compensation (salary and bonuses) being received by the highest paid executive in the company, but in any case no lower than twenty dollars per hour.

15. Every citizen shall be requested to do something at least once a day for the hell of it.

SIXTY-SIX

(From Billy Morton's *MY FRIEND LOUIE*, pp. 440–447)

Late that evening we had a party. We were all sitting in front of a campfire outside our tent; Lita, Karen, Molière, and I leaning back against the side of the tent, Sheriff Coombs, Lucas, and Jimmy cooking marshmallows over the fire, and the other FFs scattered all around. Sheriff Coombs had hooked up with us after marching with the Eastern Long Island branch of the NRA. We could see other campfires, a lot of dancing, and people moving with flashlights. Music was blasting away all around us.

We drank and chatted and joked and generally acted silly, as people often do after they've been shot at, had a lot of fun, and drunk a bit of booze. The talk turned serious when Molière and Lita began to talk about the fifteen FFs who were planning to zap themselves back to Ickieville the next afternoon. Molière and Gibberish told us it was dangerous—that about one time out of ten when FFs tried to go from one universe to another they simply disappeared forever.

So we were all stunned when Karen told us she was going with Molière to Ickieville. Molière said that two other humans were also planning to go. I couldn't figure Molière and Karen going: they seemed to love life here on Earth.

"Actually," Molière says, "I'm on a recruiting mission. I'm going to invite some new Ickies to come back with me to Earth. We've had a lot of player casualties lately."

"Karen part of your sales pitch?" says I.

"No," says Molière after a short laugh. "Ickies will find Karen stupid, ugly, and limited. You have to be on Earth a while before you can see gold in the general sludge."

"I'm pregnant," Karen says out of the blue, eyes glowing happily.

There was a long silence, unless you count the twenty-three different bits of music blasting away at various decibels all around us.

The natural question was, who was the papa? Could FFs impregnate humans? *The New York Times* science section has assured its readers on at least two occasions that it wasn't possible.

"Is it Molière's child?" Lita asks.

"We think it is," says Karen, smiling at Molière, then at Lita.

"Impossible," says the Sheriff.

"Don't be too sure, Jerry," says I. "FFs tend to know a lot more than we do."

"You're telling us," says the Sheriff, turning to Molière, "that you think you made a kid with this lady?"

"I know I'm more the father than anyone else," says Molière. A bit ambiguous it seemed to me.

Lucas suddenly stood up and looked away from the fire into the darkness.

"He's here again!"

Who should emerge from the shadows but Agent Mike Johnson. It was getting to be like a family reunion. Mike nodded at me and Lita, and stopped just behind Louie on the other side of the fire.

"Nothing to be afraid of from me, Lucas," he says to my

son. "You folks mind if I join you?"

"You planning to arrest us or drink with us?" I ask.

"I'd like to drink with you."

"So what are you doing here?" says I.

"I'm no longer working for Unit A," says Mike, squatting near the fire beside Lucas. "I've been fired. My boss didn't appreciate my calling him insane and getting him locked up in a psychiatric clinic for ten days."

"Bosses tend to be picky about things like that," says I. "You want beer, bourbon, or ridiculously expensive French wine?"

"I'd love to join you in bourbon, Billy."

As Mike accepts our flask of bourbon from Jerry, Molière bounces up from beside Karen to Mike's side.

"Mike is joining the FFs going back to Ickie," he says.

Just one bombshell after another these days.

"What's that all about?" asks Lita.

"I find myself looking for a better universe," says Mike.

"And why is that?"

"Because of the killing on Park Avenue yesterday," says Mike. "Because of that nuclear explosion that killed a lot of innocent creatures. And because of this coming week."

"What's happening this coming week?" asks Lita.

Mike took a good swig from the flask, looked a long time at Lita, then at me.

"SWAT teams from throughout the country, National Guard units from New York and New Jersey, two companies of Special Forces, a regiment of the US Tank Corps, and the Navy destroyer *Arnold Schwarzenegger*, are all about to implement a plan developed by the DOD to end the occupation of Central Park. D-Day is Tuesday morning at four A.M."

Silence.

Of course, we all knew that something like this was in our future, but hadn't had any desire to actually think about it.

"Do your guys realize that the NRA will fight?" says Jerry. "And have over two thousand weapons?"

"They're not my guys anymore," says Mike. "And yes, they know it. And they're *glad* the NRA will fight. They plan to make sure everyone knows that the Central Park Nation went to war with the United States Government. And of course you'll lose."

"We've got to get the NRA to lay down their guns," says Lita.

"They—we won't do it," says Jerry.

"Then we'll have to get them to leave," says Lita. "As long as they're among us and wanting to fight, hundreds of innocent people will get killed."

"Thousands," says Molière.

"I'm an NRA member and proud of it," says Jerry. "And it's not our fault. We're just hacking around in the park like the rest of you. It's the government that's starting it."

"That's right," says Louie. "But shooting to kill is not hacking around."

Silence.

"Why don't you and the sheriff go talk to their leadership, Billy," says Molière. "Let them know how we feel about it. See if they won't agree to march out of the park tomorrow, flags flying, without dishonor."

"We should get out too, Billy," says Lita.

"What are you—?"

"I'm not letting Jimmy and Lucas be subjected a second time to so much danger. I want them to leave. I want you to leave. Enough is enough."

"Sweetheart," I says, always tending to use that word when I'm entering into an argument with Lita I know I'm going to lose, "we can't desert all our friends here."

"I'm not sacrificing my sons for my friends. We're going."

"There's something else you should know, Lita," says Jerry. "Something I probably should have told you both when it happened."

He stands up. We all look at him.

"Two weeks ago I got a visit from a guy who claimed to be an FBI agent—showed me identification and all—who wanted to know if you kept guns in your house. I figured they were planning an arrest and wanted to know if they'd be in any danger. I told him that far as I knew you just had an old deer rifle you hadn't used in years. He looked disappointed."

The sheriff spit into the fire.

"Then he said something that chilled me to the bone. He asked if it might be possible if I, as your friend, might get you to go do some target practice shooting."

He looked around at us all to see if any of us were getting his drift.

"Billy," he says. "They want you to have your rifle out of storage, in your house, and recently fired. Can you think why?"

"They want to have an excuse to shoot him," says Lita, always a lot sharper than anyone else.

Jerry looked at me to see if I got it too. I did.

"You'd be in danger if you left the park with the NRA guys," he says. "In fact, you'll be in danger until—"

"Until I'm dead," I says, sighing. I smiled. "But then I can relax."

Lita moaned and slid a few inches down the tent.

"Is there no end, O Lord?" she says, eyes closed.

"You know," I finally say to Louie across the fire from me, "me and my boys almost got killed. Hundreds of people did get killed. My two boys got gassed and shot at. Mike here says the Feds are going to assassinate me. Are all *Fun-Ins* like this?"

"Human life is like this, Billy," says Louie.

"The deaths weren't caused by any of the people joining in the *Fun-In*, Billy," says Molière. "The deaths are caused by people who are serious, people who feel they have important purposes to fulfill, feel they have Answers. People doing things for the fun of it don't kill."

"And despite the deaths," says Gibberish, "there are nine hundred and thirty-two thousand eight hundred and sixty-six people in this park tonight. Do you get the impression that they think their lives are worse for being here?"

I looked around at the campfires and listened to the music and saw people dancing around two of the fires. Not too many people seemed to be feeling too bad about things.

"People seem happy enough right now, Louie, but how are they going to feel when the tanks move in and the explosions start and more of us die?"

"They're going to feel horrible," says Louie.

"I'm too old for this shit, Louie."

"No, Billy, you're not. You joined the march, you confronted the police, you ran when you had to, and now you're here, and I think in a half hour you'll go with Sheriff Coombs and try to get the NRA leadership to agree to leave the park and avoid a blood bath for all of us. I noticed you weren't too enthusiastic when Lita talked to you about leaving."

"Well, that may be tr—"

"I now think we should stay," says Lita. "We're safer here with several hundred thousand friends than we would be out there."

"I don't like seeing more deaths," says I.

"Don't waste your time worrying about dozens of deaths here," says Gibberish. "Worry about the hundreds of thousands of humans and other living things that are dying unnecessarily all around the world every day because of the insane system you humans have created."

"And don't forget about all the *Fun-Ins* in cities all over the world," says Molière. "They're calling us the Central Park Nation. They're looking to us to lead."

"We have to go," says Louie suddenly. He, Molière, LT, and Gibberish roll a couple of feet away. "There's a big meeting of a few FFs with your leaders in the zoo building to decide what we're going to do tomorrow."

"What are the options?" asks Lita.

"Some want us to stay here for as long as we can, others want all of us to march out of the park down Fifth Avenue to Battery Park, gathering more people as we go, but also some of us slipping away home. Then some of us would occupy Battery Park for as long as we can."

Lucas leapt up.

"Can I come?!"

"Sure," says LT.

"Go, Lucas," says Lita, "and tell them what you think should be done."

"And you, Billy," says Louie, "should go with Sheriff Coombs and talk to the NRA. If anyone can make them see that they should leave, it's you."

With my usual groan I managed to struggle to my feet.

"Never thought of myself as a pacifist," I said.

"Baloney," says Baloney suddenly appearing from wherever he'd been for the last four hours.

"You don't even know what we're talking about," Karen says to him.

"Makes no difference. Baloney."

The four FFs with Lucas in tow, begin to move off.

Lucas stops and turns to look back at us.

"We're going to be all right, Mom," he says.

"Baloney," says Baloney.

"You're too optimistic, Lucas," says I.

"Baloney," says Baloney.

BOOK TWO

THE HAIRY BALLS
AND THE END
OF CIVILIZATION

WILL BE AVAILABLE SHORTLY.
LOOK FOR IT AT YOUR LOCAL TAVERN.

ACKNOWLEDGMENTS

Without the time, effort, critical skills and support of Paul Lucas, Robert Bosler, Rob Wringham, and Steven May this novel would be a weak echo of what they helped it become. Much much thanks.

HACK
Kieran Crowley

JOURNALISM.
NARCISSISM.
CANNIBALISM.

It's a dog-eat-dog world at the infamous tabloid the New York Mail, where brand new pet columnist F.X. Shepherd accidentally finds himself on the trail of The Hacker, a serial killer targeting unpleasant celebrities in inventive—and sometimes decorative—ways. And it's only his second day on the job. Luckily Shepherd has hidden talents, not to mention a hidden agenda. But as bodies and suspects accumulate, he finds himself running afoul of cutthroat office politics, the NYPD, and Ginny Mac, an attractive but ruthless reporter for a competing newspaper. And when Shepherd himself is contacted by The Hacker, he realizes he may be next on the killer's list...

TITANBOOKS.COM

For more fantastic fiction, author events, competitions,
limited editions and more

Visit our website
titanbooks.com

Like us on Facebook
facebook.com/titanbooks

Follow us on Twitter
@TitanBooks

Email us
readerfeedback@titanemail.com